The Broken Alliance

Legend of Rhett

Book 1

Bennett Mohler

Dedication

To my Brother for starting the fire with me.

To Miranda for seeing it through to the end.

Thanks Mom and Dad for reading it first.

Table of Contents

The Legend of Rhett

The Broken Alliance (Book 1)

We are things of dry hours and the involuntary plan
Grayed in, and gray. "Dream" makes a giddy sound, not strong
Like "rent," "feeding a wife," "satisfying a man."

But could a dream send up through onion fumes
Its white and violet, fight with fried potatoes
And yesterday's garbage ripening in the hall
Flutter, or sing an aria down these rooms

Even if we were willing to let it in
Had time to warm it, keep it very clean
Anticipate a message, let it begin?

We wonder. But not well! not for a minute!
Since Number Five is out of the bathroom now
We think of lukewarm water, hope to get in it

Chapter 1

Captured

"The test begins... NOW!"

There is an old saying.

Perhaps the oldest saying.

"I am only that which others see me as, and others are only that which I see them as."

This saying transcends all races, creeds and religions that call this relatively small corner of the universe home.

In the seemingly peaceful starlit void of this galaxy, a small, V-shaped shuttle transport cruised slowly toward an extraterrestrial space station; which was constructed in the conventional fashion of two spheres connected by a bridging apparatus. Each sphere supported ten large platforms, which housed many ships, most of which appeared newer and in better condition than the small approaching shuttle. The pilot of this little shuttle, upon seeing several guard ships hovering around the station, took a deep and nervous breath then stopped the ship's engines and set the shuttle to stealth mode.

Inside the space station, two dirtied boots tapped patiently on the floor next to a scaly, blue tail. Tucked into the boots were dark brown pants held up by a light brown belt with a silver buckle. A holstered pistol blaster adorned one side and a large sheathed knife the other. Tucked in the belt was a tan, long-sleeved shirt covered with a green utility vest. A black bandana was wrapped tightly around the figure's left wrist. The shirt was just under a blue neck with a blue, scaly, reptilian head. The creature had bright yellow eyes with black slits. The right eye was slightly discolored, paler than the other with a vicious scar tearing across it. This reptilian creature was called a Hydrolette. This Hydrolette's name was Beio-Rhett.

Sitting quietly on a waiting bench, Beio-Rhett studied a data pad connected to an earpiece. Long disheveled hair covered his scarred face as he listened and read. He paid no attention to the many different creatures that walked by. The space station, like most others in the populated pockets of this particular galaxy, was a busy cosmic airport. To the numerous passersby it seemed Beio-Rhett was only reading a book. However, his data pad was linked to the station's security channel and he was monitoring the incoming and outgoing ships. None grabbed his attention except for the V-shaped shuttle, which was the only ship to remain silent among the radio chatter. *What's going on?*

On the bridge of the station, one of the officers grew frustrated in attempting to establish contact with the shuttle.

"This is Delta Sector Transit Station 23. Please identify name and pilot code," he said for the third time. There was no answer. "Something wrong? I'll try the identity scanner."

The computer started showing technical readout of the shuttle. Suddenly, a red and white sign reading "Signal Jam" in Galactic Standard script flashed on the monitor.

The Captain took off his headphones and grunted. "Shit!"

The officer's remarks drew the attention of the Captain. "What's wrong?" the Captain calmly asked.

"Signal jam, Captain,"

The Captain huffed and turned to the other officers. "I want all visual data we can get on this guy. We'll need someone to go in," he yelled. "This could be rebel mischief."

After hearing the conversation on the bridge through his earpiece, Beio-Rhett casually got up and walked to the restroom. Leaning on the corner, outside the door, he calmly dialed numbers on a communicator. He put the small microphone-like device to his mouth.

Three roughly dressed, unkempt Hydrolettes were in the fuel storage room of the same station. The only consistent element amongst their garments was a red bandana wrapped around each of the Hydrolette's necks. Besides this one unifying article, their dress made no attempt to blend in with more sociable Hydrolettes. Rather the opposite. Their hair was shaved in strange places and given unnatural colors. Their bodies were pierced with decorations and their skin adorned with tattoos. One tattoo was consistent among the three. The tattoo depicted a Hydrolette fist holding a bloody knife. The design was enclosed in a black ring. Writing in Quel-Noran, a now-extinct language of the Hydrolettes read "The people have suffered. The system has failed." This was the insignia of the Hydrolette Rebellion.

Two of the rebels operated a pumping system delivering the stations fuel stores to the group's fuel carrier pods. The one rebel who wasn't siphoning was examining his pistol idly. He heard the communicator beep and looked to where it lay on a crate in the corner of the room.

"Yo, get the comlink," he said rudely to the other rebels.

One of the siphoners looked incredulously at his partner. "Busy! You get it! You're doing nothin'!"

The rebel fiddling with the pistol disgruntledly walked up to the communicator and put it to his mouth. "Yeah, what?" he asked impolitely.

Beio-Rhett sighed in relief when his call was answered. "What's going on?"

"Filling the last pod. We're almost done."

"Good," sighed Beio-Rhett. "Look, something came up. A shuttle just stopped near this station and cloaked its ID. Thing is, it may be one of the rebels."

"So?" the rebel asked, growing impatient.

"Well, the guards are all over it and if he's one of yours' and they catch him, we're toast," Beio-Rhett replied calmly.

"Well, it's not." The rebel seemed unconcerned. "I think they would have told us if they sent someone else out here."

Beio-Rhett sighed. "Either way, I'm gonna check it out. If I get there before the guards do, we may still be covered."

"Okay." The rebel lightened up. "You want us to…"

"No!" barked Beio-Rhett. "Just continue with your task. I'll be there in a minute."

Beio-Rhett shut off the communicator and headed toward the service exit. He walked through the doorway casually. The exit led Beio-Rhett to the loading bay where the station crew were hauling supplies and driving loaders to and from stacks of crates. The area was filled with the cacophony of workers shouting, engines humming and steam hissing. Beio-Rhett walked briskly past the cranking gears and screeching machines, barely acknowledging the workers. The workers in turn ignored him.

"Stay sharp!" Beio-Rhett barked to a worker he noticed sitting down behind a crate, smoking a cigarette.

The worker stood to attention and put out his cigarette as

Beio-Rhett made his way quickly across the loading bay.

Beio-Rhett came to the end of the corridor, which led to a ladder. He swiftly slid down the ladder onto a grated floor three levels down. There, Beio-Rhett reached the coded door and set his fingers to the panel. Inside, his three cohorts awaited him.

"That the last one?" he asked, nodding towards the fuel tank.

"Yep," answered one of the rebels.

"Good," said Beio-Rhett. "Now keep your asses movin' and pack up when you're done. I'm gonna go check out our friend."

"What if he isn't one of ours?" asked one of the rebels.

"I still need to find out," Beio-Rhett said. "It's now or never. I got my own pod, so you guys just sit tight and stay quiet!"

Before any of the rebels could argue, Beio-Rhett was off. He entered the airlock and shut the seal behind him, then quickly hopped into one of the four transports the rebels had stowed away in the airlock. The transports were small and shaped like a large round-tipped bullet with wings. The outer doors of the airlock opened and Beio-Rhett flew out before the outer doors shut again. The authorities couldn't track this airlock release because the rebels put phantom readings on the entire room making it seem like nothing was happening at all. Beio-Rhett flipped the pilot controls to manual. He steered the vessel towards the troublesome shuttle still a good distance from the station. Beio-Rhett activated the cloaking system making the little ship invisible to all sensors, scopes and radar.

When he finally reached the ship, he slowed down a bit to find a docking door or an airlock for smaller crafts such as the one he was in. He found only one small loading entrance. Beio-Rhett assumed that the pilot jammed the codes to open the loading door. Fortunately, the rebels had many brilliant minds among them. Beio-Rhett's pod was armed with a code breaker. He quickly unjammed the codes to the door and opened them. The loading space looked empty, which was lucky for Beio-Rhett since that was the only way he could get inside. He flew his pod into the loading space and punched in the code to close the doors behind him. He leapt out of his ship and opened the inner-airlock doors before stepping inside and drawing out his pistol-blaster. The passenger area was empty. Beio-Rhett walked cautiously towards the bridge, checking every last corner for any sign of movement. His pistol followed his eyes as he scanned the entirety of the shuttle before proceeding to the bridge door.

The bridge door was unlocked, so he opened it. Still, no signs of movement. Not even the blue tail that stuck out from behind the pilot's chair, flinched.

Beio-Rhett smiled. He raised his blaster up to the chair and yelled, "Yo! Stand up slowly and drop any weapons you have!"

The Hydrolette calmly lifted his head up from behind the chair. Unlike most Hydrolettes, his hair was completely shaved except for a stripe across the top of his head. Also, unlike most Hydrolettes whose eyes were yellow with black slits, this Hydrolette's eyes were red. He was shorter than Beio-Rhett and sported a black, sturdy fibrous jacket. He raised his arms and walked out from behind the chair.

Beio-Rhett and the other Hydrolette immediately recognized each other.

"Dembo!" Beio-Rhett shouted. "You're alive!"

"Beio-Rhett!" Dembo shouted back, smiling. "How are you? I mean...," He forgot his words.

Beio-Rhett holstered his blaster and chuckled. "I can't believe it. We all thought you died!"

Dembo's mood darkened as he looked at the ground as though distracted by something, some memory.

"The blast at Mount Kastikae," Beio-Rhett said. "On Katoola."

Dembo looked up and finally nodded. "Yeah," he said. "Yeah, I remember. I got launched from the blast and tumbled into a swamp," he seemed distracted by the same memory. "I thought that same blast killed all of you." He looked up again, "You have no idea what I've been through! If we make it out of here alive, I'll tell you the story."

Beio-Rhett was still smiling, glad to see an old friend. "Fair enough."

At the station, the authorities were growing anxious. Try as they did, they couldn't get any information on the shuttle.

"You gotta send someone in," said the communications officer. "There's no point in trying to hack in. It's not like he's gonna turn off his signal jam."

The Captain turned to the officer. "We gotta alert dispatch. And we need to contain this as soon as possible. This could be a decoy. Reports of shuttles being attacked by rebel squads have become commonplace in this sector the last few days. They may be trying to board us from some cloaked vessel as we speak."

"Should we go into lockdown?" asked the officer

"No, maybe we can have the upper hand here. Keep the guard force focused on the public and watch their points."

A tall Hydrolette in a brown soldier's uniform walked briskly through the crowds, at the station, towards his next flight. His uniform bore a sergeant's badge and above that, a black patch that read the symbols for "M" and "P," military police. The Hydrolette was older, almost middle-aged. His face was worn and bearded and his hair was cropped short. He wore his field uniform, rather than the ceremonial.

He glanced out the long window that lined the station walkway only to see the same tenacious shuttle. Although the soldier found it strange how the shuttle was hovering just outside the station's perimeter, he shrugged it off and continued walking. It wasn't until he noticed a few station guards ahead of him listening to their earpieces intently, that he took an interest.

"Well, we should still engage." The officer seemed concerned but still calm.

"We'll send a scout. Maybe someone without colors, fool 'em into thinking we didn't notice. Let's not divert any more attention than we have to in case they're trying to spring a trap."

"And what if it's nothing?"

"Lucky us."

The soldier stepped up to the guards and flashed his ID tag, hanging around his neck on a chain.

Both guards immediately saluted, "Sergeant? May we be of service?"

"I was actually going to ask you the same thing," the soldier replied. "Mind telling me what's going on with that shuttle out there? I think I can be of some help."

"Military? Yeah, send him in," the Captain replied to the guards' request over the radio. "Guess it is our lucky day," he said to the officer.

Shortly after, the Captain turned and saw the guards escorting the military colors through the bridge doors, "Sergeant?"

"Sir, with your permission I'd like to volunteer to get a closer look at this visitor," the soldier spoke firmly but quietly.

The Captain nodded and spoke to the guards, "Get back out there and maintain crowd control." He turned to the soldier. "Glad to have you with us, Sergeant. Do you have a transport?"

"No, I'm in transit."

"Damn! Well, you can use one of ours'. I want you to engage that shuttle as fast as possible. Board it and apprehend any perpetrators should they turn hostile. You can contact us easily from the cruiser should you run into trouble. Now here's the game plan…"

The sergeant darted past the guards on one of the landing platforms towards one of the unmanned guard crafts. The vessels were small defense cruisers armed with light weaponry and room for only one pilot. Besides the few guard vessels on the landing platform, there were crates of all sorts. Some technicians were tuning up other vessels on the platforms. This was one of the smaller docking bays on the station, mainly for use by the crew.

The sergeant briefly looked up through the clear bubble that shielded the docking bay from the starlit void. He could see the vast array of stars and the second sphere of the station separated by a cylindrical bridge, which was surrounded by other bubbles protecting the several other docking bays. The sergeant could also make out the small speck that was the infamous shuttle in front of the backdrop of space. Using a remote the Captain gave him, he unlocked one of the vessels and opened the cockpit. The sergeant jumped inside the vessel just as it opened. He activated the radio as the cockpit closed

"This is Sergeant Reuk Singatt requesting permission to vacate docking bay 93." "Permission granted," the voice on the other side sounded. "You are clear of all space traffic. Proceed with caution."

"Copy that," Singatt responded. The cockpit now closed, Singatt fired up the engines. The craft slowly hovered above the platform, blowing air out from under it, which upset the techs only mildly. Red lights flashed around the perimeter of the platform as the guard ship rose. Singatt steered the ship towards the bubble wall. The thrusters lit up and the vessel sped right through the bubble without upsetting the barrier at all. Only a ripple pulsated from the point at which the vessel passed through the bubble. The technicians continued their work.

Aboard the shuttle, Beio-Rhett and Dembo were much

more relaxed.

"What are you doing here?" asked Beio-Rhett still smiling.

"Like I said, it's a very long story," Dembo insisted. "However, I am here to basically refuel and be on my way. Unfortunately, this shuttle is stolen and I don't have registration of any kind. When I saw the scanner pop up I turned on the signal jam and tried to find a way out of this before they sent someone out and then… you showed up."

"I tend to do that when people least expect it," Beio-Rhett chuckled. Before he continued he caught a glimpse of the guard ship heading towards their shuttle out of the corner of his eye. "Hey, man." He pointed towards the vessel.

Dembo spun around to see the approaching vessel. "Damnit!" he shouted.

"Well, so much for catching up," Beio-Rhett quipped. He turned back to Dembo, "What was your plan for when they did send someone out?"

"I never got that far," Dembo lamented. "This is a transport shuttle. It doesn't have any weapons!"

"Don't worry," Beio-Rhett said pulling out his comlink. "I have some back-up."

He awaited a response on the other end of the line, keeping his eye on the vessel. Finally an answer: "Hello?" one of his subordinates said.

"We have an officer approaching fast," Beio-Rhett remained calm. "We need some back-up."

"We?"

"He's one of ours', one of the first, actually. Just get out here and quickly. If you live through this, I'll explain!"

Singatt squinted to get a better look at the silent transport. Before his scanners confirmed the lack of any ballistics, he could tell by the shape of the vessel that it wasn't equipped for any weaponry, even defensive. The only thing he had to worry about was having it disappear on him, but even then, he knew his little pod could go much faster. Still, Singatt was in no mood for a chase. He lit up the shuttle and set the pod's missiles to lock on to the shuttle's engines.

In the shuttle, Dembo noticed a red warning signal on the control panel. "Shit, he just lit us up!" He scrambled towards the controls.

"Relax!" ordered Beio-Rhett. "Get the shields up and lets get outta here!"

"We can't outrun him, this is a fucking shuttle!" Dembo started to panic.

"We've got hyper drive. Make a U-turn and gun it," Beio-Rhett walked up to the control panel. "Hurry though, he's gaining on us."

Dembo sat down and brought up manual control. "Won't be easy. This things turning radius is useless!" He fired up the engines and pushed the shuttle forward banking it to the right as hard as he could. The force threw Beio-Rhett sideways against the hull, but he quickly recovered. The shuttle seemed at first to be charging the guard craft, but soon rolled over on its side to the right, making a most ungraceful turn before putting the rear engines in Singatt's face and blasting off.

Singatt's lock on the engine's faltered, but he knew it would eventually recover. He accelerated, keeping close behind the retreating shuttle. He continued scanning the vessel for any useful information. Its top speed was hardly comparable to his craft's. The shields wouldn't hold out against his weapons and it didn't even have defensive weapons. There was no reason to fire upon the shuttle, but he still needed to find a way to stop it. He was about to disarm his missiles when a laser blast rocked his vessel. His monitor flashed red text in the Hydrolette's native language of Groakor, "Emergency! Incoming Fire!" Singatt, instinctively maxed his shield power and switched to manual weapons, scanning his perimeter. Three solo attack vessels were coming up from behind him, firing rapidly.

Singatt spun his vessel around to face the attackers and lit up the three vessels, realigning his missile targeting. He manually locked on to one of the vessels, tweaking the joystick quickly but calmly till a red indicator that read "LOCKED" was flashing. Singatt pulled the trigger on the joystick without hesitation sending a proton missile straight towards one of the craft, incinerating it. Unfortunately, for the other two attackers, the craft was loaded with the liquid fuel supplies the three rebels had just been siphoning. The fuel ignited and the explosion swallowed the other two attacking crafts without incident. Singatt released a quick breath of relief before turning his craft back around to continue his pursuit.

Beio-Rhett watched the incident on the shuttle's monitors. "Morons," he muttered.

"That was your back-up?" exclaimed Dembo.

"It bought us some time," replied Beio-Rhett. "Get us into hyperspace!"

"We have to set a course!"

"Anywhere! Just punch it!" Beio-Rhett was starting to lose his cool.

Dembo turned his attention to the controls and typed in some coordinates.

Meanwhile, Singatt discovered a useful function in his craft. An engine disabler. He quickly set up the targeting system and locked on to the shuttle engine. When he got a positive reading from the targeting system, he fired the electromagnetic pulse designed for such troublesome vessels. The glowing blue pulse shot from the guard craft's stern and struck the shuttle's engines, which went dead, bringing the shuttle to a stop.

Dembo broke into a cold sweat. The engines ceased, the monitors went dark and even the lights had gone out. He tried in vain to start the engines. None of the controls were responding. "Fuck!" he shouted. "We're finished! Nothing works!"

Beio-Rhett forced his way towards the controls. "Let me try!"

Before Beio-Rhett could make any other futile attempts, they both heard the airlock door of the shuttle open. The doors slid all the way open as the two spun around revealing the unlit airlock. Beio-Rhett drew his pistol and aimed at the darkness. He fired six times. No shouts, screams or thuds, just the soft whine of the pistol recharging. "Wait here," he said softly as he walked slowly towards the airlock, pistol raised.

He leapt into the airlock and checked all the corners, his pistol following his eyes. Still nothing. There was only the guard craft, empty and powered down.

Above Beio-Rhett, clinging to the ceiling of the airlock, hung Singatt with his pistol aimed at Beio-Rhett. The barrel of the blaster was less than a foot from his head. Singatt watched as Beio-Rhett carefully scanned the empty corners of the airlock, looking every way but up. Singatt pulled the trigger.

Dembo heard a muffled blast accompanied by a blue flash coming from the airlock. He could also see Beio-Rhett's body fall forward and not get up. He was startled by the blast and emitted a short gasp, but quickly regained composure. He took a deep breath and reached under the control panel, keeping his eyes on the airlock door. He found a compartment and opened it. He reached in and pulled out a small pistol of his own. Keeping his eyes on the door, he stood up and held it forward, not letting his eyes leave the dark doorway. He stepped forward cautiously, keeping the weapon raised and his eyes open. Seeing Beio-Rhett's fall, he did not enter the airlock, but stopped just short of the entrance. His visibility was a little better, but he still couldn't discern any bodies besides Beio-Rhett's unconscious one. He could just see the guard pod, still creaking, having just landed. Still, there was nobody there. It was a small airlock and Dembo could make out the furthest corners, there were no shadows.

Dembo wasn't fooled. Someone was in there and he knew it. They were only hiding well. Still, he couldn't see them from this vantage. He had to enter the room. Keeping his eyes fixed forward and his blaster poised, he took one step into the room. He stopped for a few seconds and scanned the room again, checking his peripherals. Still nothing. He bent down slightly to see if he could make out anything under the guard craft, but he couldn't. There was only Beio-Rhett, lying a few feet in front of him. He stood back up and lifted his other foot to take his second step into the airlock, but having bent down, his balance was compromised. His other foot tripped over the lip of the airlock entrance, sending Dembo flying forward. His head hit the wing of the guard craft and he saw no more.

* * *

Singatt walked briskly through the main corridors of Bestton Air & Naval Base, the primary headquarters of Hydrolet's armed forces, located just outside of Hydrolet's capital city of Bestton. The Base was the center for tactical military decisions, flight training, and monitoring combatants. It housed the largest fleet of fighter ships on the planet and one of the largest fleets in the system. Bestton also housed one of the largest naval fleets in the galaxy, despite sea warfare becoming obsolete with the advent of space travel. Hydrolet was one of the few planets that maintained a powerful naval force, which served them well in times of warfare on their soil. Bestton was conveniently located between a mountain range and the sea, making it practically impenetrable. Most of the launch pads were built into the mountain giving a strategic advantage in air fights. Most of the brains of the base were also housed deep within the mountain, making the most important personnel and equipment unreachable by invading forces. The naval defenses were also massive: huge fusion cannons bordered the sea, poised and ready for any invading forces. Although the Department of War was housed within the Executive Building in Bestton City Center, the micromanaging and grunt work of the Hydrolet Military was performed at the base.

Singatt had a reserved spring in his step. He was walking straight and tall, saluting the various soldiers and engineers he happened across as he marched through the main corridor. They all recognized Singatt as he strutted by.

"Way to go, Singatt!" one would shout.

"You're going down in history!" said another.

Singatt came to the end of the corridor where a guard stood by a large arching entrance. He saluted the guard.

The guard saluted back and typed in a passcode behind him, which opened the sliding doors to the entrance. "The General's gonna be glad to see you." The guard stepped aside to let Singatt in.

The entrance led to a large conference room. Chairs surrounded a large circular platform, at the center of which, projected a glowing hologram of the planet Hydrolet. Sitting at the table were several high-ranking officers. A few nonmilitary executives were also present. The officers all wore similar brown and beige military outfits, each decorated with various metals and badges. One of the generals, who was significantly older than the rest, seemed more relaxed than the other officers. His outfit was purple. Lines creased his blue face and his black hair had unmistakable streaks of grey.

The only one standing was a lower-level officer. He had a laser pointer, which he used to point out certain areas on the hologram, where boxes of text sprung forth. "And over here by Ttanis, we were able to move in troops which sacked enemy locations here, here and here…" he spoke firmly, unjostled by the doors opening. However, he was soon interrupted by the older general.

"Singatt!" the general exclaimed. He immediately stood up

and walked over to Singatt.

Singatt stood to attention and saluted, "Sir!"

Artinuare saluted back. "At ease, Sergeant," he said snatching his hand and shaking it firmly. "We're all pretty damn proud of you! That little stunt you pulled at the station really turned the war around. Of all the rebels you could've happened upon… It really is a miracle. Not to take anything away from your previous performance."

"Good to see you, General Artinuare," Singatt shook his hand firmly and grinned. "But you are right, it was blind luck. And besides that, it wasn't my interrogation. I only captured the bastards."

"You only captured the uncapturable!" Artinuare exclaimed. "I wish I were there to see it. I've only heard stories of that menace. Never have had the pleasure of meeting him. But his reputation more than precedes him. I would imagine you'd be afraid to be so aggressive."

"If I'd have known I probably wouldn't have been," Singatt chuckled.

The General laughed. "Oh come now, no need to sell yourself short! You're a hero!" He patted Singatt on the back. "And that brings me to why I summoned you here."

He turned around to face the officers. "Sorry for the interruption," he said as he reached into his pocket and produced a small case. "Although I am glad you're all here as well to witness this," he turned back around and presented the case to Singatt. "Sergeant Major Reuk Singatt of the Hydrolet Space Force, I hereby promote you to Second Lieutenant." He opened the case to reveal a silver badge in the shape of a small shield.

Singatt was in disbelief. He tried hard to maintain his composure, but his eyes betrayed him. "G-General," he stuttered. "You summoned me here for this? To personally promote me?"

"Of course!" the General smiled. "I would never pass up the opportunity to personally congratulate the officer who single-handedly ended this devastating Rebellion. Of course you realize I'm a busy man, and it's hard to schedule such an event… I had to double book myself. He looked back sheepishly at the officers at the table. "Again, my most sincere apologies," he said. "We'll continue the debriefing as soon as you all show your appreciation for Lieutenant Singatt here."

As the general took the badge and fastened it to Singatt's collar, the officers and the other attendees stood up and applauded. When the General took a step back and saluted Singatt, he was saluting a Lieutenant.

When Singatt saluted back, he was saluting as a Lieutenant. He tried to stop the tears that were beginning to well up. He was described by what few friends he had as a stoic, unflappable. That's why his friends assumed he joined the military. But, all living things are alive. One can only displace their emotions, not destroy them. Singatt made it to age 78, a little younger than middle age by Hydrolette years, without ever getting married. Like most in the military, the only semblance of validation besides surviving was promotion. Singatt never admitted to himself that he had any need for human connection. His adoptive parents died in the first Hydro-Baltan War 60 years prior. He felt no deep connection to them and he believed they felt likewise. It was soon after that he joined the military, perhaps as a way to give himself the purpose that his adoptive parents didn't give him. The only thing he received from his parents was his last name. There couldn't be a more common first name in the Hydrolette race than Reuk. Singatt was his name. He never even finished school. He just joined the armed forces and worked his way up from the bottom. First as a private, then up through the ranks. His first combat experience was at the tail end of the first Hydro-Baltan War. He came out a Staff Sergeant and spent the next 25 years as a drill instructor at various academies. Once again, this occupation made it easy to detach himself from any emotional connection as it was part of his job. He had to be cold. The second, more infamous Hydro-Baltan War put him back into action where he attained the rank of Sergeant Major. He was not as active on the battlefield, but flew more space battles. He became renowned for his flying prowess and led many successful bombardments. He made it out the Hydro-Baltan War nearly unscathed, having only been shot down once. The Rebellion saw him back behind a desk, this time serving as an MP. He had grown tired in his later years of battle and preferred to serve behind the scenes. Yet, it was times like this when that displaced spirit found itself welling up. Validation. To be promoted was always the next step.

He thought, ironic how he earned this promotion. He had never seen a rebel during the Rebellion. He served the nation during this Rebellion investigating misdemeanors and overseeing court-martials and discharges. It was pure chance that he happened to be on that space station when Beio-Rhett was there. That he had encountered Dembo as well was an amazing stroke of luck. His decision to aid the station in apprehending the unknown assailant was partially a sense of duty, but there was some impulse in his decision. He didn't admit it to himself, but maybe he was tired of not seeing any action for such a long time. And here it made him a commissioned officer. Now he'd definitely not be seeing any action. Still, it was these moments where his displaced emotions had their outlet. Promotion was never his intended goal. He was fine with being Sergeant Major his whole life, and before that he was fine with being a Staff Sergeant. Even now retiring as a Lieutenant seemed like a fine career, but in the moment of that promotion, he felt like he could climb to the top. He felt like he had made his mark, especially being awarded this honor by the Grand General of Hydrolet's Armed Forces Erthon Artinuare himself.

Singatt turned and saluted the other officers, still smiling. He turned back to the General. "It's an honor," he started.

"Nonsense!" Artinuare interrupted. "It's an honor to meet the man who saved us a good ten years of trying to quell these rebels. The entire planet of Hydrolet is in your debt!"

Singatt could only smile. He looked down at his feet and then back at the General with a more concerned expression. "So General, speaking of the rebels, what will happen to the survivors."

"The not-so-Masked Menace?" the General asked. "And the other one… Dembo Bebsin, self-proclaimed Colonel of the Rebellion. Status, M.I.A., presumed K.I.A., until now that is."

"That's right, or that's what I've been told. He's been missing now for about five years," Singatt replied.

"Indeed," the General remarked. "Well, now that their interrogation is over we have no more use of them. Both of them are basically off the grid. One is presumed dead and the other is a mercenary. And besides that, they are technically your prisoners. As such, I leave their fates in your hands."

Singatt was taken aback. "Sir, I don't know what to say."

"Well, the Government's done with them, but anything you decide we will financially support, be it incarceration, execution, etc."

Singatt thought for a moment and turned back to the General. "May I see them first?"

"Of course! That's another reason I brought you here. We're holding them in this very base."

***

Beio-Rhett and Dembo sat in a white room with no defining features except for a white door, barely visible except for the shadow made by the crease around the frame. The two sat on a rather uncomfortable black couch with their hands bound by cuffs connected with an electronic beam. Their feet were also in cuffs that were bound to the feet of the couch with similar electronic beams. In front of them was a small coffee table with three glasses and a black pitcher and across from that was another uncomfortable-looking black chair. Both wore the same clothes as when they were captured: Beio-Rhett in his shirt and vest, Dembo in a plain dark outfit with a thick black fibrous jacket.

Dembo also sported a bandage on his forehead where he was struck by the ship's wing. He seemed troubled, but not worried.

Beio-Rhett was more distraught, an empty look on his face. His unkempt hair hung sparsely in front of his face covering up any expression one could discern. He took a breath and finally looked over at Dembo. "So what's with the Mohawk?" he asked.

Before Dembo could answer, the invisible door opened and Singatt, holding a folder, walked into the room. He sat down in the chair across the table from Beio-Rhett and Dembo then filled one of the glasses with water from the pitcher. He took a sip and smiled at the two.

Beio-Rhett snarled back. Dembo only stared at him intently.

"I see we're going to get along." Singatt opened up his folder and placed it on the table. "Before we get started, I want to show you something." He produced a small remote control from his pocket. "Security gave this to me. It controls the slack on your electric binds." He pressed the unlock button.

Beio-Rhett and Dembo could stretch the electric beam as far as their arms could go. They could also move their feet.

"Just so you know who's in control," he pressed another

button and the binds contracted completely, leaving Beio-Rhett and Dembo's hands completely bound. "Not to disrespect you, but I've heard stories about your attitude," he looked at Beio-Rhett, "and your deviousness." He looked at Dembo. He placed the remote on the table next to him, but out of reach of the two, "But I have no need to play power games with you, I'm just concerned for your and my safety."

Beio-Rhett's eyes followed the remote down to the table. He saw the remote placed on the "unlock" button. He didn't say anything, nor did he move in any conspicuous way. His eyes returned to Singatt as if he saw nothing.

Singatt leafed through some papers in the files. "Now, in case you haven't been keeping up on current events, I regret to be the first to inform you that the Rebellion has been crushed. Thanks to the information we've extracted from you two: we were able to locate all the major operation centers for the Rebellion, invade and sack them. We were also able to apprehend most of the ranking officers leading the Rebellion. Obviously some of the highest ranking officers were able to escape." He tossed down a picture of a very clean-cut looking Hydrolette, the left side of whose face was badly scarred from a burn. "But even though General Dresbar has escaped, the Rebellion is practically wiped out. Most of the soldiers have either been killed or captured and every leader of any sort is now under trial."

Beio-Rhett didn't react.

Dembo stared at the picture of Dresbar for a second and closed his eyes.

Singatt leafed through a few more papers and looked back at the two. "Now I've heard a lot about you," he looked at Beio-Rhett, "as has everyone." He turned to Dembo, "And you as well, Colonel Dembo Bebsin of the Hydrolet Rebellion. It's difficult to not come across your name. I'm actually surprised to be seeing you in the flesh. You've been presumed dead for the last five years."

Dembo made no motion. He continued to look at the picture of Dresbar.

"So Beio-Rhett," Singatt continued looking through his files. "56 years old, 7'1." Birthplace unknown. First known records appear under the alias Rhett in the Nielhelm Orphanage on Baltania. First registered under our grid in the second Hydro-Baltan War as a private. Quickly rose to the rank of First Lieutenant before becoming employed in the Special Operations Sector. After falling off the grid again, you resurface as the infamous Masked Menace, the most feared bounty hunter in the galaxy. After tiring of that, you decide to turn to more engaging mercenary work. Last known employers were the Hydrolet Rebellion and that brings you here."

He looked up at Beio-Rhett. "There are many holes in your life story Beio-Rhett, but you see we have very reliable sources."

"You should see the holes in my body," quipped Beio-Rhett.

Singatt only smiled and turned to Dembo, "And you. We already know your story, one of the highest-ranking officers next to Dresbar in the Rebellion. Also, it is apparent that you were instrumental in starting the Rebellion, while a student at the University of Colett. Age 45, 6'9." Dropped out after three years at University and resurfaced as one of the Government's most wanted criminals. Presumed dead after a skirmish on our moon, Katoola. We already know your sentiments of the Rebellion and you know why you're here."

Singatt put the files down and took another sip of water. "Now, given the circumstances, we all know the two of you have no reason to be alive right now and I'm sure you're both wondering why. I brought this info here to show you that I've done my homework. I am not a rash man like the two of you. After going through your files and doing some research myself, I've come to the conclusion that the two of you have invaluable skills in combat, strategy, leadership, and integrity. I came here to tell you that I admire you both."

Beio-Rhett still snarled, but Dembo looked up with a surprised look on his face.

Singatt leaned forward. "Now, to be honest, I see no purpose in executing either of you except to set an example for a Rebellion that no longer exists. The movers and shakers who have caused death and destruction to many citizens of our planet will face their punishment. The worst criminals like Dresbar here, are who we're really after. You two, although responsible for your crimes, will not set an example even if we made the most public spectacle of your executions. You aren't even a member of the Rebellion, being a mercenary." He looked at Beio-Rhett. "And you haven't been active in the Rebellion for the last five years and made no effort to rejoin their forces in that time." He looked at Dembo. "I know neither of you really have a home now that the rebellion is crushed. You've lost your employer and you just rejoined society, but you are both still very talented warriors. There is no need for that talent to go to waste. As the Government considers you both free agents, I am offering to compensate you for mercenary work, for the Planet of Hydrolet. What do you say? Why not join the winning side?"

Dembo took out a long sigh, but before he could say anything, Beio-Rhett sprung into action. Seizing his opportunity, he leapt from his chair, the electric strands trailing behind his feet but not stopping him. He kicked the table over with one foot and gave a sharp roundhouse kick to Singatt's stomach which sent him tumbling back in his chair, coughing. Beio-Rhett then leapt upon Singatt like a savage beast and put his hands on both sides of Singatt's neck, the electronic beam coursing through Singatt's flesh.

The strand was incorporeal, so it passed right through Singatt's neck, but not without doing damage. The electric charge surged through his body. The skin where the strand came through his neck glowed red. The pain in his stomach and Beio-Rhett's weight on top of him made it difficult for him to stand. That, along with the loss of feeling spreading from his neck throughout his body, Singatt knew he only had a few minutes to live, and only a few seconds before he lost consciousness. He clutched his stomach which he was already losing feeling. He was going to die. The few seconds he had left of consciousness spanned an eternity as he felt his existence come to a close. His proudest moment was now followed by his last. He thought that to act generously would be the best way to not waste the honor given to him. Offer this monster freedom, and redemption. It would've been so easy to have him killed without even meeting him, but he thought this would be the right thing to do. However, the Masked Menace was no less menacing without his mask. He was the same harbinger of death. Singatt should have known. His logic told him death was near, but he also had the spirit of a soldier. Even as he comprehended his end he searched for some way to free himself.

Meanwhile, as his fading eyes searched the room he could hear Beio-Rhett's cold, growling, animal-like voice whisper violently in his ear, "I say no fucking way!"

As soon as the words left Beio-Rhett's mouth, Singatt saw the remote had fallen by his hand. Three or perhaps four seconds had passed. He had at least three more seconds before he passed out. He thrust his hand out, as hard as it was. He could barely feel his fingertips, but he used his eyes to guide them to the "off" button on the remote.

The strands disappeared and Singatt's feeling returned almost instantly. Before Beio-Rhett could react, Singatt slid back away from Beio-Rhett and pressed the "on" button, turning the tautness of the strands to zero.

Four electronic strands sprung from the couch grabbing Beio-Rhett's limbs. They connected with the cuffs on his hands and feet and then contracted pulling Beio-Rhett off of Singatt and sending him flying back to the couch. His feet stuck against the legs and his hands were pulled to the back of the couch leaving him completely bound.

Beio-Rhett looked at his hands bound to beam emitters at the back of the couch. His plan would have been solid had he noticed these earlier. "Hmm," he remarked. "I was wondering what those were for."

Dembo barely had time to react, but seeing that Singatt had made it out alive, he only shook his head and let his head fall in his bound hands.

The doors slid open and several guards came storming in. They aimed their rifles directly at Beio-Rhett's face. One of the guards helped Singatt up.

"What's going on?" shouted the guard helping Singatt up, "Are you all right? What happened?"

"Nothing! Nothing!" Singatt gasped through hoarse coughs. "Everything' fine! Just back up! Gimme some room. He shooed the guards away from him. He noticed the guards with their rifles aimed at Beio-Rhett barking orders furiously at him. "Wait!" he shouted at them. "Don't shoot!"

"But, Lieutenant!" one of the guards replied.

"It's all right!" he shouted back, trying to stand up. "We just had a little... misunderstanding."

Dembo still had his head in his palms, but looked up when he heard this.

Beio-Rhett was also confused. He was smiling at the guards when they had their guns pointed at him, but when he heard

Singatt's words he was no longer smiling. *Why is he doing this?* His face betrayed confusion as his mind started to spin. He expected to die, by now his defiant face would be torn apart by laser blasts. He was waiting for it. He was never willing to admit defeat, to submit to his captors. *I can only be a wild animal or a dead one, never a tamed one.* He didn't expect to get out of the base alive, let alone the room. Maybe he could make it out of the holding cell, but he wouldn't make it far after that. Regardless, he had prepared himself to die. The entire time he was waiting in the holding room for Dembo, and even when they sat together, he was preparing himself, physically, mentally and spiritually. *I survived their little interrogation easily, and this post-interrogation is a fucking joke by comparison.* But there was no way out of here alive without cooperating, and he wouldn't do that. He would fight. Resist. He would press on until he spent his last defiant breath. He was ready the moment he woke up captured. It was a new concept to him, being captured. *I won't accept it!* That was why he smiled. If they killed him, he won. *They can't control me.* No one could. He had seen war, violence, and death itself. Nothing scared him. No one could intimidate him. *I'm ready.* This was how he wanted to go out.

But he didn't. There was one thing he wasn't planning on. Compassion. He ignored Singatt's words earlier, which already hinted his compassionate nature. He was too blinded by pride and resolve. But now he finally saw it. This was a *misunderstanding?* It was no such thing. *I couldn't have made my intentions clearer. But why?* Why even after he revealed he had no regard for Singatt's generosity or his life would he spare his? It sent his mind into a tailspin. His cold, grim, simplistic outlook on life began to peel away. The thought of Dembo popped into his head. *I could've gotten him killed, too.* His ego had blinded him to that fact. Sure Beio-Rhett would never admit to caring for another being, *at least not since…* But nevertheless, he couldn't deny he respected Dembo. Still, this Singatt did care. He saved both their lives, *twice!* As his jaded perception continued to crumble, something subtle started eating away at the thick layer of encrusted hatred and suffering around his heart. It wasn't a complete turnover, but a small bit of light found its way in, a growing infection. Perhaps it would never completely heal him, but it was there now.

"I'll do it," he looked at Singatt.

Singatt spun around, "What?!"

Dembo also turned and looked at Beio-Rhett confused.

"You're right," he said, trying to cover up his revelation. "I am still a mercenary. I sure can't work for the Rebellion anymore... and... I'm here anyway, so I'll take whatever jobs you have to offer." He took a deep breath.

Dembo looked over at Beio-Rhett. He was in a bit of disbelief having witnessed the whole event. Although it took him by surprise, he couldn't really say he didn't expect it. Beio-Rhett was rash when he met him and remained rash when they parted ways. It definitely wasn't Dembo's way. He never jumped into a situation without completely analyzing it. He did take chances, and put himself in dangerous situations, but they were always calculated. He had no intention of working for the government, just like Beio-Rhett. For over a decade he had been against their policies on war and colonization. His spirit was still rebellious, but he knew the Rebellion had lost its spirit. Still, he had never thought of supporting the monster he was trying to take down. He was of the same mind as Beio-Rhett to refuse to submit, but he didn't want to make a spectacle of himself. However, seeing the most rebellious, defiant soul he had ever seen submit was something he never expected.

"Really?" was the only word he could come up with to respond to Beio-Rhett.

Beio-Rhett only looked to Dembo and nodded.

Singatt turned to Dembo, "And what about you, Colonel Bebsin?"

Dembo thought for a minute. The idea of being a mercenary was something very alien to him. He was always a fighter for a cause, not for a paycheck, although he hadn't fought in a long time. He sorted through his options, of which there were none. "What if I don't?" he asked calmly.

Singatt smiled, "Well, you are still a war criminal. Just because you went missing doesn't mean you aren't on our list. You can serve your debt to society in jail if you want. I won't take your life, but I can't let your crimes go unanswered."

Dembo nodded, "Well, I guess I don't really have a choice."

"Of course you do," Singatt said. "This is the best deal you'll ever get. If you didn't have such a nice guy like me capture you, you'd both be dead now.

Dembo took a deep breath, "I know… I know…"

"Do we have a deal?" Singatt asked.

Beio-Rhett and Dembo both nodded.

Singatt turned the binders off and the electronic beams disappeared.

"Lieutenant!" one of the guards exclaimed.

"Put your weapons down," Singatt ordered. "These two are officially working for us, for now at least."

Beio-Rhett stood up slowly and messaged his wrists. He stretched his arms and neck and cracked his back.

Dembo stood up and did the same. He took a deep sigh.

The three Hydrolettes looked at each other and smiled.

Chapter 2

A Seed of Evil

"Mother Earth is pregnant for the third time… for y'all have knocked her up"

A small drop of fluffy white substance broke the calm surface of the water in the sink. Then another drop. A few smaller drops also fell into the water, before a knife covered in the substance was lowered into the sink. It was submerged and swirled around, clearing it of the fluffy substance before being lifted back up. Then a drop of thick green liquid fell into the water, slowly dissolving among the clear water.

"Shit!" exclaimed Beio-Rhett. He put the knife down and grabbed a small piece of bath tissue. He placed the small piece over the wound and looked at himself in the mirror. The green blood soaked through the paper quickly and it soon fell. Beio-Rhett grunted and grabbed a towel next to the sink. He wiped the rest of the cream off his face and dabbed the wound. The bleeding had almost stopped. He looked back into the mirror. "Good enough," he said to himself. He threw the towel in a nearby hamper and reached into the sink, pulling the plug. The water slowly drained taking with it all the cloudy froth and small bit of green. As it was draining, Beio-Rhett sheathed the knife and threw it in his small duffel bag full of his personal things found on him when he was captured. There was only a change of clothes, some sparse hygienic equipment and some rations. He turned and ran the faucet over the draining sink to help clean it out. After the sink was completely drained he turned off the faucet. Naturally a few drops of water still dripped down into the drain below. Beio-Rhett looked down as the water fell. He then noticed one of the drops was green. There was then another green drop. No more innocent, clear water, but thick violent blood. A little distracted by what seemed like a bleeding faucet, he noticed that he was still bleeding. He regained his senses, then wiped off his face, figuring it'd clot soon enough.

He looked in the mirror again. Singatt had told him to tidy up a bit since he was going to meet Grand General Artinuare. Although he didn't admit to himself that he gave a shit, he still thought it was pretty neat that he was given such an honor. Not during his tenure as a special ops agent was he ever introduced to the Grand General. And here he gets the privilege when he's a damned prisoner. His hair was still quite disheveled as always. The best he figured he could do was tie it back, although it was a loose ponytail. At least he was clean-shaven. Since he was not a soldier, he had no formal military dress. He didn't want to wear the outfit that he had been for the last few days, so Singatt gave him a standard military outfit usually given to civilians or refugees. It was little more than a simple brown jacket and pants with a black T-shirt.

Satisfied with his appearance, he slung his bag over his back and left the restroom. He ran into Dembo who had just come from another restroom. The two were cleaning up in one of the barracks private rooms on the Bestton Base.

Dembo chuckled when he saw Beio-Rhett's face. "Stupid with a razor?"

"Stupid with a knife," Beio-Rhett replied.

"You forget what century it is or something?"

"No, I'm just a badass like that. A razor can only be used for one thing. A knife has many uses."

Dembo laughed. "We're not on the battlefield anymore."

"It's all a battlefield. You should've learned that by now."

"You should've learned by now that it isn't."

Beio-Rhett laughed. "Man, you have changed."

Dembo only smiled. "You haven't."

Beio-Rhett nodded. He motioned to the exit. "Shall we?"

Dembo nodded, "You remember where to go?"

"Kind of."

The two left the private room and headed through the corridor ahead. "You still haven't told me about the mohawk."

Before Dembo could answer, the two saw a worried-looking Singatt walking toward them from the other end of the corridor.

"What's going on?" Dembo asked.

Singatt stopped just short of them still looking at the floor. He took a breath and finally looked up at the two.

"Well, I thought I'd have this meeting already set up but the truth is, I haven't spoken to the General since I last saw you."

"What do you mean?" Dembo asked again.

"Not that I can expect the General to drop everything and grant a request for an audience from a simple Lieutenant, but still, he seems to have disappeared from the base. He specifically told me that when I had drafted my proposal for the criminals, to contact him immediately and now I can't reach him. I've been up for 24 hours straight getting this file in order and he's gone. I've asked all knowledgeable personnel and they say they can't reveal the General's location at this time, though I get the sense that by 'can't' they mean 'won't.' The General even gave me authorized clearance to be patched right through to him and even that won't do it. I even took some initiative and tried my military multi-pass to the entire the War Room where I figured he may be and it denied my access. At that point, the guards came after me and told me that the General cannot be reached at this time and he will not receive any audience with anyone until further notice."

Beio-Rhett scratched his head. "Didn't you just talk to him in person, like yesterday?"

"I did…" Singatt looked back down at the floor. "I know. I know he's here, and I figured out he's in the War Room, but he's sealed himself off. Something's gone horribly wrong."

"Or he doesn't like you anymore," quipped Beio-Rhett.

Singatt smiled back sarcastically. "Anyway, they said I could wait in the security chamber of the War Room, so you guys should just follow me there.

Beio-Rhett and Dembo followed Singatt through the military complex to the War Room. Beio-Rhett and Dembo were given dirty looks from almost everyone they passed. If it wasn't a scowl, it was a look of confusion. A few of them recognized Beio-Rhett's face and stared in both awe and fear. The trio finally came to the War Room security doors. Singatt used his military tag to gain entry. Beyond the door was a large waiting room. Two guards sat behind a desk at the far end. Behind them was a nondescript door that blended into the white wall behind them. Cameras were also stationed in the corners of the room. There were a few couches to sit on as well as two monitors on the sidewalls that projected various television stations.

The two guards looked up as Singatt entered. "The General is still unavailable."

Singatt nodded. "I'm well aware, but you said I could wait here."

"If you wish, but we have no idea how long it could be. If you don't mind sitting here all day, or even all week."

"Why can't you tell me at least what he's doing in there?" Singatt asked firmly.

"Lieutenant, we don't even know. Even if we did, we're under orders not to reveal any activities occurring in the War Room unless specifically given permission to do so by the Grand General himself."

Singatt sighed and motioned for Beio-Rhett and Dembo to step in.

The guards stood up. "Why are you bringing the prisoners here?!"

Singatt held up his hands. "Stand down soldiers, they still have their binds on but only for security reasons. These are not active rebels. They are free agents."

Both guards looked to see the metal cuffs on either of the Hydrolet's hands. The electronic beams were not activated, but they both knew that Singatt could turn them on at any time. "Very well," they said, and sat back down.

Singatt motioned for the two to sit down. He then sat down himself and looked to the other two. "I hope you don't mind waiting…"

When he finished saying this one of the guards answered a comlink transmission. The transmission was private, so the trio could only hear what the guard replied.

"Yes, sir," replied one of the guards. "Yes, sir, right away." He looked over to Singatt. "The General will see you now."

Singatt and the others went to stand up when the guard continued, "The General requested only an audience with Lieutenant Singatt."

Singatt looked back at Beio-Rhett and Dembo. "You two sit here," he ordered.

Dembo and Beio-Rhett plopped back down on the couch with a disappointed grunt while Singatt walked passed the guards to the door behind them.

"Your clearance has been reactivated," the guard informed him.

Singatt swiped his military tag across the scanner and the doors opened. He walked through to find a short corridor with a mirror on the left side and a control panel on the right. A guard awaited him inside.

"Please face the mirror and confirm your identity," requested the guard.

"Second Lieutenant Reuk Singatt, MP, ID number 951137141."

"Now place your eyes and hand in the scanner behind you."

Singatt turned around and looked into a binocular-type contraption at the control panel on the other side of the wall. He also placed his right hand on a scanning panel next to the eye scanners."

A green light flashed on the control panel. A voice sounded over the speaker. "Confirmed. Send him in."

The guard motioned Singatt to the door at the other end of the corridor.

Singatt took a breath and walked through the last barrier to the War Room.

Beio-Rhett watched as the door closed behind Singatt. He had no idea how long it'd be before he saw him again. He sighed and looked over to Dembo. "You worried?"

"About what?" Dembo sighed, "Dying of boredom."

Beio-Rhett laughed. "I never thought I'd see you end up working for the Hydrolet Government."

"I said the same thing about you before you agreed to work for the Rebellion," Dembo quipped back. "At least this is something you're used to."

"I suppose so," Beio-Rhett said, mostly to himself. His attention drifted off to the TV monitors. Naturally they were tuned in to the news channel. He noticed as one of the anchors mentioned a familiar name. "Still the top story today, the End of the Rebellion. We've just received news about the Hero of the Day, Sergeant Reuk Singatt who only yesterday was promoted to Lieutenant for his honorable actions that helped end the war."

"Can you turn it up?" asked Beio-Rhett.

The guard indifferently pointed a remote by his side to the

TV turning the volume up a few notches.

The broadcast continued. "It was due to his heroic maneuver at the Delta Sector Transit Station 23 that this Insurgence, which was calculated to last another ten years, ended in only a few days. Although the chief officers have yet to stand trial, most of their forces have been wiped out and the leaders of the commanders have, for the most part, been apprehended. Yesterday, Lieutenant Singatt was awarded the Medal of Honor by Governor Elorum Nasdett. Allea Saulfa has the full story on Singatt's heroic story."

The image cut to a middle-aged Hydrolette in front of the Capital Square of Bestton. "Thank you Bora, I'm standing at the very sight where now-Lieutenant Singatt was given this prestigious honor for his actions at Delta 23. For those of you not familiar with Singatt's maneuver, a lone cruiser came within viewing distance of the station two weeks ago but failed to identify itself. Authorities, worried that the cruiser may be some distraction for an impending rebel attack, made efforts to apprehend the shuttle. Ironically, a rebel assault was occurring at the station, but authorities were unaware of its presence. Lieutenant Singatt was in transit at the station when the commotion started and volunteered to make contact with the cruiser."

The screen cut to a picture of Singatt's official military photo ID.

"Singatt single handedly apprehended both the pilot of the cruiser who was in fact a former high-ranking officer of the Rebellion, Colonel Dembo Bebsin and the leader of the rebel operation on the Station, Beio-Rhett. Singatt still insists that the nature of his capture of the two was pure luck."

"Damn right it was," exclaimed Beio-Rhett.

Dembo laughed. "Can never admit defeat."

"Back to you, Bora," the reporter said.

"Thank you Allea," said the anchor, the image having swapped back to the newsroom. "Now the Government still won't reveal the details of the interrogation process that led our forces to victory, but needless to say, they do credit Singatt with apprehending the two that made this victory possible. Here again is the footage of Singatt's reception of the Medal of Honor."

Beio-Rhett looked at Dembo. "I still don't get it," Beio-Rhett said to Dembo. "What did you tell them? I didn't tell them jack or shit."

"All my info's five years outdated," Dembo replied still looking at the TV. "Most of the important stuff I forgot... I know this doesn't sound like me, but during my time away, I lost my faith in the Rebellion. I'm surprised you stayed with them so long."

"They paid well," said Beio-Rhett. "And I knew most of the weak spots of the Government's infrastructure having worked for them so long."

Dembo smiled.

"Still..." said Beio-Rhett, "how they finished off the Rebellion with your outdated info makes no sense."

"I didn't say I told them anything," Dembo said, still looking at the monitor.

At this, the guard looked up at the two, but quickly returned to his work.

The broadcast continued of the ceremony where Singatt was honored. In the middle of Capitol Square, a large platform was raised among a huge crowd of Hydrolettes in the Capitol City of Bestton. A podium stood in the middle of the platform. An elegantly dressed older Hydrolette female stepped up to the podium. Her outfit was very ceremonial: a purple tunic with a v-collar, over which hung a green robe with silver trim bound at the waist by a black belt and a silver buckle. Her trousers were purple as well with black shoes. This outfit was reminiscent of regal outfits of Hydrolette's feudal dress centuries before. The elaborate nature of these outfits was drastically tuned down as the modern age approached, but for ceremonial occasions, Hydrolette leaders still dressed in this elaborate fashion.

Governor Elorum Nasdett spoke into the microphone. "My fellow Hydrolettes. I come before you to honor this great man whom I am about to present to you. Not only do I give my thanks to him, but I also give my thanks to the men and women who gave their lives to quell this Rebellion. It's been a long ten years, but I am happy to say that this war is finally over." Applause ensued. "It gives me great pleasure to now introduce to you the hero of this war, Sergeant Reuk Singatt."

Singatt was in formal brown military attire as he stepped up onto the platform and walked towards the Governor. Applause roared as he made his way over to her. He stopped just short of her and knelt down on one knee, bowing before the Governor in the traditional fashion.

The Governor smiled and put her hand on his shoulder.

Singatt stood up and smiled back.

The Governor turned to one of her assistants who handed her a small case. She turned to Singatt, opened the case and presented the contents. "Sergeant Reuk Singatt, I present to you the Hydrolet Medal of Honor, the highest award granted to any soldier on this planet." She took the medal out. It was a gold circle with the insignia of vines wrapped around it. A purple ribbon was folded behind it to hang. She fastened the medal onto Singatt's outfit and bowed before Singatt. More applause, this time louder, followed. The Governor stood back up. "I bow before you to show my gratitude for your efforts in this war. You have honored me, your fellow Hydrolettes and this entire planet with your bravery and your efforts in quelling this Rebellion. For this, I honor you with this medal and with my personal blessing on behalf of the entire planet."

"Thank you," Singatt said with a wide smile on his face.

"Thank you for seeing me, General" Singatt said with a concerned look on his face.

"Lieutenant, I don't mean to be short with you, but we are in a crisis situation and the only reason I gave you access to this room is because I am a man of my word and I do not forget the service you have provided our planet."

"Sir, thank you, but it's about the fate of my prisoners."

"And your decision?"

"Hire them, General."

The General was silent for a moment and looked a little confused.

"Sir, I've done a lot of research on these two. I've gone beyond the files you've provided me and have done some digging of my own. Long story short, neither of these prisoners are active members of the Rebellion. Beio-Rhett is only on the rebels' side as a hired gun. Bebsin has expressed no interest in maintaining loyalty, so now they are both technically free agents."

"Lieutenant, I admire your compassion, but I assumed it would only go so far as letting these two go free."

"General, I am not requesting this out of compassion. I am requesting it out of strategic reasoning. Like I said, I have spent the last twenty-four hours researching these two. I'm sure you know a lot about Beio-Rhett already, but…"

"Of course I do!" The General raised his voice. "Who doesn't? The man is infamous. Before he was a bounty hunter, he was a professional pit fighter. He literally fought people for entertainment. I've heard that he even killed some of his competitors. As a bounty hunter, he was ruthless, aggressive, and unnecessarily violent. When I heard that the Rebellion had successfully hired him, I was devastated that we'd have to go against him. Consider yourself lucky to have made it out alive with your encounter."

"I do sir, but don't you hear what you're saying? Were you devastated because you had to oppose Beio-Rhett, or because we didn't get to him first?"

The General paused for a moment.

"Don't you see? Beio-Rhett isn't an opposing soldier. He's a weapon. For Zala's sake, his name says it all!" Bola was the Quel-Noran word for weapon. Although the word itself had several connotations, including the use of the weapon, which was mostly used in terms of defense or guarding something. "Regardless, if you've read as much about him as I, you'll realize he is an unstoppable machine. He's not just a killing machine. He's durable, quick-witted, and has excellent leadership and strategy skills. And Dembo was one of the main coordinators of all the Rebellion's operations. He's also an excellent shot. I'm not just playing mister nice guy here. You have to believe me, General, I'm requesting this for the good of the planet. I know that these two can be a valuable asset to the Hydrolet Government."

The General sighed. "Lieutenant, I'm sure it would be, but that's not the point."

"Then what is your objection General? This is the perfect time to do so, since the Rebellion is over. We have no pressing financial crisis. Also, these two would be a good investment in seeking out the remaining Rebellion officers and sweeping up the mess."

The General raised his hand up to Singatt to silence him. "Would you like to know why I've been unreachable for the past few hours?"

Singatt stood attention. "General, if you deem it appropriate that I am qualified to handle such information."

"Since you've been such a key player in this past conflict, I find it necessary to involve you in these events," the General said. "After you received your promotion, I was informed of an urgent transmission that had clearance to reach the Capital. It had to come from some executive source, so I was informed immediately for security reasons. When I learned the contents of the transmission, I had to put it under immediate lockdown and have been working in here with my top men discussing this problem."

"What kind of transmission?" Singatt asked.

"Commander Tainock," ordered the General. "Bring up the transmission Governor Nasdett received yesterday."

A soldier at one of the many monitors in the War Room typed in a few commands. There was a large holo-emitter in the center of the room below the General and Singatt, who stood at a railed balcony at one end of the room. The emitter spit out a glowing image of the Governor of Quesgarlon II, Hynlon Missan. The inhabitants of Quesgarlon I and II and III were Quesgralions. The origin of the Quesgralion species was shrouded in legend, but it is known that they were one of the first space-faring species in the galaxy. The species refer to themselves as the Second Race. The only race that had conquered the cosmos before them was the Kitholorians, referred to as the First Race, or the Elders. While the origin of the Quesgralions is a mystery even to them, it is widely believed that they originated from Daemer, the capital planet of the Galactic Republic. At least this was the first planet that they inhabited according to surviving records.

The Kitholorians call Daemer their Planet of Origins, but some have argued that the Kitholorians actually colonized Daemer from an unknown galaxy beyond. The Kitholorians deny this but refuse to reveal their records, which are known to be the oldest in the galaxy. Regardless, the Quesgralions were a more aggressive race, which is evident by the number of planets they call their own. They were one of the first races to begin mass colonization of the galaxy. Quesgarlon I was the first planet they colonized several hundred thousand years ago and was considered their point of origin. Recent evidence showed records of their existence on Daemer before those on Quesgarlon I, now referred to as Quesgarlon Prime, or by the Quesgralions as Prime. This planet was and still is considered their home planet and became over industrialized and densely populated to the point that it could no longer support its population. After several millennia on their home world, the Second Race set out to colonize other worlds. Prime is scarcely inhabited by Quesgralions anymore and has since become home to countless races from across the galaxy, as a makeshift intergalactic crossroad. This planet is in the same system as Hydrolet and was the first planet they colonized almost 10,000 years ago. It is still officially referred to as Quesgarlon II. Quesgarlon III was recently claimed as their own 1,500 years ago and civil strife is still ripe in that area. As for Quesgarlon II, the planet has been designated the official home planet and contains the highest density of Quesgralion population. Although at the time of colonization, it was believed that the planet was uninhabited. A few centuries later that the planet did have a native race, the stocky Lieks, whom the Quesgralions left alone since their culture was housed underground. Quesgarlon II's surface became heavily industrialized over the next thousand years after colonization. A huge planet, with many different biospheres, Quesgarlon II soon became home to many different races. Although the Quesgralions remain the dominant and most populace race on the planet, the cultural diversity was staggering. Quesgarlon II quickly became one of the most industrialized and populated planets in the galaxy. Its capital city, Kashik, is the second largest city in the galaxy next to Daemer's capital and the capital of the Galactic Republic, Lemeth. The Quesgralions were a tall race, taller than the Hydrolettes who stood seven feet, on average. The average Quesgralion was between seven and a half to eight feet. Quesgralions were also cycloptic. Their one eye usually had a red, orange or purple iris surrounded by black. They retained depth perception through a type of telepathic sonar. Their vision also was shifted to the red spectrum, which allowed them to see some infrared rays, unlike the Hydrolettes, whose vision was shifted to the blue spectrum, allowing them to see some ultraviolet rays.

Despite their physical differences, the Hydrolettes and the Quesgralions lived in relative peace throughout their stay in the same system. When Hydrolettes first discovered Quesgarlon II's colonization several thousand years ago, there was initial conflict, but this never erupted into full-out war. Hydrolet had a much more aggressive attitude towards planets outside their system, especially Baltania as made evident by the two wars with the planet in the past century. Still, Quesgarlon remained an invaluable ally throughout Hydrolet's history of war, providing moral and financial support. Likewise, Hydrolet supported Quesgarlon in its conflicts with other planets. Part of the reason for their lack of conflict was an unspoken agreement of mutual dominance over the system. Both planets respected the other's massive power in the galactic field and didn't challenge that power. Although recently, since Lutyr Nok became the Senator representing the Delta Beta System in the Galactic Republic, the Quesgralions started to see themselves as the wardens of the system and began acting as such to the Hydrolettes.

Singatt looked at the paused holographic image of the Governor. "It's Governor Missan!" he exclaimed. "What's going on?"

Hynlon Missan became one of the most trusted Quesgralions to the Hydrolettes. This was good for Hydrolet since he was the supposed leader of the planet. His frozen image had a grim face. Not that Governor Missan was ever a happy man, but his face betrayed some terrible news he had to bear. His one eye had bags under it from age. Quesgralion's foreheads stretched up and split into three bone plates. They had a mouth and a nose formed of two upturned nostrils close to their eye. On either side of their eye they also had square earflaps. Hair also grew behind the bone plates and on the back of their heads. Governor Missan's hair had long turned grey and his face was prematurely aged.

General Artinuare spoke, "Play the message."

The hologram started to move. The ghost of Governor Missan began to speak. "Governor Nasdett, My congratulations to you for successfully quelling the Rebellion. I wish I didn't have to bear such terrible news during such glorious times, but I have no choice. I ask of you something that I wish I could do but am unfortunately prevented from doing so. I realize that all of your resources and abilities must be turned now to the aftermath of this conflict and that your attention must go to repairing the damage done by the Sedition. However, I have information that you must act upon to retain the harmony of this system, possibly the galaxy. As you know, Senator Nok has been the incumbent for nearly ten years. Although I supported him in his election to the seat and his actions thereafter, we both know that he has begun to see himself as the warden to this system. While I don't agree with this role he's given himself, I saw no viable candidate to replace him. I apologize for my lack of interference earlier. His political greed has turned into something far more sinister. He is now beyond my power. He has been planting seeds in the Senate to redefine his role as that of master of this system. Due to the Republic's dependence on him for our two worlds' political climate, he is succeeding with his plan. My people will not do anything since he has convinced them it is for the better, but I know your people are not as vulnerable to his propaganda since he has spent no effort to condition you. He will get away with his plan to redefine his role and I am sure his ambitions go beyond this system to the entire galaxy. Again, I apologize for not contacting you earlier, but these are my people, and I thought I could trust them to defy such obvious call for tyranny. I have failed. It is up to you. You must send a transmission…"

The hologram sputtered and faded away.

"That's it," the General said grimly. "After that, the signal was cut. I've been pouring over that transmission trying to decipher his every word. I have a whole team working on it, trying to figure out what he means. We've also had experts trying to trace the source of the signal, but to no avail."

"Whom did he want us to send a transmission to?" Singatt asked.

"That's the question on everyone's mind today," the General said. "After much deliberation, we decided he intended us to send a transmission to Quesgarlon II's embassy to the Republic. We did, but received no transmission back. We tried every contact, the military headquarters, the Capital itself, nothing. After many desperate attempts, we finally sent a shuttle to the planet to find out what was going on. We lost contact with the shuttle when it came within Quesgarlon II's airspace. That's when I put the War Room on lockdown and the Capital under red alert. Then we received this transmission. Commander Tainock!"

The Commander typed a few more commands in his monitor.

This time, one of the large screens opposite of the General and Singatt flickered on. The screen projected the image of General Vipka Kitchnok, the current Minister of Resources. He wore the traditional grey formal military uniform of the Teneman, the current military party that dominated the executive branch of Quesgarlon II. This uniform was decorated with many badges and medals. This Quesgralion had a larger brow than the Governor and stood taller. He also had a smaller chin and larger earflaps. He began to speak in a very formal, almost pompous tone.

"I understand that you have received a transmission from former Governor Missan. You may interpret this as some serious news, but believe me, it's nothing to be alarmed about. Please do not act rashly to this new information. Although the information he provided is somewhat accurate, the best course of action for your planet is to do nothing. While you may have a different opinion on how to act on this matter, we've taken precautions to make sure that you act in accordance with our recommendation for the best course of action. As of yesterday, when we became aware of former Governor Missan's transmission, we began dispatching SETs (Solider and Equipment Transports) to your location. By the time you've received this transmission, they should be well within range of your planet. They should be arranged around your planets most important metropolitan areas, ready to invade should we feel your course of actions deviates from the one suggested to you." Kitchnok looked like he was going to leave when he continued speaking, "Oh, and one more thing. Before I cease transmission, don't try to send any form of transmission to the Republic Capitol informing them of these events. I advise this because it would be a waste of time. We have perfected our research in force field technology to create an impenetrable bubble surrounding our system. This bubble is composed of antimatter fields, so any incoming force, be it a ship, a projectile, or a signal, will be destroyed. We are well aware that this means we too are cut off from outside this system. However, we have more than sufficient resources to stage an all-out invasion and annihilation of your planet if you force us to do so. So please, for your sake and ours, just sit tight. Goodbye." The screen flickered off.

The General turned to Singatt. "After that, we figured out who the Governor wanted us to send a message to. However, by the time we tried reaching Lemeth, it was too late." He sighed.

Singatt looked from the screen to the General. He knew what the General was about to say next. He wasn't happy about it either.

"It is not an option to let the Quesgralions get away with this treachery," the General said. "But resistance to their plan means war. All out, planet to planet war. So we are in a financial crisis Lieutenant. We've just come out of this Rebellion emotionally and financially devastated. Many of our major cities are torn apart by the rebel's sabotage. Our troops are scattered around our own planet, still cleaning up the mess left by the rebels. We're low on resources and moral. The last thing I need to do is waste some more of the government's money hiring war criminals."

Singatt thought for a moment, then spoke, "But General, with all due respect, you said yourself, submission is not an option."

"But neither is war!" the General responded promptly, "Not in the condition we're in now. Like I said, our soldiers are tired. And their moral is devastated, fighting on their home planet, gunning down their own kind, attacking their own cities! Now that it's over, they expect to go home to their husbands, wives and children. We can't even call reinforcements from the Capitol. It's just us, and we have come out of a war. I cannot send these troops back into combat, this time against a much stronger enemy. These aren't scrapping rebels we're dealing with. This is the Second Race. We've been lucky to be on such good terms with them until now. Not since millennia ago have we had need to come into conflict with them. Not to sound disheartening, but I can't guarantee victory against a force like this. Not in all-out combat."

"And that's why people like Beio-Rhett and Dembo can be so useful!"

The General looked confused.

"Don't you see? All out combat is not the answer. It'll just deplete our resources and destroy our forces' moral. But with the help of mercenaries like Beio-Rhett, we can destroy the quezzes from the inside out. How do you think the rebels were able to carry on the war for so long? They didn't attack us outright. They knew they'd lose. It was insurgency. It was a series of sabotages, assassinations, and bombings. The kind of thing that Beio-Rhett is good at."

"We can't just launch a covert war on them without them knowing, Lieutenant. They aren't stupid. It's still resistance, and when they discover it, they'll launch their invasion, and then we're at war again."

"General, we are at war no matter what. Unless you want to sit back and let the quezzes conduct what could be not just a coup of this system, but perhaps the galaxy. The quezzes are threatening us because they are afraid. They know we can stop them. That's why they're locking us off from the system. They're intimidating us. I know you're not considering submission. I know you hate the idea of falling back into war, but that it is inevitable. I'm suggesting we buy ourselves some time. I'm suggesting we use a secret weapon against them."

The General looked at the floor and sighed.

"General, I know you're in a bad place right now. I'm sure Governor Nasdett is too. But listen to what I am proposing. Maybe with their help we can find the generator to this bubble thing and deactivate it and get a message out to the Republic. Maybe we could even get these two to take out members of the Teneman. Think of the head start we could have in this inevitable war?!"

The General released a heavy breath. "Lieutenant you're telling me what I can't admit to myself. I know war inevitable. I just don't want to bring it sooner than it has to come."

"And that's what I'm trying to propose, General. We can either launch a public attack now, or spend a little money to launch a private one that'll do far more damage. The best part is, I'm talking about mercenaries. These are not commissioned government employees. These are private agents, contractors, privateers. It's easy for them to deny their ties to us because they have none! They aren't registered with us. Again, I realize it'll be pretty obvious who's hiring mercenaries to assassinate Teneman Ministers, but it is still a step away from all-out war!"

The General took a deep breath and held it. He let it out and looked at Singatt. "What are they asking?"

Singatt gave off a huge smile.

"Well, I think it's fair to say bed and board for now. We did spare their lives after all. We'll make an offer that the first one's free."

The General laughed. "And I thought you were a compassionate man."

Singatt walked back into the waiting room.

Beio-Rhett and Dembo immediately stood up.

"So?" asked Beio-Rhett.

"That was fast…" said Dembo.

"The General wants to draft a contract with you for operations on behalf of the Hydrolet Armed Forces immediately," Singatt smiled.

"Great," Beio-Rhett nodded. "When can we start?"

"The General's busy with some affairs right now. However, before he discusses the contract with you, he wants to have a conference with you two and a few other important people."

"Then why'd you have me dress up now?" Beio-Rhett asked.

"You call that dressed up?" Singatt remarked. "Regardless, something very big has come up that I can't tell you about now. But you will be debriefed about it during our conference."

"Before our contract?" asked Beio-Rhett. "If it's so classified, why would you reveal it to us before you've hired us."

"Because you'll need to know what's going on before we can decide how you can be of use to us. I don't think you realize what you'll be getting yourself into."

"Is that a challenge?"

"If it gets you to work for us."

"I thought you said we have no choice," said Dembo. "What was that about jail time?"

Singatt started walking towards the exit motioning. "When you find out what's going on, I won't need to force you to help us."

The two followed him out, having to pick up their step to keep up. "Follow me. I'm gonna set you two up with some spare bunkers in our barracks. You can drop your stuff off there and rest for a bit before we have to meet with the General at the conference."

Beio-Rhett ran up beside Singatt's side. "What's our compensation gonna be like?"

"I'm taking you to it," Singatt said. "Part of the agreement is for you two to carry out at least one mission for us in exchange for bed and board. I could throw you guys out in the ocean if you prefer to be unwelcome guests."

"You sure had a change of heart," Beio-Rhett quipped.

Singatt looked over at Beio-Rhett. "After all this, you're still ungrateful. I can't wait to get to know you better Beio-Rhett. See if there's a soul underneath all those scars."

Beio-Rhett stopped Singatt, stepping in front of him. "Listen, you said you wanted to hire us as mercenaries, but this deal sounds like you're putting us on retainer. What's the deal?"

"The deal is you still facilitated the deaths of hundreds of soldiers that it was my duty to protect and it would destroy my conscious to not make you pay for it in some way!" Singatt spoke firmly. "For Zala's sake, all I'm asking is for you to help us, and yes I'm arm wrestling you into doing it because you've proven to be somewhat hard to manage."

Singatt stood a little bit taller than Beio-Rhett and stared him down. Beio-Rhett was already tall for a Hydrolette, and was not used to being talked down to. Still he stared into Singatt's eyes. He couldn't read Singatt, and Singatt had trouble reading him. All Beio-Rhett could see was unbroken resolve. Singatt wouldn't budge. But he wasn't doing this out of vengeance. There was no anger in Singatt's eyes like that, which was brewing in Beio-Rhett's. He knew it was making him weaker by letting it get to him. Besides he was curious to find out what was going on. "Lead the way." He said, stepping out of Singatt's way.

* * *

Two other eyes were looking into each other. One belonged to Senator Lutyr Nok, the other to General Brunk Nimx, Minister of the Interior of the Teneman. These two eyes were far away from each other, several light-years away from each other. However, they were able to peer right at each other through a video monitor.

Nimx stood at attention in front of the monitor that was stationed behind his desk at his office at Tenamen headquarters on Kashik. He coughed nervously as he spoke. "All orders have been carried out promptly Master. With any luck, this changeover should go as smooth as you predicted and you will have full support from the people of Quesgarlon." General Nimx was a shorter Quesgralion with a weaker chin. He wore a similar Teneman uniform to Kitchnok, albeit less decorated.

The Senator was a very plain looking Quesgralion with no noticeably defining features, except that he seemed a bit young for a Senator. His dress was the traditional black formal attire of the Republic, with ceremonial purple trim. His voice was calm and deep. "Was Operation Alpha Gone completed?"

General Nimx nodded. "Yes, sir, Governor Missan was successfully assassinated leaving no traces of foul play. The official story is engine failure on his cruiser. I regret to inform you that before the operation was carried out, he had managed to send a partial transmission to Hydrolet. Although this hasn't conflicted with our schedule, it has pushed our invasion a little sooner than we would've liked."

"A minor detour," the Senator said. "I have confidence in the Teneman's ability to take care of this slight alteration in plans."

"Thank you Master,"

"And the bubble. Is it ready to be sealed soon?"

"Yes, sir," nodded Nimx. "As soon as this transmission has ended, the bubble shall be sealed, preventing further contact with anything or anyone outside the system."

"Excellent," the Senator spoke. "As for the invasion. Are we prepared to strike now?"

"Upon learning of Missan's treachery, we dispatched the SETs immediately sir. By now, they should be in attack formation around the planet."

"Good," the Senator nodded. "My final orders are that General Kitchnok be placed in command of our space forces, effectively making him Supreme Commander of the fleet. I want him leading our main watchdog fleet around the system. I also want you to accompany him Nimx. Make sure he doesn't get ahead of himself. You are to maintain a sizable battle fleet at the ready for any sign of offensive action from Hydrolet. I shall handle things here at the Senate. Keep the Hydrolettes under our wing. Ending transmission."

Nimx saluted the screen. "Hail the Master!" he said before the screen flickered and went blank. He sighed and sat back down in the chair of his office. He didn't like responsibility, but he felt left out when he wasn't given any. Nimx was a man of conflict and that is why he was seldom respected. Yet it was times like these when he was given a task of utmost importance that his conflict was most present. He was assigned the responsibility of collecting the Master's final orders. His low profile made him the best candidate. The job was a privilege and an insult, as was his position in the Tenamen since the takeover, Minster of Interior. Could there be a more meaningless title? He was the housekeeper, yet he would probably despise the duties of a more prominent position. The title was arbitrary anyway. He liked being referred to as general, a title he earned rather than received. Most members of the inner circle

were technically generals of the Old Regime, except for
Ambassador Techet, who had little power anyway. Still, he was in a
better place than Nimx. Nimx was a man that nobody liked but
everybody needed. On the margins of everyone's circle, yet in the
center of everyone's affairs. As much as he hated it, he felt
uncomfortable when he became too close with the other Ministers
and too impatient when he wasn't busy.

The buzzer to his office door went off. Nimx answered
gruffly. "Who is it?"

"Kitchnok. Open up old fellow," the voice sounded
through the intercom.

Nimx unlocked his door without hesitation. Kitchnok
walked in with an air of vanity about him as always. His uniform
was starched and clean, his boots freshly polished and shiny. They
always seemed that way. Nimx wouldn't be surprised if he cleaned
his uniform every instance he retired to his quarters.

"Sorry I grew impatient, old friend," Kitchnok said in a
loud and boisterous voice.

"I have many good years ahead of me and would never
consider you a friend," Nimx replied in his same gruff manner.

Kitchnok didn't bother to reply. He simply asserted
himself in Nimx's domain, stepping into his office, without
permission, sitting down on a chair in front of Nimx's desk and
putting his boots on them.

Nimx looked at Kitchnok's shiny boots for only a moment
before returning to whatever trivial work he had lying on his desk.
He knew Kitchnok too well to respond at all indignantly, as it
would only encourage him.

"So?" Kitchnok asked after some silence. "What are the
Master's good wishes?"

"You are to command the main battle fleet aboard the
Command Ship for the duration of this conflict, effectively making
you Supreme Commander of the Quesgralion Fleet."

"Outstanding!" Kitchnok exclaimed. His voice filled the
room.

"I am to accompany you on the Command Ship," Nimx
said in an even lower voice. "For whatever Godforsaken reason, I
know not."

"Representation!" Kitchnok replied. "The Department of
the Interior has a vested interest in the outcome of our conflict

with this interference. Resources, my friend. Enemies, when quelled, mean resources."

"Perhaps," Nimx said. "Perhaps the Teneman needs a watchdog for you," Nimx looked up from his work.

Kitchnok's expression darkened. "Either way, I will take the position with much pride. Something you should consider, what with all your dreadfully dull countenance. Here, old friend, we are part of a movement that will affect matters throughout the galaxy. These current objectives seem trivial, but you and I both know that the Master's goals reach far beyond this system. That alone should give you reason for pride. That is the nature of ambition, to know no bounds. The Master's ambition is great beyond his person. Doesn't that lust for power, that spirited drive inspire you in the slightest bit? Does it not give you pride?"

Nimx didn't respond in any physical way and continued with his work. "I prefer to remain a pessimist," he muttered. "I will salute to your ambition with the utmost sincerity, but until that ambition has a concrete effect on reality, I will not join you in the fanfare.

Kitchnok frowned. "Drab," he growled. "You'll make no effort towards the cause, but you will take all the credit and reward when the effect has occurred,"

"I will do no such thing!" Nimx replied firmly. "My lack of enthusiasm will remain until our victory engulfs the galaxy. My support to the cause is undying and unwavering. Think no less of me. I was onboard with the conspiracy from the very beginning and it was my cunning that kept Hynlon out of the loop. I did my part. I am still doing it. But throughout my duties I've kept my zeal in check with a healthy dose of realism."

"The reality is that we're winning," Kitchnok retorted.

"So far," Nimx looked up again. "I think you're forgetting where we stand in our campaign," He held up a remote and pointed it at the screen behind him and activated the monitor. He swiveled his chair around to face the screen. He pressed another button, changing the monitor to display a Quesgarlon TV station, which was broadcasting footage of several thousand Quesgralions gathered outside the capitol building in Kashik. The tall, dark, bleak fortress loomed over the angry masses. Several guards in grey Teneman uniforms stood outside to hold the masses at bay. A podium stood on a raised platform in front of the capitol building.

The podium was adorned with the executive emblem: a desert horizon with the rising sun, behind it surrounded in a gold circle to represent a compass. This logo represented the material planet and how the Quesgralions gave these raw resources direction through their superior knowledge. This emblem signified the races dominance over the planet. Only since the Teneman took over, a new planetary emblem had been adopted, a white circle on a black background. Within the circle was an eight-arrow design. The arrows were thick, black and arranged perpendicular and diagonal. Several long vertical banners graced the raised platform and two very large banners bearing this insignia were placed on either end of the podium. The Teneman officers and guards had the insignia adorning their uniform, either as an armband or collar pin for the higher officials. The executive emblem, was changed by adorning the compass with eight arrows as opposed to one facing north. Along the circling compass of the executive emblem read in Quesgralion script "Strength Through Knowledge." The podium remained empty and the crowd grew unsettled.

"First," Nimx said to Kitchnok, whose gaze was firmly locked to the screen. "We must conquer our own territory before giving mind to our plans for those foreign."

"Have you no faith in Junior?" Kitchnok asked.

"As much as any of us," Nimx replied. "But he is young and spoiled beyond his worth. Promise of wealth and power means little to one who was provided both since birth. I am not so worried about his ambition as I believe he has none. I think he knows his place, but that could lead to indifference, which does not appeal to the masses."

"You think he lacks charisma," Kitchnok said.

"I do," Nimx replied sharply. "We should rely on his youth and vigor to convince our people of his worth."

"Come now, there he is," Kitchnok said pointing to the screen.

A young Quesgralion wearing a long grey trench coat stepped up to the podium. His coat was the official Teneman wear, but sparsely decorated. The executive emblem was adorned on the collar of his trench coat. This alone signified his importance. The emblem of the Teneman was stamped on his cufflinks. Other than that, he appeared as any other Quesgralion. Not too tall. Sharp check bones and chin, subtle head plates, and a smaller, indifferent eye. His hair was longer than most and blonde, tied behind his head. He stepped towards the microphone and put his hands on either end of the podium.

"It is here, our citizens, that we face a tragedy so unruly balanced in these times of celebration. We are faced with a loss, so terrible that, the light of our victories seems only to be cancelled out. Your outrage and confusion are the only suitable response to the death of our Father, Hynlon, here, when the fruits of his governance were about to ripen. The glorious rise of the Teneman, which will bring salvation on swift wings to our people, is now without its brave leader to give direction to the raw elements strewn among us. But with our mourning, there is mirth. For Hynlon, as any wise man would, did not allow his name to perish with his flesh. No, here you see before you Missan come anew to take these elements so painstakingly collected and guide them to our almighty purpose. Our people, once lost, are now found and given more light than ever with which to guide them. Alas, the sun set too soon on our Father's day, but the night has not lasted long. Here, this day. We see the page turn to a new Chapter for our glorious planet. A planet now guided by the Teneman, which will burn through those dark substances that hinder us from claiming our sovereign chair in this New Age. The cosmos, once a ferocious wilderness of untamed materials will now submit to our will as we shine our light of knowledge upon this infinite rabble and our sun turns the desert golden!"

The crowd's previous disjointed unhappiness was swept over by a roar of zealous approval.

The young Quesgralion stood silent for a while, looking over the now-enthusiastic crowd. As an ocean wave returns the sand to its smooth form, so his words washed over the once disheveled masses to unite them in their ignited zeal.

"Our path is true and our power only growing," the speaker continued. "Hynlon's name and kingdom are not lost in the void, but instead transcended into our form. The reigns are now taken by no less competent or worthy hands. Indeed, the very same blood flows through these as our veins. And let these hands appear idle no more. The first of these obstacles, our closest neighbors, the Hydrolettes, will prove to be viable foes if roused. However, left exhausted in vigor and resources from their recent insurrection, they are unlikely to gather their forces once more, especially against our unstoppable armada. Our sometimes ally, is now a suspect of malice. While our actions are redeemed by the ideas that give them life, our planet's great purpose may seem overly ambitious. The path which we take to seek out this truth is not through appropriate means by which the Galactic Republic would see fit. The Hydrolettes, our savage neighbors, base in their deeds seem too lofty in their ideals. That same general, Commander of their well-armed force, still our friend, Erthon Artinuare - would side with the Republic in disapproval of our unconventional means.

Behind the speaker, a large hologram of Grand General Artinuare appeared, followed by boos and curses of all sorts. The hologram depicted a recording of Artinuare insisting on the Teneman's retreat from their campaign outside of Quesgarlon. The electronic voice blared over the crowd only to be met with roars of discontent.

The speaker silenced the crowd with a wave of his hand. Quickly, the ruckus died down and the speaker continued. The hologram, now muted, continued to be shown behind him. "So this swarthy warlord, ambitious in his own campaigns, feels that our glorious regime is stepping outside our bounds? This same commander who had pleaded our support while Hydrolet had launched their campaign against the Baltans twice and during their most recent insurrection. And in our generosity, we have given him and his forces the utmost support and seen him through to victory on all occasions. Yet now, our exploits are too ambitious. So much for him."

The hologram was terminated, followed by a large cheer. The speaker continued, "Our regime knows no bounds. Our borders are illusions. No planet, no system, no physical structure can contain our ethereal state. Our power transcends time and space. Yet fear not our citizens'. This obstacle, though worthy, will not impede our state. The governess of their planet is more concerned with worldly troubles than with these matters. And while Artinuare's voice is strong, he will not ignite her extinguished flame for war. But as our blood demands method and caution, our forces will stay at their borders to further encourage their neutral stance on our glorious campaign."

Another roar of approval burst forth from the crowd, this one louder than the last. A chant began, unchanged from the previous chant when Hynlon Missan was still Governor.

"Hail Quesgarlon! Hail the Teneman! Hail Missan!"

The speaker clasped his hands and shook them at the crowd in celebration. "Hail Missan!" he repeated back to the crowd. He then took his leave from the podium and was quickly escorted from the platform. No sooner did he leave the podium, then he produced a cigarette from his coat pocket, put it in his mouth, lit it, and puffed away as he walked off. The crowd was still cheering.

The cameras pulled away from the podium and an aerial view of the crowd was displayed on the newscast. A caption below reiterated the time and place of the televised event. The reporter highlighted some of the aspects of the speech as the camera panned across the crowd from different angles.

Nimx turned away from the monitor and continued with his work as if nothing had happened.

Kitchnok had a great smile on his face, looking up at the monitor. He looked down at Nimx, still smiling. "Behold, the coronation of Governor Gastus Missan. As though the keys to the government were written into his father's will."

"We should be so lucky," Nimx grunted. "The royal blood boils down to a festering cesspool in order to save the regal stature of the lineage. Such is the nature of kings, but not true leaders. That is why every society at some point or another throws off the shackles of monarchy. To spare their people from the putrid effects of nepotism as each heir is born into wealthier and easier conditions. Where they are, with each generation, bred out of leadership qualities." He tossed aside some data pads he had finished working on and in a flustered state gathered up some more. "And here our great regime is resorting to the same folly we have forsaken thousands of years ago. And perhaps for the same reason!" He started shouting. "To preserve the name!"

"You doubt the boy?" Kitchnok said slyly. "How have you come to be so sympathetic to our people? The name is everything. The name is what lets us perform this transition so smoothly. Have you forgot our purpose?"

"What purpose does the boy serve?" Nimx spat back.

"You just saw it!" Kitchnok pointed at the screen. "Words, old friend words! Gastus has the power of words. He is an orator, a poet. Metaphors and delivery are his arsenal!"

"Words cannot run a government," Nimx grumbled.

"He doesn't need to run the government," Kitchnok retorted. "Why are you so hung up on this?" Kitchnok stood up. "Gastus is serving his purpose beautifully. What more would you have from him?"

Nimx didn't reply. He just continued to work.

Kitchnok turned to leave. "Sometimes I think you just enjoy being difficult," he made his way for the exit, which opened for him. "I expect you at the bridge of the Command Ship at 01000 hours!" He barked as he walked through the doors, which promptly shut behind him.

Nimx looked up from his work once to see the doors had closed. He grunted and continued working. The work on his desk was rather trivial, but it didn't matter. He liked being busy. He was just glad Kitchnok was gone.

Chapter 3

Changing of the Guard

"You were under the impression that when you were walking forwards, that you'd end up further onwards, but things ain't quite that simple"

General Artinuare sat at one end of a circular conference table. In the middle of the table was a simple holo-emitter. Behind the General was a large black screen. Sitting to Artinuare's right was a slightly younger Hydrolet in traditional formal attire. He wasn't military. He wore a brown tweed jacket and trousers over a white tunic with a string tie clasped with a medallion of Groacorian lineage. The tribe who established the dominant language of Hydrolet, but dwindled in population warring with the Quel-Norans. They established the infrastructure and culture of Hydrolet but lost their language during the process. This Hydrolette looked Groacorian, with a heavy brow and small eyes. His hair was longer with grey streaks and was tied back neatly in a tail behind his head. He also sported a goatee. Which was almost completely grey. Opposite of this Hydrolette, to the General's left sat Governor Elorum Nasdett, the Chief Executive and Head of State of Hydrolet. She was dressed in rather informal attire compared to her ceremonial dress seen during the televised celebration. She still wore her purple suit and black belt, but without the robe. The only indicator of her position was the pin on her collar consisting of the executive emblem, a sword, encircled with vines in front of a spherical representation of the planet of Hydrolet. Wrapped around the planet read the Quel-Noran words, "Honor cannot be given, nor taken away." Her presence at the Bestton Base was quite unusual as it was usually General Artinuare who would bring military matters to her domain at the Capitol.

Governor Nasdett tapped her long black fingernails as was the natural bone color for Hydrolettes. Their teeth, claws and bones were black. She looked at her private monitor in front of her to check the time and then sighed impatiently. "Where the hell are they?" she asked the General.

"They should've been here by now," the General said equally impatiently. "My most sincere apologies, Governor. I know they're in this base. I just briefed Singatt on the situation a few hours ago. I gave ample time for this conference so that you could make it here."

"So, you're saying they have no excuse?" the Governor looked at the General humorlessly.

The General chuckled lightly, "I guess so."

Beio-Rhett turned at a corner and walked down the proceeding hallway, followed by Dembo and Singatt.

"No! No! This isn't the hallway, it has lab signs," moaned Singatt.

"Well, excuse me," said Beio-Rhett in a mocking tone. "You said 'on the hallway on your left down here!'"

"Well, I got turned around back in that charter room," Singatt replied. "All those rooms with holograms get confusing.

"Let's just go back to the charter room and start over," suggested Dembo already heading back around the corner.

Singatt and Beio-Rhett nodded to each other and walked back the way they came, following Dembo. The three of them walked back through the corridor for a bit before Singatt stopped the group. "Wait a minute," he said. "Where the hell are we?"

Beio-Rhett also looked around their unfamiliar surroundings. "Yeah, I don't remember this at all."

Dembo grunted and looked at Singatt, "I thought that you were a soldier. Haven't you been here before?"

"Zala no!" Singatt exclaimed. "I just got promoted to Second Lieutenant. You realize that we're in the Bestton Military Base? Do you think I would be invited here unless I was stationed here or had some sort of honorary invitation? First time I set foot in this building was yesterday shortly before I met you guys. Besides, do you realize the Governor herself is attending this conference? They made it hard to find intentionally. I just forgot where we were supposed to meet that escort."

"So that means we're all lost?" sighed Beio-Rhett.

Singatt grunted. "Let's just keep backtracking. Once we're in the charter room I'll be straightened out again."

The door to the conference room slid open. An executive guard stepped in, saluted, and then turned and made way for Singatt, Beio-Rhett and Dembo. "The last attendees are present Governor."

"Thank you Corporal. That'll be all," the Governor said calmly. She saluted the guard and motioned for the other three to sit down. "Please."

Singatt coughed nervously. "We apologize for being late, Madame Governor. I take responsibility."

"That's unnecessary Lieutenant, I'm glad you could finally join us," Nasdett's face still remained cold.

Singatt, Beio-Rhett and Dembo all took seats on the opposite end of the table from Nasdett, the General and the other Hydrolette. Beio-Rhett leaned back in his chair and scanned the three authoritative figures in the room. Dembo clasped his hands together and placed them in front of him. Singatt sat straight up nervously.

The General cleared his throat gruffly.

Singatt stood up instinctively, "Sir! I was unable to locate the rendezvous escort. No excuse, sir."

"Sit down, Lieutenant," the General said softly. "I didn't call you to attention."

Singatt sat down sheepishly.

"As for your late arrival, let's spend no more time on it, since we already lost fifteen minutes." He turned to the Governor. "You've already had the privilege to meet Governor Nasdett."

Singatt nodded and smiled. "It's an honor to have an audience with you again Governor."

"The pleasure is mine, Lieutenant," Nasdett said again coldly. "I cannot express my gratitude on behalf of the Hydrolet people for your contribution quelling the Sedition."

"They preferred to be called The Resistance," Dembo said very quietly as he looked at his hands.

Everyone turned to Dembo. The General spoke. "Madame Governor, these are the two that Singatt captured. I'm sure their reputations precede them. Beio-Rhett, the infamous mercenary who has been employed by the... Rebellion for the last several years and Dembo Bebsin, one of the initial founders of the Rebellion."

Dembo looked up at the Governor with an indifferent

gaze, but not as cold as the Governor. He nodded respectfully, but did not salute.

"Are you an enemy combatant?" the Governor asked.

"Not at all," Dembo stood up straight. "But I am not a citizen of this planet and would find it hypocritical to salute the leader of it."

"Yet you refer to the faction you were a part of as 'they' and also acknowledge their existence in the past tense."

"Correct on both counts, Governor," Dembo still looked at the Governor.

Governor Nasdett nodded. "You are quite the dilemma, Dembo." She turned to Beio-Rhett, "And you," she said. "I'm surprised you're behaving yourself so well."

Beio-Rhett glared at Governor Nasdett. "If you did your homework you'd realize that I dedicated five years of my life to the Hydrolet Army."

"And you spend the next twenty-three undoing your virtuous contribution four times over," the Governor retorted.

Beio-Rhett continued glaring. He had never met the Governor before. While he was a soldier and black ops agent, the Nasdett's predecessor was in office, whom Beio-Rhett also never met. As a bounty hunter and mercenary, the only opportunity to see her would have been if she was a target, which she never was. Still, for some strange reason, Nasett looked familiar to Beio-Rhett. Naturally, he had seen her on TV. But this was different. He had seen those eyes. He had seen those eyes through water.

"Anyway," the General interrupted. "I'd also like to introduce the three of you to this gentlemen to my left. This is Dr. Huji Mheages Ph.D. He was actually born and raised here on Bestton before getting his Bachelor of Science at Colett University, wait, didn't you drop out of Colett?" he motioned to Dembo. "He got his Masters in fluid mechanics at the Kashik's Academy Tech School. He received a Ph.D. in astrophysics at the University of Lemeth's Academy of Applied Science where he still teaches today."

"Then what's he doing all the way over here?" Beio-Rhett asked glaring now at Dr. Mheages.

"Sabbatical," the Professor replied. "I'm doing some field research here to study astronomical phenomenon as they were historically recorded by Hydrolette's ancestors."

"That doesn't sound like something a physicist would study," Dembo remarked. "That sounds more like archeology."

Mheages nodded. "Somewhat. I'm doing more of the indoor work of the research, although I am working with an archeologist who is currently excavating at the Quel-Noran ruins. Besides, any true scientist does not only work in one field. As an engineer I worked on physical, tangible things and contributed to our races' understanding of how things worked and what we could do with the technology available to us. I branched off more into the theoretical nature of the technology. Physics, being a similar study to engineering, are just observations of how and why things work."

Dembo replied, "Still, those seem like studies that look to the future. Why are you here looking at the past?"

"As with any academia, it is a process, a history. In order to move forward in any science, we must look to the past for answers and mistakes. I suppose in my later years, I've had a surge of interest in old ways of understanding the things we do, now. Naturally we can say that in this modern age, we understand the innermost workings of the universe. But, people several thousand years before mass space travel thought that they had the same grasp on the universe. And yet, it is their concepts that led to the ones we have now, through elaboration and correction. I am putting together a study on some of the oldest recorded instances of Hydrolette's understanding of the cosmos by drawing parallels to methods of today and every age in between."

Beio-Rhett, Singatt and Dembo were silent. It was Beio-Rhett who broke the silence.

"Yes, but I meant, what are you doing here on a Military Base?

The General interrupted. "We paid for his sabbatical."

Dr. Mheages smiled and looked at the ground. "Yes, I'm sorry I left out that detail."

Singatt, confused, looked back at Mheages. "So you work for the Government?"

Mheages looked at the General with a facetious grin. "Somewhat," he said again. "It is true that I wouldn't be here without the Government footing the bill, but I am still here for my research. However, in return for their generosity, I have been providing the Hydrolet Government with my services during my time here, which may be much longer than I had anticipated."

"What services?" Dembo asked, now looking intently at Dr. Mheages.

"Services like this," he spoke. "Helping the Hydrolet Government assess this most extraordinary situation."

"That includes helping explain the situation to you three," the General interrupted again.

"Yes," Dr. Mheages said before standing up. "I'm sure the three of you are wondering what all this fuss is about," he picked up a laser pointer sitting next to him at the table.

"Not really," Beio-Rhett said with a smirk.

Dr. Mheages disregarded Beio-Rhett's rudeness with a chuckle. "Indeed," he moved on. He pointed the laser pointed at the emitter, which then activated, projecting a hologram of the Delta Beta System. It was a normal one-sun solar system. The sun was known on the galactic map as Delta Beta, being the second star to be discovered in the Delta Sector, which had orbiting planets that could support life. The first three planets where essentially lifeless rocks: DB I, II, and III. However, DB III had shown signs of being able to support some simple bacteria. The next two planets were the main life-bearing planets, DB IV and V. Of course, they were officially named Hydrolet and Quesgarlon II. DB VI was a gas giant and DB VII was recently discovered to support sentient life. Essentially an ice planet with vast freezing oceans, DB VII supported sleek, water-dwelling, thick-hided natives known as Zorians. They had no space-faring technology, but they had developed quite the complex social structure on what was assumed to be another lifeless planet in the Delta Beta System. Dr. Mheages pointed the laser pointer at the images of the planets. "Gentlemen, this is the Delta Beta system. Most of you are from here or have lived here most of your life. Hopefully that will make it less difficult for you to learn the news that for the time being you are stuck here."

Beio-Rhett and Dembo looked at Mheages confused.

Dr. Mheages sighed. It appears that our closest allies, the Quesgralions," he pointed his laser at Quesgarlon II, "have betrayed us. They are planning some sort of coup of this system and they realize that the only way to avoid intervention from the Republic is to make sure there are no opposing voices to this takeover of the system. They were correct in thinking we'd be that opposing voice, so they've taken precautions to make sure we can't get a word to the Senate." He pointed the laser to the perimeter of the system. A gridded sphere began to enclose the system. "After spending the last few hours scanning the outermost perimeter of our system using infrared, UV, gamma and X-rays, I've created an estimation of the force field that the Quesgralions have encased us in."

Beio-Rhett spoke, "Force field?"

"Yes…" Mheages said grimly. "Unfortunately, I'm still having trouble understanding the exact makeup of this bubble of sorts. Most of my information is based on the ambiguous description that General Kitchnok has provided us in his message, or rather his threat. They claim that it is impenetrable by any transmission wavelength or object. So far, we have not found any evidence to prove otherwise. All of our transmissions to any locations outside the Delta Beta system remain unanswered. Interestingly, the frequency is not cut off nor does it show any signs of interference. However, there is no response and no evidence of the frequency being intercepted. It's very strange. It doesn't seem like a simple communications jam. There is some sort of barrier that is separating us from outside the system. My tests with various wavelengths proved that there is some field that is consistently one AU past DBVII. The wavelengths that I send also showed no sign of reception, nor do they bounce back. They just disappear consistently at the same distance. Obviously I didn't scan the entire perimeter, but I chose certain points and triangulated them to create the grid you see before you."

"So do we know what this is made of?" Singatt asked.

"I've made some guesses," Dr. Mheages said. "It could be an antimatter field, although that seems like it would be impossible to control. It could also be a highly reactive plasma field that reacts to any matter or wavelength it comes in contact with, thus destroying it. It could even be a more high-tech field that "tricks" the wavelength into thinking it's still traveling when in fact it has stopped, some sort of constant black hole. I really don't know. This is only a few hours' worth of simple tests. We're currently sending several automated probes to a few points on this invisible wall and waiting to see the results." He turned to the three Hydrolettes. "So, that is the situation we're currently dealing with."

The General spoke. "Our main objective at this point is to

find out what this bubble is and find a way to deactivate it. Being shut off from the rest of the galaxy, we are somewhat vulnerable to a condition of total war. We'd be forced to burn through all our available resources to secure victory and we just can't afford to do that right now. We need to inform the Republic. So, our primary target is the source of this bubble. We must discover the source and destroy it. If we are unable to do this, we must find a way to get past this force field or create a hole in it."

"What does this have to do with what we'll be doing?" Beio-Rhett asked.

"We're briefing you on the situation we are in, and when I say we, I mean you as well," the Governor answered. "This is the predicament that the Hydrolet Government is in. The Hydrolet Government is going to hire you to help us with this predicament. It is important that you know what the predicament is."

Beio-Rhett was silent.

"Now there's no real emergency in terms of resources," the General said. "Planets have been able to sustain themselves without support from other planets for millennia. However, what we will not be able to support is an all-out war with the Quesgralions. They already have SET's in siege position around our planet. If we give them an ugly look they have supreme strategic advantage to invade our planet. We cannot have that, especially with our military in the disarray it is in."

"And the disarray of our planet," the Governor interrupted. "Many of our major cities are still recovering from the damage done by the Rebellion. War is not an option at this time."

"But neither is submission," Dembo said quietly.

The Governor smiled for the first time. "Indeed."

The General spoke. "Lieutenant Singatt has persuaded the Hydrolet Government to divert some resources to hiring you two, to carry out some missions for us. We are explaining the situation to you to give you an idea of what goals we are trying to achieve and how we are going about achieving them."

"You want to hire us to find the generator for this bubble?" Beio-Rhett asked.

"If we knew where it was, we'd destroy it ourselves," the General said. "Believe me, we are putting all of our resources into finding out what this thing is and where it originates from. No, we have other uses for you two."

At this point, the Governor spoke up. "As you know, I have openly spoken against the Teneman Regime for some time. I've had no reason to act on this opposition since it didn't appear to affect our people. I'm ashamed that I did not see this coming. Had I not been as distracted with opposing the Rebellion, I probably could have noticed that something more sinister was at hand beyond a fascist takeover of a planet. Unfortunately, I ignored my instincts and more importantly, ignored my foreign allies. Had I been more sociable with Governor Missan, I'm sure I would've gotten him to admit to me at least that something was wrong. I fear now he may be no longer with us. While our top agents are working to take care of this force field, I am also unwilling to let the Quesgralions go unpunished for this betrayal of our trust. It would be miraculous if we were able to deactivate this force field within the next few days, contact the Republic and get this whole thing sorted out. However, even then, the Republic may still side with Quesgarlon. They attacked us and threatened our planetary supremacy. So you are correct Dembo. Submission is also not an option. While we try to break through our cage, we will lash out at our captors. Secretly. So far they have not invaded. If we do not make any move, then we have all the time in the world. Time to reorganize our troops. Rebuild our defenses. And most importantly, discover the location of the Teneman leaders and strike at them. Perhaps we can cut this snakes head off leaving the body inert."

"So you have a mission for us?" Beio-Rhett asked.

"Not yet," the General replied. "We won't have a mission for you until we have more information. Although Lieutenant Singatt informed me that the conditions for the first contract would be that we provide bed and board for you until we have a mission for you."

Beio-Rhett laughed. "He did, did he."

The Governor looked at Beio-Rhett. "Unfortunately, the conditions of the contract are up to Singatt as you are his prisoners. You may be without any assignment for a few weeks. That's a few weeks of free food and board. Seems like a pretty good deal to me."

"At what point do we stop being prisoners?" Dembo asked somewhat indignantly.

The General laughed. "Right now, as soon as you sign the

contract." He produced some sheets of paper.

"I thought you said you didn't have a mission for us," Beio-Rhett asked.

"Not yet. This contract simply states the terms of your advance compensation. You must sign it if you wish to stay housed on this military base. It also specifies that the details of your first mission will be revealed to you when we have constructed them. When the terms for the first mission have been carried out, then you will have fulfilled your obligations and every mission thereafter will be compensated monetarily."

Beio-Rhett scratched his chin. "What makes you think that I need to be housed. I have assets in banks all over the system. You forget I've been quite busy the past 20 years working for myself. And the Rebellion was very generous. Why do you think I need bed and board? If you want me to take the first mission for free to secure my freedom, just say so."

The General laughed. "Haven't you been listening? All of your resources outside this system are unavailable and all the money you received from the Rebellion was confiscated by us as soon as we sacked them. The Rebellion ran a really tight ship and kept receipts. We were able to track down the money flow and seize everything. Don't worry though. Your blood money is being put to good use rebuilding our city."

Beio-Rhett slammed his fist against the table. "Bastards!"

The General chuckled. "We're being more generous than you deserve, Beio-Rhett."

Beio-Rhett grunted. He was somewhat bluffing when he said he had assets. He wasn't one to save. He definitely lived paycheck to paycheck as he had no need for luxury. He just made enough money to buy ample food and supplies for the next mission and that was it. He did have some emergency reserves scattered about the system, but it is true, most of them were set up by the Rebellion. Beio-Rhett didn't even have a place that he could call home. He was a true nomad. He lived in motion. The only things he owned were his weapons.

"Well," said Beio-Rhett. "Can you at least give me my ship back?"

The General looked confused.

Beio-Rhett now chuckled. "You forgot already? The Donta Ryx. I know you still have it… or what's left of it. On the attack against Fort Ttanis you guys shot my ship down during the Rebellion's attack. I escaped but used the ship as a battering ram to break down the Fort's defenses. However, I saw for myself the fusion generator didn't detonate. It just made a huge hole in the wall. Still, I'm positive the ship was intact. We never took the Base, so we had to retreat, leaving the ship lodged in the base wall. I assume you guys must have kept it, unless it's been salvaged for scrap metal."

The Governor nodded. "I remember that attack well, one of our few victories against the Rebellion. We did keep the ship. It is heavily damaged, but perhaps still operable. We salvaged it for any useful material we could find. It's a good ship. I think that's why we decided to keep it."

"It is currently at a military warehouse a few miles outside of Colett," The General interrupted. "If I remember correctly, we were to auction it after the Rebellion to help fund the reconstruction. I am sure some collector would like to have it: the Masked Menace's ship."

"I got a better idea. You give it back me so I have something to carry out your missions in," Beio-Rhett.

The General looked at the Governor and then back on Beio-Rhett. "Perhaps we can write that into your contract. Keep in mind it is a dead stick and will probably cost a lot of time and money to fix."

"Well, while you're thinking of a mission for me, it'll give me something to do," Beio-Rhett said.

The General thought for a moment. "You're free to fix the thing up yourself, but where will you get the money."

"Loan it to me," Beio-Rhett smirked. "Out of the assets you stole from me. Seriously. I'll put the ship up as collateral."

"The ship is ours."

"The ship is dead. I'm going to fix it. You pay for it. I'll pay you back by working for you. If I refuse, you get a working ship out of the deal."

The General looked over at the Governor who nodded. The General turned back to Beio-Rhett. "Deal. But sign this contract first so we can secure your release. I'll have a notary draft up the conditions of you ships return."

Beio-Rhett looked at the contract suspiciously.

The Governor spoke. "Sign the contract Beio-Rhett. I'm a

woman of my word. You'll get your ship. But we need to trust you. You are not one of us, but you've agreed to work for us, so give it to us in writing."

Beio-Rhett looked through the contract, skimming through the legal jargon. "This contract is for a flat payment. It's also for one person. So if I am to take on a posse I have to divide it up among them."

"That is correct," the Governor said.

Beio-Rhett looked back at Dembo. "Well, do you want to be on my posse?"

Dembo laughed, "Sure, man. I've got nothing else."

Beio-Rhett turned back and signed the contract. "There!" he said, throwing it back to the General.

"Thank you, Beio-Rhett. You are now officially a free agent," General Artinuare said. "We will stay in touch. When we have a job for you we'll contact you."

"So where's my ship?" asked Beio-Rhett.

The General chuckled again. "Same place it's always been, the warehouse outside of Colett. If you wish to start work on it, Singatt will escort you to the site."

"I'll go too," Dembo spoke up.

"Very well," The General said. "Singatt, you are charged with escorting them to the Colett Military Warehouse. You'll also be stationed there to make sure things go smoothly."

"You're assigning us a babysitter?" Beio-Rhett asked indignantly.

"A representative for the military," the Governor said. "Lieutenant Singatt will be our representative to you and your representative for us. Lieutenant, do you accept this important role."

Singatt saluted. "And spend more time with these two? I can't wait," he said sardonically looking at Beio-Rhett.

Beio-Rhett snarled back. "All right," Beio-Rhett said. "I guess I'll get out of your hair for now."

"Dismissed," the General said. He stood up, followed by Mheages and Nasdett.

Singatt, Beio-Rhett and Dembo also stood up. Singatt saluted. "Governor, General, Professor."

The General saluted back. "Good luck Lieutenant. I've given you complete clearance to contact me. I apologize for cutting you off this morning. However, I've decided that your contributions to our efforts are invaluable and it would be a disservice to exclude you from the loop."

"Likewise," said the Governor. "Be safe Lieutenant. We'll stay in touch."

"Thank you," Singatt said.

The General turned to Dr. Mheages. "Professor, thank you for joining us. We will stay in touch."

Mheages nodded. "I'll continue my tests on the force field. Hopefully we'll get some readings from those probes soon. He turned to Singatt. "Lieutenant if you have any questions for me, I've made myself available as an advisor for the military and all its active participants in this situation, which means you three." He said.

"I'm sure you'll be a huge help," Beio-Rhett sneered.

"I'm there if you need me," Mheages said with a smile.

The Governor looked at Beio-Rhett, "Have fun fixing your ship. Singatt will provide you with the necessary resources. We'll meet again."

Beio-Rhett was upset, but nodded in agreement at the Governor before leaving the room with Singatt and Dembo. The familiarity of the Governor was killing him, but he decided to pay it no more mind.

After the three left, the General turned to the Governor. "Madame Governor, thank you for taking time to come out here. We'll now escort you safely back to the Capitol."

"Thank you," the Governor nodded to the General. "It was no trouble. I knew that I needed to be here for this. It's not a big investment, but it could be a dangerous one. I wanted to see those two for myself before considering hiring them during a crisis like this. Not to undermine your authority, General. Normally such trivial expenditures would be authorized by at least several ranks below you, but you understand my desire to approve this specific one."

"Of course," the General said humbly.

"That being said, I'm not so worried now about this Masked Menace. I now leave control over the military end of this ordeal in your hands, General. I cannot afford to ignore the reconstruction efforts any more than I have. I leave sole authority of the armed force's course of action in your hands. Unless you're planning to incinerate the whole system, you need not seek approval from the Executive Office."

The General saluted. "Thank you, Elorum. I understand when you don't want to be bothered."

The Governor laughed for the first time since arriving at the meeting room, "Oh Erthon, you always did know how to make me laugh. But you know that I cannot balance both ends of this crisis. I trust you'll take care of the military end of things."

"And if the SETs begin their invasion?" the General asked.

"Well, then this war will have come into the domestic realm, so I could only hope you'd inform me of such a disaster. But until that time, take care of it, Erthon. Do whatever you deem necessary."

At this point, Dr. Mheages interrupted. "Miss Governor, what about any further information I discover about the bubble?"

The Governor smiled at Mheages. "Once again, you will report to General Artinuare. That is a military matter. And Professor, I'm very sorry for your loss."

Dr. Mheages looked at the floor. "There is no loss. My wife and son are probably much safer on Lemeth. I only hope I'll get to see them again. This is the first sabbatical I have gone on since our son was born. Such a shame, his understanding of the word will be very skewed by this experience."

"You will see them again," the Governor put her hand on Mheages's shoulder. "The Quesgralions won't be able to contain us for long."

Mheages smiled at the Governor. "Thank you Governor. With your leave, I should be getting back to my study of this cursed force field."

"Of course, Professor. I must be leaving as well," she turned to the General. "Erthon, shall we?"

The General nodded. "Follow me."

"Where are we going?" Beio-Rhett asked Singatt. "I thought we were leaving."

"We are," said Singatt. "But you guys should get your stuff from the barracks first."

"I thought we get bed and board," Dembo argued.

"There's a barracks at the warehouse, too, that's practically unused except during major construction contracts. You guys will have some privacy and it'll get you out of the General's hair."

"You ashamed of us?" Beio-Rhett asked.

Singatt turned around to look at Beio-Rhett with a wry smile, "you could say that."

Beio-Rhett chuckled.

In the barracks, Beio-Rhett changed back into his more comfortable outfit: his brown cargo pants, beige shirt, utility belt and green vest over. He tossed the standard military outfit aside. He checked his bag to make sure he had everything. He looked at Singatt. "Now that I'm a free agent, am I gonna get my weapon's back?"

"In time," Singatt said. "They are currently confiscated, but I can fill out a request to have them sent back to you. I don't know where they are." He turned to Dembo. "What about you, do you want that shuttle back?"

Dembo laughed. "You can't dump it on me that easily. Shit's yours now." He also tossed aside his military attire, pulled out the black jacket he was wearing earlier, and threw it on over a rather nondescript red shirt and black pants.

"Is that a steph jacket?" Singatt asked.

"Sure is."

"I thought it was illegal to hunt estephons for their hide these days."

"It is," Dembo replied zipping his jacked up. "This is very old. I've had it since college. Can't you tell?"

The jacket was made of fabric, but it wasn't ordinary fabric. It seemed to be woven from very thick fibers giving it a stiff, yet flexible texture. The estephon was a creature native to Katoola, which was viciously poached for its valuable hide that could be woven into the material known as steph. Steph was an extremely useful fabric, used mostly for clothing but also served to make very durable tents and other weather-resistant fabric. Although not a native to Hydrolet, it was the Hydrolet Government that outlawed the steph trade to preserve the estephons from extinction thirty years ago. Now, only the Katoola natives, the Kakuewees were allowed to hunt estephons. Dembo's was one of the last steph jackets legally produced. It was died black and had few pockets for outdoor use. It was definitely worn. There were no tears, but some threadbare areas were apparent on the shoulders and the sleeves.

"It is in fairly good condition."

"Considering I wear the crap out of it," Dembo said. He also checked his bag to make sure everything was there. He looked over at Beio-Rhett. "I can't believe you still wear that ugly thing," he pointed at the green vest.

"Beio-Rhett chuckled." It hasn't fallen apart on me yet, so I keep wearing it. It's got lots of pockets too." He reached in one and pulled out a pack of cigarettes. He looked at Singatt. "I'm surprised you didn't confiscate these."

"Me too," Singatt said. "Let's get going,"

The trio walked through the outer limits of the base till they got to the way station, which lead out of the base at the western end of the mountain range. This was the only way in and out of the Bestton Base except by spacecraft. No private vehicles could gain entry. Only one monorail line lead to and from the station. Singatt showed his military tag to get through the last doorway of the military base. This lead to an open-roofed station carved into the side of the mountain a few hundred feet above sea level. At the other end of the platform was the monorail, supported by huge metallic arches. The monorail looped at the end of the station and converged into a two-way line that lead out past the mountain, away from the base and towards Bestton, located only a few miles away. From the platform, one could look down on the huge naval station at the shores below and the rows of hangars along the mountainside, some on ground level and some built into the mountain. The fleet below was impressive. Ships pulling in and out to transport supplies and troops. Massive fusion cannons lined the shores. Large anti-spacecraft fusion canons dotted the top of the mountain ridge to protect the airspace over the base. Other hangars and spacecraft landing stations were nestled into the mountainside of the base. The largest structure not housed inside the mountain was the Main Communication Center, a large dome built partway into the mountain, but spanned almost to the shores.

Beio-Rhett took a deep breath when they stepped out on the platform. He hadn't breathed fresh Hydrolet air in weeks. Before he was captured and confined in tight windowless quarters, he spent most of his time in space or in the Rebellion's underground facilities. He couldn't honestly remember the last time he saw Hydrolet's sky. A subtle smile betrayed his enjoyment of the fresh air.

Singatt noticed Beio-Rhett's smile and chuckled. He

looked ahead at a long train arriving at the monorail station. "Looks like we're just in time," he said. He picked up the pace. "Hurry up."

Dembo picked up his pace, but Beio-Rhett still delayed. He kept breathing in and out. He wondered if it was bad for one's health to not be exposed to the atmosphere of one's home planet for so long. Then again, he wasn't sure if this was his home planet. Maybe nobody knew where his home planet was. Seeing that the two had gotten far ahead of him, he sprinted to catch up.

Singatt was already talking to the guard stationed at the monorail. "We need to get to Colett. Does this line transfer?"

"Via Bestton, yes." The guard answered. "Your tags?"

Singatt took his tags out from under his shirt and swiped it across the scanner that the guard held.

The guard looked at the readout on his scanner. "Says here you have clearance to bring two unregistered."

Singatt pointed to Beio-Rhett and Dembo behind him.

The guard nodded. "All aboard!"

The many-unit train sped off from the station and barreled down the monorail that led away from Bestton Air & Naval Base. The monorail carried the train over the Plains of Bestton that stretched behind the small mountain range. It was only a few minutes before the monorail descended into the main metropolitan area of Bestton. The city was the largest on Hydrolet as was per tradition with most capital cities on planets. Huge structures jutted up from the horizon as the train approached the city. Soon, the whole city was in view in its full glory. Massive skyscrapers and complex buildings covered the city scape. Large buildings were connected by crisscrossing walkways. The monorail convened into a huge system of monorails that wrapped around the city landscape, clustering together at different way stations and leading up to even the highest buildings. The Capitol Square could be found on a plateau in the center of the city. This included the Capitol Building, the Governor's Residence, and the Military Headquarters. These three buildings were spread out among the plateau, which stood out as a jewel in the middle of the city. The sea bordered the northern edge of the city, which composed mostly of the Bestton Port, being one of the largest in the galaxy. Bestton was located at the northern end of the same peninsula as the Military Base, which was located at the southern end.

Beio-Rhett sat at the end of the car, while Singatt and Dembo sat opposite of him. He looked over at Singatt who was perusing over some data pads in his hand. He then looked at Dembo, who was looking over his shoulder out the window to see the view of the city below him. He decided to do the same, turned on his side and cranked his head back to look through the window behind him. The monorail was passing through the city now. He could see the busy streets below and the soaring monorails above him. The monorail had lowered to midlevel of the city, so Beio-Rhett could look up at the skyscrapers towering above him, barely being able to make out the tops. The setting sun was reflecting off of the long windows of the buildings. Beio-Rhett's gaze then turned to the Capitol Square off in the distance. It was easy to make out the top the plateau with the sparse arrangements of the buildings. Past that, he squinted at the setting sun, which bathed the city in an orange light. They were too close to ground level for Beio-Rhett to make out the sea beyond the northern edge of the city. The last thing Beio-Rhett noticed was his reflection in the window, which was also looking away, off into the distance. *That's strange.* His reflection wasn't mirroring his image, it was imitating it exactly. His head was turned away from him, also looking out at the city. *Am I that tired? What am I looking at?* (It's you) No it's not. Finally his reflection turned and looked at him.

"Are we transferring to another line?" Dembo asked Singatt, which broke Beio-Rhett's trance

"No, just stay put. We are gonna to stop at a station up ahead, then it will take us straight to Colett."

Beio-Rhett turned back to look at Singatt and Dembo, a little startled.

"It's been such a long time since I've seen Colett," Dembo said quietly.

Singatt looked up at Beio-Rhett. "What's the matter with you, scared of your own reflection?"

"Heh," Beio-Rhett forced out a half-hearted laugh. "Yeah, you know me."

The train came to a stop at one of the way stations near the heart of the city. After a short stop, the train started up again and ran along a monorail that ran west, leading out past the city and again through the Plains of Bestton's continuing towards Colett.

"What did you go to Colett for?" Singatt asked Dembo
"You couldn't dig that up for yourself?"

"Not personal information from Universities. I knew
when you started and when you dropped out, but that's about it."

Dembo chuckled. "Political Science."

Singatt laughed. "Figures," he remarked. "Fucking
idealist."

Beio-Rhett, still looking a little startled, decided to join the
conversation to forget about his little illusion. "Is this the first time
you'll be seeing the city since you dropped out?"

Dembo nodded. "It's been over ten years. I think twelve
to be exact, Whenever the Rebellion started."

"It's been ten years," Singatt interrupted. "I'm surprised
you don't remember."

"I guess I lost track of time on Katoola," Dembo said.

"You were there that whole time?" Beio-Rhett asked.

Dembo nodded. "After the blast, I was taken in by the
Kastikae Tribe, where that mountain actually got its name."

"I still can't believe you survived that blast." Beio-Rhett
said.

"I can't believe you did," Dembo remarked. "I thought I
was the only survivor from that air raid."

Beio-Rhett shook his head. "You got it all wrong. The rest
of the squad made it. We thought you got hit. But we couldn't go
looking: they were relentless with that air raid."

Dembo nodded. "They really tore up that mountain. The
Kakeuwees were not happy about it."

"They told this to you?" Beio-Rhett asked.

Dembo nodded, "Where do you think I spent those five
years?"

"With the Kakuewees?" Singatt seemed surprised.

Dembo nodded. "In Kastikae Village. After the blast, I
went tumbling off the mountainside. I got busted up pretty bad
and landed in a marsh below, where I was sheltered from the rest
of the air raid. That's where their scouts picked me up. They
cleaned me up and then stitched me up. I insisted that when I was
better I was gonna be on my way and try to reconvene with the
Rebellion. However, their scouts insisted that I was the only
survivor from the attack, that they found. Either their scouts
weren't very thorough, or you guys scattered before they got

there."

Beio-Rhett nodded. "We did. We eventually made it back to the rendezvous and took the escape shuttle out of there safely with the goods intact."

Dembo nodded back, "Well I guess the mission was a success."

Beio-Rhett chuckled, "I guess so. But anyway, why did you decide to stay?"

Dembo shrugged. "I dunno. It was very complicated. I thought that my squad was dead, which really broke me up. I didn't feel like I could go back to Dresbar with all their blood on my hands, but that wasn't all of it. After staying with the Kakeuwee's during my recovery, I... I can't explain it." He looked back out the window. "I guess I just needed to drop out of society for a while."

"Can't explain it or won't?" Beio-Rhett asked.

Dembo cracked a smile, but still looked out the window.

The monorail crawled over the mostly flat landscape, dotted with the occasional settlements and farmland. The only mountains were on the eastern peninsula where the base was located. The rest of the continent was flatlands except for the northern ridge, which separated the icy desolation of the northern half of the Bestton Continent from the South. A few miles south of the northern ridge was Colett, another thriving metropolis that broke the calm of the flatlands. Colett was located on higher ground than the flatlands, just before the land was swallowed up by the mountain ridge. The University was located at the northernmost edge of the area, just outside the city limits, practically shoved into the mountainside. It was somewhat isolated from the rest of the city, set against a backdrop of forest. The forest spread halfway up the side of the northernmost ridge, then gave way to desolate rock capped with snow. The trio's monorail did not lead into the city but skirted the southern end of it. Just outside the city limits, the monorail would take them further west to the warehouse, where the remains of Beio-Rhett's ship were located.

Dembo looked out at his hometown as the train sped past the city limits. He really couldn't make out the university as it was tucked away far to the north at the opposite end of the city from where they were travelling, but he knew it was there. He would never forget it.

Beio-Rhett watched Dembo watch the city. He wondered what it would be like to have a hometown, to come from somewhere.

The train continued past Colett to a small military complex a mile or two past the city limits. Three large dome-like warehouses were at the center of the complex with a small headquarters and a few barracks surrounding them. The monorail ended at a small way station at the eastern end of the complex.

"Here it is," proclaimed Singatt. "The Colett Military Reserve. You're broken ship is in one of those warehouses," Singatt pointed to the three large warehouses at the center of the complex.

The train came to a stop at the way station. The three Hydrolettes stepped off the train onto the station platform. Dembo turned back to see that Colett was still in sight. While he was looking back at the city, Singatt once again swiped his military tag on the station guard's scanner and once again announced that he was escorting two unregistered personnel.

"Which of these has the remains of the Donta Ryx?" asked Singatt.

The guard pointed, "The middle one, Lieutenant. It's in the same condition as when we had it delivered, 'cept all the rations, weapons, and other movable assets have been removed. I'm sure the generator is intact, but it may need a new power source. Is the Government finally gonna scrap it?"

"Naw, we're selling it back to this guy," Singatt pointed to Beio-Rhett.

The guard looked at Beio-Rhett a little startled. "Zala!" the guard exclaimed.

Beio-Rhett barked, "Whatchu looking at!"

"That's enough!" Singatt yelled back at Beio-Rhett. "Don't worry. He's actually working for us now."

The guard gulped his fear away. "Well, that's good news."

"You should feel so lucky," Beio-Rhett started snarling.

"Beio-Rhett," Singatt spoke sternly. "Come on, let's go."

The three walked towards the middle warehouse. The huge metallic dome loomed above them. Military personnel marched to and fro around the complex. Officers were transported on armed speeders back and forth. Most of the hustle and bustle revolved around the headquarters building at the western end of the complex. Several barracks were scattered around the center of the complex, with the three dome warehouses at the northern end of the complex. A few more barracks were directly east of the warehouses. Machinery and truck loaders were walking to and from the warehouses hauling large pallets of materials, from beams to cases of battle armor. Engineers operated hovering trains that had pallets of materials trailing behind them. The only defensive structures were a few guard towers around the perimeter of the complex. One massive guard canopy towered over headquarters.

The warehouses had several cavernous archways that lead inside. They were wide enough for even the largest loading machines to get in and out easily. The domed roofs also had sliding panels to allow for spacecraft access. The three Hydrolettes stepped through the archway of the middle dome to see a loud and bustling area filled with workers, loading equipment, lifting machines, and robotic cranes and arms built into the warehouse floor. Stacks of crates littered the floor. Along the walls of the dome were large offices that overlooked the main construction floor. A network of cable cars also stretched across the warehouse. Little carrier cars sped up and down the cables carrying officers and workers to and from the ground floor and even the topmost working areas.

A few damaged Gyropod and Green Arrow fighter craft we're scattered on the floor of the warehouse surrounded by robots and workers making repairs.

Green Arrows were the most common fighter craft in the Hydrolet Space Force. They carried a single fighter and were shaped like a very narrow arrow, hence the name. A small cockpit was visible from the bubble windshield that allowed a full 3D view for the pilot. Behind the cockpit was a twin ion engine, which powered the fighter. Two curved wings also protruded from either side behind the cockpit forming two arches on either side of the jet. At the end of these wings were large plasma cannons, the fighter's primary weapon. Below the front of the fighter was also a proton torpedo launcher.

The Gyropod fighter was a relatively newer model. They were also one-man space fighters. The cockpit was encased in a glass orb with a 3D monitor system that used the windshield as a surface for the readouts. Behind the glass orb was a larger single ion engine. Three wings protruded from the engine in a triangle pattern. Each wing also had a plasma cannon, which could triangulate to blast one or lock on to several different targets. In front of the cockpit was a miniature fusion canon, built to be smaller than the usual grounded fusion canons. Although this fighter had no missiles, it was still a hardy, fast fighter and proved very effective in the Hydro-Baltan War.

Another ship also sat on the warehouse floor, but this ship was not being attended to. Some scaffolding was surrounding it for work that perhaps one day was to be done, but there were no personnel around it. This ship was much larger than a fighter. It was a B-class cruiser: larger than a normal sized cruiser, but not quite big enough to be classified as a battleship. Still, it towered over all the relatively smaller fighters. It was oddly shaped. The front end of the ship was elongated, with a window that revealed the bridge at the very top and a docking port at the bottom. The front of the ship narrowed down to a more streamlined rear end, with the top of the ship remaining level and the bottom raising higher and higher until the very rear end housed only the massive twin fusion engines. On either side of the ship near the front, just behind the bridge were gunner stations that protruded from the sides of the ship. These were quad plasma canons that could be controlled by a single gunner. The ship itself was in horrible condition. The hull was for the most part, intact. One of the gunner stations was gone. The windshield to the bridge was shattered. The docking port was busted, which made the port unable to close. Massive charring was apparent all over the hull, along with several dents. The engines were still intact, which was the most important part, but other than that, the ship looked like it barely survived a nuclear holocaust.

Beio-Rhett looked at his former home and nodded. "It's in better condition than I thought it would be."

"Ever the optimist," Singatt quipped. "Come on, this way." He started walking to one of the vacant cable cars.

"Where we going now?" asked Beio-Rhett.

Singatt was already inside the cable car. "We have to talk to the foreman and get you set up here."

Beio-Rhett and Dembo followed Singatt into the car. Singatt sat in the front seat. Beio-Rhett sat in the back. Dembo sat down across from Singatt.

"Hang on," said Singatt before he pressed the lever on the

control panel forward. The car raced up the cable to one of the offices on the higher levels of the dome. The car stopped at a catwalk balcony in front of the offices and Singatt stopped the car. "Here we are," he said as he stepped out of the car. The other two crawled out after him onto the grated balcony. Along the wall were stacks of crates. A door at one end of the balcony lead to an office that hung over the wall, supported by beams below it that formed a diagonal between the floor of the office and the dome wall. Large windows lined the office walls, which looked out at the warehouse floor below. Singatt walked towards the door to the office, "This way."

"So this definitely isn't your first time here," Dembo remarked as he followed Singatt.

"I've been stationed here a few times," Singatt said. "What about you? You lived just down the street for a few years."

Dembo shook his head. "I think I came here once for a research project for school. We were just given a quick tour."

Singatt took out his tag again and swiped it by the panel on the right hand side of the door. The door slid open revealing several cubicles with secretaries attending monitors inside them. At the end of the office a Hydrolette in an officer's uniform sat at a desk. Singatt walked up to the officer. "Sir!" he saluted.

"Ah Lieutenant," the officer stood up and saluted back. "I just got the call about your arrival. So you're going to take the Donta Ryx off our hands finally?"

Singatt chuckled. "Not exactly. We're going to fix it up."

The officer laughed. "You can't be serious."

Singatt nodded. "I couldn't be more serious. Foreman, I'd like you to meet somebody," he made way to reveal Beio-Rhett to the officer.

The officer was startled when he saw the unkempt hair and scarred face of Beio-Rhett. "Dear God!" he shouted. "These are the unregistered personnel you were bringing?"

Singatt nodded, "Don't worry, he doesn't bite… not anymore."

Beio-Rhett grunted. He was getting fed up with Singatt's patronizing him.

Singatt spoke again. "These are no longer prisoners, foreman. They are mercenaries working for the Hydrolet Government. I brought them here, according to their contract,

Beio-Rhett requested we sell him back his old ship as part of the deal."

"Selling it back to him? It's a wreck!" the foreman said.

"We're also paying to have it fixed. It's all part of his contract. Actually we're just lending him the money to fix it up, which he'll pay us back by working for us."

"He's gonna fix it?!" the foreman asked.

"I know your men wouldn't mind," Singatt said. "No one's touched it in years."

The foreman looked at Beio-Rhett. "So he's gonna stay here and work on it? Around my workers?"

"He's no longer an enemy combatant," assured Singatt.

Beio-Rhett stepped forward. "I'm not going to bother your men, foreman. I just want space to fix my ship."

"Well, is the Government also gonna pay for the worker's time to help rebuild the ship?" the foremen started getting frustrated. "It's not like we're out of things to do here. There are tons of repair contracts coming in every week and we're short-staffed as it is."

Beio-Rhett interrupted, "Like I said. I'm not going to bother your men. I'm gonna fix it myself. Just give me my space and the use of your facilities."

The foreman looked surprised. "You're gonna do it all by yourself?" the foreman asked.

"Well, if Dembo wants to help," he motioned behind him. Dembo laughed, "Of course, man."

Beio-Rhett looked back at the foreman. "I've done it before. I just need use of your facilities. You won't even know I'm here since you keep that thing in the corner, with all the cobwebs."

The foreman looked at Singatt.

Singatt replied. "The Government will pay for use of the facilities and any materials that he requests. Just place the orders and send the bill to the Capitol. Also, you have some available rooms in the barracks, right?"

The foreman grunted. "Like I said, we're short-staffed. There are plenty of rooms. I'm not sure I trust these two with my men."

"I said, I wasn't gonna bother your men," Beio-Rhett started to sound angry. "Just give me some space to work."

"I'm taking responsibility if they cause any trouble,"

Singatt said. "I'll be staying here for the time being, to mediate between them and the Capitol."

The foreman sighed. "All right." He sat back down. "She's all yours."

Beio-Rhett stepped up to the desk. "I need the schematics on the ship and a full readout of the damage. I'm sure you have that somewhere on file."

The foreman looked up at Beio-Rhett, "Oh, of course," he rummaged through one of the drawers behind his desk and produced a large data pad. He handed it over to Beio-Rhett. "There you go," he said. "Have fun."

Beio-Rhett began reading through the info on the pad. "The engine and core are still intact. This won't be difficult at all."

Singatt spoke to the foreman. "Can you give us clearance on three rooms in the barracks?"

The foreman started typing on his monitor. "I'm just informing the CO of your presence here right now." He finished typing and awaited conformation. You three will be in Barracks B."

Singatt nodded, "Well, I'm exhausted, so I'm gonna call it a night. But you two are free to start working if you want."

After perusing the data pad, Beio-Rhett turned to Singatt. "You said you guys would provide the materials?"

Singatt nodded. "That is correct."

"Does it matter who I order them from?"

Singatt was suspicious.

Chapter 4

All Quiet On The Cosmic Front

"I got some groceries, some peanut butter, should last a couple of days."

A Niskan looked at an order form data pad in front of him. Niskans were the native race of the planet Drisko, which was located on the outermost orbit of the Delta Alpha system, the closest system to the Delta Beta system. Being the outermost planet in the system, it was essentially a planet-wide tundra. The whole planet was covered in snow. Whatever wasn't covered in snow was covered in ice. There was no running water on the planet, only ice, although the planet still supported a very diverse biosphere. The Niskans were the only sentient natives on the planet and developed a culture of commerce. There was no official system of government on the planet, at least not on a planetary scale. There was no planetary army, nor did they have a seat in the Galactic Senate. Rather, Drisko consisted of a cluster of loosely knit city communities. Each city basically governed itself and depended heavily on trading income. There were some governing bodies, but for the most part, mob bosses and business owners ran the cities. They provided the power, resources and protection that kept the cities running.

For this, the Niskans played a very strange role in the Galactic sphere. The planet of Drisko was abundant with natural resources. Since mass population of the desolate tundra was impossible, most of the resources were far from depleted. Useful minerals, precious stones, and even radioactive elements were practically erupting from the planet. Also, the planet's surface was a living spectrum of elemental substances. Whatever the reason for this abundance of resources, the Niskan's seized control over them and turned the planet into the galaxy's largest open market. Drisko has been called the Pinnacle of Capitalism, where businesses literally ran the planet. Naturally, this welcomed corruption as evidenced by the rampant mob activity on the planet, but for the most part, the cities were not often the backdrops of violence. This fringe lifestyle of the entire planet is the source of much debate over the Niskans' role in the galaxy. Some considered them genius entrepreneurs and others filthy conmen and swindlers. The term Ziggums became a common insult for them, coming from a corruption of the phrase Zieg Helm, which was the Niskan phrase meaning "without sovereign or leader." Still, Drisko was a main hub of galactic commerce. Many intergalactic companies relied on resources provided by Drisko to support their business. Even foreign governments conducted trade deals on the rogue planet. The planet also served as a neutral trading ground where even warring planets could cut deals with each other in a safe backdrop.

Some planets had a better relationship with Drisko than others. Hydrolet had an excellent trading relationship with Drisko. Using resources acquired from Drisko, Hydrolet was able to produce some of the most advanced weaponry in the galaxy. Indeed, Hydrolet was perhaps the top weapons producer in the whole galaxy. Drisko would always be the first planet to receive these weapons, with which they could both protect their cities and be the first to sell the weapons in the galactic field. In return, Hydrolet usually had first access to Drisko's most precious resources, which gave them an edge not only in weapon's production, but also energy research and architecture.

The Niskans themselves were well adapted to the cold climate. Their blue leathery hide was mostly covered in white fur, which provided ample warmth and camouflage in their snowy environment. The only areas where their skin was exposed was their breast, genitals, feet, hands and face. Their hands and feet were clawless. The fur on their forehead came to a widow's peak. They also had long black oval eyes. Their nostrils were turned up high, close to their eyes and were very thin, as was their mouth to reduce heat loss. Like the Hydrolettes, they also stood a little under seven feet tall on average.

This Niskan was a little shorter than average, standing a little over six and a half feet. He looked through the data pad again and sighed. "I'm sorry man, but this is all I can get a hold of at the moment," he said in a very soft Niskan accent. He handed the data pad over to Beio-Rhett. "I may be able to pull some contacts in this system, but it's not looking good. The best I can offer is a good discount."

Beio-Rhett shook his head as he took the data pad. "Don't beat yourself up, Poko, it's not your fault were all trapped here. I'm just glad you we're in this system before the bubble closed."

Poko chuckled light-heatedly. "You may be glad. I'm the one cut off from my hometown, ya selfish bastard."

Beio-Rhett cracked a smile as he perused the data pad. "Yeah, well let's make the most of it, buddy. I honestly didn't think you were gonna make it here with anything."

Poko scratched the back of his head. "Well, I was honestly rather lucky. The shuttle from Drisko took off late since the engines were freezing up. I was able to grab a few more crates of some stuff before takeoff. Good thing too, otherwise I wouldn't have had enough space fare to make it here."

"Well, even if you didn't bring anything, I'm glad you're here. It's nice to have someone I trust close by."

Poko smiled, "Likewise. Although having people I trust around me doesn't change the fact that I'm cut off from my main source."

"Do you have contacts anywhere in this system?"

"I do. They're not great. But I guess I gotta start milking them if I'm gonna make it by here. But it's not just that, ya know. It feels weird not being able to go back home whenever I feel like it… but I guess at the same time it's nice knowing none of the mob bosses can get a hold of me for some time."

Beio-Rhett laughed, "Are you ever in a bad mood."

"I am in a bad mood," Poko smiled. "Can't you tell?"

Beio-Rhett continued perusing the data pad. "This is new. Where'd you get this?" he handed the data pad back.

Poko squinted, looking at the pad. "Oh, I think I might have three of those. It's the ammo that'll cost you. I can't even think of any space faring race in this galaxy that still uses metal bullets."

Beio-Rhett looked back. "I think I'll take one. Give me a hundred rounds to go with it."

"Just punch it in on the pad, you know my memory's no good."

Beio-Rhett pressed a button on the data pad. "I think that may be it. How much credit do I have left with you?"

Poko laughed. "Don't worry about it man. I know you're

good for it."

"Not anymore," Beio-Rhett said. "These bastards confiscated all my assets. All I got is some favors I can pull and my credit line with you."

"What else do you need?" Poko asked.

"Mostly ammo," said Beio-Rhett. "I can buy the guns from the government. Plus it's on a loan, so it works out better for me."

"Well, what do they got? I'm positive I can get it to you faster, and probably cheaper."

Beio-Rhett bit his lip. "You have any of the A-5000s?"

Poko smiled, "You know it. One of my guys found a weapon's cache abandoned by the rebels before they got busted. The guy unloaded most of it on me for a decent price. If you look on the pad, I'm sure there's some A-5000s there, along with some A-250s."

Beio-Rhett looked again through the data pad. "Man you drive a hard bargain." He said. "All right, I'll take 'em." He punched in a few more things on the data pad. "So, what's that come to?"

Poko took the pad back from Beio-Rhett. "You're a little bit over… but that's fine. It's not like I need it in a hurry."

"I'll pay you back as soon as I can get a hold of some of my assets. I promise, man."

Poko shook his head. "Don't worry 'bout it."

Beio-Rhett thought for a moment and grabbed Poko's shoulder. "I got an idea! You need a place to stay don't you?"

Poko nodded. "I always have a place to stay."

"Come on, Poko," Beio-Rhett said. "Don't lie to me, I know you're a fish out of water here. I can talk to Singatt. I'm sure they can open up another room for you here."

Poko shrugged. "I'm not sure I feel comfortable living in a government facility."

"It'd be the last place anyone would think to look for you," Beio-Rhett suggested.

Poko laughed. "Thank you, friend."

"Go get your stuff and meet me back here," Beio-Rhett said. "I'm gonna go find Singatt."

Beio-Rhett ran across the airfield where the two were standing. Poko took the data pad under his arm and walked towards the shuttle he had landed in.

Beio-Rhett ran towards headquarters, where he knew Singatt was talking to the CO. He nodded to the guard at the door who recognized him and let him in the building. He jogged past the soldiers at their monitors before coming to Singatt, who stood talking to the CO next to a large interactive map table. "Singatt, I have a favor to ask you."

"What now?" Singatt asked impatiently.

"It's about that dealer I was telling you about."

"You need another loan for his stuff too? We're being very generous with you as it is Beio-Rhett. The Government is even allowing you to purchase weapons from them as a contractor for domestic prices. Do you still not trust us?"

"I don't need money. It's not about that," Beio-Rhett argued. "I need another room."

"For your dealer? Another unregistered?"

"He's that Niskan who came in earlier. He's cut off from his hometown, Singatt. He's quick on his feet, but I know this guy gets into trouble. I think he'd be safe here. I owe him anyway."

"Yeah, but this isn't your house, Beio-Rhett. You can't owe him with government property."

"It's one room Singatt! Stop being a prick. What happened to Mr. Compassionate who was gonna save the prisoners. This guy isn't a fucking criminal."

The CO barked, "That's enough! Take it outside!"

Singatt groaned, "Sorry, Colonel." He grabbed Beio-Rhett by the arm and dragged him out of headquarters. When outside, he started talking firmly, but quietly.

"Listen, I don't care if you need another room. The General gave me clearance to commandeer living space from this facility. But don't undermine my authority in front of a superior officer!"

"I'm not a soldier, Singatt! I don't have tags and I'm not on the Government's salary. I'm a weapon that you're using and you said whatever I needed, I could talk to you. I'm a free agent now. I could walk whenever I want. There are still jobs in this system you know. I'm sure the Quesgralions could use some help."

Singatt slapped Beio-Rhett across the face.

Beio-Rhett took a breath and looked back at Singatt. "What do you want?"

"I want you to behave!" Singatt ordered. "General Artinuare is coming here to see the progress of the ship's repairs. That's why I was talking to the CO."

"He's coming here to see me? I'm flattered," he said sarcastically.

Singatt grunted. "How's the ship."

"Getting along. Dembo's in there right now welding the last layer of hull patches. Why does the General care how we're doing? It's not like we're that big of an investment."

"Yeah, but I sold you pretty well to him, so I think now he's putting a bit too much faith in your abilities."

"What happened to your vote of confidence?"

Singatt shook his head. "Anyway, he'll be arriving by a private shuttle soon. I'm going to await his arrival." He started walking to one of the landing platforms.

"Singatt! What about my request?"

Singatt turned around. "I'll get your clearance. Just get back to the ship and get ready to give a tour."

The General's private shuttle arrived soon after. A large black cruiser landed on the platform where Singatt was waiting. When the craft landed, a ramp lowered from the ship's front end. General Artinuare, escorted by two soldiers, walked down the platform. Singatt saluted them and they saluted back. After brief pleasantries, the four of them walked from the landing platform to the middle warehouse, where the Donta Ryx was slowly but surely coming back to life.

After Poko had his travel bag, he started making his way towards the warehouse too. He was quite surprised to see the Grand General himself heading to the same place. Was he here for Beio-Rhett? This was some contract that Beio-Rhett had landed. Poko slung his bag over his back and started making his way in their direction.

The General looked at the Donta Ryx, now covered in shiny new hull armor. A new windshield replaced the cracked one and most of the outer damage was completely repaired. The docking port was still busted and the damaged gunning station was completely removed. Dembo was standing on one of the high scaffolds welding on the last bit of patch armor onto the ship. "Impressive," the General said.

Beio-Rhett was descending the ladder of the scaffolding.

"Thank you!" he shouted back as he dropped to the floor and made his way to the General. When he came face to face with the General, he shook out his hand.

The General laughed at the informality and shook his hand. "Been working hard I see. It's been just a week."

Beio-Rhett nodded.

The General looked back at the ship. "Singatt's been getting all the materials for you?"

Beio-Rhett nodded again. "Doesn't need much. The biggest checks your gonna have to cut are for that gunning station and the busted port. And of course a new core."

The General nodded. "How much longer do you think this is going to take?"

Beio-Rhett scratched the back of his head. "Cosmetic repairs are almost done. We still gotta order the gunning station and the new port. It'll be about another week before we can replace the core and restart the engine."

The General nodded. "Very good," he looked at Beio-Rhett. "I'll have to make sure the first mission we send you on is dangerous, this project is getting spendy."

Beio-Rhett smiled. "Speaking of budgets, how's the reconstruction."

The General's face went grim. "Luckily, I don't have to deal with that, but I know it's not going well. We can't borrow from any of our foreign allies because we can't reach them. We do have some reserve resources we can fall back on. As for my end of things, we're on the tip of our toes with our finger over the button to launch. They have their SETs waiting above the sky and we have a whole army in position, or what's left of it. There's so much friction in the air it could start a goddamn fire."

"How are the armed forces going?" Singatt asked.

"Not well," the General said. "Morale is low. Furthermore we've had to make some cuts to their salaries, which is making things worse. Luckily, we are getting many volunteers for the reconstruction efforts, which frees up soldiers to get ready for this invasion. As much as I'd like to blame the financial crisis on this project, it's just a tiny piece of the whole mess. As far as I know, the Governor is racking up some serious debt trying to rebuild the cities. Some private donors are also relieving some of the financial pressure. The Governor is doing a good job in launching a campaign of a worldwide relief effort. I guess we should count our blessings that the Quezzes haven't invaded yet." He shook his head. "Those bastards really planned this thing out."

Beio-Rhett spoke, "General, I've been through hell and back and I've been dumb enough to return there. You help me get this ship built and I can take down the entire Teneman, one by one."

The General smiled and looked up at Beio-Rhett. "The Governor believes you, unfortunately. I've never been one to resort to mercenaries, but considering the situation we're in, I really have no choice. As for you, I won't be convinced until I see results."

"You've seen the results," Beio-Rhett said. "You're fixing them right now."

The General smiled to hide his anger. "I know it. And despite all of that, the Governor is still confident in you. She must either have lost her mind under all this stress, or for some reason she thinks you'll come through for us."

Beio-Rhett nodded. "Just let me do what I do best, and you won't be disappointed."

"And when you work off your debt on this first mission," the General said. "How do I know you won't just take off?"

Beio-Rhett smiled. "Because we both know I have nowhere else to go. The Quezzes are racist. They won't care if I'm a mercenary. I'll still be an enemy to them."

The General nodded, "Maybe that's where the Governor's trust comes from. She just knows that you have no other choice."

Beio-Rhett shrugged. "Maybe. But I think we have similar goals. I don't wanna be trapped in this system forever. And on that note, I have some good news. I found another crew member."

Singatt looked at Beio-Rhett, "Crewmember?"

Beio-Rhett pointed to Poko who was just walking in the warehouse.

"General, this is Poko Sveryntes, also a former soldier of the Hydro-Baltan War. He and I were stationed at the Aulder Weapons Complex on Drisko together."

The General looked surprised. "Oh wow… I didn't realize. I'm glad the two of you made it out alive."

"We were one of the few," Beio-Rhett remarked. "Anyway, he'll be taking some of the financial pressure off of you."

"How do you mean?" the General asked.

"He's my weapons dealer. Well, weapons and other things. I'll be buying most of my weapons from him so you guys can stop lending me money."

"I thought you had no assets?"

"I have my ways," Beio-Rhett said. "Don't worry about it. It's less money you have to spend on me. He'll be staying at the bunker here too."

The General looked at Beio-Rhett inquisitively.

"I read the contract," Beio-Rhett said. "It specifically says the payment goes to me for me to disperse amongst any accomplices I should need to hire during my mission. The payment is bed and board and I'm sharing that with Dembo and Poko.

The General sighed. "I guess that's fine. I have no reason to turn war heroes out in the cold."

At this point, Poko had made it over to the group. He looked cautious around the General.

The General saluted Poko. "It's great to meet one of the few survivors from the Aulder Tragedy."

Poko smiled immediately. "Oh, forget it. We weren't heroes. We were just survivors."

"Sometimes, there's no difference," the General said reverently.

Before anyone in the group noticed, the CO himself was standing behind Singatt.

"Lieutenant,"

Singatt spun around, surprised, and stood attention, "Yes, Colonel!"

"I've come to inform you that we'll have to move you and the two mercenaries to Barracks C. Barracks B will be used to house wounded soldiers since it is closer to sick bay."

"What happened?"

"One of the platoons hunting remaining rebel outposts in the northern ridge accidentally set off a self-destruct mechanism. Most of the platoon is still alive, but badly wounded. They're being sent here since we're the closest military base."

"That's perfectly fine, Colonel. It's not like we're really set up there, anyway."

The CO nodded, "I'm more worried about our medical staff, personally. Everyone's spread so damn thin as it is. I have a biologist, for example, who was previously doing research on

Geufsta who volunteered her time to help our medics. She was nice enough to transfer here when considering the situation we're in."

"This damned cage we're all trapped in," the General grunted. "I'm glad there are people like that who are giving everything they have to help us. I'm grateful to every soldier who's been signing back up for another tour of duty."

The CO had a grim look on his face. "Me too, General... Gentlemen," with that he saluted and walked away.

The General shook his head. "It's strange to think... I was born on Kashik, you know."

Singatt turned around to face the General, "You don't say, sir. I was too!"

The General smiled at Singatt. "Funny how things change. All that time ago, I never would have imagined in my wildest dreams that we'd be at war with them... it just makes no sense."

Singatt nodded solemnly. He turned to Poko. "Well, I guess you'll be living in Barracks C for the time being."

Poko smiled, this time more subdued. He looked over at Beio-Rhett, "Your stuff will be here inside a week. You're gonna have to get clearance with the CO for an unregistered coming in."

Beio-Rhett looked at Singatt.

Singatt shrugged. "As long as they're in and out."

Poko nodded.

Singatt turned to the General, "Anything else General?"

"That'll be it for now. I'm heading back to Bestton to see if I can get the Governor to up the defense budget so I can stop cutting salaries. I'm not sure why I'm bothering, I know she's strapped as it is. Gentlemen." He saluted the group and walked off, escorted by the two guards.

Beio-Rhett turned to Singatt. "Did you put in a request for my weapons that got confiscated?"

Singatt nodded. "They'll be here today or tomorrow." He turned to Poko. "You can pick a room in Barracks C, Poko."

"Thank you," Poko smiled. "I'll see you later, Beio-Rhett." With that he walked off too.

Beio-Rhett looked at Singatt, "Well, I'm getting back to work."

* * *

The Command Ship of the Quesgralion battle fleet cruised steadily through space, accompanied by a massive fleet of battleships. Standard Quesgralion battleships were shaped like two-pronged forks with the two prongs housing massive offensive capability. Between the prongs was a docking zone where fighters could be harbored and take off from. Behind the fork were massive triple fusion engines that emitted a bright blue light as the battleships cruised forward. The Command Ship was essentially a larger version of these battleships with a third prong in the center that housed a massive fusion cannon capable of destroying entire battleships, classifying it as a warship. While the Hydrolettes were known for their weaponry, the Quesgralions were known for their mastery of spacefaring. Their fleet was the largest in the galaxy and their battleships were infamous among enemy planets. Ironically, the most infamous battleship in Galactic History, the Domalattis was in the service of Hydrolet during the first and second Hydro-Baltan Wars. However, construction of the massive dreadnought-class warship was heavily assisted by Quesgralion engineers. Unfortunately, the Domalattis met its end by means of sabotage from Baltan spies during the war. Although no ship has compared to the massive battleship since, the Quesgralions fleet was still a force to be reckoned with.

Aboard the Command Ship, a Quesgralion ensign was monitoring a virtual periscope in front of him, which received video signals from various cameras posted on the outer hull of the Command Ship. The ensign controlled the monitor with a small panel in front of him. He scrolled through different camera feeds using the panel to input his commands. After the ensign finished cycling through all the camera feeds he got up from his station and turned around to face General Kitchnok who stood in the center of the massive bridge of the Command Ship. The ensign saluted nervously, "Commander Kitchnok, I just completed visual confirmation. No sign of any Hydrolette spacecraft has been found across our controlled parameters. So far it seems they are acting in compliance with our demands."

Kitchnok scratched his chin. He turned around and sat down in the Commander's chair, still scratching his chin. "Hmmmm," he muttered. "Yes, it would seem so, but I can't tell if that's a good thing or not. It is suspicious though. The Hydrolettes are the most aggressive creatures in the galaxy. While they are masters of strategy, that doesn't change their innate barbaric nature. While I could enjoy the solace of a submissive combatant, something just doesn't smell right. Things are going too well, as it were."

"Perhaps things are just going according to plan," Nimx grunted, standing behind the Commander's Chair.

"Perhaps," replied Kitchnok. "But I am not relying on *your* judgment, General," he added sharp emphasis to "your".

Nimx nodded. "If you wish to brood over it, be my guest." He walked over to his command station set off to the side and sat down.

Kitchnok pretended not to hear Nimx. "It's only been a week by their calendar. I guess I shouldn't expect retaliation so soon."

"Starting to feel like you've been pastured?" Nimx heckled from his station.

"Ever the optimist," Kitchnok heckled back. "You honestly think that the Hydrolettes will just sit back and follow orders? The Master didn't put me in charge of the fleet to get me out of the way. Besides, we still have uncontrolled space in this system and it's my job to secure it."

"Commander!" another helmsman addressed Kitchnok.

"Yes,"

"I've just received word of eight probes en route to the force field perimeter."

"They'll be taken care of," Kitchnok dismissed the information. "Don't bother me with anything involving the force field unless it's a manned vessel."

"Yes, Commander. I also just received a positive on our control over Delta Sector Transit Stations 21 and 22."

"Excellent," Kitchnok replied. "What of 23?"

"Still awaiting confirmation sir. Communication has been jammed, but they're still putting up a fight."

"Who, the Hydrolettes?"

"Negative, all noncompliant."

Kitchnok scratched his chin. "I supposed we should have expected as much. Lots of travelers who will be pretty upset about being under martial law. Nothing we haven't planned for."

"Shall I send reinforcements?"

Kitchnok thought for a moment, "Yes, perhaps one of our battleships. Perhaps a taste of the iron fist will keep them in order."

"Yes, Commander!" the helmsmen returned to his station to carry out the order.

"That'll be the last of them," Kitchnok said to himself.

"What of DBVII?" Nimx chimed in from his station.

"What of it?" Kitchnok asked. "Nothing but savages there. They have no contacts outside this system."

"But there are research complexes set up there, and not just Hydrolette ones."

"Your point being?" Kitchnok did not turn to face Nimx. "Those scientists are used to being out of touch with society. It would seem nothing more than a comlink breakdown to them. I see no point in expending any of our force on them. We must focus on the Hydrolettes."

"Then why are you sending troops to the Transit Stations?"

"Because I'm creative," Kitchnok said. "It's important to control the traffic to this system if we are to control the system itself."

"Perhaps the Master made no mention of the Transit Stations for a reason."

"Nimx, if you're going to second guess me at all junctions during our time here, I'd prefer you to spend it in your quarters."

"I'm under orders," Nimx continued to look at readouts on his station.

"Commander, incoming message from the Capitol!" the helmsman announced.

"Clearance?"

"It's from the Defense Ministry,"

"What does that brute want?" Kitchnok muttered to himself, "Patch it through to the conference room, helmsman, I will take this in private" he said aloud. He stood up from his chair and headed towards the bridge's exit. "Nimx, shall we?"

Nimx stood up and followed Kitchnok without saying anything. The two left the bridge and walked down a short series of corridors to the conference room not far from the bridge. The conference room was plain enough, with a large round table surrounded by chairs, a holo-emitter in the center of the table and a large screen built into the wall opposite of the door. Kitchnok pressed a button on the table.

The screen flickered on. The image of General Kut Drokktayr, the Minister of Defense appeared. Unlike Kitchnok's slim, bony countenance and Nimx's stout features, Drokktayr's build was tall and firm with a broad chest and shoulders plus a strong jaw. He had no hair on the back of his head and his earflaps were small. He also sported a heavy brow over his one eye.

"What can I do for you today, Drokktayr?"

"I've contacted you to inform you that the Sal de Gughea luxury cruiser has been apprehended. Naturally, no personnel have claimed allegiance to the Hydrolet Rebellion, but I didn't expect to find any answers until more sophisticated interrogation methods have been imposed."

"Where are the prisoner's being held?" Kitchnok asked.

"Kaeko Desert Outpost 51. Although our facilities are a little over-occupied there. Our soldiers apprehended a Hydrolette platoon sweeping the desert there a few days ago."

"Probably scouting for rebel outposts," Nimx muttered.

"Perhaps, but there's no reason to take chances," Drokktayr responded quickly. "The platoon is currently being held at the Outpost, but there should be enough room in the holding cells for the personnel of the cruiser. As you know, only senior officers will be able to find what we're looking for, so until then all they can do is hold the prisoners there."

"You want one of us to go there?" Kitchnok seemed annoyed.

Drokktayr nodded, "Affirmative. I am busy taking care our conflict with the natives here and Techet's dealing with diplomatic issues. Having Gastus himself go would be too high profile, especially now with so much press on him."

"I've been stationed with this fleet by request of the Master himself," argued Kitchnok. "It would be bad form to promote subordination so soon after everything being left in our hands."

Drokktayr grunted. "Damnit Kitchnok, the Hydrolette's aren't doing squat! They're tied up with the Rebellion's aftermath right now, I doubt you'll be facing an imminent armada attack any time soon."

"Regardless," Kitchnok argued, "they are now aware of our agenda, and knowing their arrogance, they'll probably still put aside some effort to combat us."

Nimx sighed. He knew where this was going.

Drokktayr looked over at Nimx. "Send Nimx then. He doesn't need to be there."

Nimx grunted, "I was technically ordered upon this fleet as well, but I'm sure the Master won't mind if I abandon my post for a few days."

"There's some taking initiative for once!" Kitchnok said in a patronizing tone.

"Shut up, Kitchnok!" Drokktayr yelled. "Nimx, I'll alert the Outpost of your arrival. Upon finding what we're looking for, report to me personally and return to the fleet at your leisure. It's not like there's anything to do out there anyway."

Kitchnok sneered at Drokktayr's comment. "Is there anything else General?"

"That'll be all. Nimx, I expect your report soon. Kitchnok, carry on. Hail the Master."

"Hail the Master," Nimx and Kitchnok repeated back.

The screen went black.

Kitchnok turned to Nimx, "Well old friend, your company will be missed."

Nimx cracked an insincere smile. "I'm sure it will."

Kitchnok headed for the doors, "I'm sure I'm needed on the bridge. I suppose you'll take your leave now. No need for the rest of the crew to know. Be discreet with your exit."

Nimx smiled, without looking at Kitchnok, "Yes, I'll be out of your hair soon enough."

Kitchnok did not respond. He walked out of the room and the doors closed behind him.

The scent of boot polish still lingered in the room. Nimx could hear the shiny boots walk through the corridor outside. Once again, he was glad to not have to be in the same room as Kitchnok, but he was still upset to have such a pivotal responsibility assigned to him. At least it wasn't a dangerous mission. It was probably safer than staying on the Command Ship, although Drokktayr did make a point that the fleet would probably never see conflict. He briefly sighed and entered some commands on the comm station on the table in front of him.

"Docking bay A-3."

"This is Nimx, ready a shuttle for me. One escort. Don't

alert any other personnel."

"Yes, sir,"

Nimx ended the transmission and left the room.

* * *

Dr. Mheages sat at the desk at his makeshift office at the Bestton Naval & Air Base. The Government set him up there so that they'd be in direct contact with him in case of an emergency like the recent situation. It was also relatively close to the Northern Ridge, where his partner, Dr. HarRhett Yeffrej was partaking in an archaeological dig. Mheages's quarters were fairly generous. He had a large desk in the corner opposite the door, with a computer monitor in the center. The right wing of the desk was an archaic reading area, with a lantern placed above a stack of books, some notebooks with scribbles on them and a jar of writing utensils. To his right were some stacks of data pads and a design surface. The desk was in the corner opposite of the door and was placed beneath a large window over the right wing of the desk, which looked out over the eastern sea. Hand-drawn formulas, equations and various inscriptions in ancient Quel-Noran and Groacorian script text hung on the walls. On the left wall when entering the room was a much larger monitor that displayed a semi-holographic map, with a control panel in front of it. The map was currently on standby. On the right wall stood a massive bookshelf. Numerous data pads were stacked haphazardly on the bookshelf, along with several more old-fashioned paper books from Mheages's private collection. In the corner on the other side of the window on the same wall as the desk was another holo-emitter that projected a large detailed image of the planet Hydrolet. The only items in the room that showed any sign of interest, besides academia, were a Groacorian crest of arms that hung on the wall above Dr. Mheages's desk and a framed picture that sat on his desk of an older female Hydrolette and a small Hydrolette girl, both smiling brightly.

Mheages had an old-fashioned paper book in his hand which bore ancient Quel-Noran star maps. The design surface bore a similar image, only partly completed. The stylus lay, idle on top of the design pad. Mheages was not paying attention to his work right now. He was looking at the picture on his desk.

A knock sounded on the door to the office. "Professor?"

Dr. Mheages broke from his trance, "Come in,"

The doors slid open and a young technician appeared in the doorway. "Am I interrupting anything?"

"Not at all, just transcribing some old records."

"Part of that archaeology project? How is that going, Professor?"

"Mostly been copying things for the moment. Ancient star maps and such. It's quite interesting how reverently the First Race treated the Hydrolettes upon first discovering this planet. At least it seems that way from some of the scrolls I've been studying. You study much history during your time at university?"

"I got my degree in Astrophysics sir. I think the last time I read a history book was in prep school. Can't say I remember much."

Mheages nodded, seeming to stare off into the distance, "Yes, fascinating stuff should you get a chance to read any of it," he broke himself from his gaze, "Anyway, what was it you wanted?"

"Professor, the reports from the probes you sent out have finally been retrieved. They all stopped transmitting at the estimated perimeter of the bubble. We assume that they were destroyed by their impact with the force field wall as you predicted."

Mheages sighed and put the paper book on the desk behind him. He stood up from the chair. "Do you have video and audio feed intact? What was the last recorded data?"

"The feed was streaming perfectly up until the projected distance to the perimeter was reached. There were no anomalies in sight. As soon as the probes reached the estimated distance, the feed was cut."

"And the scanners."

"There is something there, Professor, we just can't tell what it is. You can look at the data yourself to try to come up with a better hypothesis. The spectrum scanners show the presence of some field at the estimated distance, but that's about it. All we know about it is that it's invisible and anything that crosses it is destroyed."

Mheages furrowed his brow in a disappointed fashion. "Where is the spectrum data?"

"Your lab on Observation Deck 12. Would you like to study them for yourself?"

"Yes, but maybe later. I need to talk to General Artinuare about sending a manned scout out to the perimeter. I may be able to draw something from the readouts, but I heavily doubt it. The only way we'll be able to know what the hell is out there is by sending someone, but at the same time I know the General won't want to spare any of his soldiers..." he paused and smiled, "I wonder if he'd be willing to use those two new mercenaries. I may finally have a job he could give them."

The technician smirked, "That's rather morbid, Professor."

Mheages looked up at the soldier. "Still, I trust your analysis is sufficient to make a report to the General. Would you mind accompanying me to his quarters?"

The technician nodded enthusiastically, "Certainly Professor! Let me grab the data pads first."

General Artinuare sat in his office at the Bestton Naval & Air Base. Like, Mheages's, it was a temporary location. His main office was at the Department of War at the Capitol Square. However, during times of crisis, he usually stayed at the Base, where he had more direct contact with the officers leading the ground and space forces. Also he could oversee strategic decisions and planning more intimately. Artinuare played a much more active role in Hydrolet's military endeavors than had previous Grand Generals of the Hydrolet Armed Forces. He was appointed to the position twenty years ago, just after the Second Hydro-Baltan war ended. He succeeded Grand General Hett Deigger, who was dishonorably discharged after the devastating outcome of the war. While General Deigger's responsibility for the disastrous aftermath was somewhat exaggerated, his isolated and detached nature regarding military decisions did cost thousands of Hydrolette and Baltan lives. Rarely did General Deigger leave Capitol Square, leaving him oblivious to the gruesome reality of the battlefield. His orders led to the destruction of the Domalattis, since he ignored numerous reports of suspicion of sabotage on the ship and led the warship to the space battle where it met its end. Also, the infamous fall of the Aulder Weapons Complex on Drisko was a direct result of Deigger's failure to prioritize the siege and send reinforcements. Due to these and other incidents, Grand General Deigger became the scapegoat for Hydrolet's failure in the war and was publicly humiliated by forcing to resign.

Artinuare was a General of ground forces during the Hydro-Baltan War, and was given the position due to his valiant performance on the battlefield and his highly successful tactics. He and General Zaedin Dresbar were the two most likely candidates for the position, but Artinuare won out for his hands-on leadership in the battlefield, which he continued to practice even as a Grand General. It is believed that his failure to be appointed caused General Dresbar to later defect and form the Rebellion, but this is highly disputed as Dresbar had shown signs of disloyalty even during the war. Regardless, Artinuare retained his hands-on attitude as a Grand General and spent very little time at the Capitol, unlike Deigger. The drawback of course, is that Artinuare was not as intimate with the Governor as Deigger was. Although Artinuare still remained one of Nasdett's closest confidants.

During the Rebellion, Nasdett entrusted nearly every aspect of handling the situation to Artinuare without exception. Part of this trust stemmed from Artinuare's seniority. He had already been Grand General for ten years before Nasdett was appointed Governor after the assassination of former Governor Orren Octtanis, widely regarded as the beginning of the Rebellion. Nasdett inherited the Rebellion and the economic mess that Hydrolet was in after the Hydro-Baltan War. Artinuare became a fast ally by dispatching many of the Rebellion's initial advances, holding off what could have been a successful coup against the Capitol. Afterwards, the conflict was slow-going and deadly as the Rebellion stayed away from any full-on attacks and resorted mostly to acts of sabotage, bombings, assassination and heavy-artillery raids. Although the following ten years delivered little success to Hydrolet in trying to snuff out the Rebellion, Artinuare's victory in defending the Capitol remained a feather in his cap and cemented Nasdett's trust in his abilities to defend the planet.

At first their relationship resembled more of that between an older brother and younger sister, but as the Rebellion pressed on they began to respect each other as peers. Although a good twenty years her senior, Artinuare never questioned Nasdett's judgement and towards the end of the Rebellion came to rely on her financial and moral support to continue what seemed like a futile effort against the Rebellion. The Rebellion took its toll on Artinuare. He looked much older than he was. His hair was prematurely grey and his face bore more lines than it should. His brow was weighed down from the years and years of stress, trying to keep the peace, not to mention the emotional stress of killing fellow Hydrolettes, young Hydrolettes as well. There was also feeling of betrayal that his main target was one of his comrades during the Hydro-Baltan war, General Dresbar. Artinuare would never admit it even to his closest friends, but sometimes the endless conflict started to make him think that the rebels were right. He fought in the Hydro-Baltan War too and he knew it was a frivolous conflict. He knew that while the lofty political motivations made sense in discussion, the thousands upon thousands that died because of those arguments could never justify those reasons. He had to bear the shame of being the leader of one of the most aggressive races in the galaxy. Wars like that with the Baltans only confirmed their warmongering nature, and he knew even as he fought in it that they were acting out the very stereotype he knew did so little justice to his race. He promised himself and others that when he took up the position of Grand General he would not find excuses to attack other planets. His career would be marked with peace. However, he was never given the chance. He blamed himself as well for not seeing the seeds of discontent earlier. He even had suspicions of Dresbar that he never let himself think about. However, the truth slapped him and everyone else on the planet's face when Octtanis was killed. And now, the Hydrolettes were the aggressive beasts whom would even kill their own kind, and Artinuare was the warlord who reigned over this slaughter.

Still, Artinuare never stepped down from his position. As ashamed as he was of his race's warrior-like tendencies, he could not ignore his own. He was a warrior, as were many of the soldiers in the Hydrolet Military. The battlefield was his home. The honor of victory was his salvation. He could never deny it. In fact the only thing now that ate at his conscious was that he was getting too old to take as active a part in warfare as he once had. The Rebellion did not help either. Soon his physical prowess would leave him, and after that, his mental, this is what caused him the most unrest. And so he remained Grand General, hoping to either die in battle or to achieve the only true happiness he knew, which was victory. After the Rebellion was quelled, he felt such bliss, but it was short-lived as the Quesgralion's treachery brought them full-circle into interplanetary war. He mused over the thought of the outcome of this war. Perhaps he would finally die now, in the battlefield, an honorable death. He would be remembered fondly and his funeral would be grand. His children would come to revere him and generations after him would speak highly of his victories.

And yet, what would happen after this war? Another Rebellion? Were the Hydrolettes really such a war-like clan, stuck in an endless cycle of conflict? Was this their only comfortable mode of existence? Perhaps it was. In ancient times they were, at least, more honest about it. Now they have the illusion of civilization, but are they any different? The Niskans are masters of commerce, the Quesgralions must dominate as many planets and cultures as they can, and the Hydrolettes must do battle. Perhaps the stereotypes were there for a reason. Artinuare didn't really care what other races thought of the Hydrolettes. It seemed silly to even consider it, but he did often consider all the death. Not every race had such a respect for death in battle as the Hydrolettes, for some, death is just death.

Artinuare's office on the base was more lived in. There were no windows. His chair faced the doorway with a large desk in front of him. Behind him was a huge monitor with a digitalized terrain map that currently showed Bestton. On either side of the monitor was a stack of shelves where several data pads were stored. A holo-emitter was set up on the right wall of the room when entering. Two chairs were positioned on the other side of the desk for guests. On the bookshelves were placed several items of personal interest. His Medal of Honor for his services during the second Hydro-Baltan War was presented on a stand. Next to it the key to the Capitol City, presented to him by Nasdett after his successful resistance to the coup. The Crest of Zala also hung from a stand, implying his faith. There was also a bust of Governor Octtanis, whom he greatly respected and was saddened by his death. The walls were not without decoration either. A scale model of the Domalattis was imprinted on a wall relief on the left wall of the room. The Quel-Noran script read "Never Forget" underneath it. There was also a wall relief commemorating General Ghealston's victory in the first Hydro-Baltan War on the other wall. Artinuare liked the two pieces as they kept him in check during times of hopeless despair and hasty optimism. Other ornaments decorated his desk. There was a small gold plated globe model of Hydrolet, with the Quel-Noran word for "home" on the base. There was also a copper plaque that read in Galactic Standard, "I am only that which others see me as, and others are only that which I see them as." Naturally, the saying was translated in almost every language in the galaxy, including Hydrolette's native tongue, Groacorian, but Artinuare preferred to have the saying in its original language. Then, besides his nameplate, several data pads, and a miniature video monitor, the only other personal item on the General's desk was a framed photograph of two young adult female Hydrolettes. Tucked in the corner of the frame was a much older photograph of an older Hydrolette female. Artinuare sat crouched over his desk perusing over a data pad on the desk in front of him when the video monitor blinked. A green light, implying proper clearance flashed.

The General took a deep breath. There was usually nothing but bad news these days. He pressed a button on the monitor to patch the transmission through.

An operator from the communications center appeared on the video screen. As the General could guess, his face was grim. "What is it, Sergeant?" he asked.

The operator saluted. "General, we've just received sat-cam readings that show a fleet of Quesgralion battle ships led by a command ship has come to a standstill in interplanetary space roughly 3.7 AUs from Hydrolet. They do not appear to be in attack formation, but they do have a pretty impressive fleet, estimated thirty to forty battle ships. They appear to be setting up some sort of vanguard for their planet in case we manage to launch an attack."

"That seems unnecessary since they have us surrounded by SETs."

"Agreed, General. They seem to be taking rather excessive precautions."

The General smiled insincerely, "It's because they're afraid, Sergeant."

The operator attempted to mimic the General's attempt at lightening the situation, "Indeed, General. What of our defensive capability?"

"We have a few hundred fighter ships ready for immediate deployment. We don't have nearly enough battleships to stage a successful attack on a fleet that big."

"I understand, General. Orders?"

The General was taken aback. "Oh, just keep watching them. There is nothing we can do. Unless they take attack formation, just sit tight. Keep collecting data from the fleet until they find and blast those sat-cams."

The operator chuckled, "Indeed, sir. Should we redirect more sat-cams to their location?"

"Negative. Let's not make them skittish. Keep whatever cam that found them retrieving whatever it can. Hopefully they won't notice it too soon."

"Yes, General," the operator saluted

The General saluted back then ended the transmission.

Artinuare slumped back in his chair and let out a long, disgruntled sigh. He shook his head and stood up. He pressed the comlink on his desk. "Operator, could you send a request to the Executive Office with my clearance. Classify the message as urgent…"

Mheages and the technician saw Artinuare walking towards them with his head down. "General! We were just looking for you," Mheages said.

Artinuare looked up surprised, but kept walking towards the elevator behind them, "I'm sorry, Professor, I can't talk right now. I have a meeting with the Governor," his voice was very gruff.

Mheages was taken aback as Artinuare walked passed him. He turned and followed him, trying to match his pace. "General, might I ask what about? It's just that I do have some important news concerning the force field."

Artinuare stopped at the elevator and pressed the button for ground floor. As he waited for the car to come up, he looked at Mheages, a grave look on his face. "Perhaps you should join me then." He paused, looking back at the elevator. "I've just been informed that a fleet of Quesgralion battleships has taken position a few AUs away from our planet, creating some sort of buffering defense force between our respective planets."

Mheages sighed in disappointed, "This is getting ridiculously out of hand. What if it's an invading force?"

Artinuare nodded. "I doubt it, they already have their SETs for that, but naturally we shouldn't rule it out as a possibility. The Governor is coming here to discuss our options, which are quickly running out."

Mheages looked at the technician, who was aghast. He spoke again, "Well I hate to say I have no good news for you. It's about the probes I sent out. Unfortunately, we didn't get much information from them other than there indeed is some perimeter around this system, with roughly the same dimensions that the Quesgralions claim it is."

Artinuare was silent. The doors to the elevator opened. "Do you have the data with you?"

"I can access the mainframe of the lab if we get to a holo-emitter," the technician interrupted.

"Excellent," Artinuare said.

The three of them entered the elevator. Artinuare spoke, "Let's hope there's no more bad news today."

After meeting Governor Nasdett at the western docking bay, the trio escorted her to the War Room, which provided the most secure environment to discuss the current situation.

The last security doors to the War Room opened before the General. The guard behind the door stepped aside to let him, Mheages, the technician and Governor Nasdett into the War Room. The doors closed behind them.

"All right, what's going on?" the Governor asked impatiently. "I'm afraid I'm a little bit short of patience today. Our foreign trade has been completely cut off, so we're literally being held hostage. We have ample resources for survival, but not for war. We've also lost contact with all three space stations in this system. I assume they've been taken over by the Quesgralions."

"Governor, I apologize for interrupting you. I understand this must be a difficult time, but I'm afraid things have taken a turn for the worse," the General said. He turned to one of the soldiers operating the holo-emitter in the middle of the room. "Bring up the sat cam images from today."

He turned back to the Governor. "Normally I wouldn't call you here for military matters. I assumed our situation would only entail dealing with those damned SETs hovering over our cities. Unfortunately, that's not all the Quesgralions are throwing our way."

The large screen in front of the group flickered and projected an image of the massive fleet of battleships. The command ship stood out amongst the other battleships quite starkly.

The General spoke, "This fleet was spotted roughly four AUs from our planet, just about halfway between Hydrolet and Quesgarlon. Based on our initial observations, it seems they've come to a standstill, keeping a safe distance from our planet. They don't seem to be in attack position, but it is clear that they have a sufficient force to stage a wide-scale invasion of our planet."

"Then why don't they?" the Governor asked, "If they want to wipe us out, why don't they just attack. What is with this stalemate they're imposing?" she seemed frustrated.

"I can't tell you, Governor," the General said. "All we know at this point is that they've mobilized a battle fleet and it's staying put. But they haven't invaded yet and those SETs haven't moved either."

The Governor turned to the General, "Erthon, have you been giving the Quezzes reason to feel defensive? Any covert attacks I should know about?"

The General shook his head, "Not at all, Governor. I've been far too busy trying to reorganize our troops. There's no action we have taken to betray any offensive tactic other than increase our anti-space craft defense around the major cities where their SETs are already stationed."

"What's the chance of success in taking out those SETs should they move in?"

"Not good. We could probably destroy a few, but they have a whole ground force ready for a full-scale invasion. Our initial defenses would only give us a head start in what would be total ground war on this planet."

"Perhaps that's what they're trying to avoid," the Governor looked back at the menacing image of the fleet. "They really don't want us to make a move. Perhaps the longer we sit here with those SETs above us, the more restless and desperate we get. By their reasoning, maybe after months of frustration coupled with a lack of options, we become forced to start firing on those SETs and start a war. Perhaps the Quesgralions aren't convinced they'd be successful when they invade our planet and that our ground forces would eventually wipe theirs out. It would take time, yes, but we are not squabbling natives vulnerable to being stamped out by their colonizing fist. Perhaps the Quesgralions know this. They also know that when we defeat their ground forces we'll move in to attack their planet, and because of our frustration and desperation, we'll throw everything we've got." She turned back to the General, "And wipe them out."

The General took a breath. "I appreciate your optimism, Governor, but I'd still prefer to do everything in our power to stop those SETs from landing."

"Me too," the Governor said, looking back at the image contemplatively. "I'm just trying to understand why they've amassed this fleet. Probably to discourage us from initiating the scenario I've just described. If we are victorious in fending off their invasion, then they now have a second line of defense to stop us before we reach their planet." She turned back to the General. "And I assure you, we do not have the capability to defeat a Quesgralion fleet."

The General nodded, "I'm well aware."

"Well, what do you want to do about it?" the Governor asked.

"That's what I brought you down here for," the General said. "What do you want to do about it? It's a military decision, yes, but this could change everything. What if that fleet decides to mobilize and just devastate our planet from above? They are obviously escalating this conflict and we may have to take some preemptive action."

The Governor looked back at the image. "We may. But we don't have to yet. They want us to sit still, than let's sit still if it makes them leave us alone. We have to rebuild our planet before going to war. Believe me, I am not saying we let them get away with this treachery, but we simply can't afford to act now."

"I understand."

"That being said, I still want you to find a way to destroy that fleet. You and I both know that our ground forces are far superior to theirs, but their space force is a different story. I don't like that fleet and I want it gone. In our supposed complacency, let's not forget to develop a plan when this stalemate is inevitably broken."

"Yes Governor."

The Governor turned to Mheages, "And you had some information as well?"

Mheages nodded and turned to the technician. "Can you bring up the data from the probes?"

The technician punched in some commands on the control panel below the monitor. The image was much less interesting, just depicting the starlit void of space. "There's your problem," the technician said with a slight grin. "That's the force field."

"Invisible then," the Governor said. "How are you sure it's there at all?"

"Two reasons," Mheages said. "One, the spectrum scanners detect interference with Non-visible frequencies, implying that there is indeed a field there."

The image simulated an illustration of different wavelengths leaving the probe and stopping before an unseen wall.

"That just gives you an idea of what is happening to the rays the probe sends out since you can't see it yourself. It does explain why we lost contact with the Republic. Our normal transmission waves are stopped by this barrier."

"But light passes through," the Governor said. "It's a shame we haven't invented a transmission signal out of light yet."

The technician chuckled. "Indeed, but I don't think that would be much help to us either. See look at the visual data on the monitor."

The Governor complied.

"Now I'm going to put a distance timer in the bottom left of the monitor here," the technician said. "This tells the distance from the supposed location of the barrier. It's counting down as the probe gets closer."

The Governor watched as the distance rolled down to zero. No sooner did the timer reach zero that the image turned to static.

"And then we lost the feed," the technician said. "This same thing happened for all the other probes we sent out. There's definitely something there."

The Governor sighed. "That doesn't really change our situation at all. You've just confirmed that there is a force field there. What do you know about it?"

"Nothing much," Mheages said. "I'd have to analyze the spectrum data a bit more closely to get a decent report. However, I did want to speak to the General about possibly sending a manned probe out to the force field to get a more comprehensive study."

The Governor laughed. "Are you willing to volunteer?"

Mheages shook his head. "Not fly into the damned thing and be destroyed, but at least get near it, run some tests, attempt to send solid projectiles through it to get more information."

The General shook his head. "I'm afraid that's out of the question. We can't spare any of our pilots right now, plus I don't feel comfortable sending anything off this planet as it may spook the SETs. I'm afraid you'll just have to work with the data you have."

Mheages sighed. "Well I can't promise much. As for leaving the planet, haven't there been private vessels coming and going?"

"Probably," the Governor said. "But the Quezzes probably know military signatures and haven't moved because of it. We've kept all of our armed forces stationary. In fact, we still have outposts and bases out on other parts of this system left over from the Rebellion. Right now we have to work on getting those soldiers back here. Some have returned unscathed, so the Quezzes don't seem to be completely heartless."

Mheages spoke, "What about the new mercenaries you hired."

The Governor smiled. "Send them to their execution after all? I'm afraid I do see potential in those two and would like to keep them for something a bit more useful. As for a manned probe I'd suggest you send one of your own technicians or interns, but I can't in good faith, knowing it would most likely be a death sentence."

Mheages shrugged, "Maybe. There just simply isn't enough data to find any real answers. Then again, it depends on what your focus is. If you want to get through that force field then we should send people there and focus our efforts on finding out what it is and where it originates from."

"That is our goal," the General said.

"But you'd rather focus your military strength on Quesgarlon itself."

The Governor spoke. "They are the architects of this force field, so it makes sense that they'll be the ones that know how to shut it off."

The General spoke. "Not to downplay your efforts Mheages, but as much as we'd like to get out of this bubble, I don't think the Republic would be of much help to us. For all we know they're completely on board with the Quezzes' plan.

Mheages shrugged, "Fine by me. You're the one who wanted my help. I'm just trying to offer it as best I can. I'll continue to study the data we have, but like I said, it won't reveal much."

"Thank you, Professor," the Governor said. "It's all we can do right now. Maybe as this situation escalates, we'll be able to make some attempts at crossing that barrier, but right now, we wait. We are in this on our own, and so we will go it alone."

Mheages sighed. "I understand. I'll probably have a report by the end of the week. I warn you it'll be based mostly on speculation."

"Whatever you can do will help," the Governor spoke softly.

Mheages grunted. "What about sending more probes? Obviously there's something there at the projected distance, so there's no need to attempt to cross it again, but perhaps a droid probe could be stationed just outside the barrier to do further scanning."

"We've already lost eight probes," the General objected. "Those things aren't cheap."

Mheages huffed, "Artinuare, I'm just trying to help. You want my assistance but you gotta give me a leg up every so often. If you want me to work with my hands tied behind my back, the results aren't going to be what you want. I'm just saying, don't complain to me later when you don't get the information you're looking for!"

"Huji," the Governor interrupted. "We'll send one more droid probe for observation."

Mheages took a breath. "Thank you Governor. I'm just feeling sort of helpless right now."

"We all are," the Governor said. "We are all caged beasts. Let's not turn against each other. That is exactly what the Quezzes are hoping for."

Mheages nodded. "Thank you for understanding."

"Thank you for your help. You should focus on your research to take your mind off things. The truth is right now, we can't do much of anything."

"I know, but it's hard to focus knowing that we are under siege. Knowing that I can't go home."

The Governor patted Mheages on the back, "It's just as bad being under house arrest."

Mheages smiled. "Well, I'm gonna start pouring over those readouts. Thank you for your time, General. Miss Governor, thank you for your help." He saluted the General and bowed before the Governor.

Mheages and the technician walked towards the exit and the guard escorted them out of the War Room.

The Governor looked at the General briefly and then at the screen. "Bring up the image of the fleet again," she ordered the operator. She looked at the image of the menacing fleet. "General, we must start planning how we are going to take care of this threat. I have no interest in alarming the Quesgralions to attack, but that fleet will be devastating if it reaches us. Even if it means initiating their ground force invasion, we have to destroy that fleet."

"Agreed, Governor. Are you suggesting a preemptive strike?"

The Governor sighed. "Not exactly. We have to direct all of our space force at that fleet, which would distract our air defense if they invade. We still would not be able to leave much of a mark on that fleet."

"We should build another Domalattis," the General quipped.

"And build it without their help this time," the Governor went along with the joke. "In all seriousness, we do have to focus our attack on that fleet. What are our options?"

The General had a data pad ready with the information. "At our immediate disposal, we have two hundred Green Arrow fighters and one hundred Gyropod fighters. There are some other fighters unaccounted for on DB IV and DB VII, but I don't know if we'll be seeing those again. We have over 1,000 transport units available, but that won't do us much good against a fleet. We also have 20 battleships, in commission, currently docked. Three are on patrol and are returning. We've informed them of the Quesgralion fleet and told them to avoid it at all cost."

"And our ground capability?"

"Much more impressive as you can guess. Our anti-space weaponry is equally impressive. It would almost seem a better move to lure them here and take down their fleet from the ground."

"In theory, except that means the destruction of our planet. Their ground forces will already be occupying us."

"I understand, Elorum, but you and I both know our strength is with our ground forces, so either we fight them on our ground or theirs."

The Governor lowered her head. "I know Erthon, I know," she sighed, and leaned over the railing before the screen. After a few seconds she stood up. "Maybe Mheages had a point. What about the mercenaries?"

"What about them? Send them up against the fleet alone?"

The Governor smiled. "Not exactly, but there must be some sort of use for them. Think of something. The first step is we have to find a way off this planet without them knowing it. We need to find a way to start attacking them without starting the war. Not that we can put it off indefinitely. They will attack, and they will attack soon, but we need a leg up."

"What do you suggest?"

The Governor looked back at the image of the fleet. "I don't know, Erthon. That will have to be your job. I'm still busy trying to rally support."

"Indeed. My primary focus is reorganizing our troops. We have to get those battleships back here before that fleet finds and destroys them. We also have to recall all of our troops scattered throughout the system."

The Governor turned around to face the General. "What about our troops on Quesgarlon?"

The General nodded, "Those especially. Two platoons stationed there have actually made it back successfully. Although they were stationed in uninhabited areas searching for hidden rebel bases so they were unaware of any Quesgralion activity. They were also lucky enough not to be spotted by any Quesgralion forces."

"Are there any others there?"

"We're trying to look into that Governor. It's been a long ten years and we've been stretched all over the system. But I'll do my best to find the rest of them on Quesgarlon."

"I'm not talking so much about bringing them in, but see if they can find anything out."

"Governor, that's out of the question. These are soldiers, not spies. They'll be completely vulnerable in what is now designated as an enemy planet."

"I know, I'm just thinking about options." She was silent for a while. "Find out what troops are left on Quesgarlon II and get in contact with them immediately. In the meantime find out our capability for sneaking off of this planet without alarming the SETs."

"Yes, Governor."

"I'm still trying to get in contact with allies on DBIV and DBVII. We need to get some forces off this planet. I'm also trying to get in touch with the three Delta space stations, but to no avail. If we can break their focus from just one planet, we may stand a chance. As for the mercenaries, let's keep them in mind."

"I'm sure I'll think of something."

Beio-Rhett leaned on his knee on a catwalk underneath the docking port of the almost-revived Donta Ryx. He wore a protective mask as he took a welder to the joints of the port door, which had finally come to the base yesterday. The bright blue flame sealed together the remaining joints where the new port door joints would be attached to the ship's hull. The blackened metal folded into itself neatly as the blue fountain poured over the joints. Satisfied with his weld, Beio-Rhett turned off the torch and took off his mask. With the blasting sound of the torch off and the mask now uncovering his ears, he could hear Singatt yelling at him from the ground floor.

"Beio-Rhett! Goddamnit, take your…"

"What?!" Beio-Rhett called back after hearing his voice.

"Your weapons that we confiscated finally arrived," Singatt said. "Zala, Beio-Rhett I've been barking at you from down here for almost five minutes.

Beio-Rhett put his tools down and started to descend the catwalk. "You could've come up and tapped me on the shoulder."

"I don't exactly trust you with fire."

Beio-Rhett leapt down the last few ladder rungs to the ground floor. "So where's my stuff?"

Singatt motioned behind him. "In the mail room. Just give them your name, they're expecting you."

Beio-Rhett looked up to the gunning station of the Donta Ryx, where Dembo was assembling the weaponry. "Dembo! I'm taking a break!"

Dembo simply waved his hand, signaling that he heard Beio-Rhett.

Before Beio-Rhett headed for the mailroom he turned to Singatt, "Feel free to help out any time."

Singatt only smiled and went his way.

Beio-Rhett walked towards the exit of the warehouse. The mail room was inside headquarters, a few paces past the warehouse. He walked briskly past the various workers and soldiers muddling about the warehouse, not making eye contact with anyone. The workers in turn tried their best to avoid any eye contact with him. He stared straight forward, looking at the headquarters building, which was just barely in sight behind the archway of the warehouse. As he walked closer to the gaping archway, the headquarters came more into view. He stared forward, keeping the edge of the building in sight, like the sight of land giving hope to a drifter at sea. Beio-Rhett had spent the last two weeks either around his broken ship or in his room. He ate in the mess hall apart from the others with Dembo, Poko and sometimes Singatt. He woke up, ate, worked, sometimes took a break in the middle of the day, worked more, ate more, and slept. The monotonous grind distracted him from the fact that he was trapped. Trapped in this base, trapped by the government, trapped on the planet, trapped in the system. It was easy to stay focused on one simple goal. *Fix the ship*. Why? *So I could start working again*. For whom? *Hydrolet*. It didn't matter. There was no reason to be upset about it. But he was because he took his capture personally. It didn't do any good to think about it. That's why he stayed focused, focused on one goal. *Fix the ship. Get to the mail room*. That was his goal now. *Walk forward, don't look at anyone, don't talk to anyone*. If he didn't bother anyone, he'd make it out. He was working for these people, but he knew he was a prisoner. He was underwater, holding his breath, swimming to the mail room. He told himself he was not intimidated. He just had no reason to create relationships with these people. He would be gone soon enough. He could get back to what he did best. He was almost out of the warehouse now. The headquarters building was in plain sight. There was a loading vehicle coming into the warehouse, taking up most of the archway. Beio-Rhett stepped over to the right of the vehicle, so he was close to the right side of the archway. He kept walking forward, keeping towards the right edge of the archway, still looking forward, only briefly glancing at the loader to avoid it, looking forward at the headquarters building. He walked closer to the edge of the archway, still looking forward.

He had successfully avoided everyone in the warehouse. He stepped past the archway into another person, a Hydrolette, a female, walking perpendicular to him across the archway from the outside. Beio-Rhett was no longer underwater.

The two Hydrolettes were walking at an equally brisk pace, hurrying towards their destinations before smashing into each other with such force that both of them fell backwards. Even Beio-Rhett's larger stature than the female didn't save his balance as he was taken by such surprise. Their torsos smashed into each other at right angles, they stepped onto each other's boots tripping the other. The female held a stack of data pads up to her breasts that jammed into Beio-Rhett's chest before they went flying into the air. Their heads also bumped into each other from the impact. As they fell, their legs became twisted after having stepped on each other.

Beio-Rhett got back up almost as soon as he fell. He checked himself to see that he hadn't sustained any serious injury, except for his head, still a little sore from the impact with hers. He looked down at the female who was on the ground, obviously a bit more shaken from the impact. In the few seconds before he decided to express his discontent with her he looked her over to get a quick idea of who she was. Her clothes said little about her as she was dressed in the standard civilian jacket and pants offered to any civilian guests of the base and a pair of standard army boots. No information there except she wasn't military. She did have an ID tag, so she had some purpose on the base. Her hair was long, a little longer than shoulder length, but not particularly stylized, rather plain. He watched as she quickly rolled over and searched for the data pads that had scattered before her. Before she even had a chance to look at Beio-Rhett and say anything he barked, "You clumsy bitch! What the fuck were you thinking?!"

"Whoa, chill out!" the woman said as she gathered her things, "It was just as much your fault as it was mine."

"Bullshit, watch where you're going!" Beio-Rhett barked again.

"Listen, I'm sorry, okay. I'm in a hurry, alright?" she picked up the last data pad.

"Sorry my ass, Goddamnit!" he rubbed his forehead where a bump was starting to form.

At this point, Singatt ran over to the archway. "Beio-Rhett..."

"Shut up Singatt, she's not military!" Beio-Rhett shouted then turned back.

"Listen, I'm sorry. I should've paid more attention," the woman said.

Her acquiescence fed into Beio-Rhett's rage. "I don't care if you're sorry. Do you know who I am?! You're on a fucking military base and you're just bumping into random people, you could've just bumped into the wrong perso…'"

Beio-Rhett couldn't finish his sentence. The woman gave up trying to reason with the rambling brute before her clenched her fist, gathered as much strength as her small stature could grant her and thrust it straight into Beio-Rhett's face.

Beio-Rhett was on the ground again. This time his injuries were somewhat more severe. He slowly lifted his head up and looked at the small woman, now towering over him with her fist still clenched. He felt the lukewarm wetness of blood running from his nose. His upper lip was throbbing. He grunted and wiped the blood from his nose with his hand, confirming that he had been struck as hard as he thought. He looked up at her again. She was still clenching one fist. She seemed to be breathing heavier. Her breasts heaved. A few beads of sweat broke from her forehead. Perhaps she regretted what she had just did. But Beio-Rhett couldn't sense fear. She looked more surprised than anything else.

"Listen, I'm sorry," she said. "But you seriously have to calm the fuck down."

"Beio-Rhett, this is one of the medical volunteers the CO mentioned!" Singatt shook his head, embarrassed as he spoke.

Beio-Rhett looked up and saw the red cross insignia on her armband that he failed to notice before. He sighed and looked up at her sheepishly.

The woman looked at Singatt, "Beio-Rhett? Holy shit, you're one of the mercenaries they have stationed here. I'm kind of surprised I haven't run into you yet."

"What are you talking about? You just did," Beio-Rhett spit blood on the floor next to him.

The woman's face brightened. She cracked a short laugh then unclenched her fist. She held it out for him, "I guess I have."

Beio-Rhett wiped more blood from his nose before looking up at the hand. He hesitated for a moment only before reaching out and grabbing it.

The women pulled Beio-Rhett up to his feet. "I'm sorry about the…"

"Oh, that's fine. Happens all the time. My fault, really," Beio-Rhett resorted to his dismissive sarcastic tone.

The woman laughed again. "I probably took it too far, but I didn't know how to shut you up."

Beio-Rhett was a little taken aback by her smile. He realized he wasn't as upset anymore. In fact, he couldn't figure out why he was so upset to begin with. He had forgotten what he was so focused on before.

"I'm very sorry, miss. He's not very good with people," Singatt said.

"Don't apologize for me, I can do it myself," Beio-Rhett grunted.

"It's okay, I'm not either," the woman said.

"But you're a doctor," Beio-Rhett said.

"I'm actually a biologist. I just arrived from Geufsta before the bubble closed, I guess just in time. I got called here to assist the medical staff since they were shorthanded."

"I'm also here cause they're shorthanded," Beio-Rhett finally cracked a smile.

Singatt sighed and made his exit, "Miss, I'm sorry about him, he's a bit short tempered. Beio-Rhett, try not to get in another fight on your way to the mail room."

Beio-Rhett chuckled, "Yes, boss." He turned back to the woman. "I'm sorry about that… I was just… I actually don't know what I was thinking." He shook his head. "I'm not used to staying in one place for too long."

"Me neither," the woman said. "It's alright. I'm sure you were frustrated about something. I am too. I have these medics yelling at me, left and right, because they're frustrated too and I probably just wasn't paying attention."

Beio-Rhett wished he were frustrated about something. He decided to go along with it. "Yeah. I… I'm not sure why I snapped. I don't even know you and I… I think you were just the first person to literally cross my path… miss…" he noticed the medic ID tag, which only listed a last name. "…Jemenae."

"You can call me Prellina."

"Prellina. I'm…"

"I know who you are. Everyone does. It's nice to meet you

Beio-Rhett… or maybe not."

Beio-Rhett chuckled. "Don't worry, I've been declawed."

Prellina smiled. "Well, I have to go get yelled at some more. Thanks for letting me take it out on you."

Beio-Rhett smiled. "Yeah, hey, I'll buy you a drink and make it up to you sometime."

"Where? The mess hall?"

"Well, next time you get leave. Don't they let you at least get out to Colett?"

Prellina, "I'll see. We don't exactly get weekends here."

"You know where to find me."

"Just around the corner." Prellina walked off as briskly as she had when she smashed into Beio-Rhett.

Beio-Rhett smiled and watched Prellina run off to the barracks where she was perhaps gonna help some of the imported injured soldiers. He watched her tail sway back and forth as she ran and thought briefly about the last time he made love. *It has been a very long time.* An image of a naked body, a naked female. *Wait…* That was for sure. But he thought it strange how quickly he could put it out of his mind. Some say that Hydrolette's lust for blood will overshadow their lust for flesh. Perhaps that was truer for some Hydrolettes than others. God knows Beio-Rhett's bloodlust was rarely unsatisfied. But maybe there was something else. *No, I'm not gonna go there.* A naked body lie in bed beside him. *Stop!* He tried to regain his focus and looked forward at the headquarters building. It had been a week after Singatt had said the weapons would be there the next day. *Quite the efficient system.* At least he had his weapons back, or at least one weapon in particular that he was glad to have back. Maybe not having it was what was making him so agitated lately, as if he was missing a part of himself.

Chapter 5

The Diamond Knife

"In my thoughts I have bled from the riddles I've been fed."

"Target eliminated," shouted one of the helmsmen of the Quesgralion Command Ship.

"Bastard sat cams!" Kitchnok exclaimed from his Commander's Chair. "I don't know why we didn't think about the satellites that they had on other planets."

"With all due respect, Commander," the helmsman said. "It's really not that bad. They can't act on information about our position seeing as how they're currently under siege."

"This is true," Kitchnok said calmly, "But I worry that their knowledge of our position may come to their advantage should they decide to engage in open conflict. Also, although they are under siege, we must always consider the possibility of undercover sabotage."

Kitchnok paused for a moment scratching his chin. He took a few moments to examine his previous words and thought about their effect on the men. "But we shouldn't worry about such preposterous scenarios. This is merely a precaution. It would never actually occur. You know well the Teneman has orchestrated this scenario for over a decade. We are in control because we know what we're doing. Everything will go perfectly according to plan. What we are doing is making sure we stay one step ahead of them. The less they know, the better off we are. Knowledge, gentlemen, is the only true power! To acquire more of it is to become more powerful and to keep it from others is to render them powerless." Kitchnok stood up from his chair.

"It is unfortunate that they had to discover our little surprise party for them, but we may still recover our advantage. Take our fleet 12 parsecs starboard, behind the sun to Hydrolet's current position... around DB III, where the Hydrolette's only control one satellite. We will reposition our fleet there and perhaps create an even more elaborate obfuscation."

"Yes, Commander," said the helmsman

"Yes!" Dembo exclaimed, looking into the freshly opened crate, the smell of gun oil still lingering. "I've never actually held one of these. I've just been shot at by them." He lifted a large rifle blaster out of the crate. "So this can take rope magazines of any size?"

Poko nodded, "As far as I know. I think rounds are about 80 shots. Four bolt bursts."

Beio-Rhett picked up another of the same rifle from the crate and inspected it. "Standard issue A-5000 assault blaster, double barrel compound laser bolt action with top mounted rocket launcher and infrared side scopes for both barrels."

"You said these were from a rebel cache?" Dembo asked Poko.

Poko nodded.

Dembo looked on the side of the mounted rocket launcher to see a decal of the rebel insignia. He laughed silently. "I guess they finally acquired these after I went AWOL. Shame."

Beio-Rhett put down the A-5000 and opened up another crate, revealing boxes upon boxes of power cells for hand blasters, rope ammo for the A-5000s and regular magazines for the older A-250 models. He laughed aloud upon looking at the rebel insignia stamped on the boxes in various locations. "Hey, if we ever get caught we can just say we're a leftover rebel squadron."

Dembo kept looking at the rifle in his hands. "Yeah, and then we can just say we'll work for their side," he smiled deviously.

"I wouldn't joke about that," Singatt's voice sounded behind the group.

Beio-Rhett and Dembo spun around to see Singatt standing behind them. Poko was already facing him, but paid his presence little mind.

"You obviously don't have a sense of humor," Dembo calmly went back to looking over the rifle.

"No, just not yours," Singatt said. "What the hell is all this?"

"I told you!" Beio-Rhett was a little irritated. "I was gonna order some equipment from my own sources."

"Yeah, but I wasn't expecting a whole arsenal."

"Zala, Singatt, what does it matter? You want me to go out

and shoot shit up for you? How do you want me to do it? A wooden stick? You gave me clearance to bring this stuff here. It's not costing you anything."

Singatt grunted. "Whatever. Just please don't do any target practice on the base."

Beio-Rhett refused to respond. Singatt walked away mumbling.

Dembo was looking at the rifle for the duration of the brief exchange. "Man, these are way different from the A-250s. It may take me a while to get used to these."

"Speak of the devil!" Beio-Rhett exclaimed as he opened the third and final case. He pulled out one of the five A-250 blaster rifles in the case. A-250s were Hydrolet's standard assault blaster until the Rebellion when the A-5000s became standard issue. The A-250 was the tried and true standard through both Hydro-Baltan Wars. They were also in use by several other races throughout the galaxy because of their durability, mass availability, and user-friendliness. They were simple angular blaster rifles. The barrel was rectangular and had a cubic tip. The entire rifle was the same thickness, making it easy to store. The top was formed into a trapezoid cut diagonally on both sides. The rear end of the trapezoid displayed a tiny screen with a digital counter of how many shots were left. A triangular shoulder rest was mounted in the rear with a hollowed out trigger guard the joint between the shoulder rest and the rest of the rifle. At the front of the trigger guard was the magazine clip. In front of the clip was the pump-action handgrip to load rounds.

Dembo looked over to Beio-Rhett holding the old classic. "I'm glad you got a few of those. Something I'll be a bit more familiar with. What else is there?"

Poko answered for Beio-Rhett, "Some pistols, crunchers, a crate of plasma grenades and an ion rocket launcher."

Dembo nodded in approval. "Very nice."

Beio-Rhett took out a strange looking blaster and placed it in his side holster without saying anything.

Dembo looked at it for a moment, but decided to pay it no mind. Before he looked away, he noticed another weapon on the other side of Beio-Rhett's utility belt. It looked like a sheath with a beautifully carved handle sticking out of it. Dembo had a slight recollection of the weapon from their time working together, but the memory was too distant to grasp. He decided to stop grasping and continued to pour over the rifle in his hands.

"How's the ship coming along?" Poko asked.

"Pretty much done except for the core, which will have to be restarted eventually. Now that most of the repair work is done I'm starting to get some wild hairs about making some upgrades."

"Don't fix what ain't broken," Dembo commented, putting the rifle back in the crate.

"The ship is broken," Beio-Rhett said with a smile. "Or was. I'm actually talking about weapons. It's a B-class cruiser, but it's fairly large and while we do have the gunner stations I'm starting to realize that the thing can't do any major damage on its own."

"What are you talking about?" Poko asked.

"I'm thinking of mounting a huge anti-ground fusion canon on the rear, right before the engines."

"That's a bit of a gamble," Dembo said.

"Not really. It's been done."

"Yeah on massive warships," Poko argued. "And that's a rarity. It's mostly ground-mounted anti-space weapons' cause it has such a kick. A decent fusion canon's gonna be spouting high-energy plasma blasts that could backfire and tear your ship apart. Plus, where are you gonna get the energy to operate such a canon?"

"I guess I could mount a fusion reactor behind the canon somewhere."

Dembo was putting the lid back on the crate and moving on to the next one when he looked up. "Wait a minute. You have a fusion reactor. The ships engines are fusion powered. You could find some way to tap into the reactor for the engine to power the canon."

Beio-Rhett and Poko both nodded.

"Nice," Beio-Rhett said. "I'm not much of a physicist, but that sounds like it would work."

"It should," Poko interrupted. "Most ground-mounted canons have a miniature reactor similar to the one already installed in the ship. Naturally an engine reactor is much bigger, so I think there might be a way to harness some of that energy for this canon."

"Yeah. It may only work if the ship isn't moving though," Dembo thought. "I don't know. We'll need to get an expert on the subject. But I can't imagine it'd be too difficult. Maybe take a smaller battleship-mounted canon and slap it on the rear of the ship, wrap some tape around it and plug it into the core."

"I might be able to find you a fusion canon," Poko said. "May not be in the best shape. Then you just gotta wire it up to the core like he said.

Beio-Rhett chuckled. "Yeah, that simple. I wonder if we can get the government to help us out with it," he looked around behind him. "Damnit where's Singatt when you need him."

"That Mheages guy. He mentioned being under the government's wing. I wonder if we're important enough that they'd let us use him," Dembo mused.

Beio-Rhett nodded. "It's worth asking. As long as we're just sitting around here, I don't see why not get our shit really together before we go off on whatever suicide mission they send us on." He stared off in the distance thinking about how he'd phrase the request to Singatt.

Dembo finished putting the lids on all three crates. "Well, should we load this in the armory?"

Beio-Rhett broke out of his train of thought, "Yeah, sure. Poko, wanna lend a hand?"

Come lunchtime, Beio-Rhett had a game plan for how to approach Singatt with his request for two things, a plasma canon to mount on his ship and an engineer that could help him successfully mount it. He talked it over with Dembo while organizing the interior of the ship, which was essentially completely repaired. The only place that took significant damage was the bridge and the exit port, which were located in the front of the ship, where it crashed. Other than being ransacked by Hydrolet, the rest of the interior was in good shape. The kitchen and mess hall were put back in order, but they were still unstocked as the ship wasn't going anywhere soon and there was no need to let unused food spoil. Beio-Rhett's personal addition to the ship from when he previously owned it was a small SEL, or Simulated Exercise Level, which served as a holographic gym. Various environments would be displayed by the holographic projectors to simulate anything from races, to battles, to a relaxing exercising environment. The user would be in a virtual world, but the strain and conditioning of the body was real.

Naturally, this room was useless now without a power

source for the hologram. The armory was in the worst shape after being raided upon salvage, but was returned to its former glory fully stocked with Beio-Rhett's newly acquired arsenal. The small room contained two rifle racks on the right wall where Beio-Rhett and Dembo placed the A-5000s and A-250s. A crate for ammo sat beside these. The wall across from the door sported some shelves for other weapons, mostly explosives. Two other crates containing heavier duty weapons sat in the upper left corner of the room. A vault was also built into the left wall adorned with a large red X, beside it was a control panel. The group put the most dangerous explosives in the vault where they wouldn't do much damage. After loading up the armory, the group did a quick sweep of the living quarters, also left unstocked since they were not yet lived in. Although Beio-Rhett and Dembo both planned on moving their stuff to the living quarters when the power was on. As for the bridge, it was almost completely repaired, the biggest problem being the busted windshield, which was finally repaired. The bridge seated four comfortably. A wide control desk lined the bottom of the windshield in the front of the bridge. In the center was the piloting station. To the right facing out the windshield was the main weapons station and to the left was the navigations station. In the center of the bridge up against the rear wall on a raised platform was the main communications center. Severe damage was sustained on the bridge, but most had been repaired. The group went in to finally install the chairs for the four stations, which Beio-Rhett ordered from a depot for destroyed ships. Naturally, each chair was slightly different, giving the bridge a more disjointed feel, which was emphasized by the welded-on plate repairs made to the controls. Beio-Rhett didn't care much for cosmetics.

In the cafeteria on the base, Beio-Rhett sought out Singatt. He ate in the cafeteria without exception. Sometimes he would join Beio-Rhett, Dembo and Poko, and other times he would eat with other soldiers. He was a very social person in an antisocial manner. Beio-Rhett wasn't looking forward to this. While installing the chairs, he discussed how to phrase this request over and over again with Poko and Dembo, but that's not what bothered him. He hated having to ask for something. He made it by in the base without having to ask for much, just necessary materials that the government expected him to use for repairing the ship. He even succeeded in avoiding a request for weapons from the

Government, thanks to Poko. He didn't like the idea of the Government knowing they had something he wanted. He continuously crafted the illusion that it was all owed to him and he didn't need any of it. To admit that he needed something from them would be a sign of weakness. He already felt uncomfortable eating their food and sleeping in their dorms. It was hard enough convincing himself that he was independent. He knew he wasn't. They had him. *And now they'll finally prove it, damnit.* Perhaps he really didn't need a fusion canon attached to his ship. Too late, they were already standing next to Singatt.

Singatt looked up from his trey. "Gentlemen," he said softly.

"Can we take our lunch with you?" Poko spoke first.

"I don't see why not," Singatt said.

The three sat. Poko sat next to Singatt. Dembo and Beio-Rhett sat across from him.

Beio-Rhett took a breath and dove in. "Listen, Singatt. I don't know what the status is on getting us a job, but the ship is nearly repaired."

"Excellent. You guys are welcome to stay at the base till we have a mission for you. It's probably safer than floating around the system, even if you can get past the SETs. Especially now that there's a huge Quesgralion fleet out there scouring."

"What?" Beio-Rhett's dive was interrupted.

Singatt merely nodded and took a bite from a hunk of meat on his tray, his eyes still on Beio-Rhett.

Beio-Rhett shook his head. "Well, that's not what this is about, although that does put a monkey wrench in my 'floating around the system' plan"

Singatt snorted.

"Anyway, I have a request I want to put in for the Government."

"Wow, you actually need something from us? I thought asking for help was below you."

Beio-Rhett grunted. *You're not gonna make this easy are you, boss?*

"Listen, I'm not gonna let you make a fool of me. I'm trying to help you too. Help you kill these bastards. You're sending me out into God knows what death trap with a B-Class cruiser. Either you want me to get crushed or you have a bit too much faith in that thing. I'm talking about giving it some heavy artillery, something that could stand up to a battleship if I ever was unlucky enough to be in such a situation. And from what you've said about that fleet, this may be a better idea than I thought."

'A fusion canon?!" Singatt coughed. "On that thing?"

"We've thought it out," Dembo said. "We're gonna hook it up to the fusion reactor of the engines. We use the core as a direct power source for the weapon."

Singatt thought for a moment. "Yeah, I guess that could work." He took another bite. "So you want us to buy you a fusion canon?"

"I can get that," Poko said.

Singatt frowned. "I'm glad none of your shipments have been apprehended by the SETs."

Poko shrugged, "I don't work with fools."

Singatt looked back at Beio-Rhett. "Well, what the hell are you talking to me for?"

"Like you said, you guess it could work. We guess too," Dembo explained. "None of us know how to hook up a fusion canon to an engine reactor."

"I mean, physically, we can do it," Beio-Rhett explained further. "But none of us are physicists. We need an engineer to design the canon's power source and give us a blueprint on how to hook it up."

Singatt nodded slowly, finally gathering the purpose of the visit. "I see, you need a brain."

"Exactly," Beio-Rhett said. "I mean, anyone will do. We just need to see if it can be done and then how. Can the Government help us out with that? I'm asking because you seem to have some faith in us. If you do, I imagine you want us to also survive out there."

Singatt just kept nodding slowly.

Beio-Rhett grunted heavily. "Look Singatt, don't make me do this. I'm trying to cooperate here. I'm contributing. Thinking of ways to help you guys out."

Singatt just kept nodding.

Poko smiled silently.

Beio-Rhett sighed. "Singatt, listen, I appreciate what you're doing for us okay? I realize this is a better alternative than jail or... death."

Singatt smiled. "That's very nice of you, Beio-Rhett. Not sure what prompted you to say that. I'm all on-board with your fusion canon idea."

Beio-Rhett lowered his head, closed his eyes and sighed. "Ugghhhh," he moaned.

Singatt laughed. "Oh lighten up, no shame in being polite once in your life."

Beio-Rhett's head still hung low. After a brief moment he opened his eyes. Head still lowered, underneath his hands out of the corner of his eye he spotted the female he bumped into a few days ago. *What was her name? Prellina!*

Beio-Rhett's head shot up to get a better look. It was definitely she, dressed in the same standard civilian outfit with the red cross armband. Except now, she had a tray of food instead of some data pads. He stared at her for a few seconds before she turned and noticed him. It was too late. He couldn't look away. She had made eye contact. He wasn't sure if he should smile or wave.

Prellina recognized him immediately. She waved *and* smiled.

Now Beio-Rhett was obligated. He didn't want to have to explain to the other three who she was. He hesitated as long as he could, but finally knew it would be more awkward not to wave. He raised his hand, waved briefly and nodded in place of a smile.

That didn't end the exchange. Now Prellina was walking towards their group.

"Who's that?" Poko finally asked.

Before Beio-Rhett could answer, Prellina was standing next to the group. *She sure walks fast.*

"How's your nose?" she asked.

"Fine," Beio-Rhett grunted. "How's your... day... been."

Prellina laughed. "Terrible. Can I sit with you guys?"

Singatt answered for him. "Sure."

"Oh, you were there when I punched him."

Dembo and Poko chuckled.

Singatt nodded. "I was... it was a good punch."

By now Prellina was sitting next to Beio-Rhett.

Beio-Rhett looked over at her. "It was a good punch," he finally cracked a smile. It wasn't so terrible attempting to socialize.

Singatt looked closely at Prellina. "Wait a minute. You're the biologist from Geufsta aren't you?"

Prellina nodded.

"I thought I recognized you the other day, I knew you were one of the volunteers. I forgot I escorted you from the shuttle, from Geufsta when you arrived."

Prellina took a sip of her drink nodding, "Still me."

"Where on Geufsta?" Poko never had a problem making conversation.

"It was a village a few miles north of Enduras. I was there alone, too. I had a liaison on the planet that cleared my stay with the natives there, but when he introduced me, he took off. I didn't even have a translator."

"Can you speak Rhukin?" Poko fanned the fire.

"Some, but they didn't even speak that. It was some ancient dialect spoken only by scattered tribes in that area. It was similar to Rhukin, I guess, but I was mostly talking to them with my hands. Things went somewhat smoothly, though I think towards the end of my stay they wanted to eat me."

Dembo chuckled a bit.

Prellina smiled. "Obviously I made it out alive."

"Other than wanting to eat you, did they treat you alright?" Poko asked.

Prellina nodded. "Oh sure. They were mostly curious. Having a tiny blue thing in their midst must've been exciting. I honestly never felt like I was in any danger."

"Kisgats are pretty intimidating," Singatt said. "Not to mention huge."

"Yeah, and we're pretty huge and intimidating compared to the Kakeuwees. What's your point?"

Dembo chuckled again. "Funny you mentioned that. I just got back from staying at a village on Katoola."

Prellina nodded, impressed. "What were you doing there? You're not a scientist are you?"

Dembo shook his head, "No, I never even graduated from University. I guess you can say I was hiding out there. The Rebellion wrote me off as dead, so I just sort of took advantage of being off the grid for a while."

When's he gonna explain that mohawk?

Prellina's mouth popped open in a silent gasp, "You're the other mercenary. I guess I should've figured that out. You were an officer in the Rebellion, weren't you?"

Dembo nodded.

Prellina took another sip from her drink, eyes wide with a sincere, yet light-hearted amazement. She looked across the table at Singatt. "And you're the soldier they were talking about who captured these two. You were on TV a few weeks ago… and that's why I thought I recognized you when you escorted me from the shuttle."

Singatt smiled awkwardly.

Prellina looked around at the people sitting around her once more. "Well you guys must be quite the clique then."

Singatt chuckled, "You gotta make friends during times like these, otherwise you won't last very long."

"Yeah, but if you don't make the right friends, you won't last at all," Prellina spoke while looking down at her food.

Beio-Rhett couldn't tell if that was a jab at him or at Singatt, or perhaps everyone. He wasn't even sure if that was meant to be a joke, or if she was sincerely giving everyone some sound advice. It seemed a rather morbid statement compared to her cheery expression.

"Yeah, the world kind of turns upside down when your closest ally up and declares war on you," Singatt responded.

Beio-Rhett hadn't even thought of that reference. *It seems like she didn't think of it either.* He watched as she looked up from her tray a little uncertain.

"Yeah," she said half-heartedly as though she figured that could also be what she meant. She didn't look at anyone to confirm that she was perhaps speaking about something a bit more specific. *But she did give Singatt a glance to validate his comment,* Beio-Rhett thought.

"What are you guys doing here?" she asked honestly.

"They're fixing Beio-Rhett's old ship that we commandeered a few years back," Singatt answered for them.

"Oh, so you guys are just hanging out till they got a job for you?"

"Basically," Dembo answered.

"What are you doing here?" she asked Singatt.

"I got assigned as their military liaison," he said looking at his tray. "Obviously the soldiers on this base are busy enough as it is, so I'm the one attending to them while they fix up their ship."

"So you're like their babysitter?"

Beio-Rhett smiled.

Singatt coughed a bit as he took a sip of his drink. "If you must know, I personally fought to make the government hire these guys. If it wasn't for me these two would probably be dead."

Prellina blushed. "Oh... wow... well,"

"Believe me, I regret the decision more every day," he looked over Beio-Rhett and Dembo with a playful smirk.

Dembo didn't seem to notice.

Beio-Rhett smirked back. He liked Singatt more with each passing day.

Prellina watched the exchange and looked back at Singatt, "But... why? I mean. I don't know. I guess it isn't my business."

Singatt shrugged. "Other soldiers give me a hard time saying I got a soft spot. That I let my sensitive side through a proper, hardened soldier's exterior, and I let them have their laugh. In all honestly, I don't think I made a more calculated and reasonable decision in all my life. I didn't feel any sympathy for these two."

Beio-Rhett scoffed. *What're you doing, boss?*

"But I wasn't gonna just have them killed out of a vengeful rage for all my friends and fellow soldiers they killed. That's not fulfilling my duty as a soldier, that's murdering someone for revenge. The more I thought about it, the more immature the idea seemed. And the more I brooded over what terrible things they did, the worse I felt about the idea of executing them. I did my best to act as a proper soldier and a servant to my planet," he looked at Beio-Rhett. "And if you know anything about the Masked Menace, you know he's a force to be reckoned with. If he truly is a mercenary, then he would have no problem working for us. And God knows we really need an ace in the hole in this shit storm we've got ourselves in."

Beio-Rhett finally spoke, "And I thought you loved me, boss."

Singatt didn't respond. His eyes were lost in thought, struggling to hold up his heavy, creased brow.

Prellina was silent for a moment. "Wait, what do you mean 'we've gotten ourselves into?' How the hell could we have known that the Quezzes would fucking attack us? There's no way. No way at all. What could we have possibly done to stop this? It's like your neighbor, or more accurately, your very best friend randomly shooting you in the leg."

"We got ourselves into it because we let it happen. We were distracted. We're always distracted... by war, and finally by our own kind. If we weren't so busy trying to quell the Rebellion, we would've seen the treachery of the Teneman long before they finally seized control of the planet. We would've blown the whistle on our Senator's corruption long before he silenced us. If we spent more time building our relationship with Quesgarlon, Missan would've let us know about this menace and we could've helped him rid their planet of it."

Dembo looked up from his tray at Singatt. He seemed greatly disturbed.

"So why don't you blame the Rebellion?" Prellina asked.

Dembo looked back down at his tray.

"You can't go through life finding someone else to blame for everything that goes wrong," he took a sip of his drink. "Eventually, you have to take responsibility."

The whole table fell silent.

* * *

The whole bridge fell silent on the Command Ship. Kitchnok stood in front of his Commander's chair, back straight, feet spread apart, chin held high, shoes shined. He looked out at the starlit void through the main portal of the bridge. The light from Delta-Beta's sun shined brightly in the left end of the portal. The sun itself was just out of view due to the ship's direction. The entire fleet slowed, the glowing blue engines of the battleships dimmed, and the fleet came to a stop.

A soldier stepped up to Kitchnok promptly. "Commander, we are exactly 12 parsecs from our original position at the desired location next to DB III. Should we hold position?"

Kitchnok turned away from the soldier and walked towards the periscope operator. "What is the Hydrolette sat-cam's position?"

"Currently the satellite is behind DB III, we're in the clear," the operator said, looking up from his monitor.

Kitchnok nodded slowly and turned towards the portal. "Ensign! Give the order!"

The Ensign nodded and pressed a few buttons on the

panel in front of him before speaking into his headset. "This is the Command Ship. Kitchnok orders are to hold our position by DB III. Resume sentinel protocol at predesignated location." After relaying the orders, the ensign turned to Kitchnok, "Commander, should we send a fighter to dispatch the sat-cam?"

Kitchnok looked out at the lifeless rock of DB III as it eclipsed the distant sun. "No," his voice surprised the Ensign and everyone on the bridge. "I have a better idea. We are going to disappear."

"Commander?"

"If we destroy that sat-cam, we will avoid visual confirmation, but the Hydrolettes will soon know that their DB III satellite has been destroyed which would be a generous clue as to our position. No, if we want to stay hidden, we'll have to be a bit more creative than that."

"Yes, Commander, but disappear? How?"

"During our little jaunt through space, I've done some calculations in my quarters regarding the bubble. We will use a similar force field, but instead of aligning the frequency of it as it is, we will rearrange the makeup for visual obfuscation."

"Can that be done, Commander?"

'We'll find out, won't we?" he produced a data pad from his coat pocket. He walked over to the helmsman and handed him the data pad. "Here, helmsman. You will apply these modifications to our force field generator."

Y-yes, Commander," the technician grabbed the pad nervously and perused it as swiftly as he could. "This seems to be plausible Commander, but…"

"But what?!" Kitchnok's voice grew firm.

"This may not be a safe idea, Commander," the helmsman grew more anxious. "You're just rearranging the frequency inhibiters, but many things could go wrong. The field is designed to bend light now, but it could magnify starlight and incinerate us, or have some magnetic effects," he stuttered, picking up the pace of his words after hearing no response. "Th-these modifications are only hypothetical. We don't know if the changes will work on our shield generators either. It's a long shot."

"So check my modifications!" shouted Kitchnok. He stopped for a moment and took a breath. The helmsman remained scared, yes, but Kitchnok could not lose his composure. It was a delicate balance. He cleared his throat and stabbed the helmsman with his gaze. "Run the modifications through the shield generator and do a test readout." He looked back towards the main portal and walked towards the center of the bridge. "They spotted us once so they can spot us again. I don't care if we have them cornered. If they know where the main fleet is, they have an advantage, even if it is slight. We must render them completely impotent if we are to guarantee our success. As I've said before, the best way to do that is render them ignorant." Kitchnok crafted his words to emphasize the noblest of intents, and he was partially sincere when he gave his logical reasons for hiding from a caged animal. He would never admit to cowardice, even if it seemed obvious that was his primary motivation. He owned his words so much that he believed them himself. He didn't fear the Hydrolettes. He didn't fear them. He wasn't hiding. He wasn't. He could tell himself that all day. Whatever it took to believe his own words to the men.

"Gen – um - Commander, we're getting a transmission from the Capitol," a communications technician spoke fearfully

"Clearance?"

"Officer's only. I need your clearance to even access it,"

"Those must be the codes to access the force field's schematics. Move aside," he stepped up to the technician's station and hunched over the control panel. After a quick and vicious glance to see that the helmsman was not looking at his hands, he proceeded to punch in his five-digit code that appeared as a sequence of identical dots on the screen. The screen flickered and then displayed in text, "scanning."

Kitchnok sighed impatiently.

The screen then displayed, "Transmission accessed."

"Now download the data on a disc so I can input the changes manually," Kitchnok ordered calmly.

The technician grabbed a small disc and inserted it in the station. He punched in a few commands and watched a bar slowly filled with red on the screen. The codes didn't take long to download and the technician ejected the disc promptly afterwards. He handed it to Kitchnok who walked the disk over to the first helmsman. After handing it to the helmsman, still shaking from their first encounter, Kitchnok stood erect behind him awaiting a speedy execution. The technician grabbed the disc, a little confused that Kitchnok would need to access the bubble generator manually, but didn't hesitate a moment as he struggled to insert the disc in his station. The helmsman's screen displayed the text, "Accessing codes," soon followed by a flashing text that "access denied." The computer's voice sounded, "Access restricted. Confidential material. Unable to…"

The helmsman panicked.

Kitchnok interrupted the computer, "Override. Authorization, Kitchnok, Vipka, Minister of Resources, Supreme Commander of the Quesgralion Fleet, access 125367A, Teneman clearance," his voice was impatient with a hint of anxiety.

The computer voice stopped. The screen flickered. The voice continued, "Restriction overridden. Decoding encryption." The screen now displayed five sets of six numbers in Quesgralion script.

"Type those codes into the generator's mainframe," Kitchnok ordered, the anxiety becoming slightly more apparent.

The helmsman looked from the screen to the numbers touch pad, where he typed in the five codes, double checking the screen between each code.

"Faster, faster," ordered Kitchnok as he snapped his long, bony fingers.

The helmsman jolted but continued to type, looking back and forth from the screen to the touch pad feverishly. Finally, after the helmsman finished inputting the last code, the touch pad displayed in flashing text, "Locked in." "We've accessed the generator's software, Commander."

"Input my modifications," ordered Kitchnok.

The helmsman picked up the data pad that Kitchnok handed him earlier and checked it one more time before rewriting the programming. Looking back and forth from the touch pad to the data pad, the helmsman furiously typed in the modification, giving only one brief frightened glance at Kitchnok still looming behind him. "Done!" he exclaimed triumphantly after completing his task.

"Good," replied Kitchnok. He turned and walked back to the Commander's station in front of his chair at the head of the bridge. The station was elevated a few feet above the rest of the bridge so everyone could see who was in charge. Another officer was waiting for him at the station. He wore a look of confusion, but felt no need to question Kitchnok's actions.

Kithcnok wondered *why the officer would question his actions in the first place* and wore a look that made these sentiments obvious. He stood next to the officer and looked down at the main station where two slots looked back up at the two. Kitchnok produced a key card from his uniform's right pocket. He looked at the officer next to him, holding the key up. The officer reached in his pocket instinctively after coughing timidly. Kitchnok placed his card over the slot and waited for the officer to do the same.
"Synchronizing… three, two one," he spoke firmly before both placed the card keys in their respective slots. A square metal panel at the center of the station slid open to reveal a touch pad interface for the force field generator.

Kitchnok looked at the pilot, "Order all our forces to hold position."

"All vessels hold position until further notice," the pilot said into his comm station as soon as Kitchnok finished speaking.

Kitchnok tapped the interface and activated the force-field emitter, now altered by his codes. Before he pressed the execute function, he hesitated for a second, but not enough to let the men see. He carried through.

The top of the Command Ship housed a smaller version of the force field emitters that the Quesgralions had placed around the system to enclose it. This emitter was a more portable version used on the larger ships to test their success for blocking out incoming wavelengths to create an impenetrable shield. The emitter lit up and spout forth some sparks of ungrounded electricity before spewing forth a difference type of shield, a shield of light. A blanket of nothingness poured forth from the emitter and shot above every ship. When it reached the length of this dimension, it spread outward forming a wide circle, engulfing the other two dimensions of the fleet, bubbling forth like a liquid mirror. The starlit cosmos bled its person over the fleet, covering one battleship, then another, then another. The blanket came cascading down over the fleet after expanding to the outermost diameter of the ship. The painted veil, black and star-studded, draped over the entirety of the Quesgralion Fleet, leaving it completely invisible to all manner of instruments, mechanic and organic.

* * *

Dembo was eating his lunch later than everyone else, sitting on some of the supply crates next to the ship. He was busy programming the SEL when the lunch hour came around and decided to work through and take a quick one afterwards. Ever the industrious one, Dembo did not spend his lunch hour simply fulfilling his nutritional requirements. In one hand he held a data pad where he pondered over a mysterious transmission sent to his personnel files a few days ago. The transmission was encrypted with the galactic standard symbols for "X" and "Y." This was the only clue as to what the message contained or from whom it was sent. Dembo had given up trying to decode the message after a few hours of receiving it. Every so often when he found a space moment, he brought up the transmission and stared at it blankly, hoping something would come to him to make the meaning of the strange message clear. He was finding no such luck this time around.

Singatt was inspecting the older, but functional fusion-powered plasma canon that had just come in through customs. He didn't expect any foul play, but he wanted to make sure that it at least looked sturdy enough to not explode when they turned on the ship's core.

Poko stood behind him with his same old data pad, racking up more credit on Beio-Rhett's tab. He looked up at Singatt every so often to make sure he wasn't touching anything he was supposed to.

Beio-Rhett was standing in one of the offices built into the higher walls of the warehouse. He looked over a monitor that Dr. Mheages sat at, pondering the professor's highly technical language and asking him repeatedly to break down into simpler terms how to hook up the canon to the generator.

Prellina walked by the entrance of the third warehouse and could see all four scenarios quite clearly. She was in between gofer jobs and it would not upset her superiors too much if she took a few extra minutes between one beverage run or another. Poko and Singatt were closest to her. Beio-Rhett was up high in the offices, but his imposing silhouette was quite visible behind the window. Dembo was perhaps the furthest away from her, but the most approachable.

Dembo looked up from his portable meal and data pad to

see Prellina walking towards him. He quickly remembered her from the cafeteria the other day and that she seemed unusually cheery for sitting next to two former combatants, a soldier and a weapons dealer. She was probably the first person to interact with their little group since they had arrived on the base. Maybe it was because she wasn't a soldier. Even the medical staff were technically military personnel. She was just a day trader, one could say a mercenary like them. Except he remembered Singatt also saying she was a volunteer. Ah, there's the difference, Dembo thought. She's not a mercenary, just a good samaritan. Although it wasn't like they were getting paid, and he assumed she was also getting bread and board, so technically they were the same for the time being.

"Hey, you!"

She walks fast, Dembo thought. He remembered they had something in common having lived on primitive planets for a time... although it didn't seem to affect her the same as it did him. Quickly, he switched off his data pad, turning the screen which once displayed the mysterious symbols of "X" and "Y" blank, and set the device aside figuring he wouldn't get any further with that dilemma at this moment.

"What's your name again?" he asked.

"Prellina," she smiled. "You're Dembo right?"

Dembo nodded.

"So, why are you guys doing this? Weren't you like the leader of the Rebellion at one time?"

Dembo smiled and took another bite from his meal. "We don't really have a choice. The grounds for our release were that we would be employed by the Hydrolet Government for the time being."

"You mean you can't just up and leave?"

"Well... I guess we could, if we wanted. We technically owe them at least one mission for bread and board... at least that's what Beio-Rhett signed on for. But even then, when this ship is finished."

"It could be finished," Prellina interrupted. "I've been asking around and it looks like Beio-Rhett's been tacking on more and more little upgrades. It seems like he's looking for an excuse to stick around."

Dembo chuckled, "I guess you could look at it like that."

"Why can't you just admit you want to help us out?"

"What are you talking about?"

"Listening to Beio-Rhett earlier... he made it seem like they were holding you guys to this, and you said the same. Are you really? If given the chance would you two just up and leave? Regardless of that bubble thing?"

"Well, probably not. We don't want to be trapped in this system forever, so I guess it's in our best interest to help out... at least to find a way out of this cage. It's still for selfish reasons," Dembo smiled.

"You seem pretty light-hearted about the whole thing," Prellina said still smiling. "Which is strange, 'cause I figured you would be the one who would be hating life right now and Beio-Rhett wouldn't give a shit either way."

Dembo looked confused.

"Unless I've just misunderstood completely, you were a high-ranking colonel in the Rebellion? I looked up some of your speeches and even threatening transmissions you've sent to the Capitol. I don't know about now, but you sure as hell hated the Government back then. Now you're apathetically going along for the ride, looking for excuses to appear a selfish mercenary when you obviously want to genuinely help. Meanwhile, from what little I know about Beio-Rhett, he harbored no ill feelings towards the Government and didn't really seem passionate about any cause during his time as a mercenary, but he quite clearly has a problem with working for Hydrolet now. It's just strange."

Dembo was not prepared for this at all. He sat looking at her a little slack-jawed. He had to think of something. "Well, me... I... I gave up on the Rebellion after I was M.I.A. on Katoola. I still haven't talked about it with anyone, so it's hard to put into words what made me completely change my sentiments about the whole thing, but I did. You should know, living with a different race, especially an indigenous one, really opens your eyes to things you've never seen before. I can't explain it. I was only living with the Kakeuwees for a little over five years, but it was enough. By the time I decided to leave, I forgot all about the Rebellion. And it wasn't like I was against it, nor did I abandon those ideals I preached so readily. I just understood those ideals better and I realized the Rebellion was not the way to materialize those ideals. It used to be, but I grew up." He took another bite. "And even though I know many of my friends, other officers and soldiers of the Rebellion are now being persecuted, some executed... it's not like it doesn't bother me. It's just that I accepted it as inevitable." He chewed for a while. "I realized we all signed our life away when we started the Rebellion, you have to with something that big."

"But you got out alive," Prellina pried.

"Yeah," Dembo let out a heavy sigh, "Didn't see that one coming. And I guess Beio-Rhett didn't either. That was so obviously the end for us. It's been strange trying to adjust to the fact that it's not. I think that's what's upsetting Beio-Rhett the most. That's probably why he has such trouble admitting that he needs help, that he wants to help."

Prellina nodded. She looked over to the office window where he stood and then back at Dembo. "How long have you known him?"

Dembo took another bite. "Not that long, and I hadn't seen him or anyone for those five years. And before that, well... I'd only known him for perhaps a few years, three or four at the most. I met him about a year after the Rebellion started. It's funny, we grew quite a reputation together during the Rebellion as a veritable wrecking crew, but we never were acquainted that long. He and Poko were friends long before I ever met him."

"You had a reputation?" Prellina asked playfully.

"Well, maybe not on your side. I'm not sure how the media presented us. I never paid much attention. I didn't care. We weren't terrorists. We had an objective. But on our side, we were recognized as quite the team."

Prellina nodded. "You ever get to know him well? He seems to treat you pretty nice, compared to everyone else... well, except for Poko. Why are you so close to him? How did you meet?"

Dembo thought on it for a while. "Why don't you ask him?"

"Because I'm talking to you," she never stopped smiling. "He doesn't seem like the kind of person who would open up to a complete stranger, or at least I don't think so. I only know him as the Masked Menace. Doesn't seem like such a great idea to get on his bad side."

"He's not as bad as everyone makes him out to be," Dembo chuckled.

"Well, what is he like?"

Dembo paused. He wondered if he really knew. "I don't know if I can answer that. It depends what you want to know. Like I said, I met him after the Rebellion. He was already a legend then."

"What is the legend?" Prellina asked. "I mean, I may sound stupid, but why is everyone scared of him? I know about the Masked Menace, but nothing specific. He was a head hunter or something like that?"

Dembo sighed. He wondered why it was his job to tell Beio-Rhett's life story. "I know as much as the next guy about it. I mean, I guess you can say his infamy started as a pit fighter. At least that's where the mask came from and the name, for that matter. I heard that he was a soldier before that, a high ranking one, and he used to be called Rhett. I'm not sure. He never talked about it much. In fact, he was pretty adamant about not talking about it. Sure he would tell stories from the second Hydro-Baltan War, but it was always so trivial. Nothing important. He would only tell it if something funny or a gruesome death was involved. But I do know that he became a pit fighter after that for some reason. His mask was the same one that he wore when I met him. Crimson red with black stripes. There were only two small holes for his eyes surrounded in black and a few slits near his nostrils, no opening for his mouth so his voice was always obscure. As far as I know he always had long wild hair. I think he had dreadlocks back then too, but he doesn't now. He fought in all kinds of matches, even death matches. He never lost. He became a hot ticket. That's where his reputation started. He would mutilate his opponents. Not that that's unique for a pit fighter, but he would really get into it. The difference was he didn't seem to enjoy it as much as the audience did, but maybe that's because he always wore the mask. Who knew what he was thinking behind that mask. Maybe he did get off on it, but from the fights I saw footage of, there was a very vicious apathy to his style. He was obviously making enough money as a pit fighter, and even traveled to some of the top underground tournaments in the galaxy, but I guess he was done with it after a while. I used to joke that he went on to head hunting so that the people he killed would provide more of a challenge. He never found it that funny. But I'm not sure how it started. Maybe a sponsor was upset with a debtor or something and figured Beio-Rhett would be the guy to squeeze it out of him. Either way, he became a bounty hunter shortly after, and that's the Masked Menace that everyone knows. He definitely collected Government bounties, but I could tell he was much more interested in the prices of mob targets, maybe because those prices were almost always dead or alive. He did straight up assassinations as well… oh wait, I think that's what he used to do when he was in the army, anyway… yeah, he was brutal. He became pretty well known as one of the deadliest bounty hunters in the galaxy. He was hard to get a hold of, but if you could, you knew whomever you wanted would be in your lap within a week, or if you wanted someone dead, you could write their death certificate while waiting for the call. This is almost exactly how someone else described him to me when I first heard about him. Of course everyone had their own way of blowing up his reputation. This is just mine. I researched him for a bit before I decided to recruit him for the Rebellion. Like you, I figured it probably wouldn't be safe to just walk up to this guy. He really made himself an unapproachable figure. You think he's stand-offish now? Besides the mask, he wore a pitch-black coat and dark attire under that. He never used very heavy weaponry, usually a pistol blaster. I remember he would sometimes use pistols with metal bullets, but he rarely used guns." He snapped back to the present, "That's what that is!"

"What?"

"Oh nothing, I was just wondering about something earlier, a weapon I saw Beio-Rhett carrying. It looked familiar, but I couldn't remember what it was."

"What is it?"

"A knife. A knife with a blade made entirely out of diamond. That's the weapon he used most. He never killed anyone that he wasn't in pretty close proximity with. For a big guy, he was surprisingly discreet. Almost without exception he would finish off his marks with that knife. It eventually became as infamous as him, this glimmering flash amidst a dark backdrop. He would even use it in open battle. Sometimes he would find himself in tight situations and he would shoot his way out, but using just that knife, he would hack his way out. That's the thing about Beio-Rhett. He could never be captured. He was a tenacious bastard. Never caved. That's part of why he was in such high demand. People could send him out and know that he would make it back. He wasn't necessarily the strongest warrior or the fastest. He wasn't the most brutal or efficient. He could never be caught, though. Even if they had him locked in a cell, which he was, he'd find a way out, somehow. He must've had a guardian angel."

"Well, not anymore," Prellina giggled.

Dembo shrugged, "Well, he's still alive, ain't he?"

"I suppose."

"Either way, that's what made him stand out. And he had gone out of bounty hunting into straight mercenary work by the time I had finally gotten in touch with him. He was doing jobs of all sorts around the galaxy, always on the move, which made it hard for me to track him down, let alone interest him in working for a rag tag group of rebels back home. We were well funded. At the very least I could offer him money, but I wasn't entirely sure that was his primary motivation. Maybe it was just the quenching of his bloodlust... but there was definitely some of that to be had in the Rebellion, so I felt fairly confident."

"You found him?"

"It wasn't too hard. He doesn't necessarily hide himself, he just doesn't make himself readily available. However, I managed to pick up from the grapevine that he frequented a cantina on Kaliekae. God knows why, maybe because it was so out of the way. I've only been there twice, including the time I went there to meet Beio-Rhett. The first time was for University, for some environmental study. I remember never wanting to go back. Where was I? Oh, right. I *did* end up going back. This cantina was sweating with corruption and villainy. It probably deterred me more back then than it does now. Sure I was a full-ride University boy, but it wasn't like I hadn't found my way into the underbelly of society. Especially after joining the Rebellion, I was thrown into some of the scummiest parts of Hydrolet. I know Colett doesn't have many 'slums' but we did a lot of recruiting on Bestton and Ttanis. The problem with a planetary Rebellion is that you really only have your home planet to draw from."

"Is that why you went after Beio-Rhett?"

Dembo thought for a minute, "Maybe, I hadn't thought of that. Mostly because of his reputation, but I guess yeah, I didn't even realize that he was also a Hydrolette, although, he's never confirmed it. He may be a Baltan for all I know."

"What about Baltans? Were there any of those in the Rebellion?"

"Some, one of our head officers was actually a former Baltan General, Stoph Auximott. But anyway, besides the home planet and Baltania, I didn't have much of a reason to travel outside the system, except for this guy. Like I said, this place was bad. I guess the further away from the core planets you get, the more fertile the land is to cultivate such scum. I was alone too. I decided to go at this alone, partially because we couldn't spare any men and partially because I thought Beio-Rhett would probably have more reason to listen to my proposition if I dared approach him all alone."

"And it worked obviously," Prellina interrupted.

Dembo chuckled. "You already know the end of the story, why do you need me to finish it."

"I'm sorry," she said as she blushed.

"But naturally, he did accept," Dembo continued. "I tried not to be too forward with him. I began by asking him,

'You know about the Rebellion back home?'

'What makes you say that's my home?'

'You used to be a soldier there didn't you?'

'What of it?'

'You're not anymore?'

'That should be obvious.'

'You didn't leave for any particular reason? There's nothing they've done to turn you against them have they?'

'Do you want something from me?'

'I'm saying you wouldn't be opposed to turning against them would you?'

I finally got him to look at me at that point. I don't think he cared much either way about the Rebellion, but I also don't think he ever considered taking a job that would be openly opposing Hydrolet. I know that he had collected bounties for the Hydrolet Government as well. But so far he hadn't taken up any work from the Government against us.

'You're lucky you got to me before they did.'

'You saying that if they got to you first you'd work for them against us?'

'If they paid well enough.'

'I think you're lying.'

'You think I care about your petty little cause?'

'I didn't say that. I just said I don't think you care about money.'

Again, I caught his attention. I think if there's one thing that Beio-Rhett really can't stand, it's when people read him right. Or maybe he just hates when people read him at all. At least when I first met him, he seemed to want to keep every relationship simplified into a business transaction. Probably a healthy and stress-free way of going about life, but you and I know that no race in the galaxy can really survive that way."

"Were you trying to be his friend?"

Dembo laughed. "I was trying to get him to fight for us. But I guess if I just wanted that I could've handed him a stack of cash. Nah, I think part of me wanted to tame the beast. I wanted him to want to fight for us."

"What's the point of that?"

"Maybe I did want to be his friend. What do you want from me? Honestly, he just fascinated me. I was hoping to understand him better if he fought for us, but beyond that he's just a good guy to have on your side. Think of the alternative. I hated the idea of having to fight that motherfucker down the road."

"So did it come down to a stack of cash?" Prellina's smile turned sardonic.

"Not exactly. I tried my best to explain where I was coming from with the Rebellion. Really, all I had to go on was that he was a soldier during the Hydro-Baltan War. I figured he witnessed all the horror and injustice that I had only read about at University. Sure I could've just hired him for a job, but that wasn't enough. For one, this guy was hardcore enough that he'd definitely play turncoat. He'd blow up a base on Ttanis for us one day and then assassinate one of our officers the next. Maybe I was a little over-paranoid about that, but I really wanted him to fight *for* us. I tried to make him see that Hydrolet needed to be brought down. It's painfully ironic that we're back here working for them. I think I kept him listening simply because I wasn't afraid of him, although I was definitely on my guard. That and I wasn't trying to sell him anything. After a few drinks, I think he saw that I was truly passionate about this.

"Beio-Rhett drinks?"

"Like a fish, or at least he used to."

"I thought he was this hardcore, undefeatable warrior."

"Yeah, a warrior, not a monk. Like I said, the guy's tough,

but doesn't have a lot of finesse. His body is no temple as you can see from how hacked up it is. But a few drinks wouldn't stop him from tearing the first guy into quarters, who gave him a funny look. Anyway, he didn't necessarily cave, but he understood that I was for real. He understood that what I really wanted him to do was join us.

'I'm never gonna fight for another side, never again. I understand how much you believe in this, but that doesn't mean I do.'

'I know you don't, man,' I was a little drunk at this point, 'but you're a mercenary! You can at least fight for us!'

'I didn't say I wouldn't do that, I'm just not gonna commit to you guys.'

'Why not? Yo-you gonna take jobs from the fucking Government?'

'I didn't say I'd do that, but it's a huge galaxy. There's jobs everywhere.'

'But why not have a little stability in your career for a while? You don't think we can afford to keep you on retainer?'

'It's not that either, I'm just not gonna fight for anyone anymore.'

'But you are fighting for people, whether you want to believe it or not. You're fighting for governments all around the galaxy, and if it's not governments, it's mobs. The point is, you're fighting for everyone!'

'But I'm not loyal to anyone.'

'Who are you loyal to?'

'None of your business.'

'Well, whatever, never mind, I don't care… the thing is, what if, think of the job as winning the Rebellion for us!'

'That's a tall order.'

'But it's an order. What if we didn't hire you for something small like taking someone out or blowing up a weapons facility, but for taking down the whole fucking Hydrolet government?'

He laughed at this point. I think this was the first time he laughed during our whole interaction. Either way, I was getting through to him, or he found me amusing. Maybe a bit of both, but I think the fact that I was so persistent made him keep listening. Most mercenaries at that time, especially after the Hydro-Baltan War, would usually play one side during the war. Especially if it involved one of their home planets, not that Beio-Rhett was necessarily a Hydrolette, but still, there weren't many turncoats simply because it was too dangerous. Especially during a war, you could take jobs from both sides, but eventually, they'll figure out the guy that blew up one of their battleships was the same guy they hired last week to take out some hidden barracks. Usually that results in them never hiring that mercenary again, or they seek out and kill him!"

"But he didn't betray anyone. He's a mercenary," Prellina argued.

"I didn't say he did," Dembo continued. "But do you see how the situation can make people a little ticked off. All I'm saying is it's dangerous. And I know that Beio-Rhett was the kind of guy that would do that. Not for Hydrolet though. In fact, I don't think he did any job for Hydrolet since he left the army, for whatever reason. He fought on both sides of skirmishes all around the galaxy though, and he turned in Republic bounties, but the Hydro-Baltan War was over. Far as I know he hadn't taken a job on either side of any huge war. This was different. Hydrolet is a huge force in the Galactic Republic. Sure we were just a small Rebellion, but we had ten percent of the population on our side and several defected members of the military."

"You were getting the sense that he planned on playing both sides of this war?"

"No, I think he was planning on not getting involved at all. At least, that's why I think he was so resistant. I realize now that most jobs he did take involved outer rim systems, with the exception of Republic bounties, which paid really well. He didn't do much work for Baltania either, like he was trying to leave the whole thing behind."

"And that's why he frequented places like Kaliekae," Prellina put it together for Dembo.

Dembo nodded, "Yeah... I suppose I never thought of it like that. But the funny thing is, most people who defect want to get away from the violence and horror of war. Beio-Rhett, if anything, made a nosedive into more violence and horror. Pit fighting for Zala's sake! But he wasn't angry with Hydrolet either, 'cause I tried playing that angle with him and he didn't seem to care. No matter how much I spouted my bit about the corrupt regime of Octtanis and Deigger's inefficiency and lack of sympathy for the real soldiers like himself. None of it got to him, so he obviously didn't leave for that reason. He just didn't want to be a part of it. All of this was made much harder by the fact that he was wearing a fucking mask the whole time."

"How did you get him to join?"

"'You're not trying to hire me, you're trying to recruit me,' he said to me.

'No, I'm trying to hire you. And a regular mercenary wouldn't turncoat a thing like this.'

'I just don't want to commit myself to a whole war, especially one back on Hydrolet.'

'So why not take them down?'

'I don't want to do that either. I just want to keep doing what I'm doing.'

'Damnit, man! What do you want out of life? You want to be famous? You got that. Everyone's terrified of you. You obviously don't want money. Don't you want to be a part of something?'

'That's just it kid, I don't want to be a part of anything. That's why I do what I do.'

'Who're you calling kid?'

If I was sober, I would never under any circumstances pick a fight with the Masked Menace. I was just drunk enough and I'd been talking my head off about shit that makes me angry sober that I wasn't gonna take that kind of talk. I was 36 at the time and too old to be called kid anymore, yet too young to be the bigger man and let it slide. I vaguely remember the latter part of that conversation since I got increasingly drunk, but I do remember standing up with my hand above my pistol. I didn't really want to fight, but I was getting frustrated and thought if I showed off, he'd take me a bit more seriously.

'What are you doing? Sit down.'

'No, stand up. I'll give you first draw. You wanna see how fast a kid can shoot?'

'I didn't mean anything by it, kid, now sit down.'

'Now you're just pissing me off. Come on, stand up.'

I couldn't tell, but I think he was laughing behind the mask.

'Alright, fine,' he stood up, 'Listen, I don't want to hurt you.'

'Who says you're gonna? Go ahead and draw. You won't even graze me.'

'Let me put it on safety first.'

'Don't bother, you won't get a shot off.'

I think I was finally getting to him. I got tired of trying to cater to his ego, and drunkenly tried to attack it instead. Maybe he never intended to shoot, or maybe he did. I never asked him afterwards. I remember he looked at me long and hard. I think he took my threat seriously or he was just curious to see what I was gonna pull. Either way, I was ready. My mind was a little compromised, but muscles don't get drunk, and most of my target practice was done drunk anyway. He finally drew. I knew he wouldn't be fast enough. I took my pistol out and shot his out of his hand, clear across the cantina floor. I'd pulled off my trick, so now it was a matter of whether or not he'd work me over for ruining his pistol.

'You son of a bitch!'

'When was the last time you saw a kid shoot like that?'

He was fine except for a bruise on his hand. His pistol was fucked. He looked at me after considering the damage that was done. Finally I could hear him laugh behind the mask.

'What's your name so I can call you something else?'

After that we became friends. It wasn't like he became friendlier or anything like that. He was still a hardass, and quite the introvert. God forbid I ever learned about his life prior to his infamy. But after that point, I got the sense that he trusted me and it didn't seem like he trusted many people. I'm not even sure if my little stunt worked or he was planning on joining us all along, but something about violence gets his attention, like it's a language he speaks. Either way, it's how I finally got through to him. And once again, all I got him to do was work for us as a mercenary. He didn't join our cause, nor did he ever express any loyalty towards us. But he did fight for us and he planned on doing so until we won. So I guess you could say he was loyal, in a sense. Still, he cost us a small fortune but he was worth every bit of it. The money let him continue to think he was a mercenary, but he only fought for us those next few years. He and I stuck by each other on every mission. We were quite a success too. Every complex, facility, or base that we targeted was destroyed without exception. That's where our reputation that you never heard of came from."

Prellina giggled.

"So yeah, that's pretty much how we started to get along. We never talked much. Most of the time we spent killing people or running from them, but I guess that's a way to connect in and of itself. You really learn to trust someone as both of you are being shot at."

Prellina looked back up at Beio-Rhett who still looked frustrated trying to understand Mheages's techno-babble. She smiled and looked back at Dembo. "Well, that all adds up except for one thing…"

Dembo's expression asked what it was.

"When they captured him, he was still working for the Rebellion. From what you tell me, it seems the only reason he stuck around was because of you. Yet when you were considered dead, he kept fighting for the Rebellion, even until he was captured. Why?"

Dembo took another bite from his meal and chewed on it as well as the question for a while. "I never thought about it," he finally said. "You're gonna have to ask him, yourself."

Prellina nodded with an unsatisfied smirk. "I think you know why,"

Dembo didn't respond to Prellina. Prellina looked back up at Beio-Rhett. Beio-Rhett finally turned and noticed her through the window. *Why's she always hanging around?* He turned back to the monitor and sighed. "I think I get it, how long do you think it'll take to rig up?"

Mheages spun around in his chair and looked up at Beio-Rhett, "How many people you have working on this?"

"Myself and Dembo, maybe I can get two others to help,"

"A week at most, if you really crack the whip. It may take some jerry rigging since you're not plugging into the ship's power source normally like other appliances. You need a direct line. Luckily you want to mount this canon in the rear of the ship where the core is already located, so you shouldn't have to do much heavy surgery."

Beio-Rhett nodded. "I think I'm getting it. Can you write up a grocery list for everything I need to order besides the canon?"

Mheages chuckled and spun back around typing away on the monitor. "Of course. I'll come back in a week to make sure you hooked it up right. You are in no danger fiddle faddling with it now. As soon as we restart that core, everything better be perfect or we're in trouble."

Beio-Rhett was starting to think the fusion canon wasn't all that necessary. "Trouble? And what do you mean 'we'?"

Mheages spun around again. "You're tapping a direct power source into a fusion generator core. If that power line isn't completely sealed, the core will become unstable and you'll create a small star here in the warehouse, which of course would incinerate us and everything else in a mile radius."

Beio-Rhett tried to hide his concern by bottling it down to a short, apathetic, "Shit."

"So I'm gonna come down to make sure you hooked everything up correctly and oversee the core activation myself."

Damnit, now I got to thank you too. "That's pretty considerate of you. Don't you have more important things to do?"

"A simple 'thank you' would suffice," Mheages smiled. "I like doing this. It's a good mental exercise. Besides I've hit a bit of a brick wall with my other assignment. The government's taking care of me, so I might as well give a hand wherever I can."

Beio-Rhett nodded slowly, trying to figure out what Mheages's story was. "Weren't you a professor of... astrophysics or something?"

Mheages smiled. "That's all this is. Physics. You forget I also have a degree in fluid mechanics. Don't worry about these specs. They'll work. Just follow my instructions and you'll be fine. Plus, I'll personally check the results before we do the dangerous part."

Beio-Rhett nodded again, slowly. As hard as it was to follow Mheages's complex dialect, it was even harder to not look at Prellina who still insisted on looking up at him from way down below. *What is she still doing here?* Beio-Rhett never let himself think that he was very intelligent, but he was good at noticing anything that was happening around him. He tried not to care too much about the fact that Prellina was staring up at him. *Is she talking to Dembo?* Yet, he also couldn't follow Mheages's train of logic well enough to not keep from staring out the window.

"Well, good luck," Mheages broke Beio-Rhett's train of thought as he stood up from his chair. "I gave you my private contact info right?"

Beio-Rhett checked the data pad in his vest pocket. "Yep,"

he confirmed.

"Okay, feel free to call me with any questions. I'll be at my office on the Bestton Base, so I won't be able to pop by often. I'm sure you won't have any problems that can't be discussed over the phone."

"I'm sure," he said as he shook the professor's hand on his way out the door. After Mheages shut the door behind him Beio-Rhett looked at his hand that had just shook the old man's. He wasn't terribly old, perhaps younger than the General, but old, nonetheless, somewhere between middle and old age. Beio-Rhett never really noticed how old he was, until he touched the other's hand. The cracks in the professor's palms were more defined, his skin dryer, but they were still gentle. Beio-Rhett's hand was far from gentle. Even though it was younger and more elastic, it seemed as dry and cracked as Mheages's, only not from age. Besides the oily stains from constantly working on the ship, creases from his never-ending grip on a weapon striped his palms. Callouses discolored the flesh near his fingers' joints a lighter blue then the rest of his hands. There were also the numerous cuts, bruises and scars that dotted his hands. He turned his hand around to see the back of it, just as roughened as the palm. He looked back through the window to see that Prellina was gone and Dembo was hopping off of the crates to get back to work. *What was I just thinking about?*

Singatt turned around to see Beio-Rhett walking towards Poko and himself.

"Is that gonna do boss?" Beio-Rhett smiled as he walked towards the pair. As soon as Singatt replied, Beio-Rhett's attention drifted about the warehouse.

"No need to be snide, I'm just making sure that it's safe,"

"Well, I wouldn't worry about that. It's hooking it up that's gonna be the dangerous part." He produced the data pad the professor gave him from his vest pocket. "These are the blueprints that Mheages gave us, so if we follow directions we should be good."

Singatt looked over the canon one last time and then back at Beio-Rhett. "I suppose. You need anything besides the canon?"

Beio-Rhett pulled a smaller data pad out and handed it to Singatt, "Just some insulation, routers, and heavy wiring. I wrote it all up with Mheages."

Singatt looked over the data pad. "Shouldn't take too long, a few days at least. What else is there to do on the ship?"

Beio-Rhett turned around and looked up and down at the ship, scratching his chin. "Not... much... else, actually."

Poko stepped up to Beio-Rhett and handed him the data pad, "Wasn't cheap. Luckily, that rebel weapons cache I was talking about included two of these. I'm pretty sure it used to be an anti-spacecraft canon, probably for some guard tower."

Beio-Rhett took the data pad and looked at the price before slightly gasping. "Zala, you weren't kidding. Well, I can't pay you up front now..." he looked up at Poko sheepishly, "I know my tab is getting pretty steep,"

"Don't I know it," Poko said with a smile. "Don't worry man. Thanks for giving me a place to stay for the time being," he looked over at Singatt, "or should I say thank you." He grabbed the pad back from Beio-Rhett, "But when you get out there and start kicking ass, it'd be nice for you to pay at least half of it when you get some capital. I had to pay for this thing upfront."

"Absolutely man, when I get some cash. Thanks again," he opened up his arms and leaned in to embrace Poko.

Poko reciprocated and grabbed Beio-Rhett tight, patting him on the back, "Always, man,"

"I didn't know you could be so sweet," Beio-Rhett could hear Prellina's voice behind him.

Beio-Rhett immediately pulled away from Poko and turned around to face Prellina. "There you..." *Don't be stupid!* "... haven't seen... um... where've you been?"

Prellina smiled, "Around. Hey remember when you said you'd buy me a drink for being such an asshole that day?"

Beio-Rhett smiled and lowered his head in shame, "Yes... I do," he said quietly.

"Well, I just got a 48 hour leave so I was thinking of heading to the city to relax."

Beio-Rhett scratched the back of his neck, still looking down, "Well I have to..." he looked back at the ship. *No excuse.* "I'm... actually waiting for some parts to arrive before I can attach this thing, so I guess I can take a break and head to the city. If that's okay with you, boss?"

Singatt smiled, "I don't see why not. In fact, I think I might join you. Since you won't be on the base, I don't really have any obligations here for the time being. It'd be nice to take a break."

Beio-Rhett glared at Singatt. "You think I'm gonna bail?"

Singatt laughed, "That's part of it. But I've been here working my ass off just as hard as you. I haven't had a drink all month. Besides, it's good to travel in a group in these tough times. I want to protect my investment."

Beio-Rhett chuckled and looked at Poko. "What about you, man?"

"Let's do it," Poko smiled. "Any excuse to get off this fucking base. Not my style at all."

Beio-Rhett looked back at the ship to see Dembo walking towards them, "Dembo! We're taking a leave and heading to Colett to have a night on the town. You down?"

Dembo was taken back by the suggestion. "I... guess. I just finished uploading the data for the SEL, so yeah, I guess there's not much else to do until we can hook up that canon," he thought for a moment. "Wow, I haven't been to Colett in forever. So, who's all going?"

Beio-Rhett twirled his finger around signaling everyone around them.

Dembo looked at Singatt, "Ha, you drink?"

Singatt huffed. "Come on, let's go before I change my mind."

"Well now it's a party," Prellina quipped. "I didn't realize you guys came as a package deal."

Why didn't you talk to me later when no one was around? "Not usually, but there's a first time for everything," he said looking around at the other four. He wondered if he would be spending more time with this little posse than he originally thought.

Prellina laughed. "Well, I've never actually been to Colett, so who knows the town best?" she turned her gaze to Dembo.

"I think I know a place," Dembo smiled as he spoke, "That is, if it's still there."

The place was still there and it was called Sy's Hideout. It was a fairly rowdy establishment, but not particularly dangerous unless one was either looking for trouble or didn't know how to avoid it. The five of them walked in looking like they were important, but the other patrons seemed like they couldn't care less. Everyone there had more important things on their mind, whether it was a good time being had or a terrible loss being lamented over. The bar itself was loaded. Almost every table was occupied. The cantina itself was rather large. An incomprehensible hubbub of dozens of voices in different languages filled the room. Colett was almost as large as Bestton and the city center, in particular, was excessively diverse. Hydrolet was not a particularly multi-cultured planet. It wasn't as exclusive as some other planets such as Zynoth, but Hydrolettes for the most part, kept to themselves. The city of Colett was the exception. It served as a cultural way station and socially liberal oasis in an otherwise military-centered society. Naturally, this clashing of multiple cultures made for a somewhat tense environment in the inner city and places like Si's Cantina were not exceptions to this atmosphere of conflict. A menagerie of species cluttered the shadowy recesses of the cantina. Naturally, it was mostly Hydrolettes, but one could spot a few Baltans from their unique eye color and even some Niskans as well. There was actually a group of Kitholorians sitting in the corner discussing matters they considered far too complicated for other races. There was even one of the reclusive Dynothoxans all the way from the race's secluded home planet in the Outer Rim, Zynoth. A band of Kakeuwees were performing on a raised stage tucked in the upper right corner behind the bar which dominated the center of the cantina. Their exotic instruments provided a mellow sonic filler between the cacophony of voices.

Dembo stepped in front of the group and muttered to himself, "This place hasn't changed a bit."

"You came here as a little dark blue-skinned brat?" Beio-Rhett chuckled.

"I used to do my homework here," Dembo said, bulldozing right over Beio-Rhett's jab. He smiled as he allowed memories of the place and his days at University to flood back. "It's not dangerous. Just a downtown haven for brawlers, bawlers and bastards."

"I hope they make their drinks stiff," Beio-Rhett spoke as he walked up behind Dembo, who was busy scanning the cantina for a place to sit. He was lucky enough to spot one empty booth tucked away in the opposite corner of the stage. He simply pointed and led the way.

The table was circular and wrapped around by a cushioned

seat that sat five comfortably. Above the group hung a black-shaded lamp. Dembo took one end of the seat to claim an outside spot. Poko darted to the other side and scooted in making room for Prellina who slid in next to him. Before he knew what he was doing, Beio-Rhett went for the seat next. *Wait, shit!* He scooted up next to Prellina before realizing he was tucked neatly in the back with Prellina before Singatt sealed the deal by taking the other edge seat.

After settling in, the five looked around for a waiter, but accepted that it may be a while. Beio-Rhett leaned forward to get Dembo's attention. "Can we smoke in here?"

"You could when I used to go here, I don't know how the laws have changed," He looked around the table for an ashtray without success. He finally found one under the table after accidentally kicking it. "Here we go," he said as he plopped it on the table.

Beio-Rhett picked out a cigarette, placed it between his lips and lit it. "I haven't spent this much time in one place in a long time," he took a drag.

"You'll be gone soon enough," Singatt spoke looking around for the waiter. "Right now the military base is the safest place you can be."

"How so?" Beio-Rhett tapped some ash in the tray. "We're sitting on a target. It's probably much safer floating around in space."

Singatt shrugged. "Gimme a cigarette,"

Beio-Rhett turned to Singatt with eyes widened. "Did I hear you right?"

Singatt sighed and looked at Beio-Rhett with a smirk. "I quit ten years ago. But I figure in these times I'm not gonna last much longer. Besides, if I have to deal with you much longer I oughta start again."

Beio-Rhett grabbed his pack and handed him one with a bright smile. "I think we're gonna get along much better now," he said with the cigarette between his lips. After Singatt grabbed one, he moved the pack around to the others at the table. Dembo had his own as did Prellina. Poko didn't smoke.

"It's been a drag not being able to smoke on the base," lamented Dembo.

"There's a lot of combustibles lying around. It's not that

unreasonable," Singatt said.

Dembo shrugged and took another drag. His eyes wandered around the room before spotting a rather attractive female making her way towards the table. It wasn't until she pulled out a data pad that he finally realized she was the waiter they'd been waiting for.

"What can I get y'all tonight?" she asked in a gruff manner.

"Bring a round of the best stuff on tap on my tab," Beio-Rhett spoke before anyone could say anything. The rest of the group was somewhat taken aback.

"Name?" she asked.

"Beio-Rhett,"

The waitress's eyes darted up at hearing the name put to the face. A little startled, she quickly looked back down at the data pad punching in the information. She pretended she didn't notice the name and quickly applied the charge to Beio-Rhett's tab. "Be right with you," she said before she walked away quickly.

Singatt watched the waitress walk away and then turned to Beio-Rhett, waiting for him to say something.

Beio-Rhett knew what Singatt was thinking, but only smiled and took a drag. *Didn't see that one coming did you?*

"Why are you in such a good mood tonight?" Singatt finally asked.

"It's good to get off that base," he let out a puff of smoke, "I'm trying to make the best of a shitty situation. Call it a bit of gratitude. You did save my life, after all."

Singatt smiled, "Thank you,"

Prellina took a drag of her cigarette and let it out with a heavy sigh, "Well, I was hoping to talk to you in private, but I guess it doesn't matter in front of these guys."

The rest of the group all leaned in towards Prellina who sat perfectly in the middle of the five.

"I was wondering if you would hire me to work on your ship."

Beio-Rhett coughed up a bit of smoke. "What?!" He never would've guessed that was coming as long as he lived. He thought with his friends around it would be easier for her not to get too personal, but there was no preparing for this. "Work on my ship? Work what? We don't even have a job yet."

Prellina shrugged, "I know, but you will soon, right Singatt?"

Singatt blew a puff of smoke, "Soon as we find something for them to do, yeah."

"Exactly," Prellina said. "I seriously regret leaving Geufsta when I did. It's not like I don't care about my home world, I really do, but I just don't feel like I'm doing anything being an assistant to the medical staff. I know I'm helping and I volunteered because it seemed like the right thing to do, but I think we all know that this isn't going to be a quiet conflict. War is gonna break out and I don't want to be stuck on some base in Colett getting drinks for stressed out medics, while we stitch up thousands of soldiers before they die anyway. I just can't do it."

"Prellina, don't think you aren't helping us out any less," Singatt tried to console her.

"I don't think that," she said. "That's not the point. The point is I don't want to get stuck. I was happy on Geufsta doing my research completely cut off from civilization. When a wire came through about the medical staff being understaffed because of the Rebellion, I felt like I owed it to my home world to go back. Like I was being selfish way out on this jungle planet. But now I feel like I should've stayed. I know it sounds selfish, but I just don't think I came back for the right reasons."

Singatt grunted, "Prellina, in these dark times, we have to think about the bigger picture."

Beio-Rhett just stared and listened.

"I know it sounds childish," Prellina said softly. "It's just… I don't know. The point is, I don't want to just run away. I do wanna help, but I think I can be more help if I worked for Beio-Rhett, went along on his missions. You are hiring him to help against the Quezzes, right? This just seems like my chance to get out of a potential rut."

Beio-Rhett looked down at the table. The smoke trailed up from the tip of his cigarette broken by the stream of light from the lamp above.

"Before I got my degree in Biochemistry, I was in pre-med for a while. I can serve as a medic on your ship!" she said. "I know you're a hardy mother fucker, but be realistic. You're gonna go flying around in suicide missions in a little cruiser and you don't think you're gonna get shot up? Every ship needs at least one person with some medical expertise."

Beio-Rhett finally tapped the extensive ash at the top of his cigarette. *Didn't see this coming at all.* "Well, um…" he tried long and hard to think of a reason to say no. Then he tried long and hard to not think about why he was trying to say no in the first place. His train of thought was stuck in a downward spiral as Singatt broke him out of it with his words.

"Prellina, don't think that your help is not appreciated at the base. We need all the help we can get. It's very stressful for everyone involved and we end up treating each other worse than we normally would. Especially with the medical staff, they're dealing with people dying on their watch every day…"

"Goddamnit I know that," Prellina barked. It seemed to be the first time she raised her voice since the rest of the group met her. "That's just the thing. It's too big a project. I want to work on something smaller, something I can manage. I can actually save lives if I work on a ship, cause I only have a few people to worry about. I'm not… I don't know, I don't have to explain myself, I just want to do something different," she took a breath and then a drag. After letting it out she looked over at Beio-Rhett. "I mean, it's your call, it's your ship. I don't wanna try to get all buddy buddy with you, I just genuinely think I can be of help."

Beio-Rhett took a drag from his cigarette before letting his eyes wander about the bar in search of the waitress. A few more seconds of distraction as she returned with their drinks. Beio-Rhett concentrated on making it seem like he was stalling to appear cold and indifferent, upholding his dangerous, tough-guy persona. What a tragedy it would be if she figured out he was actually more embarrassed about admitting that he would absolutely love to have an excuse to see even more of her.

"That's five on your tab… sir," the waitress said.

Beio-Rhett rifled through his pockets for a few seconds before succeeding in finding a card. "Here," he said handing it to her. "Keep it open."

The waitress walked away with the card, again quickly.

Singatt looked at Beio-Rhett suspiciously.

"I told you I have some accounts even you don't know about. One, I use specifically for occasions such as this," he gave a wry smile.

Singatt grunted. He couldn't tell how much of what Beio-

Rhett said was indeed true.

"Well?" Prellina persisted. There was no more putting it off. *Best to answer quickly and sharply, like it doesn't matter to you either way, and you've already forgotten the whole thing.*

"Sure, whatever," he finally said.

Prellina seemed a little hesitant at first to believe Beio-Rhett, but finally smiled and raised her glass. "Well, cheers to that, boss."

Beio-Rhett never called Singatt "boss" again after that moment.

The five of them lifted their glasses and brought them together with a triumphant cling.

"To darker times," Beio-Rhett said sarcastically.

Singatt humored Beio-Rhett with a smirk.

"Ow," muttered Prellina looking down at her backside. "Watch your... what is that?"

"Oh, the fucking strap broke," Beio-Rhett looked down at his backside as well, seeing his knife sheath had a broken leg strap, causing it to jut into Prellina's thigh. He unbuttoned the whole thing and placed it on the table. "I'll get that fixed later. For right now it'll scare off troublemakers," he said before taking another drink.

"What is that?" Prellina's curiosity was piqued.

"My most prized possession," Beio-Rhett said through his teeth with his cigarette still in his mouth. "I've had that thing for twenty-five years and it hasn't failed me once."

Poko looked at the sheathed blade curiously. "Oh, that thing! You still have that?"

Prellina looked at Dembo and then back at Beio-Rhett. "Is that the... the diamond knife?"

Beio-Rhett tapped his ash on the tray, "So you do know who I am?"

Prellina shot Beio-Rhett a wry look, "Actually, Dembo told me about it,"

Beio-Rhett paused, feeling a bit foolish, "You two been getting along then?" he recovered.

"Nah, I was just asking about you," she said confidently. She looked at the sheathed knife, then back up at Beio-Rhett, "Well?" she asked honestly, "Can I see it?"

Beio-Rhett casually put his drink down, and with cigarette

still in his mouth, unbuttoned the leather holster. The handle was gorgeously crafted in dark red wood from Katoola, glazed over with a smooth varnish finish that reflected only slight streaks of light from the lamp. It was capped with gold at the pummel and the hilt was steel, which wove into the handle as though it grew out of the wood. The hilt also curved around the front to secure the user's index finger and up into the still hidden blade as Beio-Rhett slid it out of sheath. A pure white flash reflected off the blade as Beio-Rhett unsheathed the knife. The blade shimmered not just white, but all colors came across it, infused in the indestructible crystal. As Beio-Rhett pulled it out and swung it back around to the center of the table, light danced around the blade and shot off in all directions. The blade was indeed made of diamond.

"Holy shit," Singatt whispered.

"It's beautiful," Prellina said, gazing at the blade.

Dembo smiled and took a drink. He'd seen it before, but was amused by the reactions of those who hadn't.

Poko chuckled, "I'm surprised that thing has held up… that was one of my first experiments with that carbon bonding catalysts."

Prellina's gaze shot over to Poko, "Wait… you made that?"

Poko nodded, "I put all the parts together… but it was definitely a group effort… heh, if I remember correctly, I made Rhett here do most of the work for me,"

Beio-Rhett snorted trying to hold back a laugh, "Damn right you did, man. I don't think you ever heard the whole story of the shit you put me through for a fucking knife."

"You said it was your prized possession! Why you knocking it now?"

"I'm just saying you made me jump through way too many hoops…"

"I didn't mean to…"

"Doesn't matter…"

"Hey, you saying it's not worth it? Like I said, that shit is still working for you,"

"Wait, wait, wait, stop! What're you two talking about?" Prellina leaned over the table to get her face up in Beio-Rhett and Poko's. "Slow down, what shit? Tell me a story!"

Beio-Rhett took a drag. "You tell it, man, I wanna hear

your side of it."

"Dude, I honestly don't remember. You tell it, you're the one who has the story. I was just caught up with shit, believe me, I didn't mean to send you in circles around the galaxy."

"Shut up and just tell the story!" Prellina raised her voice but kept her smile.

Beio-Rhett paused and looked at Poko, "Where to start?"

"I remember you were a government assassin at the time… so after Drisko, for sure," Poko mused as he sipped his drink."

"So, this is when you were… or it's gotta be before the whole Masked Menace thing, right?" Prellina asked.

Beio-Rhett hesitated for a moment and then took a drag, "Yeah before. Poko and I met at the ill-fated Aulder Weapons Complex on Drisko during the Second Hydro-Baltan War. We were both stationed there. I was a soldier and he was a technician, God knows what he was doing there."

"Even I don't remember, man," Poko said. "I've been a mercenary longer than you have. I think I must've been smuggling raw materials for some syndicate."

Beio-Rhett snickered, "Heh, yeah. As you can see we both made it out of there alive. I lost track of Poko for a while when I got shipped back to the frontlines. But I wasn't out there for long before I was called out of action for a special rendezvous. Back then, I was much better at following orders, so I complied without question and was sent to a small space station where I was brought to an important looking colonel. He gave me a bunch of talk about how my performance on the battlefield was impressive and said I would be much more effective in the Black Ops Program,"

"An assassin," Prellina clarified.

"Essentially. I did some non-lethal contracts as well. I was still technically a soldier as the Black Ops Program is still under military funding. Most of my contracts involved either sabotage or apprehension. There were some assassinations, especially near the end of the war when several Baltan figureheads were starting to lose hope and go into hiding. Much of the war at this point was fought in the shadows, as you remember. I had been through the frontline warfare that had been raging for years before. I'm not sure if I preferred that to the cloak and dagger stuff. There was a lot more responsibility on my shoulders as I usually flew solo missions. I guess I learned to be a much more self-sufficient warrior during those times... but anyway, what was I talking about... the knife! Right, so as an assassin, I traded most of my heavy artillery for smaller, silent weapons. I'd never used blades much on the battlefield. When you have to make a silent kill, you sometimes have no choice. So I started using knives and swords. I wasn't inept at blades, but I certainly got better during my time in Black Ops. Anyway, I think it must've been almost a year before I finally got in touch with Poko."

"Yeah... I was pretty busy after Drisko, like always," Poko interrupted, "But you also weren't easy to get a hold of either."

Beio-Rhett sipped his drink during the interim, "Fair enough, but yeah, Poko here finally got in contact with me, to ask me for a favor of all things. I felt a little unsure about it at the time, since I worked for such high command in the government, but he assured me I'd get something out of it. I decided to go for it. I was currently going into a weapons facility, underground some mining caverns on Daemer. Where the Baltans were producing new chemical weapons. I was supposed to set a thermal detonator on the power generator to bury the place. Poko needed some important formula from the facility. He said to just grab a sample before leveling the place. I didn't see any harm or difficulty in this, so I went ahead and grabbed some before setting the detonator. He said something about the substance being an important carbon bonding formula to make infused crystal bonds with long chains to reduce brittleness. It was some technology that the Baltans were experimenting with that Poko wanted to get his hands on to make improved blade linings,"

Poko only nodded, impressed that Beio-Rhett had remembered his techno-babble so well.

"Getting the stuff wasn't too difficult. I just had to make a quick detour through the facility after setting the charges, using some directions Poko gave me. The only added obstacle was a group of scientists who didn't put up to much of a fight. I found a vial of the formula and carried out the mission without incident. After my debriefing, I got a call from Poko saying he couldn't receive the formula from me in person. Why I don't know."

"You know why," Poko interrupted. "I always used middle men and you know it, especially for something as top secret as that. Course, I didn't expect everything to spiral out of control like it did. In retrospect, I probably shoulda just picked it up in person."

"Damn right you should've!" Beio-Rhett barked with a smirk. "Anyway, he wanted me to drop it off at a merchant on Drisko. So between missions, I went to Drisko and followed directions to the merchant's station. He knew who I was and took the formula, but it didn't end there. He was surprised to find out that the formula was unstable. In twenty-four hours it would crystallize and become useless. Luckily, he said he knew a Kitholorian chemist all the way back on Daemer that had a carbon stabilizer formula. It should work, that is, if I got it to him in twenty-four hours. Naturally, I was pissed off and asked why he couldn't do it, and like any other Niskan, he said he was grounded on Drisko because of mob ties. I was trying not to get angry with Poko as I flew halfway across the galaxy, back to Daemer."

"Dude, cut me a break. I had no idea the stuff was unstable. You gotta realize that I'd only just heard of the stuff. If I..."

"I forgive you, man," Beio-Rhett said. "The merchant gave me a note to give to the chemist to expedite the process. When I made it back to Daemer, I found the chemist and he gave me the stabilizer without question. I raced back to Drisko only to find that the merchant had disappeared! Now I was getting really pissed. However, someone recognized me, probably a partner or accomplice of his. He told me that the merchant got in trouble with the mob and had to skip the planet. He did say that if I returned I could find him on Geufsta. Racing to Geufsta with only a few hours left, I was starting to wonder if Poko's present for me would even be worth all this trouble. But, I was so invested at this point I knew I was going to carry through. On Geufsta, I found the merchant and gave him the stabilizer. He told me it would take three days to create the proper solution using the stabilizer. At this point I wondered where Poko was or if I was ever going to hear from him again. He wasn't returning my calls either," he shot a glance at Poko.

Poko laughed, "Dude, if I knew any of this was happening I would've intervened, but I couldn't risk getting involved. I trusted that merchant to let me know if anything went wrong and the sonobabitch never said a word."

"Whatever," Beio-Rhett smiled. "Anyway, I got the solution and to add insult to injury, he said I had to deliver the solution to Poko myself. Now I was angry at Poko since I didn't see the purpose of the middle man at all."

Poko smirked. "That pissed me off too. I think he was in more trouble than I thought and wanted to go into hiding as soon as possible. Meeting me was not a good idea if you're in that much hot water."

"When I finally got in touch with Poko he told me to meet him on Hydrolet. I gave him the formula quite irritated. He was surprised and asked why but I was in way too bad a mood to tell him just then. He took the formula and said he'd have something for me inside a week. Luckily, I didn't have any missions during that time so I took a mini-vacation to unwind. Finally, he gave me a call and presented me with a wooden case. I unlocked it, opened it and saw what you're looking at right now. It really washed away my bad mood. I finally had a weapon that I could call my own. And it's never left my side… well until this guy fucked things up!" he pointed at Singatt.

Singatt chuckled and took a drag from his cigarette. "We've come so far," he said.

Beio-Rhett thought to respond with some snide remark, but his eye was caught by the shimmer of light reflecting from the blade he was holding. The colors that reflected off the blade seemed to defy the laws of physics. He was only looking at the blade out of the corner of his eye, but he swore that the dominant color dancing off of the blade was green. He knew it was just a trick of eye, or it was perhaps the reflection of the greenish overhead lamp, but the green seemed to glow stronger than a simple reflection. Beio-Rhett was afraid to turn his gaze on the blade directly. His mind was playing tricks on him. The drink was getting to him. *Don't look!* It was definitely green. There were spots of green, dark green, the color of blood. The knife wasn't reflecting the green, green was blocking the light. *Don't look! Put it down! Don't go there!* He couldn't listen to reason. His eyes finally turned towards the blade. It was dripping wet with blood, Hydrolette blood. *No it's not!*

"Can I see it?" Prellina's voice broke him from his trance.

Beio-Rhett couldn't respond for a second, then finally turned towards Prellina. "Here," he said bluntly handing her the knife with the handle facing her, trying to keep his eyes on her and not the blade. "Don't cut yourself, I gotta go to the little girls' room." After handing her the blade, he put his cigarette out in the ash tray, turned the other way and pushed his way through Poko and Singatt to get out of the booth seat. It appeared to the others he was about to be sick, so they quickly slid out of his way before he made his rushed march to the lavatory.

Trying to appear nonchalant, Beio-Rhett stood straight up and faced forward, keeping the doorway to the lavatory in sight. His eyes drifted only slightly to his left and right, mostly to make sure he wasn't about to run into anyone. He briefly paid notice to the lone Dynothoxan standing alone next to the bar. *Was he looking at me?* Beio-Rhett shrugged off the thought and tried to focus on getting to the lavatory. Now he was just being paranoid.

Bursting into the lavatory, he bumped into a Hydrolette stepping out. The other Hydrolette saw that Beio-Rhett was much bigger and quickly ran off hoping Beio-Rhett wouldn't make a scene of it. Beio-Rhett had already forgotten about the other patron and rushed to the sink. He hung his head low over the sink. He knew that he was only hallucinating the blood, but that didn't change the fact that it was bothering him. He wondered if he needed to vomit, but found no such need. He knew this would happen if he let his guard down. He had to focus. Working on the ship kept him focused. It kept him distracted. That's all that this was. After taking a few breaths, he looked at himself in the mirror. *Zala!* Beio-Rhett realized he never looked in the mirror much (Are you afraid?) *No! What?* He hung his head back down and turned on the faucet, splashing water in his face. The sound of the running water slightly masked the creak of the door, but Beio-Rhett didn't care enough to look to see whomever it was that walked in. They would probably just assume that he was feeling sick. Beio-Rhett decided to ignore it until he felt the barrel of a pistol press up against his back.

"What are you doing in a place like this?" the voice was Dynothoxan. There was only one Dynothoxan in the bar.

"What do you want?" Beio-Rhett kept the water running. *Fuck, I left the knife at the table! Way to go, asshole!*

"You!" the Dynothoxan replied. "There's a bounty on your head that you can see from space."

"What the hell are you talking about?" Beio-Rhett decided to turn the water off so he could hear a little better.

"You thought no one would find you if you were safe in a

jail cell? No one thought they could get a hold of you. I'm actually amazed I found you. I was on my way to the Colett Base thinking they we're holding you in custody there. I had a tip. Never thought I'd run into you before I got there. Maybe Dresbar will even throw in something extra for being so prompt."

"Dresbar!" Beio-Rhett shouted. He turned off the water and stood up slowly, making sure not to spook the bounty hunter. "Where's that son of a bitch been hiding? And more importantly, what's he got against me?!"

"Part of the reason he agreed to hire you was that you would never get caught. You expect him to believe that you were just overpowered? Bullshit, man. Dresbar smells a rat, and figured he'd sic every bounty hunter in the system on you."

"He's blaming me for getting caught?"

"Don't be smart, asshole! He knows you didn't get caught. You turned yourself in cause they offered you more than him and you sold the whole Rebellion down the river!"

Beio-Rhett sighed. "Good God, I knew that guy would eventually lose it. Listen man, I was just in the wrong place at the wrong time. I didn't do shit."

"Tell that to Dresbar then," the pistol dug itself deeper into Beio-Rhett. "I just want the reward."

Beio-Rhett hung his head low and sighed. "Well, I better go let my friends know they have to pick up the tab."

The bounty hunter laughed. "Yeah, cause I'm gonna fall for that," he jabbed Beio-Rhett in the back. "Come on! Let's go."

Beio-Rhett pushed himself from the sink knocking the bounty hunter back a few paces. He spun around with his hands up to show he didn't intend to make a break for it. "Relax!" he said with a smirk.

The bounty hunter regained his footing and lifted up the pistol to Beio-Rhett's face. He was starting to shake. "Don't fuck with me!" he shouted. He was dressed in a fairly thuggish manner as was normal for most bounty hunters, but he didn't seem to have any visible weapons on him other than his pistol. Of course there were the four venomous tentacles recoiled beneath his jacket that anyone who knew even a little about Dynothoxans knew to watch out for.

"I was just trying to give myself some breathing room. Damn, you're jumpy."

"Let's go. I'm not fucking around now," he was definitely shaking now.

"Listen, if we walk out of here with you following me with a gun to my back, my friends are gonna wonder what's going on. Most of them aren't very nice, and you may be asking for trouble if you act so bold."

The bounty hunter tried to steady his hand, slowing his breath. Finally, he let out a heavy breath. "All right," he said coldly. "But turn the fuck around and don't look back. I'm gonna be behind you the whole time with this gun pointed at you. You try anything and I will shoot. I won't kill you 'cause the bounty is for you alive, but I will make you bleed and drag your ass out of here."

Beio-Rhett kept smiling and just nodded, "Fair enough," he said. He turned around to face the mirror again. He could see the bounty hunter in the mirror and looked at him in the eyes through the reflection. "Follow me,"

Beio-Rhett walked out of the lavatory calmly with his hands in his pockets. The bounty hunter followed, looking especially shady, with his pistol held at point, but low and inconspicuously. The duo made its way slowly back to the table.

Prellina was looking over the knife as the two made their way back. She ran her finger over the dull edge softly, as if she was caressing it to the deadly tip. After gently touching the tip with her finger she twisted the blade in the light to make the colors dance again. Seeing the others look at her in a patronizing manner, she smiled and shoved the blade back into its sheath tossing it back on the table. "Don't look at me like that," she said. "It's beautiful."

As Beio-Rhett walked back to the table, his mind raced with options. This wasn't going to be tough at all, this guy was nervous. He would easily slip up, but Beio-Rhett needed to be careful and act fast or he would get shot, possibly killed. This guy was definitely scared and sometimes that was more dangerous than someone who was calm. He tried to make out the table where his comrades sat. *Why the fuck did I give her the knife?* He didn't have enough time to get it back. He had a few seconds at the table to make a move before the bounty hunter got suspicious. If he could grab the knife, he'd be okay, unless the bounty hunter saw it first. *Oh shit!* He would definitely see it since it was out of the sheath. *You can see that thing from miles away!* Beio-Rhett hoped the bounty hunter would be so nervous he wouldn't pay any attention. They were only a few steps away from the table. His eyes darted about the table for the knife. There was no flash, no shine, no dancing of colors. *Where was it?* Finally after walking within reach of the table, he saw it safely put in its sheath, lying invisible to the bounty hunter on the table, but within Beio-Rhett's reach. Beio-Rhett cracked a confident smile and turned slowly to face the bounty hunter, "Just a sec," he said. He placed his hands on the table to lean over as if he was about to whisper to the group. His right hand slowly made its way to the knife handle, while the other came upon the sheath. There was no way the bounty hunter could see any of this since it was so dark. Beio-Rhett spoke to Prellina with the same confident tone, "Thanks for putting it away when you were done with it."

Before Prellina knew what he was talking about or the bounty hunter could react, Beio-Rhett slid the knife out of its sheath and whipped around to his right, flinging the knife sideways. It spun in a deadly whirlwind towards the bounty hunter who was still a few steps behind Beio-Rhett. The bounty hunter only saw a flash of brilliant color before the shimmering blade embedded itself into his neck. The Dynothoxan's red blood shot forth in cadenced spurts, giving a rather graphic visualization of his heartbeat. The knife had made an all-too-lethal incision in the main artery of the Dynothoxan's throat, starving the bounty hunter's brain for oxygen almost instantly. He could not even squeeze the trigger of his pistol before he lost feeling in his hands, then his feet, then all his limbs before the world finally went dark around him. His body stood for a moment before slowly collapsing, his neck pumping out blood in a slower rhythm until finally the fount had dried up.

All of Sy's Hideout fell silent for a moment. The band stopped playing. Singatt and Prellina tensed up, clenching their hands on whatever was closest to them. Poko looked concerned, but made no bodily show of his apprehension. Dembo remained relaxed through the entire ordeal, responding casually by taking a sip of his drink.

Beio-Rhett grabbed a nearby rag from one of the glass deposits and leaned over the dead bounty hunter, jerking his knife from his neck. He glanced over the blade briefly. *Red, not green.* He wiped the blade clean until it shimmered once more and threw the rag to their waitress who happened to be standing close by, shocked and motionless. "Just put that on my tab."

The waitress clutched the rag to her chest where it landed and ran to the kitchen. The band continued playing, the voices in the bar returned and the silence passed.

Beio-Rhett motioned for Singatt to scoot in so Beio-Rhett could now sit at the edge, further away from Prellina, "I guess we should go soon," he quipped as he took out another cigarette and lit it. He inhaled and let his muscles unwind as he let out a relieved cloud of smoke.

Singatt chuckled, "You make enemies everywhere you go, don't you?"

Beio-Rhett smiled. "I guess so, 'cept this guy had nothing against me. Apparently there's a price on my head, which is gonna make it hard to finish working on the ship," he sipped his drink after speaking.

Dembo cocked his head in interest, "Who? By now, everyone should figure you're dead."

"I guess word got out," Beio-Rhett said as he took another drag. "It's Dresbar."

A cold wind washed over Dembo. He seemed to shiver slightly, but not in fear, as if a menacing revelation came over him all too fast. "Dresbar? Put a bounty on you?"

Beio-Rhett shrugged. "I'm as confused as you, man. I was just a hired gun, but I guess he's choosing to blame the fall of the Rebellion on me. I warned you that guy was paranoid."

Dembo only nodded, but had no words to offer.

Prellina looked back and forth between Dembo and Beio-Rhett and took a drag from her cigarette, "Well, let's finish our drinks and find another bar, before they ask us to leave."

Beio-Rhett smiled and raised his glass, "I'll cheers to that."

The rest of the group raised their glasses. Dembo hesitated for a moment, but finally raised his glass as well.

"And they will know us by the trail of dead..." Beio-Rhett said with a vicious smirk on his face.

The rest of the group looked down at the dead Dynothoxan. Singatt finally spoke, "As long as they're not on our side," he shrugged.

Dembo finally spoke, "You're gonna have to watch your back with that price on your head,"

"I know" Beio-Rhett said before he downed the rest of his drink, "I know."

Chapter 6

The Missing Platoon

"No change, I can't change, I can't change, I can't change, but I'm here in my mold."

Two sliding doors opened for General Kitchnok as he walked into a very gray, very drab meeting room. Many important looking Quesgralions in similar dark grey Teneman officer uniforms sat in identical metal chairs around a circular table. Two guards in contrasting black uniforms stood by the door he used and greeted him as he entered.

Most of the men at the table represented the inner circle of the Teneman, only those most trusted by Senator Nok. Naturally there was Governor Hynlon Missan's son, Gastus, in his simplest of Teneman attire; the uniform-standard trench coat, belted but lightly adorned except for the executive pin on his lapel. General Drokktayr, now Minister of Defense, was there also in his more decorated uniform, displaying his many achievements on the battlefield. Ambassador Jedka Techet, now Minister of Foreign Relations was present wearing similar Teneman garb only sans decoration considering his lack of any military service. Besides the Teneman coat, he appeared as any other politician in formal Quesgralion dress. Three other Ministers of lesser importance were also there. These men were still important officers in the Teneman, but not considered part of the true inner circle.

As per tradition, Kitchnok raised his hand in the new Teneman salute, followed by a loud and sincere, "Hail the Master!" The grey company at the table responded with the same salute and phrase. Kitchnok then looked briefly over the table before meeting eyes with Gastus.

"Welcome, Kitchnok," Gastus said calmly, "Late as always,"

Kitchnok tried to cover a snicker with a polite smile, "Hello Governor, glad to see the polls were in your favor,"

Gastus only nodded, "You may call me Prime Minister. Governor is a title my father referred to himself as."

Kitchnok broke out into an innocent chuckle, "Of course… Prime Minister," he said staring straight into Gastus's eyes.

One of the lesser Ministers interrupted. "And where is Nimx?"

Kitchnok prepared to answer but was interrupted by Drokktayr's deep, commanding voice, "I've sent him on an important errand. He will not be joining us for this meeting."

Kitchnok only cleared his throat and sheepishly found his seat.

"Well then, shall we finally get back to business," another one of the Ministers insisted.

Gastus nodded towards the Minister and proceeded to produce a pack of cigarettes from his coat pocket.

The Minister continued, "The Republic won't stand for this! They will see it as a fascist movement that can't…"

Another of the lesser Ministers interrupted, "As long as we keep the Hydrolettes under our wing, we're fine! The Republic relies on what we tell them about the status of this system."

The first retorted, "But it will seem suspicious if the Hydrolettes show no report for themselves. It's not like they can just disappear!"

Gastus finally spoke, "They won't be missed. The Republic relies on the Senate for information. As long as we control the representation of this system, we are perfectly safe."

The first Minister spoke, "And what of Drisko? When they realize the trade routes have been severed, they'll send a report."

The third lesser Minister finally spoke, "You know that our informants on that planet shall take care of that complication should it arrive. The Niskans are scum, they won't care anyway."

The first shouted, "But they will! Hydrolet and Drisko have not only strong diplomatic relations but underground ties as well. The festering underbellies of both worlds are heavily linked and both will notice such a drastic halt in communication!"

Gastus lit his cigarette and took a drag before speaking calmly, "It will only be a whisper in the wind. Even if Drisko sends a report, the Republic won't even bother. Besides, the final decision rests with the representative of the system, who is in fact the architect of this entire design. The Senate won't even consider the report. The Republic is not the issue here. Leave that to the Master. We must focus on our part."

The first Minister, now sweating, spoke again, "And what if the proposed bill doesn't pass? Besides, it goes against everything the Republic stands for. We'll be stuck with Hydrolet. We can't just entrap them forever."

Drokktayr's voice boomed, "The bill will pass. Do not disregard the Master's influence on the Senate!"

The first Minister fell silent, but the third spoke, "Of course, no one here does. However, even if the bill does pass, do you think the Hydrolettes will just roll over? We must not open the barrier once we've won. As soon as we do, they will surely bring this matter straight to the Senate.

Gastus blew a faint cloud of smoke and replied, "Once the bill passes, the Hydrolettes will have no diplomatic power in this system. They will be nothing but subjects."

The first Minister shook his head, "That won't stop the Hydrolettes from sending a report to the Senate, perhaps even a personal messenger. The Senate will see the truth and we'll be crushed. The Hydrolettes won't submit."

"They will or be destroyed," said Kitchnok. "Besides, even if the Senate agrees that we did declare war, it will not be hard to convince them that the Hydrolettes were being unnecessarily aggressive as they are so well known to be."

The third spoke, "Still, we must deal with them here and now. They have been almost too cooperative. They may be planning some sort of resistance. If they carry through with a successful offensive strategy, the Master's plan will fail and we will be ruined."

"That won't happen," said Kitchnok standing up. "Our numbers are too many for them and our weapons are too strong. We have the upper hand here. We are in control. They can't make a move without us knowing. Our finger is on the trigger. If they do attack, we will crush them without hesitance. Should espionage become an issue, we will tighten our defenses. They have nowhere to hide. Already I have sent interceptor teams from my fleet to almost every moon and planet in the systems. Plus, by order of the Master himself, I am valiantly patrolling the system with one of the largest interstellar fleets in galactic history."

"Which is another reason why you were summoned to this meaning," Drokktayr's voice was softer but still deep. "Was it also the Master's orders that you use the force field codes entrusted to you to create a highly experimental visual shield for your fleet?"

Kitchnok cleared his throat and sat back down. "I admit I was acting somewhat recklessly in trying to execute my innovation to our force field technology, but the results were a success, were they not?"

"That's not the point," Gastus spoke through a cloud of smoke, looking at Kitchnok with apathetic eyes. "Why did you deem it necessary to cloak the entire fleet, which you just finished informing us was doing such a commendable job patrolling the system?"

Kitchnok glared at Gastus, "If you had as much battle experience as I, then you would realize that the most dangerous of enemies is the one you cannot see. My successful reconfiguration of our force field technology has provided my fleet with yet another advantage to keeping the Hydrolettes at bay."

Drokktayr barked, "Did a satcam scare you, Kitchnok? What advantage do the Hydrolettes have knowing the location of your fleet? Let them know of our massive fleet. Perhaps it will discourage them from making any of these futile plans that the Minister here was talking about."

Gastus backed up the conversation, "Battle experience, Kitchnok? Are you talking about your extended tenure at the ivory tower of Wilhuff Military Academy? Or perhaps your time spent AWOL during the Geufsta Proximity Wars? Or was it your time as a bureaucrat in the Air Force?"

Kitchnok furrowed his brow heavily as he stared at Gastus, "Please Prime Minister, let's not lose focus from the issue at hand."

"This is an issue at hand!" barked Drokktayr. "I will follow the Master's wishes even until my death, but I am unsure if we can entrust the most impressive fleet in the history of this planet to someone who does not trust us!"

Kitchnok was broken from his staring contest with Gastus. "I was only trying to expedite what I thought would be a lengthy process due to unnecessary red tape!' he seemed to grow nervous.

"Kitchnok, we don't really care if you find it necessary to hide yourself from a sieged planet," Gastus said before he took a drag, "However, in such uncertain times, it is important that the Master's most trusted accomplices are indeed…" he stared right into Kitchnok's eyes, "trustworthy."

Kitchnok sighed as he gave Gastus an obligatory smile, "Of course… Prime Minister."

Techet finally spoke in his usual timid manner. No one in the room was surprised when he tried to play the middle ground of the argument, "Indeed, there is much reason to be cautious of the Hydrolettes aggressive nature. They could plan an assault on the fleet if they know its location."

"The Hydrolette's aren't stupid!" the first Minister called out, "They won't go down without a fight. The only reason they haven't engaged us is the aftermath of the Rebellion."

"Which is exactly why…" Gastus interrupted in a calming tone, "they will not win. Why do you think we attacked them after the Rebellion? They'll never muster an assault worth our concern. With our current ground troops and an equally impressive Air Force ready, at my word, to invade their home planet, I am not concerned with their offensive capability. We will not, in any scenario, be conquered."

"I still say we should have held the siege when the Rebellion was in process," the first Minister said.

"We wouldn't have had to hold the siege at all if your father had kept his mouth shut," said the third Minister.

Kitchnok interrupted before Gastus could speak, "Well now, we must deal with it and deal with it we shall. Let us continue protocol for now."

Gastus finished his cigarette and put it out in an ashtray set in front of him. "Kitchnok, return to the fleet and continue your *valiant* patrol," his sarcastic inflexion of the word was all too obvious, "Drokktayr, keep the troops' morale high. Everything will continue according to plan. The Hydrolettes have not struck so there is no need for concern. If they do, we shall reconvene. Until then, we will proceed as scheduled. Dismissed."

Kitchnok paused for a moment, took a quick breath, stood up, saluted and made his exit as dignified as he could. Techet left with a brief, half-hearted salute. The first Minister did the same, only coughing nervously as he exited. The second Minister left quickly with all the necessary salutations. The third was the last to leave, smiling as he saluted Gastus before making his hasty exit as well.

Gastus and Drokktayr remained. Gastus produced another cigarette from his jacket pocket and lit it. "That one should learn to be more respectful," he said pointing to the doors after they slid shut. "If he compares me to my father again, I will be forced to demand of his disposal."

Drokktayr looked over to Gastus, "Please, try to refrain from abusing your power so early in your candidacy. It will make you appear paranoid, first and foremost, which will make both the Teneman and the public lose faith in you."

"You really don't get my sense of humor," Gastus said as he took a drag. "But on a serious note, I don't see much of a reason for keeping those not in the inner circle up to date with these trivial group therapy sessions."

"The point is to keep them on board. We cannot do this alone and you know it. The Master cannot do this alone. That is our job right now, to keep the masses on our side. The last thing we want is dissent. You know your role. Keep the other Ministers convinced that everything is going to plan and keep the people convinced that this is all for the greater good."

"Everything *is* going according to plan and this *is* for the greater good," Gastus blew a puff of smoke in Drokktayr's direction. "Is there any reason I should be concerned?"

Drokktayr simply shook his head.

"Nimx?"

"Checking out our lead. I have not received a report."

Gastus only nodded, "It'll keep him out of everyone's hair for now," he took another drag. "But to talk seriously for a moment, Kitchnok is starting to get on my nerves. I understand that we are all equal pawns in the eyes of the Master, but for the sake of the other Ministers and my public appearance, I would appreciate it if he treated me as though I am in charge. It is my face that the public will look up to and my voice that will be conveying the words of the Master. Plus, I am the one controlling the machinery."

Drokktayr cracked a smile, "No one is denying that, Gastus. Kitchnok irritates us all and there is little we can do to change that."

Gastus tapped the cigarette ash into the tray with one hand and scratched his chin with another, "I just want him to know his place. You needed me to make this work. You needed me in order to kill Hynlon. You need me to keep the people from revolting. I am the keystone to this whole scheme and if you piss me off I can destroy this whole thing!" his voice grew in malice with each sentence.

Drokktayr face became serious again, "Gastus, calm yourself, please. We all realize this. Do not let Kitchnok reflect the rest of the Teneman's opinion of you."

"I don't care what Kitchnok's opinion of me is," his voice was still venomous, "I care when he tries to upstage me in front of the other Ministers. If you care so much about keeping morale up among the officers, don't you think it's important that the inner circle maintains a firm sense of who their leader is?"

"Yes, Gastus," Drokktayr tried using as calming a voice as he had.

"Does Kitchnok think he can be the phantom head of the Teneman? Or is he trying to press our equality under the Master by humiliating me? Does he perhaps even doubt my loyalty to the Teneman? To the cause? Would I have killed my own father if I didn't believe in this?!"

"Gastus!" Drokktayr shouted as he stood up.

Gastus looked up to Drokktayr, startled, and took a deep breath. He took another drag and regained his composure. "I'm sorry, Drokktayr, you're correct. It's outbursts like this that will certainly damage my image amongst the inner circle."

"Exactly, Prime Minister," Drokktayr sounded relieved.

* * *

Beio-Rhett was submerged in one of the engine compartments of the Donta Ryx. He was doing some last minute maintenance and making sure that the core was properly engaged with the main thrusters. The ship was essentially completed. The parts for the fusion canon arrived on schedule and were assembled precisely according to Mheages's designs. After the canon was successfully attached, Mheages helped activate the core as promised. The CO showed some concern for the process as it was indeed a dangerous process hooking up what could be considered a small star to an energy focuser. Luckily, Mheages's design was sound and the activation was without incident. With the core activated, Beio-Rhett could finally get around to rebooting the computer systems. Navigations and life support were finally operational, making Donta Ryx officially ungrounded. Beio-Rhett already moved what few belongings he had into one of the living quarters he claimed for his own. Dembo did the same. Prellina also moved her duffle bags worth of clothes and other personal items into the ship to make it harder for Beio-Rhett to double back on her position in his crew. Beio-Rhett did indeed consider reneging on his offer, but found it harder to do when she started sleeping in the ship. There were only four proper living quarters in the ship and Beio-Rhett only intended to use two of them. Now three were called for and it seemed that Singatt was heavily suggesting that he would accompany Beio-Rhett on his first job.

"Why?"

"You still have to make good on the advance of your contract. Like I've said, I'm protecting the government's investment."

"You don't trust me."

"I am also looking for some action."

"Sure you are,"

"Beio-Rhett, stop treating me like an enemy. I'm your liaison for your employer. I'm here to help, not watch over you, and as for the missions I suspect you'll be assigned, I think you'll need some extra manpower."

"Feeling left out?"

"I'm still on the Government's payroll, it's not like I'm trying to rip you off."

"I just don't want any tourists."

The matter was never clearly resolved, but Beio-Rhett decided to let it go. He knew that he would do better with a group than he admitted. Still, he felt like his ship was being hijacked and he hadn't even gotten off the ground. He decided to bury himself in the engine compartment to once again distract himself from everything else. It was hard enough trying to put the price on his head out of his mind. He regretted not asking the Dynothoxan what the exact price was.

As he tried desperately to put all these bothersome ideas out of his head, an officer approached him and looked down into the engine compartment trying in vain to make eye contact. Finally, the officer cleared his throat.

Beio-Rhett lifted his head at the sound, only for it to be whacked by a rebar above it. "Fuck!" he shouted before grabbing his forehead in pain, "What the fuck do you want?!"

"I am to deliver you a message from General Artinuare himself," the officer said nervously, handing Beio-Rhett a data pad.

Beio-Rhett glared at the data pad as he rubbed his forehead. After a few seconds, he reluctantly grabbed the data pad.

The officer saluted and walked off through the corridors of the Donta Ryx.

Beio-Rhett grunted and opened up the text message stored on the data pad. It read, "To: Beio-Rhett, From: General Artinuare. I have very important information concerning your contract. Meet me in the main engineering office at base HQ."

Beio-Rhett's brow rose after he finished reading the message. *Finally!* He was running out of things to stay occupied. 'Concerning his contract' could only mean that he finally had a job, but Beio-Rhett didn't want to jump to conclusions. He didn't want to get excited just yet, but wondered whether or not he should tell his makeshift crew. He put the data pad in his pocket and hoisted himself out of the engine compartment, making his way towards the elevator at the front of the ship. The strange design of the ship located the engine room on the second level, just below the bridge and the center room. Beio-Rhett walked through the elevator doors after heading up from the second level. The center room tied the entire Donta Ryx together. On opposite sides of the room were portals to the bridge and engine room. The kitchen and lavatory were on the opposite side of the weapons cache. The room itself had a simple beverage table placed in the middle of an "L" couch. The table also served as a game table and had a smaller holo-projector in its center. In the corner opposite of the "L" couch was a two-monitor computer station for miscellaneous work.

Beio-Rhett opened the door to the center room to find Singatt *of all people* sitting at the computer station. Before he mentioned anything about the message, he wondered why Singatt hadn't delivered the message and why the General contacted him directly. He stood in the doorway, ignored by Singatt. After staring into the middle distance for a while, he decided maybe he wasn't supposed to tell anyone.

"Bored?" Beio-Rhett was broken from his trance at Singatt's words. "What are you doing here?" asked Beio-Rhett.

"Checking your system uplink for any bugs. I tried sending the ship a message and was having some trouble, so I'm making sure your network's up."

Beio-Rhett tried his hardest to come up with some snide comeback, but he didn't have the spirit for it. He was distracted by the General's message. He instead scratched the back of his head leisurely and decided to wander around the warehouse for an hour before going to headquarters. He made his way to the headquarters to find some extra guards posted outside, to no surprise. After recognizing Beio-Rhett immediately, they let him pass to reveal the General sitting with the CO at the main operations table. The two stood up as soon as Beio-Rhett came to the table. Out of some strange sense crossed between habit and respect, he saluted the General as soon as he stood up.

"Finally," the General said with a smile, "Some respect."

Beio-Rhett immediately regretted the involuntary gesture. *Why did I even do that?* He put his hand down and grunted.

"I'm sorry," the General said, still smiling. "I was trying to match your sense of humor. But on to more important business, I'm sure you're awaiting the information I have for you."

"Yes, General," Beio-Rhett said.

The General turned to the CO and motioned for him to leave the two alone. He then pulled out a data pad. "We've recently received a report from communications that a platoon on a routine sweep of the Quesgralion Desert, Kaeko, hasn't sent in its progress report in over a week. All attempts to establish contact with it have been in vain. Naturally, our goal since the siege has been to recall all outpost troops, and for the most part, the Quesgralions have allowed them to return. However, this particular platoon has gone AWOL and we suspect foul play. Standard protocol states that we should immediately investigate, but as you know this situation creates a bit of a dilemma."

Beio-Rhett nodded. "But, General, haven't there been other platoons stationed on Quesgarlon that have made it back safely?"

"There have been," the General's face turned grim. "However, those platoons returned over a week ago, without incident. The same goes for other platoons scattered throughout the system. However, this particular one has not returned and has not sent any manner of report concerning their condition."

Beio-Rhett scratched his head. "Sounds bad… but I don't see why the Quezzes would want to capture a platoon leftover from the Rebellion. Are they trying to prompt you to engage?"

"That's our best guess," the General shrugged, "But we can't let that happen. That is why I am personally giving you the details for this job."

Beio-Rhett was scrupulous, "You came all the way down to a warehouse to give a mercenary details on a rescue mission contract? Was the governor on that platoon or something?"

"Don't be smart with me," the General responded. "Don't you see? The less people know about this, the better. That messenger didn't even know the details of why I sent for you. After I heard of the platoon's disappearance, I classified the report and decided the best way to keep all-out war from erupting would be to take care of this situation myself. I remembered you were still looking for a way to fulfill your end of the contract and this seemed like a perfect opportunity. I need that platoon back without alerting our people that they went missing in the first place and alerting the Quezzes that we ever sought them out."

"What the hell do you want me to do? Scour the entire Kaeko Desert? Like that isn't gonna attract attention," Beio-Rhett was getting irritated.

"Relax," the General maintained a calming tone. "I wouldn't assign you a wild goose chase. We do have one lead. There is a large Quesgralion military base located in the Southeast quadrant of the desert. It appears to be a top-secret facility, as it's not listed in any of the Quezzes public records. We only know about it from satellite imagery. The platoon wasn't even aware of its existence according to their last report. However, their last reported location was dangerously close to that base. We believe they may have spooked the personnel at the base and were apprehended. It doesn't make much sense why, maybe there are ulterior motives not concerning us. Whatever the reason, I want that platoon back. They are the only unaccounted-for military personnel."

"You want me to break into a top secret military base, with maybe hundreds of guards and rescue an entire platoon?" Beio-Rhett was in disbelief.

"And I want every soldier in that platoon back alive," the General continued, "That is if the platoon is being held at the base, which I am positive they are."

"What about the space stations?" asked Beio-Rhett. "I've heard the quezzes are taking over those around the system. Why haven't you sent us to go rescue the Hydrolettes caught there?"

"Those are Republic property and it's a damn shame that the Republic hasn't done anything about it. These soldiers, however, are my responsibility so I have no choice but to take action."

"You mean, make me take action."

"Beio-Rhett, don't think so highly of yourself. I would go myself if not for the fact that it would practically be a declaration of war. If you're captured, you have no military ID, no rank, and no allegiance. You're just a wayward pirate stirring up trouble and if you point a finger at me I can easily deny it because you have no official connections to this planet."

"I'm so glad you trust me now."

"Beio-Rhett, do you want the job or not? You still owe the government a lot of money."

"That doesn't matter, the contract says that my accommodations would be paid in full by a mission of your choice. That includes the parts and working space for fixing my ship."

"Agreed, that's why I'm giving you this one. I realize it won't be easy."

"You expect to have the Quezzes take me off your hands?"

"I expect you to prove what your worth."

Beio-Rhett sighed and scratched the back of his head. "All right, I'll take it."

"Excellent," the General gave Beio-Rhett the data pad. "Here are the details. I suggest you go over it with your crew before the debriefing tomorrow, here at Colett Base Headquarters."

Beio-Rhett glanced at the data pad before shoving it in his pocket and nodding at the General hesitantly. He turned and walked out of headquarters. As he shoved his hands in his vest pockets trudging back to the warehouse, he noticed some moisture on his nose. He looked up to notice that there was a very slight drizzle approaching. The sky was a blanket of grey, with darker more menacing clouds approaching on the mountain horizon in the distance. The sky was blotted out, letting no sunlight through, only cold, filtered illumination. Fall was coming, and Hydrolet had very wet Falls that brought heavy rain lasting until the end of Spring. There was little difference in the Winter except the rain would give way to hail, freezing rain and sometimes snow, though the climate didn't allow for snow except at the poles and the mountain tops. Beio-Rhett wiped his nose and looked to his right at the distant Northern Range and the oncoming storm beyond it. He breathed in the chilled, moist air preceding the first rain of the season, thinking again about how long it's been since he walked around the surface of his home planet, whether or not it really was. He could hear faint thunder coming from the Ridge as he walked through the arch of the warehouse where the Donta Ryx stood in all its former glory. It wasn't as shiny as when he first acquired it, but it was just as durable, if not more so. The miscolored hull patches and welded repairs looked like scars on a war-torn soldier. In the back of Beio-Rhett's head he made a mental checklist, which dragged his memory through his time fixing the ship. The hull took the most grunt work, but not a whole lot of mental exercise. Waiting for parts to arrive also added to the stress of hanging around his former combatants. The core was naturally a nightmare, seeing as how there was the slight possibility of a fusion reaction going unstable and causing a meltdown, but luckily everything went according to plan. Beio-Rhett was realizing more and more that his ship was finally done and he now had to hold up his end of the bargain. The fusion cannon helped put off sitting around the warehouse with nothing to do, but now it was official, he would go back to working for the Hydrolet Government. *23 years*. He never thought he'd see the day, or live to see the day. He stopped just before the docking port of the ship, looking up at the ship. *It's done.*

"Going up?" Mheages's voice approached Beio-Rhett from behind. He spun around to see the plainly dressed professor. "Just about to. What are you doing here?"

"Came to see how the system uplink went. I heard Singatt was having trouble accessing the network so I came to make sure everything was configured correctly."

"Oh, well that's good. We may have to disembark soon, so I hope it's something that you can fix overnight."

"It probably won't involve fixing anything. Just making sure things are linked up all right. I'm glad the cannon was successfully hooked up to the core without incident, but that doesn't mean it could be hindering the core's energy supply to the mainframe. Shouldn't take more than a power source configuration."

Beio-Rhett stared at Mheages blankly for a while before scratching his chin. "Well, I won't stop you, come aboard."

The two entered the docking port elevator and rode up to the top floor where the bridge and center room were located. Singatt cranked his neck around to see the elevator open, surprised to see Mheages there in mid conversation with Beio-Rhett.

"I'm surprised the system works at all. We finished it in such a short time that I didn't have much time to check for bugs," Mheages said as he stepped out of the elevator.

"Well," Beio-Rhett said in a low voice, "I'm sure it's fine. I have to round up my... crew and talk to them about something important. If you want to run a check, that's fine."

Mheages stepped up behind Singatt, who was still at the main computer station in the center room, "May I?" he asked.

Singatt stood up immediately, "Of course,"

Beio-Rhett stepped up to Singatt, "I need to talk to you and the rest of my crew. I finally got a mission and I want to go over it with everyone..." he looked around, "And on that note, where is everyone?"

Singatt shrugged, "Beats me. There's not a lot left to do on the ship, so everyone seems to be bumming around."

Beio-Rhett walked through the kitchen, which lead to the living quarters. He banged on the door that he remembered Dembo claiming as his own. After a few seconds, the automatic door slid open, revealing Dembo in casual, unkempt attire.

"You napping?" Beio-Rhett asked.

"Reading," Dembo answered, "What's up?"

"We got a job. Where's Prellina?"

Dembo looked to his right and left outside his room. "Try her room."

Beio-Rhett grunted thinking about the concept of Prellina having a room of her own *on my ship*. It didn't upset him too much, but he was somewhat disgruntled by how swiftly she made herself at home, and with little to no resistance from him.

He walked one door down and knocked. No answer. He tried the next one. Before he moved on to the third, he could hear the elevator open behind him. He could hear a faint voice addressing Mheages. It was Prellina. He walked briskly back through the kitchen to meet her in the center room.

"Oh," Prellina said surprised. "There you are. I was looking for you."

"I just got back from a private meeting with General Artinuare," he looked behind him to see that Dembo had put some shoes on and walked out into the center room, plopping himself down on the "L" couch in the corner of the room. Singatt was also standing in the doorway to the kitchen. Beio-Rhett looked over to where Mheages was sitting. "Professor, cover your ears," he said with a hint of dry sarcasm.

Mheages laughed. "Don't worry, the General trusts me. I think they consider me part of their 'inner circle' now, or at least they let me think that."

Beio-Rhett nodded. "Okay, you three," he waved his finger across Prellina, Dembo and Singatt. "I'd call Poko in too, but I'm not sure he really wants to fly a mission with me. He gets in enough trouble as it is so I don't think he'll like putting himself in it voluntarily. Anyway, the General contacted me directly for a mission he wants to keep hush hush," he pulled the data pad out of his vest pocket. "A platoon stationed on Kaeko Desert on Quezz II went missing a few weeks ago and the General thinks they are being held at an outpost there in the southwest," he looked at the map provided by the data pad for a few seconds before spotting the flashing red dot on the topographical map of the desert. He handed it to Prellina first as she was the closest. "So, the mission is simple. Fly in, infiltrate the outpost, grab the prisoners, fly out. The reason we're getting the job is that nobody on our side or theirs' knows that we are making a first strike. Plus, as mercs, we have nothing tracing back to Hydrolet."

"Except that you are Hydrolettes," Singatt said.

Beio-Rhett nodded. "I'm not saying it's gonna work. This is just the mission. I'm asking who wants to go."

Dembo yawned and stretched while still reclined on the couch. "I'm definitely going. Plus, I can just say I'm a holdout of the Rebellion." He slipped the sweater he was wearing over his right shoulder to reveal the hand and bloody knife standard of the Hydrolette Rebellion permanently inked onto his skin.

Prellina raised her hand. "I'm not a soldier. I'll definitely go."

Beio-Rhett sighed. *Of course she's going.* "You realize this will not be easy."

Prellina nodded, "I'm not going into the base. But you need a medic in case something goes wrong. Plus I can stay with the ship."

Damnit, she's got a point. "Alright," Beio-Rhett looked over to Singatt. "I know you want to see some action, but you realize that if you go along, you could jeopardize the mission, and the state of the war."

Singatt sighed. "I realize. But at the same time, you cannot infiltrate a top-secret Quezz base with only two people. You'll need another soldier. You know it."

Beio-Rhett grunted. "I've infiltrated some of the most secure bases in the galaxy on my own. I don't need an extra hand."

"Yeah, but you're not blowing this place up. This is a rescue mission. Do you know how many soldiers you'll be responsible for?"

"Soldiers! Not civilians."

"Beio-Rhett, you don't care about the state of the war. Just let me go. I said from the beginning I would be your liaison, at least for the first mission. It's not that I don't trust you either, I just want to make sure the mission is a success. I don't think it'll be detrimental to have another experienced soldier for this mission. Plus it's not like I'm gonna take a cut of the pay."

"There is no pay, remember? This one's free."

"Not exactly, you have your ship."

Beio-Rhett grunted. "Fine, but you know you can't wear your colors."

"I may be dumb, but I ain't stupid," Singatt said with a smile.

Beio-Rhett sighed. "All right, we have our team. I wish I could get Poko to go, but I know he wouldn't. Anyway, the General says he's gonna give an official debrief tomorrow morning, so everyone get some sleep."

"The General himself?" Prellina was surprised.

"I know," Beio-Rhett shook his head. "He's pretty serious about this one."

Dembo stood up. "Good deal," he started heading towards the kitchen. "I'm gonna make dinner if anyone wants any. My grocery list finally arrived. Mheages, you want anything?" he asked before walking through the doorway."

Mheages was glued to the monitor, fingers furiously typing away. "I already ate, but thank you."

Besides starting revolutions and being an excellent shot, Dembo also had made a hobby of cooking since his days in college. It wasn't anything he took too seriously, but usually in whatever group he found himself in, he would inevitably end up being the cook. He made a simple stir-fry of vegetables and lean meat cuts for himself, Prellina, Singatt and Beio-Rhett. Beio-Rhett took his plate back to the engine room to continue the grunt work he was doing before the General contacted him. Prellina and Singatt ate in the center room, after which, Prellina retired to her quarters and Singatt left the ship to turn in for the night at his bunk at the barracks. Dembo stayed with Mheages, watching him check the network of the ship, hoping to get a better understanding of the programming that would be keeping him alive while floating in a vacuum.

After Beio-Rhett exhausted every possible excuse for staying in the engine room, he grabbed his bowl and eating utensil and pulled himself up out of the engine compartment and walked back to the center room. He saw Mheages and Dembo staring intently at the monitor.

"Still at it?" he asked as he threw his dish in the sink of the kitchen.

"Yeah," Dembo replied. "You can get some sleep if you want. I'll stay up with Mheages."

"You sure?" Beio-Rhett asked.

"Sure," Dembo said. "Prellina's already bailed."

Beio-Rhett nodded, "Alright. Goodnight." He walked down the hallway to his living quarters. He came across the door to what he thought was Prellina's room. He went to press the intercom button, but hesitated. *What am I doing?* He could just go to bed, or make an effort. If he went to bed, he'd regret making the effort, but if he made the effort, he'd regret going to bed. *Too late.*

He pressed the intercom and spoke into it, "You tucked in?" he asked.

Prellina's voice on the other end spoke between laughs, "Yes, you want to come in?"

Beio-Rhett paused briefly. "Um… sure."

The door slid open. Prellina was dressed down in sweat

pants and a black tank top. "You're up late," she said.

Beio-Rhett only nodded while looking at the ground. "Just making sure everything is ready for takeoff."

Prellina walked over to the table in the corner of her room and sat down. "Would you like to sit down?" she said with a smile.

Beio-Rhett walked over to the table, which only had one other chair and sat down. "So," he said. "What do you think about living on a ship?"

"Well, it's not really a first for me," she said causally. "But I know it's something you're definitely used to."

Beio-Rhett nodded, "I guess I never really had a choice... but I never minded it. It is convenient having everything you own compact and ready to go. You're never tied down anywhere. It works for me," he looked over at Prellina whose head was lowered to get a better look at his face. "But... are you... sure that you're ready for this?"

Prellina reclined in her chair. "Of course it sounds dangerous, even lonely. Maybe it really isn't the life for me, but I'm willing to try it for a while. Not to say I'm gonna bail on you or anything. Don't worry about that. I'm definitely going to stick with you till this conflict is over. It seems like the safest place to be in the system."

Beio-Rhett was finally able to crack a smile, "Don't be so sure."

Prellina laughed, "You think that'll scare me off this ship?"

"I'm just warning you,"

"You don't think I've ever seen the 'horrors' of war" she graveled her voice for dramatic effect.

"Where were you during the Hydro-Baltan War?"

"Where do you think?"

Beio-Rhett shrugged.

"I was perched in the ivory tower."

Beio-Rhett chuckled, "You and Dembo,"

"Not everyone's a soldier, big guy."

Beio-Rhett shook his head, "That's not what I mean, I..."

"I know what you meant. You just don't think I know what it's like getting shot. Well, just because I was a university gal doesn't mean I was sheltered. After I graduated, I spent the next decade or so traveling the galaxy, practicing medicine abroad. I worked as a doctor in some of the saddest, most dangerous, forgotten corners of the universe. Planets plagued by economic chaos, civil war or a combination thereof. The Hydro-Baltan War wasn't the only thing going on in the galaxy then, but if you really care to know I did work at a clinic on Kaliekae, where there was some proxy warfare."

Beio-Rhett took a breath. He couldn't think of anything to follow up with. Was he trying to scare her off the ship? "I uh... I didn't mean to..."

Prellina couldn't hold back her laugh any longer, "Relax, chief, I'm just teasing you. If you're *actually* concerned for my safety, don't be. I'm not gonna run out in the middle of a firefight trying to be a hero. I've been shot at. I've seen all manner of injury. I've seen death. I just want to try something different. I think this'll be a good experience. If you think it's cause I have a crush on you or something, dream on."

Why am I bothered by this?

"I dunno, I'm just not used to... never mind," he stood up from the table. He was defeated. "Listen, I actually came in to apologize for earlier."

Prellina was still smiling looking up at Beio-Rhett, but she looked genuinely confused. "For what?" she asked.

"For being such a prick when we first met. That was very uncalled for. I was just angry... not at you of course. You were just the first person I saw that I could take it out on. But I shouldn't have, and I'm sorry."

Prellina sat there for a moment without smiling, seeing the sincerity of the apology. She looked down at the floor for a second before looking back up with that same, warm smile. "Forget about it. I was the one that decked you, right?"

Beio-Rhett couldn't help but smile. "Yeah," he said softly. He took a breath. There was no more to be said, "Well, goodnight."

"Goodnight," Prellina said as she stood up to see Beio-Rhett out of her room.

The next morning, Beio-Rhett awoke to find Singatt, Prellina and Poko eating breakfast in the kitchen. Dembo slept in and skipped breakfast since he was up most of the night with Mheages. When he did awake, he informed the rest of the crew that the ship's network was up, running, and bug-free. Singatt came to the ship to eat breakfast and make sure that the crew would be prompt for their appointment with the General. Beio-Rhett convinced Poko to at least come to the debriefing to see if he really didn't want to go. The crew arrived at headquarters a little after sunrise to find the General was already waiting for them and had the CO reserve one of the basement rooms to keep their meeting private. In the basement room, Artinuare stood with a Hydrolette Major, by his uniform, and a Niskan diplomat

"Good morning," the General said. "Take a seat everyone."

The five of them sat.

"Now," said the General activating the holoscreen in the table that stood between the two groups. "As you all know, a platoon headed by Lieutenant Eileknous Ttaurel has stopped sending their reports and we have failed to regain contact with them. Their last known position was reported here," the holo-screen depicted the Southeast quadrant of the Kaeko Desert. A flashing green dot marked the location. "As you can see, this location is notably close to a secret Quesgralion military base here," A red flashing triangle marked the location of the base on the screen. It was indeed noticeably close to the green dot. "Now it is vital to our current situation that we rescue this platoon from this base if that is indeed where they are being held. The soldiers could have acquired important information about the Quesgralions during their stay at the base that we could never hope to have access to. Naturally, I am also unwilling to allow for any of our soldiers to become POWs in a war that hasn't even begun, but keep in mind the valuable information that these soldiers may have access to and ensure their safety at all costs. I expect all surviving members of the platoon to be returned to the Bestton Base as soon as possible," the General manipulated the holographic map some more, causing it to turn to project a horizontal image of the desert. "Now, I hate to tell you how to do your job Beio-Rhett, but keep in mind that we have more powerful instruments than you do and the tower's radar is going to be effective within a hundred-mile radius, so I suggest you drop altitude before coming into this radius," a bright red circle appeared around the triangle. "Also, their visual capability doesn't seem like it will extend past two miles unless there are underground sensors that we haven't detected," a smaller yellow circle appeared closer around the triangle, "But just to be safe, I highly suggest landing outside this perimeter and engage the base by foot."

"That's gonna be a long walk," Dembo quipped.

"That it will," answered the General.

"Do you expect a clean getaway with this mission?" Beio-Rhett asked.

"Not at all," the General replied. "Even if you do manage to successfully infiltrate the base without setting off any alarms, you're still going to be escaping with a large group of prisoners that won't go unnoticed for long."

Prellina raised her hand, which the General found amusing. "Wouldn't such a bold move be cause for mobilization? They won't be fooled who's rescuing Hydrolette prisoners. They'll move to invade if they find out."

"That is correct," the General said. "We aren't in denial about the consequences of executing this mission. We cannot hope to stop the possibility of full-scale war, but we can delay it further and have our missing platoon back. When you're in the base, try to find a way to jam their communications temporarily. Do not attempt this until you have the prisoners and are on your way out. If their communications are dead for too long, they'll either fix it, or send out a scout to alert other Quesgralion forces. After you jam their communications, place a thermal charge on the power source for the base, plus any other areas that are important to the structural integrity of the base, get the soldiers on your ship, get outside their blast radius and set off the charges.

"You want to destroy the base?!" Singatt exclaimed. "Then the Quezzes will definitely mobilize. How are they going to miss a missing base?"

"They aren't," the General said. "Yes, this does mean full-scale conflict, but I think at this point we all knew that it was inevitable. And as far as I'm concerned, they fired the first shot when they captured my platoon, even though we obeyed all the terms of their siege. Our only other options are to leave the platoon in that base to rot, which I won't let happen, or leave with the prisoners only to have the Quezzes strike within an hour of them first noticing their disappearance. Destroying the base will buy us more time than you think as it is a top-secret base, and based on our wavelength scans, it does not send very frequent reports to the capitol. Whatever, they're doing out there, they're doing it on their own."

"Besides," the Niskan diplomat interrupted. "The time has finally come to end this disgraceful submission. The Executive Council has decided, with Drisko's support, to mobilize for a defensive strategy."

The General nodded, "That is correct. We have no intention of waiting out this siege any longer. In the past month, we have mobilized ground troops all over the planet to intercept their invasive forces. We have an arsenal of anti-space weaponry at our disposal. We are ready to take their first blow.

There was a long pause that Beio-Rhett broke, "You're ready for the war to begin… and you want us to set it off?"

The General was silent.

Beio-Rhett nodded to himself.

"It would not only be a tactful strike against the Quezzes, it would be a humiliating one. Can you think of any greater disrespect than a small group successfully infiltrating and destroying one of their top-secret bases?"

Dembo gave the first positive reply, "That would be quite the blow,"

Singatt looked uncomfortable. "I suppose if the Council has already decided on this course of action, I'm in no place to argue, I'm just a little surprised."

"As you should be," the General assured him, "The point of this mission is that nobody, including our side would ever expect it. It will catch the Quezzes off guard and put them in a state of unrest, giving us the upper hand."

"For a moment," Singatt argued.

"It's all we can ask for," the Niskan ambassador said.

The General spoke again, "Now I hate repeating myself, but I find it necessary to clarify the priorities of this mission. First priority by far is to retrieve the captured soldiers. None of them are expendable. Second priority is to jam communications. Make sure no signal gets out of that base. Third priority is to leave no combatants alive."

"You're talking about blowing the outpost?" Beio-Rhett clarified.

The General nodded, "Correct. If it comes down to it, leave with the prisoners alive. We will simply be thrown in to open conflict sooner than scheduled."

Singatt slumped in his chair tossing the situation around in his head.

The General waited out the short silence, then continued, "A few other things to know before you go is that there are a few friendly transit stations in the system that may be a safe haven should you run into trouble, or not be able to return to the planet."

"Friendly?" Singatt seemed skeptical. "The Quezzes took over the system, what havens are there?"

"It is true they have seized control of two of our three major transit stations, for whatever reason I don't know. Considering those stations are technically Republic property, they should have no reason to attack them unless they're declaring war on the whole Republic, which they very well could be. However, 25 still confirms Republic control, and there are also Hydrolette outposts stationed in orbit of DBIII and DBVII, which the Quezzes have not yet detected. Point being, should things go south, you're not alone out there."

"Good to know," Beio-Rhett said.

General Artinuare shut down the holo-emitter, "Well, that's all the relevant information I have for you. I expect you to disembark post haste. Singatt has my personal contact information so I suggest you bring him along. As for the rest of your crew, I leave it up to you. Return the soldiers to the Bestton Space & Naval Base. You will be cleared for landing there. Good luck. Godspeed."

"Wait," Singatt interrupted. "What about the blockade? How is the ship going to get passed the SETs? Sure it's an unregistered ship, but that can't fool them for long."

"Ah, thanks for reminding me," the General said. "In the data pad I handed Beio-Rhett yesterday, there are coordinates for a small chink in their armor, a hole in the blockade near the southern pole. Due to the lack of urbanization there, there are almost no siege ships around. As long as you are quick, you should be able to slip out without alerting them, as long as you punch the hyper drive as soon as possible. Are we clear?"

Beio-Rhett nodded for the group.

"Dismissed," the General said.

Beio-Rhett stood up first, followed by the others and the five of them exited the basement. Singatt walked out ahead, followed closely by Dembo and Prellina. Beio-Rhett fell to the back of the group with Poko.

"So?" Beio-Rhett asked Poko with a smirk, "You gonna come?"

Poko sighed. "I really don't want to. But at the same time, I don't want to stay at this military base all by myself. I ain't paranoid, but it just doesn't seem safe. Then again, this job seems like a suicide mission."

"So stay on the ship," Beio-Rhett coaxed.

"Why you want me there so bad?" Poko asked with a smirk.

Beio-Rhett chuckled. "I'm just looking out for you man, that's all. I don't need you to go in there with us, but I do want someone I can trust back with the ship," his voice lowered significantly.

"You don't trust Singatt? Or the girl?"

Beio-Rhett sighed, "It's not that I don't, but I just don't know either of them that well. Normally, I wouldn't sweat it, but we are going into quite the death trap and I wanna make sure I have a guaranteed exit strategy."

Poko grunted, "Shit man, I understand. I'll grab my bag from my bunker. I can conduct business from your ship for a while I guess. It's probably better than doing it from a damn military base."

Beio-Rhett smiled, "Thanks man. Get your stuff, I'm gonna warm up the ship," he said before sprinting ahead of the group.

Beio-Rhett leapt into the entrance elevator first, followed by Singatt, Dembo and Prellina.

"Is Poko coming?" Singatt asked, watching Poko run off towards the barracks.

Beio-Rhett only gave a quick smirk and nodded.

On the bridge, Beio-Rhett immediately took the center pilot station and placed his headset, "Dembo," he called out just as Dembo walked into the bridge, "Can you head to the engine room to keep an eye on the energy delivery, make sure it's calibrated right and adjust if necessary."

"On it," said Dembo, spinning around and heading back out of the bridge, almost bumping into Singatt as he stepped through the door.

Singatt apologized to Dembo before asking Beio-Rhett, "You trust me to do anything up here?"

As Beio-Rhett flipped a few switches and pushed some buttons, activating the core power supply and starting the engines, he pointed his thumb behind him. "Hop on the communication tower and make sure we're clear for takeoff with HQ,"

Singatt nodded and stepped up onto the raised communication station in the center back of the bridge. A large control panel surrounded the raised panel, leaving an opening on the side of the platform next to the entrance to the bridge. The panel contained a massive switchboard capable of picking up almost any channel for communications. There were two video monitors and a holo-emitter also, along with a regular computer monitor to access the ship's network and communicate with other networks outside the ship. Singatt opened up a channel to hail the control tower and threw on a headset, "HQ, this is the Donta Ryx, requesting permission for takeoff, repeat, this is the Donta Ryx, requesting permission for takeoff."

Prellina walked in next and leaned in the doorway, "Can I be of any help?"

Beio-Rhett turned around to face Prellina, then quickly went back to doing a quick systems check, "Can you work a navigation computer?"

Prellina nodded, "On simple cruisers," she looked over to the navigation station to Beio-Rhett's left and gave it a quick once-over. "I can work that," she said as she plopped down at the station.

Beio-Rhett took the data pad out of his vest pocket and handed it to Prellina, "The coordinates for the hole we're gonna punch through in the blockade is on here. Plug them into the system, so we have a course," he didn't look at her as he spoke. He didn't admit to himself that he was trying to make her nervous.

Prellina perused the data pad and found the location of the weak point in the blockade. It took some blank starting at the screen before she figured out how to upload the coordinates into the system, "Looks like we're good. The route is set for you to follow."

"Awesome," Beio-Rhett said, still watching the energy levels of the thrusters. He put his hand up against the headset to hear better, "Dembo, how're the engines doing?"

"They're rattling, but it looks like they're holding together. Energy flow is stable," his crackling voice sounded from the other end.

"Gotcha, I'm gonna punch the thrusters in a bit right now so hold on," he turned around to face Singatt, "Are we clear?"

Singatt waited, listening on the headset, "Air traffic is clear, they're clearing the ground space right now of personnel and opening the sky door. Give them a few seconds to clear personnel and we're good to go,"

Beio-Rhett nodded and turned back to his controls. The engines appeared to be running smoothly and the core was sending power successfully. His breathing grew heavy, but he tried not to show it, taking long, slow breaths through his nose. He looked out the windshield at the warehouse below, watching the engineers get clear of the Donta Ryx as the stabilizer thrusters blew hot air all around the perimeter of the ship. The air around the floor behind ship seemed to ripple from the heat coming off of the thrusters. This was it. "Where the hell is Poko?" he said aloud to himself.

As soon as the thought grazed through his mind, he could see the white figure running toward the ship with a large duffel bag slung over his back. He quickly made it to the elevator port running past the last engineer clearing the area, giving him a wink and a nod.

"Finally," Beio-Rhett commented, he punched in the code to unlock the port. When he saw the green light indicate that the port had closed with someone inside, Beio-Rhett was satisfied. He was jostled by the sound of the hangar doors overhead beginning to slide open. The massive gears that opened the doors started to crank with a mighty clang, followed by a low, metallic groan. The hangar doors creaked open, letting in the cold, grey light above. Beio-Rhett cranked his head up to look at the thick blanket of clouds above. It was getting darker and he could see droplets forming on the windshield, "Shit," Beio-Rhett muttered. He turned to look at Singatt again, "Can you open the weather channel to see what's up?"

Singatt opened up an audio channel for the weather in the area. After a few seconds he spoke. "We're okay for right now, but we better take off soon. There's a hell of a storm coming."

"Damn straight there is," Beio-Rhett said under his breath, "Are we clear?"

Singatt flipped the control tower channel back on, "HQ, are we clear for takeoff?"

Beio-Rhett cranked his head up again to look up at the dampening sky. He could make out the faint rumble of thunder echoing from the Northern Ridge beyond. His train of thought was broken by Singatt's words.

'We're clear," he said. "We may takeoff when ready,"

Beio-Rhett spoke in his headset, "Hang on, Dembo,"

"Gotcha," Dembo's voice said.

Beio-Rhett pressed hard on the throttle, firing up the engines to maximum upward thrust. Right as he was about to disengage the stabilizer thrusters, the door to the bridge opened to reveal Poko.

"Bout time!" Beio-Rhett said sarcastically, "Better grab a seat quick!"

Poko ran to Beio-Rhett's left, the weapons station, just as Beio-Rhett disengaged the stabilizer thrusters and the Donta Ryx lifted up out of the hangar. Beio-Rhett maneuvered the ship gracefully, first pulling it up out of the warehouse, far outside the base's air perimeter, then turning it around to face the southern pole of the planet. "Prellina, you send those coordinates?"

"Yup," she said, looking over the route on her screen. "You can take it manually or just set a course,"

"I don't trust the computer with this one," Beio-Rhett said. "I'm not sure how big a hole we're dealing with." With that, he fired up the rear thrusters and blasted the ship southward, just under the last layer of atmosphere. It didn't take long at all for the ship to reach the southern tip of the planet, where they would be able to break through the atmosphere and escape the treacherous siege.

Prellina watched the route the ship was taking from her screen. "Okay, the blockade is coming up here. I can see the hole on this screen. Just stay on the course. You'll probably want to speed up a bit. We should slip right through without them noticing."

"You gonna activate the cloak?" Singatt asked.

Beio-Rhett shook his head, driving the throttle further as he took the ship up away from the planet, "It may trick them, but they must have other wavelength sensors. If they spot us on one of those and see that we're cloaked, it might look suspicious, but…" he pushed the ship to full throttle, shooting up through the atmosphere into the dimly starlit void of space, "If we just run right through, they'll think we're nothing more than some unregistered smugglers, or pirates, probably skipping the planet for our own reasons." The SETs were barely visible in the peripherals of the windshield, but Prellina could see their location clearly on her screen. Beio-Rhett gunned the ship as far as it could go until Hydrolet was little more than a small blue speck behind them. After reaching .005 AUs from the planet, Beio-Rhett eased off the throttle and let out a breath he had been holding since breaking through the atmosphere. He slowed the Donta Ryx to a steady cruise and looked over to Prellina, "Are we clear?"

Prellina checked through some read-outs on her screen. "No apparent response from the SETs. I think we fooled 'em."

Beio-Rhett took another breath and then spoke into his headset, "You all right back there, Dembo?"

"Shit held together all right," Dembo said. "Looks like she'll pull through, especially after a run like that."

"Well, we still don't know how it'll take hyper drive."

"Probably better than that bullshit, I'm coming up to the bridge."

"All right,"

Beio-Rhett took off his headset and leaned back in his chair.

"Congratulations," Singatt startled him. "I guess you do know how to fix a ship,"

Beio-Rhett sighed and leaned forward in his chair, "Yeah, but it'll have plenty more opportunities to break," he looked over to Prellina. "Will you set a hyperspace route to Quesgralion II?"

Prellina nodded and punched in a hyper drive route after another series of blank stares trying to figure out the slightly different input controls from what she was used to. "There we go," she said. "Should be a straightforward enough route."

Beio-Rhett leaned over for a brief examination of the route. He shrugged, "Looks good. No asteroids as far as I can see," he smiled at her.

Prellina glared at Beio-Rhett, but kept a playful smile, "This isn't the first time I've done this, you know."

Beio-Rhett chuckled, "You better grow a sense of humor if you want to survive on my ship," he leaned back into his seat and uploaded the route onto the pilot station. He grabbed his headset again and put it up to his ear, "Dembo, I'm…"

Before he could finish, Dembo walked onto the bridge. He looked around the bridge, then at Beio-Rhett, "You need more chairs up here."

Beio-Rhett smiled, "I'm making the jump to hyperspace."

Dembo nodded, "Okay, You don't need me down there for this. Plus, I like watching the slip into hyperspace."

Beio-Rhett shrugged, "Good deal, but be ready if the core indicator starts flashing red.

Dembo nodded.

Beio-Rhett stared forward. "Okay, prepare for the jump to hyperspace," he said as he pushed the hyper drive throttle forward. "Engaging…" the engine ports behind the Donta Ryx lit up bright blue before being sucked away into space, successfully slipping through space and time into hyperspace.

Chapter 7:

Day One

"How did one straw break the camel's back? Here's the secret, the million other straws underneath it. It's all mathematics."

Beio-Rhett started out into the spiraling blue vortex of hyperspace as the ship was safely passing through it. He brought up the engine's schematics on his main monitor. He ran through a few readouts before saying, "Hyper drive seems to be functioning properly."

Prellina pulled up the hyperspace map on her monitor and followed the brightly lit course through a detailed star map. "Our trajectory seems like it'll be safe. No readouts of any Quesgralion signatures within a few AUs of our path, but who knows what kind of cloaking technology they have. If all goes well, we should reach Quesgarlon II within an hour."

Poko was fiddling with the controls of the weapons station, trying to pull up the target scanner, "That is unless we get intercepted. You don't see any Quezz readings, but they could have signal jammers, or worse, they could've hired mercenaries themselves to intercept incoming hyperspace routes."

Beio-Rhett leaned back and chuckled, "Ever the optimist, what are you doing over there anyway?"

"Just checking how you hooked my cannon up. Can you work it from here?"

"You can work everything from there except for the gunner stations," Beio-Rhett rifled through his vest pocket, happy to find a pack of cigarettes with a few left.

"Nice," Poko said, finally getting the interface to work, "I'm gonna leave the weapons system online just in case we do get intercepted."

"Good idea," Beio-Rhett said through his teeth as he took a drag off his cigarette. He lifted the pack above his head and shook it, "Singatt, you want one?"

Singatt laughed, "Trying to help me quit I see?"

Beio-Rhett lowered the pack, "Trying to be friendly," he said after blowing a puff of smoke.

"I didn't say no," Singatt said with a smile.

Beio-Rhett turned around and smiled back. He threw the pack up towards Singatt who caught it easily. "Is our channel to HQ still open in case we have any problems?"

Singatt nodded as he took a cigarette out of the pack. "We got a clear channel, plus our distress signal is ready to go should something go wrong."

Beio-Rhett turned back around to watch the ethereal spiral of hyperspace, "Good deal."

Singatt didn't respond as he was distracted by a flashing light on the switchboard. "Hmmm," he said as he took a drag. "We're getting a signal from Hydrolet. It has a high clearance, but it's not from HQ. It's not the General either."

Beio-Rhett leapt out of the pilot's seat and ran up to the communication station, "Well, patch it through, I'm sure they're friendly."

Singatt sent the signal to the video monitor, which flickered on and produced an image of Professor Mheages, sitting in his office.

Beio-Rhett smiled at the familiar face. "Hey, Professor, please don't tell me you found something wrong with the core now that we've taken off."

The Professor laughed, "I wouldn't have let you take off if that was the case. I actually just thought I would give you a word of caution. I took the liberty of doing some astronomical research of Quesgarlon II's surface. I thought you should know that based on some readings of the weather patterns I've assembled, I think it'll be a clear sky around the Southeast quadrant of the Kaeko Desert. You may want to push that two mile radius a little further out since the base's guards will have better visibility."

Beio-Rhett nodded. "Well, thanks for the tip, prof. Anything else we can do you for?"

"Just that, sorry to bother you, but I figured I'd do my part to help out. I've informed the General that I know about the mission and he wants you to know that should you have any non-protocol questions, you can field them to me."

"Will do," Beio-Rhett said before taking another drag.

"Be safe," the Professor said before ending the

transmission.

Prellina swiveled her chair around to face the group. "Well, what do we do for an hour?"

Beio-Rhett chuckled, "Well, since this is a suicide mission, I'd like to have a shot beforehand."

Singatt shook his head, "Not everyone's out to kill you."

"Most of the time, they are," Beio-Rhett said with a slight smirk.

Dembo chimed in, "Might as well treat every mission like a suicide mission."

"Why's that?" Singatt asked.

"So you can do a shot before each one?" Prellina shrugged.

Beio-Rhett laughed, "You're a keeper! And on that note, let's do a shot!" he made his way towards the door.

"You can't be serious?" Singatt said, standing up from the communication station.

"You don't have to have one," Beio-Rhett yelled from the center room as he continued on to the kitchen.

Singatt shook his head and looked up at Prellina who was smiling. "I regret this more and more every day,"

"Then why'd you come along?" Prellina asked standing up and turning to look at the swirling ether out the window.

Singatt took another drag from his cigarette, "For this very reason. I want to make sure this mission goes down without a hitch, and it seems that Beio-Rhett's trying to make that impossible."

Prellina laughed and made her way out of the room, "You came for the same reason I did, to get off that base… and particularly off of that planet."

Singatt shrugged and took another drag before being startled by Beio-Rhett's voice.

"Singatt! Get in here! We gotta make our game plan!"

Singatt walked out of the room followed by Dembo and Poko, who looked at each other with a child-like smile.

In the kitchen, Beio-Rhett had a few shot glasses set up and a half bottle of an aged Baltan liquor. When he saw Poko walk in, he lifted the bottle up to cheers him, "Remember when this stuff was contraband?"

"It still is technically," Singatt said. "There's just not really any pressure on the embargo since the war ended. At this point it's just on paper."

"Well, Poko got this for me while the war was still going on, so it's special," Beio-Rhett said. "Now," he said as he popped the cork off and poured some of the dark liquor into one of the shot glasses. "Who's doing a shot?"

Dembo raised his hand, as did Poko and Prellina.

Beio-Rhett poured three more and shot Singatt a glance, "Well, if you insist on being so responsible," he said as he passed the others their shots. "Now, Dembo and I are going in for sure, because we've done this kind of thing before. Poko, I know you don't want any part of the gunfire, so you stay with the ship. Prellina, you should probably stay too just cause it's gonna be hell out there. I don't know how well you can shoot."

"Not very," Prellina said with a smirk.

"Exactly," Beio-Rhett said. "Plus, it'll take two to pilot the ship. One to fly it out of here and another on the weapons station to blast any unfortunate bastards who want to tag along after we split. So, that leaves you Singatt," he looked over at Singatt and pointed at him with his shot glass. "If you want to come with us to get the prisoners, you can, but I think it'll be too much manpower."

"Too much?" Singatt asked. You're infiltrating a top secret military base and you think you can do it with just TWO people?"

Beio-Rhett nodded, "You said the magic word, 'infiltrate.' We aren't trying to storm the place. We gotta be discreet, that is until we blow it up. But, three people is six sets of footsteps, and I don't want to attract any more attention than we're already going to get."

Singatt grunted. "Yeah, but with two people, you only have so many strategies. You could use a third to possibly set the charges. Speaking of which, do you even have enough charges to level this place?"

Beio-Rhett scoffed, "You act like I haven't been doing this for a living the past 23 years. Come on, man,"

"All right, settle down. I was just checking. The point is, this is a multi-objective mission and you may need to do a few things simultaneously, not to mention rescuing and escorting an entire platoon of soldiers out of there."

"Escorting? These are soldiers, you don't think they can

take care of themselves?"

Singatt had finished his cigarette and put it out in the nearest depository. He rubbed his forehead in frustration and took a breath. "Beio-Rhett, I'm just trying to help. You have to start treating me like an ally sooner or later."

Beio-Rhett sighed and looked over at Dembo and Poko who offered no help at all. "All right, you'll be with the ground team, but try to keep up and stay quiet."

Singatt smiled, "Glad you'll have me."

Beio-Rhett poured one more shot and handed it to Singatt, "But only if you'll have a shot with me."

Singatt smiled and shook his head, "Fine."

Beio-Rhett saw that everyone had their shots and raised his glass. "All right! Here's to us making it through the day, alive."

"You mean the next few hours," Dembo said with a smirk.

The rest of the group raised their glasses, clinked them together and all downed their respective shots.

Singatt took his without flinching, as did Poko. Prellina was a bit put off, but didn't let it daunt her. Dembo shook his head a little as did Beio-Rhett before looking over to Dembo. "Damnit dude, what is with that fucking mohawk?!"

Dembo chuckled. "Why does it bother you so much?"

"Just tell me, is all. It's hard to ignore. Why are you so secretive about it? Zala dude, it's a haircut, I'm just asking what it's about?"

"It's just hard to explain and it's a long story,"

"Is it about Katoola?" Prellina chimed in.

Dembo nodded, "Yeah, but I just don't want to talk about it now."

"Why not?" Beio-Rhett shrugged. "We got an hour. It can't be that long a story."

Dembo grunted.

Singatt slapped Dembo on the back, "Come on, even I want to hear it now."

Beio-Rhett leaned forward on the table. "Dude, at least tell us what happened after the blast on Kastikae. Even I haven't heard that story yet."

Dembo sighed, "Fine."

Beio-Rhett slammed the table with his fist, "Finally."

"So," Dembo began looking at the rest of the crowd.

"Beio-Rhett and I were on a mission on Katoola. We were leading a small squadron of rebel forces to a Hydrolet base stationed on that moon. We also had the cooperation of a low-lander Kakeuwee tribe whose village was located at the base of Mount Kastikae. They lead us up through a mountain pass to get to the base, which was nestled on the other side of the peak. Beio-Rhett already knows this part, but I'm gonna reiterate for the rest of you. Unfortunately, not all the Kakeuwees were down with our cause. A scout from a different tribe that agreed to help out the Hydrolet forces saw our small squadron mustering at the base of the mountain and informed the base. As we made our way through the pass, a very steep trail up the ridge, we got ambushed by Hydrolet forces. First a bomber made a pass and dropped a fusion charge, which luckily missed us, but really set us in disarray. Hydrolet troops swarmed us and a bloody battle ensued. Naturally, we kicked ass. Beio-Rhett led the front assault and slaughtered most of them. I tried to regroup our forces and held the rear. They killed a few of our forces, but we definitely held them off. When they started to retreat we thought we had won the skirmish, but after we heard the engines of the bomber getting closer, we knew they were just getting out of the way before the next charge dropped. This time the bomber didn't miss. Our Kakeuwee scouts disappeared immediately. They probably knew all sorts of secret escape routes. Beio-Rhett lead the surviving troops forward trying to outrun the blast. I don't know how they managed to escape, but I fell behind trying to regroup the remaining troops."

Beio-Rhett interrupted. "We just pressed forward. Those Hydrolet forces kept shooting at us to stay within the blast radius, but they failed. We cut through them easily and made it around the corner of the ridge into a small outcropping where we were safe from the blast."

"Well, now I know how you survived," Dembo shrugged. "I thought for sure you were all goners. I knew I couldn't outrun the blast, so I looked around for my options. I couldn't even give the last few rebels around me any orders. I just told them to run as fast as they could. I was no longer their leader. I was just trying to be a survivor. I don't think any of the rebels left behind with me made it, but I found a small mud puddle at the edge of the pass. It was a reservoir for a small mountain creek that got damned by the rubble from the pass. As far as I knew it was the only option for me. I held my breath and dove in. Luckily it was deep enough for me. I couldn't see a thing in there. I don't know if it was because of the murky water or all the blood in my eyes. All the gunfire and shouting was blotted out as soon as I submerged. When the charge dropped on the pass, I felt the shock wave. It rushed through the water and broke through the rubble that dammed the creek. I went down the mountainside with the water and the rest of the rubble. It felt like I slammed into every obstacle on the way down that mountain. Luckily I stayed in the creek and the slope wasn't too bad. The creek emptied into a lake near the base of the mountain. The pressure from the fall sent me deep underwater, but I managed to garner enough strength to surface and paddle my way slowly to dry land. Obviously, I immediately passed out as soon as I made it to the shore. This is probably why the surviving rebels never found me. That creek took me clear to the other side of the ridge, which was opposite the side we ascended. When I woke up, I remember seeing faint beams of sunlight cutting through the dense foliage above, then looking down and seeing the murky darkness of the forest floor. It took a while to figure out that I was not only alive, but I had been carried a few miles from the shore to a highlander Kakeuwee village located up in the trees. I was surprised that I had remained unconscious for the whole trip, including being carried up into the trees. The healer came out to greet me and handed me some hot herbal drink. When I tried to move, I realized I was wrapped up fairly well in bandages made of hand-woven cloth, with a splint of wood tied to my leg. There was little of my body that didn't hurt, especially my leg, which was broken. I understood the language well enough to communicate with the healer. He took it slow with me, nonetheless, and explained that the village council would like to speak with me. I didn't have a good enough grasp of their language to ask where I was or how I was brought here. The healer quickly figured out what I was yammering on about and apparently the village was called Kastikae. I still never figured out whether or not the mountain was named after the village or the village was named after the mountain as they referred to Mount Kastikae in their tongue only as 'The Mountain.' I tried repeatedly to ask 'what happened?' in so many words, but the healer spoke cryptically. He said something to the effect of…

'Death chased you down the mountain, but it couldn't catch you. You were too swift. But when you stopped, it caught up with you. If we had not found you when we did, it would've taken you, but we took you from death."

At first this kind of talk was frustrating, but I sort of caught onto it later. They handed me a crutch and I found that I could walk. The village council was comprised of most of the people in the village. I think a 'town meeting' would've been a more appropriate title. The chief's name was Ikanan. He was relatively young for a chief and I found out later that he had only been appointed the chief a few years ago. They knew what I was, they even seemed to know a little bit about the Rebellion and which side I was on thanks to my tattoo which they recognized. The communication barrier was growing frustrating for everyone. One of the council, a younger woman whom they referred to as a high priestess of sorts, revealed that she actually spoke our language of Groakor. She kept it a secret in case her knowledge drew attention from either side of the Rebellion, but through listening to me at the council, she learned to trust me. Her name was Alaia. It was finally from her that I got the whole story. Scouts went to investigate the lakeshore after the blast. They found my limp, bloody body washed up on the sand and thought I was dead. They carried me up to the village, telling the healer that my 'spirit was departed,' but the healer corrected them, saying that my 'spirit was still with us, only it was laying dormant in your body.' The healer and the priestess said that it took both their power to successfully 'awaken your spirit.'

I did my best to express my gratitude and tried to explain my duties to the Rebellion and how I would have to leave them when I healed. They understood and told me that I would be welcome to stay with them while I recovered, on the condition that I did not bring any more of my kind to their village. Not that I really could, since all my equipment was destroyed in the fall. The scouts only found some pieces of weapons. My clothes were ruined too. The villagers lent me some simple robes to put over my bandages and the artisans stitched together some simple clothes. I really didn't know how to respond to their boundless generosity. At the end of the council, I had one last question, which of course was if there were any other survivors. They told me that I was the only one found at the lakeshore. The scouts did not venture up the mountain since they feared that 'only death could be found up there.'

They were probably right. Until recently, I thought I was

the only survivor. I didn't realize Beio-Rhett pushed past the ridge and avoided the blast. I'd be lying if I said I wasn't distraught. I was eternally grateful for the village's hospitality, but I felt guilty for letting my squadron down and for not helping the Rebellion. Every day I was laid up in that hammock I felt like more of my men were dying. It was terrible. My body was slowly healing but I felt like my conscience was slowly withering away. I constantly wondered if anyone would come rescue me. They couldn't hail me since my communicator was broken, but at the very least I thought Dresbar would know if his second-in-command went missing. A month went by with no word. I even learned what the scout's schedules were and waited for their return, hoping they'd mention something about more Hydrolettes, even though I promised I would bring 'no more of my kind.' Alaia soon figured out why I would watch the scouts return and confronted me about wanting to be rescued. She understood and wished me the best of luck in finding my friends after I was healed, but she insisted I must complete my healing process here and that I meet my comrades away from the village, because 'they will only bring death.'

I agreed with her verbally, but I didn't really mean it until a few weeks later. Of course I wanted to be rescued. It wasn't that I hated the village, I just felt that every minute I spent there was another I wasn't helping the Rebellion. It became an obsession… or, actually, it became a goal. It gave me something to focus on. I had to get better so I could get out of there and get back on the frontlines. The first month, I was waiting to be rescued. The next month, I was waiting to get better, but all the while I couldn't help but notice the world around me. Everyone knows that Katoola is a beautiful planet and that the Kakeuwees are such a peaceful race. There's something sublime about it when you see it up close, when you're living in it. There's a harmony I witnessed that I really couldn't comprehend until then. Not just a harmony with the planet, but with each other. Everyone understood each other in a very simple, yet intangible way. But after a few months I noticed something else. These people were happy where they were. Something not a lot of races have the ability to feel. And I think that is what separates the more technologically advanced races from the more primitive ones, not time, but that dissatisfaction with one's current state.

That's what I realized was the true difference between

them and me. I wanted to be somewhere I wasn't. I wanted something I didn't have. It's that constant state of desire that pushes us forward. Having something to strive for. Having a reason to press on, to grind on, even if one never reaches their goal, their desired state. And then I realized that the goal is not the point, and that it is the endless grind which perpetuates these races forward to create cities, ships, conquer space and then other races. Good things come out of this desire, but so do bad things. The Kakeuwees don't have that desire, I realized. They can be content with where they are. This doesn't mean they are lazy or unmotivated. The hunters hunt, the farmers farm, the healers heal and the artisans make clothes every day. At first I was disgusted by them, seeing them as inferior for not striving for something more or for having some sort of goal. Then I realized that they do hunt and farm and make clothes every day like other races. They do perform the mindless grind that we do, except that the Kakeuwee's aren't fooling themselves thinking it'll get them somewhere they want to be. They just realize that the grind itself is where they want to be. They don't need to put up some almighty goal on a pedestal to give them a reason to get up in the morning. They just get up in the morning because they enjoy living. They enjoy what they have and where they are. I'm not sure how long it took me to come to this revelation, a few months at least. I remember I just got my splint off and my leg was starting to work again. Then I realized that my mind and spirit healed along with my body. I was no longer trapped by some sense of unrest. Then I realized that I was happy in this village too."

"Wow," Prellina exclaimed. "I didn't know this would be a 'going native' story."

Dembo laughed, "Part of why I didn't want to tell it. It is kind of cliché. But, I hope you realize what I was thinking at the time. It just seemed like the right thing to do. Everything I valued wasn't important. And it didn't mean that I lost interest in the cause and forsook my comrades. Not at all, I just figured out that if I truly wanted to overthrow the evils that I thought the Government represented, I would start with myself. I realized that going up against them was just creating another unattainable goal to strive for to give oneself a reason to live. It became so clear. I requested permission from Ikanan to be admitted into the tribe. He seemed very pleased to have me, despite the fact that I very clearly was NOT a Kakeuwee. That didn't seem to matter at all. Alaia was pleased with me. She seemed to know exactly what had gone through my head. She gave me this necklace,"

He pulled a polished red stone amulet bound in a leather necklace from under his shirt. The red stone had etched into it a Kakeuwee symbol, stained in black ink. "The closest translation is *understanding*," Dembo continued. "She said that it was given to her after completing her apprenticeship as a high priestess. She said she gave such an important trinket to me because she felt that such understanding of the ways of the universe was uncommon among their people and even less so to an outsider, according to her.

They are somewhat homocentric. Regardless, I had no choice but to take it as an unfathomable honor. I took up an apprenticeship as a scout, so that I could get to know the area better. I would've liked to take up an apprenticeship with Alaia, but such an apprenticeship was only deemed necessary when the current high priestess's life was ending and Alaia was still young. However, she recommended me to the village's scouting guild. It was a small group that consisted mostly of hunters and trackers. Part of me probably wanted to join so that I would eventually find my way off of the planet, but I think I'm just projecting that onto the story. Mostly, I just wanted to get out of my hammock and outside the village.

The scouts weren't the main breadwinners for the village. Since they were the only group that went outside the village boundaries, they provided the village with their meat. The hunters would take down the larger animals they encountered, usually bagging three by the end of the day, which would last the whole village a few days. The trackers not only helped to locate prey, but they also were able to tell if people from other tribes had been scouting the area, or if more dangerous people were encroaching. I was quite surprised that they never found tracks of any Hydrolettes around the area. It was pretty intense terrain on that side of the mountain and navigated at a Kakeuwee's height, but I still persevered. The trees were easy enough, but down on the forest floor, there was hardly anything you could call solid ground. The swamp seemed to go on forever. On the east side of the village, the swamp led to the lake where I was found. This was perhaps the only area around the village where sunlight came through. Beyond that was the ridge, which the scouts avoided since the Hydrolet

Government set up base there. Out west, the forest stretched for miles. The scouts never ventured to the end of it, but they had an expansive area that they covered. Our routine trips would last no more than a day – we would be back by nightfall.

Sometimes at the request of Ikanan or Alaia, we would venture far beyond our turf, usually to investigate some disturbance they felt. I was always surprised to find that they were right. Either it was another scouting group from some distant tribe that was lost in the forest, or a messenger from even farther. Other times, it was a dilapidated ship, though never a Hydrolette, and usually there were no survivors. That was pretty much the bulk of how I spent my time for the next five years. I got to know the forest region west of Kastikae very well, to the point where I could even navigate it myself. Mostly I learned to just be quiet and stand still. The only way to survive in such an unwelcoming terrain is to become a part of it. And to be a part of it, you have to blend in. The quieter animals killed the louder ones. Anyway, that's what the mohawk's all about. Living with the Kakeuwee's for that long, you start adopting parts of their culture. I felt sort of strange with my hair the way it was and decided to cut it in their fashion. I started dressing like them as well. After completing a year of apprenticeship with the scouts, I was given this," he lifted his shirt up over his left arm to reveal a design of interlaced bars forming a band around his bicep branded into his skin.

"Ouch," Prellina exclaimed.

"I suppose you could call it their version of a tattoo, which doesn't really work with them since they're covered in fur. Instead, they brand designs on their arm to reflect their role in the village. They're usually simple designs since the fur will just grow around it. As you could guess, this is the symbol for the scout guild."

Beio-Rhett nodded, "Wow, you've been busy."

Dembo chuckled, "You could say that."

Prellina leaned forward on the kitchen counter, "Still, it just seems weird that you would just up and leave the Rebellion like that... I mean, I get that you were stranded and I'm not giving you shit about that, but you didn't stay there forever, right? I mean, you got off and then what? All of a sudden you don't care about a Rebellion you started?"

Dembo lowered his sleeve, then his head and took a

breath. "See, this is why I was reluctant to tell you where I was the past five years. I can tell you what happened, but I can't explain how or why it happened. It was all very internal, and the change that I went through is hard to really put into words even now. I guess it doesn't really make sense, and that's why I don't like telling the story, cause I feel like a fool."

Singatt leaned back on one of the cabinets, "Still, how did you end up getting out of that swamp?"

Dembo had not lifted his head yet. He picked the empty shot glass on the counter in front of him as the point of focus and stared into it thinking about how he would craft his response. The surreal nature of his experience seemed to be amplified when he crafted it into words. He knew it had happened. At the same time that short chapter of his life seemed like a dream, bookmarked by the explosion on the ridge at the beginning and at the end by…

The alarm in the room began to flash red, followed by a piercing siren. Dembo's gaze down the empty glass was broken as he was violently shaken out of his trance by the flashing lights and loud noises. He looked up at the screaming alarm, "Shit!" he exclaimed.

"It's incoming," Beio-Rhett said looking Dembo, "That can only mean one thing!" Beio-Rhett took one last swig from the bottle and slammed it on the counter, "Everyone, get to the bridge!" he shouted as he ran past the others out of the kitchen.

Prellina ran after him, "I checked for Quesgralion signatures before I charted our route! We can't possibly be intercepted!"

Beio-Rhett was already at the pilot station of the bridge bringing up the readout for the alarm on the monitor, "Well, it looks like we are. The Quezzes come up with new shit every day."

Prellina plopped down at the navigation center and brought up the hyperspace route on the monitor. "Shit, they were hanging out right by our route! I didn't see anything even resembling a Quezz signature."

'Why is it showing up now?"

"They're scanning the weapon's signature since we've been lit up."

By now, Singatt, Dembo and Poko entered the room. Singatt ran up to the communications station, "Should I hail them?" He asked.

Beio-Rhett was frantically bringing the hyper drive stats up on his monitor, "You can try, but I don't think they're interested in talking. Poko, get on weapons! You know how to use that cannon?"

Poko slid across the bridge into the weapons station, bringing up the targeting system. "We gotta get out of hyperspace for this thing to be of any use,"

"Working on it," Beio-Rhett responded. "How long do we have?"

"I'm tracing the weapons signature," Prellina said, frantically typing away at her computer. "We'll be in range in less than a minute."

"Bring up a timer!" Beio-Rhett ordered.

"What are you doing?" Dembo hovered over the pilot seat, "Pull out of hyper drive before they fire!"

"We're not in range for another minute," Beio-Rhett explained. "If we pull out too early, they'll be way out of range. If we wait till the last minute, we'll pull up right next to them and be able to engage."

Dembo bit his lip, "All right, man."

Beio-Rhett looked at the timer in the upper right corner of his monitor. He placed his hand nervously on the hyper drive throttle. "Poko, are weapons system ready?"

Poko nodded, "I've even fired up the turrets, should it get ugly."

"Let's hope it doesn't," Beio-Rhett grunted. He kept his eye on the timer and his hand on the throttle. "Hold on everyone," He glanced briefly at the ethereal spiral out the windshield before returning his steady gaze at the timer. He waited patiently, watching the timer run out. As soon as he saw the timer reach one second, he pulled the throttle back as fast as he could. The atmospheric stabilizers kept the crew from feeling the monstrous shift in momentum, but the structure of the ship definitely felt it as the blue vortex dissipated in front of the windshield to reveal the placid dark starlit void. Beio-Rhett's eyes scanned the homogenous canvas before him, unable to spot any tiny anomalies. He turned to Prellina, "Scan the area, quickly before they find us!"

Prellina frantically brought up the scanners on her monitors for every imaginable spectrum. The ship was older so her options were limited. She brought up maps of the area using different frequency scanners. Finally, an infrared scanner spotted the heat signatures from the weapons of a few fighters, which showed up as several red dots on the screen. "I see them," Prellina said, with fear starting to creep in her voice. "There are six, wait seven. And they're coming in fast."

Beio-Rhett took a breath, "Cloaked?"

"Probably, I only spotted them cause their canons were heating up, but I don't think they fell for your trick, they're coming in to take us out head on!"

Singatt chimed in, "Their not answering to our hail and it looks like they've encrypted their channel."

"Zala, the Quezzes aren't fucking around," Beio-Rhett grunted, "What the hell are they up to that they're so goddamn jumpy about." He strained to look out the window, but couldn't make out anything beside stars. "How far?" he asked Prellina.

"A few parsecs, closing fast... oh shit, wait, they're separating. They're trying to surround us!" Prellina exclaimed.

Beio-Rhett slammed the front panel of the pilot station. "Shit!" he looked over at Poko, "Can you get a lock on with our front guns?"

Poko brought up the targeting systems, "Definitely, but I can probably only hit one, maybe two before they start chewing us up. I'm picking up their signatures right now."

"They must be fighters, the heat signals are tiny."

"Shields up!" Beio-Rhett announced as he brought the deflector shields up to one hundred percent. "Brace for impact."

Prellina watched the red dots on the screen, "Two are circling around, four are coming in for a direct attack. We don't have any rear blasters?"

"This isn't a battleship," Beio-Rhett argued. "Do we have visual yet?"

"Negative!" Poko said, staring at the targeting monitor, trying to get a lock on the incoming signature, "They must be cloaked."

"Well, you'll be able to lock as soon as they start firing," he directed all reserve power to the front deflector shields, "Moving all reserve power to our front shields. Come on you fucks, make your move!" he taunted the invisible assailants.

Dembo peered out from behind Beio-Rhett before seeing the incoming yellow flashes, "There!"

A stream of bright yellow blasts came towards the ship. The small bolts of light bounced harmlessly off of the deflector shields, but not before rattling the ship up some.

Poko finally locked on the heat signatures and fired the front guns. "I see ya!" he shouted as he pulled the trigger. Larger, brighter blue beams shot forth from the front plasma canons of the Donta-Ryx, they locked on to one of the incoming fighters, which became briefly visible before being swallowed in a small inferno as the plasma beams tore through the fighters' brittle hull.

After one was destroyed, the other three fighters lowered their cloaks, revealing themselves to be standard claw-wing fighters of the Quesgralion Armada. These specific claw-wings had a slightly different shape, designed for hyperspace interception. Their yellow blasts continued to pummel the Donta-Ryx's shield as the claw-wings flew closer.

"Come on, you bastards!" taunted Beio-Rhett, keeping his eye on the claw-wings. "They won't get through the shields on their first sweep. Where are the other three?"

"Coming around the rear," Prellina barked.

"I can't lock on, they're coming in too fast!" Poko's voice began to show concern as he struggled to get another one of the four approaching fighters locked on.

"Hold on!" Beio-Rhett ordered as the claw-wings flew up and over the Donta-Ryx still firing, out of sight from the windshield. The shields held, but the ship rocked violently.

Dembo tried his best to hold his ground, but was knocked off his feet from the impact of the blasts over the top of the ship, "Our shields won't outlast em!" Dembo grunted as he fought his way back to his feet against the rumbling floor.

"The rear fighters are in range!" Prellina shouted, seeing the two red dots on her map close in on the ship from behind.

"Diverting reserve power to rear shields," Beio-Rhett informed the crew as he did so. The ship rattled again with the blasts from behind. "Goddamnit!" Beio-Rhett shouted as he held tight to the pilot chair, straining to stay in place. After a generous pummeling of laser blasts, the two other claw-fighters flew into view of the windshield as they passed over the ship before banking opposite directions of each other to come around for another attack.

"They're attacking from all sides!" warned Prellina.

Beio-Rhett checked the shield power, which was currently at 79 percent and draining fast. He punched in a quick command to diffuse the shield power equally, "I'm diverting our shields equally around the hull!"

Frustrated, Poko switched the auto targeting system off and grabbed the joystick to fire at the fighters manually. The two front guns fired a rapid stream of blue plasma beams, following Poko's motions with the joystick. The blasts trailed just short of the retreating fighters before they flew out of the gun's limited range, "Fuck!" Poko exclaimed, giving the joystick a sharp whack out of irritation. "Beio-Rhett, you gotta get to the gunner stations. They're flying in to close and too fast."

Beio-Rhett glanced at Poko and nodded. He turned around and looked at Dembo. Without exchanging words, a simple nod on both their parts made it clear who was going to the gunner stations. He got up out of the pilot seat and turned to Prellina, "Keep the shields up and equally diffused. Hopefully we'll finish them off before the shields go down."

Prellina nodded and brought up the shield generator controls on her monitor, "Hurry!" she yelled behind her shoulders as the two ran out of the room.

Beio-Rhett and Dembo almost collapsed onto each other as they piled into the elevator. Beio-Rhett slammed his fist into the button for the second floor. In a matter of seconds, the elevator doors closed and opened to reveal the second floor. Beio-Rhett ran out and to the left, Dembo to the right. At either end of the second floor main room were two long corridors that lead to the gunner stations. The glass gunner stations were somewhat vulnerable. Each consisted of a double-barreled photon canon that had near complete 360 degree mobility, protruding from a glass orb which surrounded the gunner seat and controls. The seats where attached to the controls, which consisted of two joined joysticks that were attached directly to the double canons. A simple targeting screen was mounted just above the joysticks. Beio-Rhett leapt over the back of the seat and plopped down at the station, quickly strapping himself in and throwing his headset on. He tapped the earpiece to make sure it was working and then spoke, "Dembo, you in?" He heard Dembo's voice confirm so through the headset. He grabbed the joysticks and yanked them in a few directions seeing the canons in front of him follow his movements.

Dembo finished doing the same. He tapped a few commands on the targeting screen, setting the range. After a brief flickering, six red triangles appeared on the targeting screen with a cursor hovering over them, which represented the business end of the photon canons. Dembo watched the cursor move about the screen, trying to follow the red triangles as they darted about. "I see 'em," he spoke through his headset.

Prellina's voice came through Beio-Rhett and Dembo's headsets, "They're coming back around again!"

Beio-Rhett swung his cannon all the way to the right to trail the fighters as they flew across his line of sight. He kept his eye on the cursor and kept it roughly over one of the red triangles. There were two on his side of the ship, but for now he focused on only one. He glanced up outside of the turret briefly to see the two fighters were in sight. The fighters' persistent yellow blasts started to spout forth from their front canons. The blasts struck the side of the ship, but luckily, they did not hit the vulnerable turret. Satisfied with the cursor's placement over the triangle, Beio-Rhett opened fire. Green photon charges shot forth from the double-barreled canons. At first they flew off to the right of the closest ship, but Beio-Rhett adjusted the canons slightly to the left. The two fighters broke off the shoot out and separated, one flying up and above the ship and the other below, out of Beio-Rhett's range, "Shit!" he shouted, frustrated. "Dembo! Above and below!"

Dembo was already following the other two fighters who were flying around to his side of the ship to make another frontal attack. He couldn't get a steady enough shot, before he heard Beio-Rhett's voice. He then saw the other two fighters fly out from behind him, one from above and the other from below. He placed his cursor right between the two triangles on the screen as the distance between the two closed. He glanced up to see them flying out away from the ship, guessing they would split apart to come around for another attack. Without hesitating, he opened fire, tilting his canon up towards the top fighter first. It only took one photon blast to the fighter's main thruster to obliterate the fighter, sending debris to the fighter below. The blast threw the lower fighter off balance, damaging its wings in the process, but not destroying it. The fighter pulled hard to the left to swing around for another attack, but not before Dembo quickly swung his canon hard to the left, still firing. The remaining fighter couldn't outrun the photon charges, and was incinerated before it could even get a shot off.

"Got 'em both!" Dembo shouted triumphantly.

"Show off," Beio-Rhett muttered, as he kept his eye on the targeting screen.

Beio-Rhett noticed the remaining four triangles pulling around to the front of the ship, heading in for another frontal attack. They were out of his range for now, but he cranked his turret as far to the left as he could to get a shot off near the front of the ship. He spoke into his headset, "Poko, you asleep or something?"

"I can only get 'em when they're in front, man."

"Try to get at least one, I'll finish the others off as they pass over."

"What's your range above and below?"

Beio-Rhett cranked the turret up and around to face the ship as far as he could, "Not a lot, but they can't just fly around the top of the ship. We'll get 'em."

Yellow laser bolts started to strike the front of the ship.

"Prellina! How are shields?"

"62 percent and falling fast," Prellina tried to maintain composure in her voice as she delivered the bad news.

The front plasma canons blasted blue shots at the command of Poko. The blue shots trailed one of the fighters, but did not make their marks before the fighter pulled up and to the right, flying over the top of the ship, followed by another. The other two banked to the left and flew under the ship.

Beio-Rhett pulled the turret up as high as it could go firing blindly at the two fighters passing over the ship. He swiveled the torrent around, trying to follow the fighters to no avail, "Fuck!" he shouted.

"Pick up the pace," Prellina shouted, "The shields are going fast."

"You think I'm trying to miss?!" Beio-Rhett was getting frustrated. He stopped firing and swiveled his turret to face the rear of the ship. He kept his eye on the red triangle as it flew into the range of his cursor. He squeezed the triggers to his controls releasing a blast of green photons that caught one of the two claw wings as it flew past the rear of the ship. Beio-Rhett watched as the fighter was swallowed in a fiery blast, "Three more to go!" Beio-

Rhett shouted triumphantly.

Prellina kept a close eye on the digital representations of the fighters on her screen, "Finish 'em off fast, we got half of our shield power before they start tearing up the hull." She watched as the two who flew under the ship begin to make their return for another attack. "Dembo!" she called into the headset, "Watch your left, they're coming in for a rear attack!"

Dembo cranked his turret to the right, seeing the two fighters fly up from below the ship and pulling out to circle around for another attack. He brought the cursor as close as he could to the two red triangles on his screen and squeezed the trigger. He could adjust his aim later. He trailed one of the assailants, jolting it sharply to the left to get ahead of it. The green photons strafed across the front fighter, tearing through its hull and successfully eliminating it from the increasingly perilous scenario, "Got one more!" Dembo called out.

"Keep it up!" Prellina called back, "I'm getting some higher heat readings from the one on Beio-Rhett's side. Beio-Rhett, take it out quick!"

Beio-Rhett kept the triggers down, trying to follow the remaining fighter on his side flying away from the ship. It quickly dove up, spun around and headed straight back for the ship. Beio-Rhett struggled, to keep the fighter in his sights, but was growing nervous as the fighter's head-on attack took him by surprise. As Beio-Rhett tried to gun down the fighter, the claw-wing fired all five of its photon torpedoes. The bright blue orbs glided towards the side of the Donta-Ryx. Beio-Rhett kept firing at the claw wing as it pulled away to let the torpedoes do their damage.

Prellina saw the incoming heat signals, "Brace for impact!" she shouted over the intercom. The ship rocked furiously as each torpedo exploded on the shields. Prellina watched in dread at the flashing red light indicating shield failure. The last two torpedoes struck the ship's hull, one only grazing the corner near the front. The impact from the two blasts sent Singatt flying out of the communications tower to bang his head on the edge of the panel, rendering him unconscious. Prellina fell off her chair, but regained herself quickly. Poko was knocked to the side, but managed to stay in the chair. Dembo and Beio-Rhett were secured tightly in their respective stations, but were still rattled around quite viciously.

"Fuck!" Beio-Rhett shouted against the pain of the seat

straps strangling his chest as he was thrust forward. "Get the fuck away from my ship!" he screamed to the fighters in vain.

"You gotta finish them off!" Prellina shouted through the intercom. "Our hull can probably outlast their blasters, but we can't take another torpedo assault."

Beio-Rhett grunted and looked out from the turret at the remaining two fighters beginning to circle around the ship like sharks closing in around a wounded animal. Beio-Rhett tried to follow one of the fighters, but they were moving too fast. They weren't attacking anymore, they were taunting. Beio-Rhett waited with his canon poised around the corner of the ship waiting for one of the fighters to come around. As soon as he saw the nose of the fighter pass around the corner, Beio-Rhett started firing. He kept the canon a few paces ahead of the ship, hoping one of the blasts would hit its target. The fighter took notice and began to fire on the Donta-Ryx, it banked left to make a direct attack on the turret. Beio-Rhett knew he was vulnerable without the deflector shield. The claw wing's laser bolts struck the side of the ship, leaving small carbon scoring marks running up the side of the ship to the turret. Beio-Rhett swung his turret slightly to the left causing a small spread of photon blasts, hoping one of them would hit the tenacious fighter. After seeing the bright flash, Beio-Rhett sighed in relief knowing that one of the blasts did indeed hit the fighter. He was so focused on the incoming fighter, he didn't notice the one that was still circling around the fighter. It was too late to gun it down himself as it was already making its way to the front of the ship. "Poko!" Beio-Rhett yelled in the headset. On your three, one's coming around, you gotta get it!"

Poko saw the fighter on his targeting screen. He kept the cursor for the front canon over the fighter long enough for the targeting system to confirm a lock; after the targeting system flashed red, Poko pulled the trigger. The two front canons fired a few blue plasma bolts that incinerated the fighter as it flew past the front of the ship. "We're clear," Poko said calmly after taking a long, shaky breath.

Beio-Rhett sunk into his seat, "Zala," he said through troubled pants, "Thanks man." He quickly tore off his headset and unbuckled his harnesses in the gunner station. The doors to the station opened behind him and he climbed out of the seat to make his way out. At the other end of the corridor, he ran into Dembo who had just walked out of his station. The too shook hands and pulled each other in for a quick embrace and a pat on the back, "Nice shootin'," Beio-Rhett said.

"You're not so bad yourself," Beio-Rhett replied with a smirk.

"Guys," Prellina's voice sounded over the ship's speakers. "You better get back to the bridge. We've got problems!"

The two ran to the elevator as soon as the crackle of Prellina's voice faded over the speakers. After a few seconds that felt like an eternity, the elevator doors opened to level one, where Beio-Rhett and Dembo tumbled out of the elevator and bolted around the corner to the bridge finding Prellina at the navigations stations frantically running through the ship's schematics and Poko picking up Singatt's unconscious body, trying to prop it up against the front wall of the communications station.

Beio-Rhett noticed the blood trickling down his forehead, "What happened to him?"

"He took a nasty fall," Poko replied using a handkerchief to wipe some of the blood away from Singatt's face, "Might have a concussion. No good at his age. Should get some water."

Beio-Rhett sighed, looking at Singatt, but was distracted by Prellina.

"We took some excessive damage to the front hull," she said browsing through the readout on her monitor.

Beio-Rhett walked over to her, "Are we going to survive?"

"I'm not certain," Prellina replied, "But I know for sure that we can't engage the hyper drive. With that frontal hull damage, we'll disintegrate if we try to slip through hyperspace. I've been trying to reroute power to the shields so that at least we aren't sitting ducks."

"Wait," Dembo said, "If we can't engage the hyper drive, how will we reach our destination?"

"Shit," grunted Beio-Rhett. He chewed on his bottom lip for a moment. "Well, at the very least, we need to get the shields back up. How's that coming, Prellina?"

"I'm trying," Prellina didn't take her eyes off the monitor. She typed rapidly at the controls, looking at different readouts, sapping power from every possible location on the ship that wasn't absolutely necessary. Even taking power away from lights, and heat in every room but the bridge, she couldn't get enough to recharge the shields. Beio-Rhett could tell she was growing frustrated as she typed away.

"Fresh rations? Bathrooms? What do you not mind loosing?"

"All of it," Beio-Rhett snapped back. "Get the shields back up now."

Prellina grunted, "Fuck it, it's not gonna be enough." She sighed and hung her head below her shoulders. After a second of brainstorming, she threw her head back up. "I got it!" she exclaimed.

Beio-Rhett nodded, "I'm listening."

"I'm gonna shut off the gravity," she said, already entering the commands into the monitor. "That'll give us more than enough power to turn the shields back on."

Beio-Rhett smiled, "I should give you a raise,"

Prellina looked over her shoulder at Beio-Rhett and returned the smile, before shooting her gaze back at the monitor. After completing the command, she rested her hands for a moment, "Got it," she said.

A low humming sound echoed throughout the ship. Beio-Rhett and Dembo began to slowly levitate. Prellina tried to stay in her seat and continue reading the power schematics, but was finding it increasingly difficult, "You gotta get some harnesses for these seats," she muttered.

Beio-Rhett chuckled as he began to hover over Prellina's shoulder watching the schematics as well. The main readout displayed the shield power, which Beio-Rhett, Dembo and Prellina watched nervously. Poko looked around his person as he noticed himself begin to float. Singatt also rose, his blood now floating away from his forehead.

Prellina tapped her fingers against the controls without pressing any buttons, waiting for power to return to shields. Finally she saw a green indicator flash over the shield power, "Finally," she said with relief. "Now, that should give us about 40 percent on the shields right now. If we stay put with the gravity off, we should have them recharged in a few hours."

Beio-Rhett took a breath, "Well as long as no one finds us, we should be fine. Since we can't engage the hyper drive, we're gonna have to look for a friendly station or ship."

"Friendly?" Prellina asked. "The Quezzes probably control

the system. We just left the only friendly rock in orbit."

"Just look…" Beio-Rhett was about to order, "Wait, no." he turned to look at Singatt. "I need you to get him to sick bay and stitch him up. I forgot that's why you're even here. Dembo, you check around the ship for any internal damage. Poko, get on the com station.

"We should send a report back to Bestton," Prellina suggested as she shoved herself from the navigation station over to where Singatt was floating. "Just to inform the General of our condition."

"But he can't send a rescue squad," Dembo said, trying to move himself towards the doorway. "It's bad enough that those fighters saw us. We're supposed to be doing this covertly."

"No," Prellina argued as she took Singatt from Poko's arms. "We should just send a status report. I know we're on our own, but he should know that we will be delayed."

Dembo nodded as he pulled himself out of the bridge, "Fair enough, holler if you need me."

Beio-Rhett looked over to Poko, "Can you get on the tower and shoot a message to the General?"

With no more than a nod, Poko pulled himself up over the control panel for the com station and began to type out a message as Beio-Rhett pulled himself down to the navigation station, "I'm gonna scan the area and see if we can't find someone who's got a docking bay and some tools.

Prellina took Singatt's weightless body over her shoulders and pushed off the wall down the through doorway towards the sick bay via the center room. "Good luck guys," she called out as she floated out of the bridge with Singatt.

Poko typed away at the comm station, looking at the monitor intently. "Shouldn't we just ring HQ directly for something like this?" he asked.

Beio-Rhett was staring at the virtual star maps intently as he replied, "Why take the time? They can't do anything to help us. Just let them know we'll be delayed… where the fuck are we?" he muttered to himself.

Poko shrugged and kept typing, "You know it just occurred to me, man. What if those interceptors sent a transmission back to Quesgarlon?"

"What if? Just a couple of space pirates en route to the

home planet. Why would they bother?"

"Why should they intercept us in the first place?" Poko was looking at Beio-Rhett now.

Beio-Rhett stopped trying to navigate the star maps and paused for a moment. He turned to face Poko, "Why were there so many? That was a full on, strike force waiting for us." He looked down and gritted his teeth together, "You think maybe this isn't just a suicide mission, but an execution?"

Poko chuckled, "Man, you're too paranoid. If they wanted you dead, they would've done it a long time ago. I'm more worried about the Quezzes now. They're way too wound up about this shit. Seven interceptors for one pirate ship? Either they're playing it way too safe, or they know who you are and they know you're coming." He gave Beio-Rhett a very sincere look.

Beio-Rhett only nodded slowly, then returned his gaze to the monitor, "Why do you always gotta get me worrying about these things?" he said through a troubled smile.

Poko smiled and continued to write his message to the General, "You gotta plan for the worst."

Prellina wiped away the rest of the blood on Singatt's forehead. A rather gnarly gash graced the flesh above his right eyebrow. She took out some disinfectant and doused a cloth with some before applying it to the gash. Singatt was roused by the sting of the sterilizing liquid. "Ow!" he said groggily.

"Be still," said Prellina. "You had quite the fall," she said softly, while dabbing the wound with the disinfectant.

Singatt blinked and rubbed his forehead, next to the gash. "So we made it?"

"Barely," Prellina said, trying to concentrate on dabbing the wound. "But we can't make the jump to hyperspace due to the damage. Beio-Rhett's looking for a friendly station right now."

Singatt grunted at the sting of the disinfectant, "Any good news?" he asked.

Prellina smiled brightly. "We're alive," she said in a warm tone.

Beio-Rhett scanned the visual readout in front of him, looking for familiar star patterns without avail. "We're still in the system, I don't know why I can't find a fucking reference point."

"Pulling out of hyperspace so fast probably jolted the nav system," Poko said as he typed away. "Give it a second to reassess and it should give you the stopping point of Prellina's trail…" he typed in a few more keys. "Message sent."

Beio-Rhett took a breath and stopped his search for a moment. He scratched the back of his head and grunted. "Man, you really are a shitty shot."

Poko leaned back in the com station chair, "Fuck you man. I sell guns, I don't shoot 'em."

Beio-Rhett chuckled. "You're gonna have to learn to if you want to roll with me."

Poko smiled, "I didn't want to roll with you, you asked me to."

Beio-Rhett nodded, "I guess I did. At least I know that you got my back in a fist fight."

Poko nodded, watching the communications monitor waiting for a positive signal readout. "Always man. It's that girl who you should be worried about. I wouldn't take her out in the field if I were you."

Beio-Rhett turned around in his chair, "I don't intend to. Don't worry about her. She seems to know her way around a ship's system and we'll see how well she stitches Singatt up to see if she's worth keeping around as a medic."

Poko slowly floated above the com chair and began to turn backwards until he was upside down. "That gravity idea was pretty sharp."

Beio-Rhett only nodded in reply before the navigations monitor flickered. "Now we're talking. Looks like the ship's figured out where the hell it is." He typed in a few commands and scrolled through recognizable signatures. "And it looks like we're definitely in the middle of fuck-all… which is good since I figure the Quezzes control almost everything in the system now."

"There's gotta be some independent stations somewhere," Poko mused

"I'm looking," Beio-Rhett said as he continued to scroll. "Oh hey," he said.

Poko turned himself right side up and pushed himself towards the front of the bridge, "What's up?"

"Here's we go," Beio-Rhett cracked a smile. "It's a Hydrolette signature, probably a military outpost. DB Docking Station H-3. It's a couple of parsecs away, but we should be able to make it there at high speed within the hour. Then we can make repairs and be on our way." He clapped his hands together and then spoke into the ship's intercom. "We found a safe haven. It's a Hydrolette outpost. We'll be there in about a half hour."

Prellina looked up to the speaker in sick bay after hearing Beio-Rhett's voice. "Well, I guess we can kick back for a while," she said going through the medicinal supplies looking for some antiseptic ointment. "Still, even when we get to that station, it'll be a while before we get all fixed up." She paused before applying the ointment to Singatt's forehead. "I hope we aren't costing any lives."

Singatt looked up as she spread a small dab of ointment on his wound, "How do you mean?"

"The prisoners," Prellina clarified. "The General didn't mention if we have a time table on this mission. What if they're executing them as we speak?!" She began to raise her voice.

Singatt shook his head after the dab of ointment, "I guess there's no way to know. The General knows just as much as we do. I can't find any reason that the Quezzes would be executing a small squad that they happened to find roaming the desert for reasons that had nothing to do with their little coup."

After smearing the ointment a bit and wiping up the last bits of blood, Prellina produced an adhesive strip from the drawer. "Yeah, but they don't know that. The Quezzes are acting fucking insane right now. They could be convinced that that squad was planning on spying or sabotaging the Teneman regardless of any verbal or physical evidence to the contrary. She slapped the adhesive strip on and pressed against it to make sure it stuck. "Looks like you won't need stitches."

Singatt rubbed the bandaged wound gently. "You're good," he said.

"You're lucky," Prellina retorted. "I was going to be a doctor before going into biology full-time."

"So I heard," Singatt said while nodding, "I'm gonna head back to the bridge. Thanks," he said gently rubbing his forehead above the wound.

Prellina nodded in reply, but didn't seem to acknowledge Singatt in any other way. She started off into the middle distance of the room, seeming in deep thought as her body began to float aimlessly.

After a very long half hour of cruising through empty

space, the Hydrolette outpost was finally in sight. Beio-Rhett was slowly rotating above the pilot's seat with his hands crossed behind his head. His eyes were open, but he didn't seem to be looking at anything. Poko had hooked his leg under the communications panel so that he would stay put as he dozed off with his arms folded in front of him. Prellina remained in sick bay with the same blank stare whilst Singatt was floating around the center of the room having grown tired of waiting to reach the station at the bridge. Dembo continued checking the engine compartments and core for any serious internal damage, for the duration of the short trip.

While right side up, Beio-Rhett spotted the very small ring-shaped space station in the distance. Beio-Rhett immediately broke out of his trance and pulled himself down to the pilot's seat. He turned on the intercom and put his mouth close to the microphone. "Rise and shine everyone!" his voice rung throughout the ship startling Prellina and Singatt and rousing Poko from his nap. "The station is in sight. I'm gonna attempt to hail them, so everyone be ready for anything."

Beio-Rhett opened up a channel on the main monitor and pressed the hail button. "This is Captain Beio-Rhett of the Donta Ryx, requesting permission to land," he held on the button waiting for a response as the hail indicator flashed green indicating a clean channel.

Poko snickered, "Captain?"

Beio-Rhett took his finger off the button, "It's my fucking ship," he said with a sneer before pressing the button again. "Repeat, this is Captain Beio-Rhett of the Donta Ryx, requesting permission to land, do you copy?" He watched the green indicator continue to flash. "Oh for fuck's sake," he finally exclaimed. "It's a clean channel! Come on!"

A voice crackled through static before becoming clear, "This is DB H-3 Station Control, copy, please repeat your identification."

Beio-Rhett repeated, now rather disgruntled, "Captain Beio-Rhett of the Donta Ryx."

There was a pause, "Um… Captain, your ship is definitely registered in our landing archives, but the most recent status update indicates that ship was destroyed several years ago."

"Well, obviously your status update is not the most

recent," Beio-Rhett snidely remarked.

"Apparently," the voice continued as though it didn't notice Beio-Rhett's sarcasm. "The ship looks the same, but there's a completely different signature."

"It was just rebuilt," Beio-Rhett clarified. "The government may have wiped the original signature from the military database, and I haven't reregistered the ship since," he let his hand off the channel button, "Nor do I ever intend to," he whispered with a smirk to Poko.

The voice on the other end was silent, "Well, if that's the case, I'm afraid I can't allow you to land, Captain. We are a military installation and during a time of crisis such as we are now in, it would be very unwise to allow an unregistered ship to dock."

Beio-Rhett grunted and pressed the channel button again, "I understand, but I am currently under contract with the Hydrolette Military. I'm on a mission that is of the utmost importance to General Artinuare himself and we were delayed by a Quesgralion ambush. We need safe haven to make repairs."

Poko tried not to laugh too loud, "Say 'please,' man."

Beio-Rhett shot Poko a quick look of annoyance before returning to the tenacious Station Officer.

"Captain, with all due respect, there is no reason for us to believe that you are under contract with the Hydrolette Military," the voice informed.

"It's gotta be on file. Can't you request it or look it up?" Beio-Rhett began to show some desperation in his voice.

"I could send a request, but it may take a few hours, even days to hear back a positive report. Paperwork for mercenary expenditures is usually under the table and records are kept in locked cabinets."

"Call the General himself!" Beio-Rhett grew frustrated.

"Captain," the voice remained calm, "If I were to bother the Grand General of the Hydrolette Forces with every pirate that came across our station, I don't think he'd..."

"Station Officer, this is Lieutenant Reuk Singatt, MP," Singatt's voice interrupted that of the station officer. "Go ahead and look up my file, I am registered and active," he said as he floated into the bridge.

There was silence on the other side of the channel. Finally, the voice responded, "Lieutenant Singatt, we have a positive ID.

Might I ask what you are doing on an unregistered ship with a group of mercenaries."

"Military liaison for situations like these," he responded calmly.

Beio-Rhett looked up at Singatt and nodded, impressed.

"Well, you show a positive ID. We are obligated to let any vessel containing active military personnel dock with our station. If you take responsibility for this ship's crew we will grant permission to land."

"It's a deal," Singatt said with a smirk.

The voice was silent for a moment. Beio-Rhett looked at the green indicator light, then up at Singatt, then back at the light. The voice continued.

"Captain Beio-Rhett, you are clear for landing on platform C-4. I'm glad to see you guys made it past the siege."

"I'm glad the Quezzes haven't wiped you guys out," Beio-Rhett responded, now relaxed.

"Well, they can't take us all out," the voice responded, also in a light-hearted tone.

"Glad to hear it," Beio-Rhett said. "Setting a manual course for landing pad C-4."

"Proceed," the voice responded.

The Donta Ryx's thrusters flared for a moment before the ship cruised towards the station at a moderate pace, turning on a slight axis to make for a smooth contact with landing platform C-4. Inside the ship, Beio-Rhett maneuvered the controls delicately, following the preset course displayed on the monitor. As he followed the green wire readout in front of him, the bridge doors opened to reveal Dembo and Prellina floating in.

'We clear to land?" Prellina asked.

"Yep," Beio-Rhett replied as he continued to bring the ship in closer to the platform. "Could you actually run a quick check of the ship's systems?"

Prellina pushed herself from the wall towards the navigation station and pulled herself down into the seat. After typing in a few commands, a brief summary of the ship's status appeared on the monitor in front of her. "We're doing okay. Ship is holding together. The hull is definitely a wreck, but the shields are almost completely recharged.

"Good," Beio-Rhett said, still focusing on the green wire

image in front of him. "Dembo? Any serious damage?"

Dembo hovered behind Beio-Rhett, "Nothing serious. Some shit got knocked around from the impact, but other than that, we're okay."

Beio-Rhett only nodded and continued his descent. The Donta Ryx made a smooth entry into the station's gravity field before slipping through the force field of platform C-4. The ship's anti-thrusters slowed the ship's descent as the landing gear protruded from the bottom of the ship making for a safe, successful landing. After a final blast from the stabilizers, the ship's engines grew quiet. Hydrolette technicians who were already milling about the platform looked up in awe at the significant carbon scoring along the front of the hull. They watched as the indicator lights around the entrance portal began to flash. After a grinding metallic hum, the portal doors opened to reveal the entrance elevator bearing four Hydrolettes and one Niskan. A stepping platform lowered from the portal, providing a convenient exit for the five strangers.

The doors to platform C-4 opened to reveal several Hydrolettes in formal military attire. One Hydrolette bearing commander's colors walked briskly in front of the group. Stopping just short of the group of five strangers, he saluted them. "Welcome," he said. "My name is Commander Scaerott Ttak." He was tall for a Hydrolette, a little shorter than Singatt.

"Beio-Rhett," he saluted. "Thanks for letting us land."

"Of course," said Ttak warmly. "I am happy to see other Hydrolettes have successfully evaded the siege."

"Barely," Beio-Rhett responded. "How are you guys holding out here?"

Ttak shrugged. "Barely. The threat of the Quezzes coming in to crush us is constantly hovering above our heads. But it's important that Hydrolet maintains active outposts throughout the system to maintain some ability to monitor the Quezzes' activity. So far we've been lucky, but we never know what tomorrow holds."

Beio-Rhett nodded, "Yeah it's tough," he replied gruffly. "Well, as you can see, my ship is a wreck," he motioned over to the obviously ravaged ship. "Lieutenant Singatt can confirm that we are currently under contract with the Hydrolette Military on a time sensitive mission. Would it be too much to ask to occupy one of your landing platforms to make repairs?"

Ttak smiled and shook his head. "If what you say is true, it would be my honor to have my men repair the ship for you while you rest. I can see from your hull that you must have had quite an eventful day. Please feel free to take safe haven at this station. We have open quarters that you may use whilst your ship is being repaired."

This more than generous display of hospitality took Beio-Rhett by surprise, "Um... wow... um, thanks," he finally managed to get out. "I um... well, this is my crew, should you have any reason to address them. Lieutenant Singatt, whom you should know from pulling up his file. My good friends Dembo Bebsin and Poko Sveryntes, who are both unregistered, so don't bother looking them up. And this is Prellina Jemenae, who's the most recent addition to my crew."

Prellina smiled and nodded while Poko and Dembo gave colder salutations. Singatt saluted in the proper fashion. After a less than awkward silence, the party continued back towards the door to the platform and made their way into the station.

Inside the station was a hustle and bustle of activity, although an air of dismay hung over the industrious personnel, which consisted mostly of Hydrolettes in military garb. However, several other species scurried around, perhaps transients or other mercenaries.

Beio-Rhett tried to keep his eyes forward and not make eye contact. He trailed behind the group, keeping his eyes on his crew and more importantly, this rather friendly Ttak who led the way. *Too friendly.* He took a few quick glances at the personnel around him. They went about their business as though it was like any other ordinary day, only a few stopping to look up at the strangers. Still, there was an air of unrest that flowed throughout the station. *Something's wrong.* Of course something was wrong. Their home planet was under siege, but even if that was the case, *why are they acting like it's okay?* Beio-Rhett considered his own situation. He knew the art of trying one's best to ignore surrounding torment. *Everyone has their own coping mechanisms.*

"Through here," Ttak's voice drew Beio-Rhett's attention to a door in front of the party.

Beio-Rhett's crew walked through the door along with the officers to what looked like a dining hall. A long dining table was set up perpendicular to the door with a long window looking out into space beyond it.

"Oh," Prellina was the only one of the group to mutter anything.

Ttak walked towards the head of the table, "This is the officer's mess hall. It's somewhat more secluded than our larger mess hall, and I assume you're crew would like some privacy after such a rough encounter. Please, make yourself at home, there are refreshments at the other end of the room and an open bar.

Beio-Rhett looked over to the right of the room to see there was indeed a buffet with one cook attending and a small bar with another staff member tending it, "Zala," Beio-Rhett exclaimed. "I thought you guys didn't like pirates."

Ttak smiled as he made his way to the bar. "Forgive my crew's initial hesitance to let you aboard. You understand that these are dangerous times, and especially in an outpost so vulnerable to a Quezz attack, I didn't want to put my station in jeopardy. I had my station control officer lie somewhat about the time it would take to look up your contract. The General did indeed forward a copy of the contract to all outlying military outposts in the system. The nature of your mission remains confidential, but the contract gave me reason enough to believe you and your crew are legitimate. It seemed strange that the General himself would arrange the contract with a group of mercenaries. Usually, that kind of paperwork is left for lower ranks."

Beio-Rhett kept his eye on Ttak, "Yeah, I guess he really wanted to make sure the job was done right."

Ttak grabbed a plate and began to pile some food on, "I would assume so. Regardless, I decided that should the General hold these mercenaries in such high regard, I should have no reason not to do so also. I had catering prepare the officer's mess hall as quickly as I could."

Poko made his way to the food first, followed by Prellina.

Singatt spoke, "That's very kind of you, but I assure you this generosity is unnecessary,"

"Nonsense!" Ttak retorted. "The least I can do for Hydrolet is provide food and shelter for its heroes."

Beio-Rhett made his way to the bar, "We're not heroes, just hired guns." He pointed to the drink on tap that he wanted and turned to look at Ttak as the bartender drew him a glass, "Well, at least four of us are."

Ttak chuckled as he brought his plate to the table, 'Indeed, this Lieutenant seems somewhat out of place in your midst. I remember checking your file briefly before meeting you," he turned to Singatt, "You're still active, correct?"

Singatt nodded and made his way to the food as well, behind Poko and Prellina, "Correct sir. I decided I could be of help on this particular mission and volunteered my services to Beio-Rhett here."

"Strange," said Ttak. "Well, either way, at ease Lieutenant, you are also an honored guest at this station. For whatever reason you decided to brave this mission I consider you a hero as well."

Beio-Rhett shot a glance at Dembo before taking a sip of his drink. "We haven't exactly done anything heroic yet," Beio-Rhett said getting in line for food with his drink.

Dembo finally made his way to the bar.

"Well, you came across some dreadful ordeal just now? How else was your hull so badly damaged?" Ttak asked.

"We were intercepted," Prellina said as she plopped down on the table with her plate. "It was no picnic."

"I imagine," Ttak said. "How many?"

"Seven," Prellina said before starting to chow down. "We were lucky."

Beio-Rhett shot a glance at Singatt who was now piling food on his plate. *Should we trust this guy?* Beio-Rhett hadn't really trusted anyone in a long time. He was still having a hard time trying not to view Singatt as an "other." But he kept a close eye on Singatt to see if he was noticing anything strange.

After Singatt was satisfied with the food on his plate, he made his way to the table, where Poko and Prellina sat next to each other. "It was quite unfortunate," he said. "We were perhaps halfway to our destination when we detected the interception. Luckily, we pulled out of hyperspace in time and these two were pretty useful with a turret."

Ttak nodded, "Quite unfortunate. Will this delay to your mission be detrimental?"

"I sure hope not," Prellina said under her breath.

"It's just a rescue mission," Singatt said. "As far as I know the Quezzes aren't exactly known for executing POWs."

"Well, they are full of surprises these days," Ttak said

smiling, "How much further do you have to go?"

"Just to Quesgarlon II," Prellina said.

Beio-Rhett shot Prellina a glance, then one at Ttak who remained smiling.

Ttak nodded slowly, "My, this is a mission of utmost importance. Into the belly of the beast eh?"

Beio-Rhett sat down next to Singatt across from Prellina who sat next to Poko. Ttak sat at the head of the table. Beio-Rhett scanned those at the table than watched as Dembo finally made his way to the table. "Yeah," he replied at last to Ttak's comment. "It feels like a suicide mission."

Ttak laughed, "You may be right," he took a sip from his drink. "Don't think I don't know who you are. The Masked Menace. I am still dumbfounded that the General would not only spare your life but hire you for a mission as important as this."

Beio-Rhett smirked, "I guess I should've seen it coming."

Singatt smiled, "Oh come on, Beio-Rhett, no one is trying to kill you."

"Except for those fucking interceptors," Beio-Rhett shot back.

Singatt chuckled, "Fair enough."

Ttak smiled, "Well I hope for your sake, it's not a suicide mission. Although it does seem like quite a bold move for the General to send someone straight to the home planet."

Beio-Rhett nodded, "Bold indeed."

Singatt interrupted, "Better some pirates get caught then Hydrolette personnel," Singatt clarified.

"Yes, but don't you jeopardize that aspect?" Ttak asked. "You're active military personnel, what happens if you get caught?"

Singatt sighed, "I know it's irresponsible of me sir, but I felt the benefits of my presence outweighed the dangers."

Ttak nodded. "I'm sure you have your reasons, and the best of luck to you for sure. I wish I could be of more help to you, but unfortunately all I can do is provide some food and a bed before you're on your way, so please don't insist that this hospitality isn't necessary."

Singatt smiled and nodded, "Yes, sir."

Ttak turned his attention to Beio-Rhett, whose attention was turned to his food, "And you. I must ask, how does it feel to be working for the government you recently opposed?"

Beio-Rhett grunted, "I didn't oppose anyone. I was only doing a job, just like I am now..." he took a few more bites, "Besides, it's not the first time I've worked for them."

"You worked for the Hydrolet Government before?" Ttak asked. "The Masked Menace?"

Beio-Rhett nodded, keeping his gaze forward, away from Ttak. "Yes. I was a soldier, then an officer, then a black ops agent... I guess an assassin would be the more appropriate term. This was back during the second Baltan War."

Ttak nodded, seemingly impressed. "You were awfully young then."

Young? I guess I was kind of young. Still, that's a weird comment. "I was old enough," he said carelessly. He took a sip of his drink and thought more about the comment. "But, I guess it was probably not the best idea to work in such high places at such a young age. I definitely had my fair share of bad experiences that left me..."

At this point, Prellina finally saw it, a faded but sure enough scar over Beio-Rhett's right eye. She never noticed it before. It was so faint and healed over that unless she wasn't scrutinizing, she probably wouldn't see it at all, but now that she noticed, it almost became luminescent. How could she possibly have missed it? It tore straight over his right eye from the top of his temple to just above his jaw. It branched out near the corner of his eye towards his nose as well, perhaps from some attempted surgical repair. Now seeing the scar, she also noticed a slight discoloration of Beio-Rhett's right eye. The yellow of his eye was very pale and the lid slightly drooped over the right corner. How could she possibly have missed this? She didn't say anything because Beio-Rhett never brought it up and Prellina wasn't sure if she wanted to open up this can of worms just yet. She thought about his reputation as the Masked Menace. Was that why he had the mask? That scar? It seemed strange. First she thought it was just theatrics, but according to records Prellina read, it was popular belief that his face was horribly disfigured. Maybe it was. That scar looked like it used to be quite the wound. She was starting to put it all together, taking stock of all the times she noticed that Beio-Rhett's hair would always fall to the right side of his face, like he was still trying to hide that scar.

"...scarred," Beio-Rhett continued turning his gaze to

Ttak. "But it's funny you would be concerned with how old I was for such a job."

"Just curious is all," Ttak said, trying to end the conversation.

Beio-Rhett kept his gaze on Ttak as he continued eating.

Prellina tried to stop from staring at Beio-Rhett's scar. Now that she noticed it, she couldn't take her eyes off it. It was mesmerizing and what bothered her more was why she didn't notice it before. She didn't say anything, but it was the only thing on her mind. She continued to make a conscious effort not to look, not appear like she was avoiding looking at Beio-Rhett's face.

Dembo noticed immediately that Prellina was staring at Beio-Rhett, but was more interested on keeping his eyes on Ttak. He knew Beio-Rhett felt like something was off and felt somewhat uneasy about the whole scenario himself. It seemed like Ttak wanted something. Whatever it was, Dembo figured he would find out soon. He had his weapon on him, and he knew Beio-Rhett did as well. If anything went down, they would be ready.

"How long will the repairs take?" Beio-Rhett inquired, "It's really no trouble for me to help out."

"What is the extent of the damages?" Ttak asked.

Beio-Rhett glanced over at Dembo to confirm, "Just the hull, right?"

Dembo nodded, "The core's a bit drained, it could do with a charge if you wouldn't mind. The engine's intact and the hyper drive still works."

"Nothing but cosmetics," Ttak said with a shrug. They should be done overnight, perhaps a bit longer. Please feel free to use our quarters to take a rest."

Beio-Rhett nodded and took a sip of his drink, "I could definitely use a nap."

Ttak took a sip of his drink and continued to stare at Beio-Rhett, "Have I seen you somewhere before?" he asked suddenly.

Beio-Rhett tried to ignore the abruptness of the question. 'I doubt it," he said. "I never made many friends in my past professions, and when I did, I'd remember them."

"Yes, it would seem," Ttak said still looking at Beio-Rhett.

"I know they're my friends if I haven't killed them," Beio-Rhett remarked with a mischievous smirk as he looked up at Ttak.

Poko chuckled a bit, followed by the rest of the crew. Ttak

didn't laugh but continued to smile.

"Is that always true?"

Beio-Rhett started to cough in the middle of laughing and dropped his fork. He coughed rather violently as he bent down to grab his fork while the others continued to laugh, as though they didn't quite hear Ttak's comment. Beio-Rhett finally grabbed the fork and rose up, his hair, once again to the right side of his face. "Sorry," he said finally clearing his throat.

"Something wrong?" Ttak asked.

Beio-Rhett shook his head, "I forgot how to chew is all," he joked, trying to keep up with the light-hearted mood.

Ttak continued to smile and look at Beio-Rhett.

Beio-Rhett kicked off his second boot while sitting on the simple bed in one of the station's modest quarters, perhaps made for officers or guests. He stood up and unzipped his vest, placing it on the bedpost after removing it and proceeded to take off his utility belt. *Man, I'm tired.* He hung the belt on the other bed post and looked at the sheath where the diamond knife was safely nestled. *Glad to have you back.* He then unbuttoned his shirt and slid it off. His naked torso revealed many scars and burns. War had marked him well. On the left, upper corner of his chest was a distinguished photon burn. Across his stomach on the right side was a visceral scar. His upper arms were well scarred as well. On his back was a tattoo of two crossing duelist swords over a rather elaborate rendering of a Krognot, a winged beast of Hydrolette lore that represented great strength and cleverness. Some believe this creature was based on an actual native creature on Quesgarlon, but no empirical evidence has supported this. Beio-Rhett walked over to the simple sink at the corner of the room and ran some water over his hands. He ran his wet hands through his hair in an unmotivated attempt to clean it. He glanced up at his reflection in the mirror for a moment before turning away towards the bed.

There was a buzz at the door followed by Dembo's voice through the intercom, "Hey, let me in, man."

Beio-Rhett walked over and pressed the entrance button. The doors slid open.

"Going somewhere?" Dembo asked, mocking Beio-Rhett's attire.

"Very funny," Beio-Rhett responded. "What's up? I'm exhausted."

"I went to the head engineer of the repair crew," Dembo said quietly. "They said that they have overnight workers who can make adequate hull repairs by tomorrow morning."

Beio-Rhett nodded, "Wanted to talk to someone who was actually handling the ship?"

Dembo nodded, "Exactly. The guy looked honest. And I know what you mean. That Ttak guy really bothers me for some reason," his voice dropped to a whisper.

Beio-Rhett nodded, "Well, at least the ship is actually being repaired. I don't want to sit around here for long, just waiting to have my throat slit."

"You're actually sleeping tonight?" Dembo asked, surprised.

"Like I said, I'm exhausted," Beio-Rhett grunted. "If you want to stay up to keep watch, be my guest."

Dembo smiled, "I just might."

Beio-Rhett chuckled, "Singatt doesn't seem to be worried and he's military. I figure he would be able to notice anything off about another officer, ya know?"

Dembo nodded, "Fair enough, but that doesn't mean I don't trust my gut." He turned and made his way down the hallway. "Good night, man."

"Good night," Beio-Rhett said as he closed the door and walked back towards the bed. Just as he was about to lay down, the buzzer went off again.

"Go away Dembo, I'm fucking tired!" he yelled in a joking tone.

"It's me, Prellina," her voice carried over the intercom.

"Oh," Beio-Rhett shot out of bed, "Hold on," he grabbed his shirt from the foot of the bed and threw it on quickly. He walked over to the door and opened it.

Prellina stood in the doorway, leaning on the frame, "Hey," she said simply.

'What do you want?" Beio-Rhett asked, rubbing his eyes, pretending he had just gotten up.

"I just wanted to see if you wanted to talk..." Prellina said. *Seriously?* "But if you're tired I'll..."

"No, it's fine," Beio-Rhett said. "Come in," he made way for her to enter the quarters.

Prellina walked in and sat down on the lonely chair in the

corner of the room. Beio-Rhett sat across from her on his bed.

"You think Ttak's bad news?" she asked suddenly.

Beio-Rhett was startled, "Umm… I dunno. You know me by now. I don't trust anyone."

"Well, you weren't too rude at dinner, so I guess you're getting better with your manners."

Beio-Rhett smiled, "Thanks for noticing."

"Well, anyway," Prellina started. "That wasn't exactly what I came here for. I was actually wondering… I mean, I don't mean to pry, but … well, maybe I shouldn't be asking this… I just."

Seriously?!

"Go ahead," Beio-Rhett reluctantly coaxed.

"Well…" continued Prellina, "I was just curious… and I thought now when no one was around."

There was a very long, very awkward pause.

"Where did you…" Prellina paused again, "… get that," she pointed to Beio-Rhett's right eye, "scar?"

Beio-Rhett froze up instantly, "I have a lot of scars," Beio-Rhett immediately regained himself. "There's nothing special about that one."

"It's just," Prellina said. "That one interested me the most."

"I'm surprised you noticed it," Beio-Rhett said. "Not many people do. I don't exactly show it off."

"Why?" asked Prellina. "I mean, unless you don't want to tell me."

Beio-Rhett sighed, "Maybe some other time," Beio-Rhett said abruptly, "Is there anything else you wanted?"

"Um… no," Prellina looked disappointed. "I'll let you sleep," She stood up and walked out of the room. Beio-Rhett went up to the door and closed it. He ran his hand down the right side of his face. *Seriously?* He walked back towards the bed, lay down and turned the lights off.

Chapter 8

Out Of The Frying Pan

"Make sure your rope is real strong when you hang me. Better make sure that I die."

Sleep overcame Beio-Rhett quickly. Not having had a moment's rest since early that morning, he passed out without time enough to worry about the troubles he would face tomorrow. He slept deep and began to dream. Like any dream, he found himself in a place that he had no memory of a void. And as if it had always been there, a mirror appeared in front of him. He was looking at himself. However, his reflection was looking back. Beio-Rhett looked around himself, but his reflection didn't move. He moved his hand, but his reflection remained the same, staring at him. Then, as though they had always been there, a sea of dark shapeless creatures surrounded him. Their forms shifted throughout the void, as though they were a part of it. The creatures reached out for Beio-Rhett, violently, attacking him. Beio-Rhett parried their advances in vain. There were too many. He looked in front of him to see that the mirror was still in front of him. *Huh?* His reflection began to smile. Beio-Rhett was not smiling. He turned and tried to run away, but he could not. The mirror remained in front of him. He ran and ran, but his legs carried him nowhere, and the mirror remained, the reflection smiled. Beio-Rhett looked around himself to see that the shapes had retreated, and instead, as if they were always there, an endless sprawl of dead bodies, smothered in blood surrounded him. All races. As far as he could see there was a landscape of death. The shapes were now part of the bodies and they advanced again. The mirror was always in front of him. (Aha) His reflection bore a more sinister smile now. However, blood now ran down his reflection's face. It trickled down his left eye to his jaw. Beio-Rhett quickly reached for his face, but felt no blood. The blood continued to gush from the reflection's face. Beio-Rhett now saw that the blood was coming from the scar over his right eye, only it was his reflection's left. His old wound, reopened. *Mmm…* *No!* By now the dark creatures had him in their grasp, piling over him, tearing at his flesh, pulling him into the void. Beio-Rhett thrashed away to no avail. He saw in the mirror all his old scars, reopened, pouring forth blood. Beio-Rhett tried to run, but he felt his legs grow heavy with the shapes engulfing him. He looked and saw the dead bodies began to rise and walk towards him, still suffering from the wounds that killed them. His reflection in the mirror was covered in blood. Its skin began to peel off. The dark creatures chewed at Beio-Rhett's flesh. Beio-Rhett thrashed away and tried to run, but he felt his limbs go numb and lose all strength. Suddenly, he looked up to see his mirrored image appear fine, all the blood gone, wounds healed. (Look) Except now his reflection wore an all-covering black mask. Beio-Rhett, felt his limbs again. The dark creatures were no more. The dead bodies had vanished. Beio-Rhett reached into the mirror to take the mask off his reflection. There was no barrier, no mirror. He could feel the reflection in front of him. His fingers touched the mask, as real as his own flesh, and removed it to find not his face, or the face of a Hydrolette, but of a Quesgralion. *NO!* (Wait…) Beio-Rhett jolted awake in a cold sweat.

He quickly turned the lights on and rubbed his eyes before looking around the room. He was breathing hard and his whole body was beaded with sweat. He wiped his forehead and tried to slow his breath. He wiped the hair that was stuck to his face away, sat up and walked over to the sink. He ran water and splashed some in his face. After brief hesitation, he looked up at his reflection in the mirror and checked his face. Before he could examine it too closely, the lights in the room went out. Beio-Rhett turned around to check the room for any intruders. The door remained closed. After a few seconds the emergency blue lights came on. Beio-Rhett went to the bedpost and quickly clothed himself. He put his utility belt on and drew the strange looking pistol he had taken from Poko's crate. He held his pistol forward and walked toward the door, opening it with one hand while the other held the pistol steady. The doors opened to reveal nothing but an empty blue-lit hall. He looked on either side of his door, finding nothing. *Maybe just a power out.* He knew that his friends quarters were to his left, so he cautiously stepped out of his room and made his way there, pistol raised.

As he slowly walked down the hall, he saw Singatt turn the corner, pistol at his side, but not raised.

Startled only for a moment, Beio-Rhett put down his blaster and asked, "What are you doing down here? What's going on?"

"I'm not sure," Singatt said calmly, "Did you see Dembo walk by here?"

Beio-Rhett looked behind him, "No…" he checked again behind his back, "Where'd he go?"

"He woke me up and told me that the head engineer needed to see him. He wasn't clear on the details, but he seemed concerned," Singatt said.

"Shit," Beio-Rhett grunted. "Why'd he go alone?"

"He said he didn't want to attract any attention. Something about Ttak," explained Singatt. "He did go armed."

"Well, that was smart," Beio-Rhett replied. "I hope the repairs to the ship haven't been delayed. I don't like it here. Where's Prellina?"

"She's with me," said Singatt.

Prellina walked from the corner, holding her own pistol, "Are you all right?" she asked. "You look pretty tense."

"Oh… just he lights," Beio-Rhett said, now wondering if he looked tense, "Where's Poko?"

"In his room," Singatt explained. "We were about to go get him."

Beio-Rhett nodded and rubbed his eyes. "Did the lights go off before or after he left?"

"After," Singatt explained. "That's when we got worried."

"Well, come on," encouraged Beio-Rhett. "Let's go find him and get the hell out of here before something bad happens."

The three crept back down the hall towards Poko's room. The three had their weapons drawn and walked cautiously. Before they came to Poko's door, they were surprised to find it slide open, followed by Poko's head peek around the corner. Seeing familiar faces, he stepped out, relaxed.

"What the hell's going on?" he asked.

"We're trying to figure that out," Beio-Rhett responded, lowering his pistol again. "Dembo's gone missing."

Poko took a breath, "Shit, man," he looked around. "What's the plan?"

"We go find him, and get the hell out of here," Beio-Rhett insisted.

Poko nodded, "All right, none of us really know this station well."

"Let's just backtrack from where we came," Singatt said. "That way. And I think soon as we get out of this corridor, we'll be in the main loop of the station. We should be able to follow that to the docking bay where our ship is."

Beio-Rhett nodded in agreement, "Yeah, we shouldn't be too far, but we still gotta find Dembo."

Everyone nodded in agreement. Singatt added, "Well, let's just head in that general direction. We should get moving."

The group walked down to the end of the corridor, where they found the exit to the lodging sector of the station. They found it was not locked, and opened it easily. However, the doors opened to a most gruesome sight. A display of carnage lay before the four. Dead Hydrolette's in military uniform lay all over the adjacent room which appeared to be some navigations center. Carbon scoring decorated the walls along with sparse green splatters of blood. Still-wet green stains dotted the flickering map screens. The floors as well were wet with blood. Nothing short of a massacre had obviously taken place.

Beio-Rhett had seen enough violence in his life to not be terribly moved by the sight, as did Poko and Singatt. Prellina wasn't shocked by the sight, but it did cause her to flinch at first.

"Good Zala," she said. "Is Dembo here?"

Beio-Rhett quickly scanned the room. "No," he said calmly. "I'd recognize him. All these guys are wearing military uniforms. Dembo would stand out.

"What happened here?" Singatt asked, stepping out in front of the group with his pistol at the ready.

"A firefight for sure," Prellina replied. "But I would remember hearing that."

"Soundproof walls?" Singatt wondered out loud. "Maybe you're suspicious about Ttak was right. But I don't see why he would turn on his own men, especially at times like these."

"Everyone's trying to survive," Beio-Rhett said coldly. "Some do it better than others."

Singatt was offended by Beio-Rhett's comment, but paid it no mind, "Should we keep moving?" he asked.

Beio-Rhett nodded, "That's probably a good idea."

The four crept over the dead bodies to the door on the other side. It opened to reveal the main loop. It was the same broad passage they walked through when they entered the station. Only now, there was no hustle or bustle. There was only death. The bloody scene that lay before them was eerily illuminated by the emergency blue lights. Dead Hydrolettes littered the wide passageway. Across from the door where the four came in was a long window that looked out into space. There was nothing of interest outside except for stars and the occasional outcropping of one of the landing platforms.

Beio-Rhett held his pistol forward and walked out into the walkway, checking his blind spots. Prellina and Singatt did the same while Poko hung back peeking around the corner. Being unarmed, he remained more cautious than the others.

"Looks like we're clear," Singatt said quietly.

"What the hell's going on?" Beio-Rhett asked.

Singatt looked out the window, then stepped forward. He looked down the main loop, which curved beyond his sight. "This station is shaped like a circle," he said. "If we take the main loop this way, we should reach the bridge. We may be able to find out what's going on there."

Beio-Rhett walked a few paces down the main loop. He saw through a window, on the inside of the loop, what looked like a hub of sorts further down the curved tube of the main loop. "All right," he said. "It doesn't look like anyone is alive here, so we should just make our way through this walkway quickly. Come on!"

Beio-Rhett led the way as the group followed behind, briskly. Prellina quickened her pace to get alongside Beio-Rhett and looked around at the bloodshed. "Do you think any of them are alive?"

"Doesn't matter," said Beio-Rhett. "This isn't our fight. We gotta find Dembo."

The four continued to run faster down the main loop. Soon, the large arched portal to the bridge was in sight. The group quickened their pace. Beio-Rhett knew it was necessary, but it didn't stop him from glancing down at the dead bodies, looking for any sign that one of them might be Dembo. *Not today.* He knew Dembo wasn't dead, but he could never get rid of that shred of doubt. *Not again.*

The four finally reached the door. They stumbled slightly having come to such an abrupt halt, but promptly regained themselves. Prellina stepped in front of the group and looked over the door controls. "It looks like it's unlocked," she said.

Beio-Rhett shook his head. "I don't like this at all."

Poko took a breath, "See man, this is why I hate rolling with you."

Beio-Rhett looked over at Poko and gave him a quick smirk. He looked back at Prellina. "Okay, Prellina, on the count of three."

Prellina nodded.

Beio-Rhett took a breath. "One,"

Singatt raised his blaster.

"Two,"

Prellina held her pistol up while she got ready to input the open command.

"Three!"

Prellina punched the button and the doors slid open to reveal only darkness. Not even the menacing blue glow of the emergency lights illuminated the room.

"Shit," Beio-Rhett exclaimed.

"Well," Singatt said, keeping his pistol raised. "Maybe we can switch the lights on from the inside. We have to go in there."

Beio-Rhett nodded and led the group into the room. First Beio-Rhett stepped in, feeling around the walls for any semblance of a switch or button. Prellina followed, along with Singatt. Poko was the last to enter the room. When he stepped completely into the room, the doors slid shut, cutting off the only source of light.

"Fuck," Beio-Rhett said.

Suddenly, the lights on the bridge flashed on and the blast shields of the bridge windows were withdrawn letting in the faint starlight from outside as well. Beio-Rhett, Prellina, Singatt and Poko found themselves surrounded by armed Quesgralion soldiers and several Teneman officers as well. They stood in single file ranks along the walls of the bridge and up on the elevated ledges and command centers above. A few Teneman officers stood directly in front of the captured group, along with Ttak, who stood in front of them holding a Zynoth assassin pistol directly at Beio-Rhett.

Beio-Rhett pointed his pistol at Ttak, "Why am I not

surprised."

The Quesgralion soldiers raised their rifles at the four and cocked them.

"I would drop your weapon if I was you," Ttak said calmly.

Beio-Rhett dropped his pistol and raised his hands. Prellina, Singatt and Poko did the same.

"I suppose you're here to reclaim your silent friend," said Ttak.

Two Teneman officers pushed Dembo forward from behind Ttak, one of which was holding a rifle at his head. Dembo had his hands behind his head. His face was bruised and his lower lip bleeding. There was a distinct rip in his black steph jacket. Another officer held his weapons belt.

"He put up quite a fight before my soldiers overpowered him," explained Ttak. "He even killed five of my men."

"Could've killed more," Dembo said while smiling.

"Shut up, you!" Ttak shouted losing his composure for a moment only. He proceeded to smack Dembo's face with his pistol. "Your friend here was heading for the engineering room when we caught him. He was talking to the head engineer. One of my officers overheard. Silly head engineer didn't realize that that officer was one of mine, otherwise he would've kept his mouth shut. But his troubles are over, along with the troubles of everyone else here."

Prellina lunged forward giving Ttak an angry glare, but she stopped at the sounds of the rifles being raised.

"Please settle down," Ttak said in the same calm voice. "The engineer was only trying to warn Dembo of our presence. Dembo met him before and was innocently asking him if they were indeed repairing your little pirate ship. The engineer was smart enough not to say anything then because he knew that my guards were afoot. He did say that he was fixing the ship, which would be appropriate to get Dembo to go back to sleep. We wouldn't want you to suspect anything so soon."

"Well, you blew that at the dinner table," commented Beio-Rhett.

Ttak sneered. He raised his pistol to Beio-Rhett's head.

Beio-Rhett laughed. "I've known some stiffs in the military, but none as stiff as you, man. You were being way too polite."

Ttak retaliated, "Your friend wasn't that smart either. He walked straight into a trap. As did you."

"You were gonna kill us anyway," Dembo retorted. "By now, you should know that the engineer really did fix our ship. Beio-Rhett, it's ready on the landing platform where we arrived!"

Ttak whacked Dembo's face again with his pistol.

"You could've died peacefully in your sleep, but now your passing will be painful," Ttak snarled. "Whether or not your ship is fixed, you'll never get to it."

"You should've taken me with you," Beio-Rhett was speaking directly to Dembo.

"Nah," replied Dembo. "I knew that if this happened, you'd come. Now I know we can get out of this for sure."

Another blow was given to Dembo's head by Ttak's pistol.

"What was it all worth, Ttak?" Singatt seemed to be holding back a building rage this whole time. "Giving up your honor? Your pride? Your men? Your planet?! What was the promised prize for you?"

Ttak smiled, 'My honor?" he began to laugh. "My pride?" his laugh grew more vigorous. "My men? My planet?!" He began laughing uncontrollably. He finally settled down a bit. "My dear friend, you let your eyes deceive you too quickly. I have no empathy for Hydrolet or its people, because they are not my own."

Beio-Rhett stepped back with a confused look. *Wait...* "Who the hell are you?"

Ttak began laughing again. "Beauty..." he said, "is truly in the eye of the beholder" He pulled aside his Hydrolette military coat to reveal a small, electronic device on his belt. He pressed a button on it.

Hydrolette's were not the most technologically advanced race in the galaxy, but they were by no means the least. They were quite advanced in fields of applied physics and mathematics as well as highly respected in the fields of biology and chemistry. They had mastered hyperspace travel, harnessed plasma and even been able to control nuclear fusion. Whatever technology they had not mastered themselves, they had surely witnessed by the Quesgralions or the Kitholorians. But, Beio-Rhett and his crew had never seen anything like what they were about to witness. The image of Ttak's Hydrolette countenance melted away into a flutter of holographic pixels that quickly dissolved from sight. Parts of his body seemed to expand while others seemed to shrink. He grew taller. His head expanded. His tail shrunk. His eyes conjoined into one. He was not a Hydrolette. He was a Quesgralion.

Beio-Rhett was not sure what to make of what he just saw. Prellina and Singatt sported similar looks and loosened their aim. Poko, holding no weapon, only took a step back, squinting and shaking his head trying to see if some visual trickery was afoot. Dembo could only see the spectacle from behind, but was just as shocked.

"Commander Letak of the Quesgralion Military Intelligence Forces at your service," he said simply.

Beio-Rhett couldn't find any words. *How?*

"The latest in shape-shifting technology," Letak explained. "If I might say so, it's most definitely perfected. You may have suspected me of some fowl play, but I am quite confident you never in your wildest imagination thought for a moment that I was not a Hydrolette."

Beio-Rhett still couldn't find any words.

"Quite the ingenious combination of holographic and biomechanical engineering. Not only were you fooled by my disguise, but by those of all my soldiers as well," he signaled to the soldiers standing around the group, holding them at gunpoint.

"Before you so miraculously took out that interceptor squad, they managed to send us a warning transmission. Although it was a shame they failed their job, we found it a perfect opportunity to create a little trap for you. Already having this station under our control, all we had to do was put our disguises on and make sure the occupants didn't try anything funny on pain of death. Apparently, you people don't take threats very seriously."

Beio-Rhett's rage took over his shock and he was able to able to shoot back, "Finally, you're right about something," he said while cracking a smile, making eye contact with Dembo. He waved his tail back and forth for his crew behind him to see.

Dembo nodded slightly without arousing attention of the officers restraining him.

Letak turned around and walked over to Dembo. Stopping a few feet in front of him, he raised his pistol to Dembo's face, while looking at Beio-Rhett. "You think that's something to be proud of? You arrogant brutes! Do you not take this threat seriously, either?! You would let your friend die just to prove you're tough?!" Letak began to lose his composure again.

Beio-Rhett lowered his head, before lifting it up smiling. "No," he responded, his hands falling to his side. "It's just not a very serious threat."

Dembo kicked as high as he could, knocking Letak's pistol out of Letak's hand. He then gave a full swipe across the ground behind him with his tail, knocking both officers to the ground immediately.

Beio-Rhett drew his diamond knife instantly and rolled forward after shouting, "Scatter!" He leapt up right in front of Letak and embedded the knife into his chest before he could even get out one last angry word. The only response he had the strength for was a slight shiver, a slack jaw, and eyes wide with rage as he slumped forward toward Beio-Rhett. Beio-Rhett lifted Letak up and used him as a shield against the spray of laser blasts coming from the other guards. The guards fired at Beio-Rhett, but Letak's now lifeless body absorbed the blasts as it shook from the impact. Beio-Rhett knelt down, still holding Letak up and picked up his pistol. He shot from behind the body shield, killing two soldiers with well-aimed shots.

Prellina ducked behind one of the bridge's navigation stations and shot from behind the safety of the thick steel of the control panel. Singatt followed suit and ducked behind the stairs to the elevated command platform of the bridge. He fired at the soldiers from behind the stairs. Poko's martial skills were elegantly displayed as he dived for the closest soldier and quickly disarmed him in a flurry of quick hand motions. He then gave the soldier a fatal blow with the butt of his own rifle before gunning down the line of three soldiers behind him. Dembo dropped to the floor as laser bolts whizzed by his head. He followed Beio-Rhett's suit and lifted one of the dead officers in front of him to absorb the incoming blasts. He quickly grabbed the officer's weapon, a compact rapid fire blaster, and killed the other officer that was trying to stand up. Grabbing the second officer's blaster, he made a break for the command platform strafing blaster fire as he ran, taking out a few more soldiers. Dembo dove under the platform safely, getting away with only a photon burn on his jacket. Having sufficient cover, he took a breath and peeked out from under the platform to see Beio-Rhett still standing in plain sight in the middle of the bridge, capping off soldiers from behind a now-mutilated Letak. Poko was crouched behind a pilot station holding his newly acquired rifle above the control panel and firing blindly at the solders on the elevated platform above. "Beio-Rhett, get out of there!" he shouted.

Beio-Rhett kept firing his pistol, making sure his shots counted. The metal ammo for the pistol wasn't cheap and he normally wouldn't be using it so frivolously, except it was the only weapon he had. He was distraught to hear the click that meant his pistol was empty. "Shit" he exclaimed. He stayed behind Letak's body and looked around for his next move. Seeing that Poko was the closest, he threw Letak's body towards the soldier and leapt behind the pilot station, collapsing in front of Poko, "Shit!" he yelled. "Shit, shit, shit!"

"That the Rhaekul?" Poko asked, as he continued to fire blindly over the panel.

Beio-Rhett grunted as he loaded another magazine from his utility belt and slapped it into the pistol, "Yeah, goddamnit."

"Shit, man. You just emptied 100 credits worth of ammo at those fuckers. Those shots better have counted. Metal bullets ain't cheap."

Beio-Rhett nodded, "I know," and wheeled around from behind the pilot station to put two more bullets in the heads of two more officers. Their bloody carcasses fell from the command platform of the bridge to the ground floor below. Beio-Rhett glanced over at Dembo who was trapped under the platform. He then saw Singatt close by under the stairs and Prellina behind him in back of the navigation station. "Stay low!" he called out to Prellina, knowing the others could take care of themselves.

Prellina kept firing blindly over the station while crouched behind, "Planning on it!" she shouted back.

Dembo was safe, but couldn't get any shots at the soldiers from his position. Frustrated he shouted at Beio-Rhett and Poko, "Cover me!" he shouted.

Poko and Beio-Rhett heard loud and clear, nodded at each other and stood up from behind the pilot station firing at the remaining guards. Poko held the trigger on the assault rifle spraying laser bolts at the soldiers' general direction, killing a few. Beio-Rhett took more time as he fired, killing four more with well-aimed headshots.

Dembo meanwhile rolled out from under the platform and grabbed his weapons belt that lay next to the two dead guards. He continued to roll towards a different station next to Poko and Beio-Rhett's

"Clear!" he shouted

Poko and Beio-Rhett quickly retreated back behind the raised panel.

Singatt continued to fire from under the stairs with his pistol, "How many more?!"

Beio-Rhett peeked around the side of the panel to take a look, managing to pull his head back before a laser bolt tore straight through it. "Eight or nine!" he shouted. He looked at his Rhaekul, "I can't waste any more bullets, man."

"Grab one of theirs, man!" Poko yelled over the sound of gunfire behind them.

Beio-Rhett looked around and saw that one of the Teneman officers Poko had slain had a battle sword strapped to his back. "Here we go," he said as he yanked the sword from the back strap. He looked at Poko, "I'm gonna rush 'em. Draw their fire."

Poko nodded. He looked back at the rest. "Let 'em have it!"

Dembo was the first up. Submachine gun in each hand, he sprayed a flurry of laser bolts at the remaining soldiers. Prellina stood up and continued to fire, aiming in their general direction. Singatt did the same, creeping up the stairs to get level with the remaining soldiers. He managed to get a few good shots off, before they drew their fire to the stairs and Singatt had to retreat. Poko slid from behind the pilot station and fired madly into the Quezzes' ranks as well as Beio-Rhett, who ran from the other side and charged up the stairs to the command platform at the bridge. The sword was a standard issue double-handed blade used for close quarters combat between soldiers. Usually only Teneman officers carried such weapons, and amongst their ranks, it was usually the lower ranks. Beio-Rhett hacked through the Quezzes like warm butter, slicing through their vital organs, removing limbs, and even one unfortunate soldier's head.

The remaining Quezzes didn't know whom to focus their fire towards; the flurry of photon blasts coming from the lower level or the raging madman hacking right through them. Beio-Rhett cut down the second to last Quezz and stepped on the body to remove the blade. Before he could get the blade free, the final Quezz held his rifle up and used this moment to aim straight for Beio-Rhett's head, but the rifle did not fire.

Having killed most of the soldiers on the ledge, Singatt had made his way back up the stairs and planted one well-aimed laser bolt in the final Quezzes head.

Beio-Rhett looked up to see that Singatt had made the final shot and saved his life again. "Thank you," he said.

"Finally," Singatt said, smiling. "You're getting better at that."

Beio-Rhett smiled, wiping the sweat and Quesgralion blood from his brow.

"All right," said Dembo replacing the clips for the two submachine guns. "The ship's at landing platform C-4, remember? If we leave this way through the bridge, we should be able to keep going through the main loop and I think it'll be the third platform on our right."

Beio-Rhett nodded. "All right. Reload, everyone! Get some more weapons. Let's get the hell out of here!"

Singatt made sure the battery was charged on his pistol and grabbed one of the Quezz soldier's assault rifle. Prellina did the same. Poko reloaded the one he picked up. He also rifled through one of the soldier's belongings to find a few plasma grenades. Beio-Rhett sheathed his Rhaekul and grabbed a back scabbard for his sword. He strapped the sword on his back and grabbed an assault rifle for himself.

Beio-Rhett looked around to see that everyone was ready. He gave Prellina an extended look over to see if she was okay. He made eye contact with her and exchanged a nod to confirm that she was ready to go, although she did seem somewhat shaken up. "Let's go," he ordered.

The five ran out the door opposite the one they came in, to find more dead Hydrolettes and a few more Quesgralion soldiers milling about the bodies looking for survivors. They barely had time to lift their rifles up to the charging crew before being gunned down by either Beio-Rhett or Dembo, who took the lead.

"How many are there?" Prellina called out from the rear of the entourage.

"More than I wanna deal with," Beio-Rhett snapped back, capping another Quezz as the group rounded further around the corner of the main loop. "Keep moving, before they call reinforcements!"

After a few more paces, followed a few more encounters with patrolling Quezz officers, Dembo noticed on one of the main archways to his left the symbols for C-4. "Here!" he shouted, veering quickly to the right. Singatt leapt ahead of Dembo, "Let me," he said, moving Dembo aside, "You cover me. I may have a few access codes to try in case they put the whole place on lockdown."

Dembo nodded and covered Singatt's right, holding both submachine guns at point. Beio-Rhett aimed his rifle down the loop to Singatt's left, watching for any incoming soldiers. Poko and Prellina did as they were ordered and stood behind Singatt keeping watch all around in case any Quezzes popped up from unexpected corners.

"We in trouble?" Beio-Rhett asked, still keeping his gaze fixed down the corridor.

"Not yet," Singatt said. "Just military clearance, which I have," he took out his tag and inserted it into the receiver on the door panel. "Clear!" He held up his rifle and pointed it at the doors as they slid open. Dembo followed suit, pointing his two submachine guns at the doors, ready to gun down whatever lay beyond.

On the landing platform, several dead engineers were strewn about the platform. Several guards were standing, waiting for the group as they burst through the door. One of them was speaking into a communication device, "Ground Captain to control, lock down landing platform…" but his message was cut short by a flurry of photon blasts that tore through his face and the communication device.

Dembo charged forward, emptying the clips of both guns at the guards ahead. Singatt held back taking shots from a distance, making sure there were no guards hiding out of sight. Beio-Rhett rushed passed him, "Come on! We gotta get to the ship!" he shouted as he held his assault rifle in front of him, killing the few guards who remained.

Dembo was the first to the ship and quickly punched in the access codes to the boarding port, "Come on!" he shouted in vain at the elevator doors as they slowly slid open. He looked behind him to see Singatt, Poko, and Prellina hanging by the entrance. "Hurry!" he shouted to them, "Before more of them come, hurry!"

By now Beio-Rhett skidded to a stop in front of Dembo and spun around to make sure the remaining three weren't being followed. He pointed his rifle up towards the observation decks to find no soldiers, then darted his aim quickly around the landing platform, making sure he didn't miss any hiding soldiers waiting to cut their escape short. *Almost out of here.*

He stood aside for Poko, Prellina and Singatt to leap into the elevator. Dembo backed up into it, followed by Beio-Rhett, who kept his assault rifle aimed outside. After taking his last step into the elevator, still holding his rifle with one hand, Beio-Rhett pressed the button for level one and the boarding port doors closed. In a matter of seconds the doors behind the group slid open to level one. Beio-Rhett bolted out of the elevator and tossed his rifle in the middle of the center room before charging around the corner to the bridge. He leapt into the pilot's seat and fired up the ship's engines. Prellina was close behind and plopped down in the navigations station.

"Are we golden?" Beio-Rhett asked as he powered the engines, waiting for the ship's systems to boot up.

Prellina did a quick check of the ships status. "Efficient hull integrity. We can engage the hyper drive."

"Good enough," Beio-Rhett said. He fired up the thrusters and gave the ship a rocky lift-off. Still, the thrusters worked and the engines were showing 100% efficiency. "Ha!" Beio-Rhett laughed aloud in relief. "You can't fucking trap me!" he screamed out at the dead Quezzes below. He brought the ship around to face the exit to find his relief short-lived. The thick, metal blast doors were closing over the force field exit.

"You spoke too soon," Dembo said as he sat down at the weapons station.

Beio-Rhett grunted. The exit bay was not too far away, but the blast doors were closing fast. "I'm trying to charge the thrusters, we'll go to slow at normal speed."

"Fucking gun it! They're closing fast!" Singatt yelled from the communication station.

Beio-Rhett pushed the throttle to the max, hoping he wouldn't stall the engines. His grip tightened over the throttle waiting for the ship to lunge forward. After lighting up, the thrusters finally blasted and shot the Donta Ryx forward, clearing the blast doors right before they hit the protruding gunner stations.

Beio-Rhett's grip on the throttle loosened and he let out a breath he appeared to be holding since he powered the ship on. "I never speak too soon!" he shouted in triumph.

He sighed and then turned to Prellina, "Can you set up a new hyperspace course?"

"Already on it," Prellina responded, rapidly punching in commands trying to map out the rest of the distance to Quesgarlon.

Dembo, brought up the station's schematics on the targeting monitor. "We need to blow up the station before they send a transmission," he said as he searched the schematics for the ship's power center.

"What?" Prellina exclaimed, turning around. "You can't do that!"

"Listen," Dembo said, still mapping out the station on the targeting monitor. "Everyone is dead anyway, except for Quesgralions. If we don't destroy that station, they're going to alert the whole fucking planet to our arrival."

Prellina took a breath, "It's too big!"

"We got that fusion canon remember?" Dembo said. "If I can locate one of the power reactors and blast it, I could start a chain reaction. It's a small station, one of their reactors should take the whole bloody thing out."

Prellina paused for a moment and took a breath, "Okay," she said. "I'll finish this course, while you target it."

Beio-Rhett nodded. "I'll stay close for you to get a good shot with the canon, but Prellina we gotta make the jump as soon as he fires."

Prellina nodded as she typed frantically, "Working on it."

"I got a lock!" Dembo said. "Fusion canon charging."

"We can't jump until you fire, there's not enough power," Prellina barked.

"Is the course set?" Beio-Rhett eyed the hyper drive throttle.

"Almost."

"Canon charged."

"Prellina?"

"I got it... I hope."

"Hope?"

"I got it, just fire."

"Firing canon, two bursts, if that won't take it out, nothing will."

The fusion canon gathered a massive glowing bluish-white orb in front of the canon before releasing the destructive energy blast towards the station. Another white orb gathered in front of the canon before being released soon after.

"Locked on, let's go!" Dembo shouted

"Hyperspace course is locked in," Prellina called out.

Poko scratched his head nervously, "Don't get me killed, man."

"Engaging hyper drive!" Beio-Rhett shouted.

The core energy levels began spiking in the red, "Come on," he pleaded. "Hold together, baby."

"I'm increasing the rear deflector shields to max," Prellina said.

The core read positively for engaging the hyper drive, but it wasn't yet ready for Beio-Rhett to accelerate into hyperspace.

"Shit!" Dembo cried, watching the monitor. "Quezz signatures leaving the station. They're sending fighters!"

Beio-Rhett heard Dembo, but kept his eye on the core readout, waiting to accelerate the hyper drive. *Come on.*

The two vicious white orbs struck the power reactor at one end of the circular station. The orbs struck causing a massive white explosion that engulfed one end of the circle. As planned, a chain reaction caused by the power systems connected to the core set off explosions down the circle until the entire station was engulfed in a bright white mini supernova of expanding energy. The blast radius immediately engulfed the incoming fighters and the shockwave from the initial blast was coming fast towards the Donta Ryx.

Beio-Rhett saw the indicator of the hyper drive turn positive, "Hold on!" he shouted. He thrust the accelerator forward and the ship started to be sucked away into the slipstream between the void. The last physical elements of the ship peeled into hyperspace just as the shockwave nipped the rear end.

"I hope those repairs hold up," Singatt said as he gripped the seat of the communication station.

The Donta Ryx tore through the void of space successfully

achieving hyper speed, and was on its way to Quesgarlon II as the shockwave rippled harmlessly outward.

Chapter 9

The Desert Outpost

"Two riders were approaching and the wind begins to howl."

Beio-Rhett was greatly disappointed as he looked out the window from the center room where he was sitting. At first he couldn't tell what he saw. There was just a big beige blur. It could have been that they were still at the edge of the atmosphere. Beio-Rhett knew that couldn't be right. He saw Quesgralion's three moons getting smaller. He was relieved that his ship had made it to the planet without any other interruptions. Still something was wrong.

A sandstorm? He banged on the control panel and walked over to the computer station at the other corner of the room. After typing his clearance in, he brought up the video monitor and dialed in a contact. After seeing the channel go through, he waited impatiently for a response. "Come on, man…" he said gruffly. "Why'd you give me your number unless you wanted me to call you?"

The video monitor produced a negative reading, but an audio signal was coming through. "Beio-Rhett? This is Mheages. Sorry I can't see you in person, I'm away from my computer in the lab right now. How can I be of assistance?"

Beio-Rhett was in a bad mood for other reasons, but unfortunately, Mheages would be the one to receive the brunt of his attitude. "Assistance? Well, this call is regarding your previous assistance. I believe you were the one who predicted a clear desert night when we would arrive."

"Yes, why?" asked Mheages.

"You're off by a whole fuckin' sandstorm!"

Beio-Rhett tapped some numbers on a screen and rerouted the comlink to show images from the outside cameras. After a moment, Beio-Rhett switched the transmission back to audio.

"How the hell can you explain that?!"

"Well," thought Mheages, "it's probably the ammunition exhaust from the Quezzes' weapons. Perhaps a lot of action going on down there. The formula stirs up the weather a bit. I'm sorry Beio-Rhett, but even with as many scientific advances as we or any other race has achieved, the weather will always be one of the hardest things to predict."

"Damnit Mheages, we'll be flying blind! This isn't some little setback."

"Look on the bright side. You can bring your entrance point a little closer since the Quezzes will have next to zero visibility."

"Yeah, but neither will we!"

"Beio-Rhett, I'm sorry my predictions were off. Your ship's navigations system may still be able to track the outpost's location. Have you even checked if they're working properly?"

Beio-Rhett switched off the transmission with a grumble. He marched off furiously to the ship's elevator. He opened the door, walked in and closed the door. He pushed the "bridge" button and sped upwards to level one.

The door of the elevator opened to level one, where Beio-Rhett stomped out. He turned the corner to make his way for the bridge. He saw Singatt sitting in the pilot seat, punching in commands to bring up manual control of the ship's course.

"Why switch to manual?" asked Beio-Rhett who popped up behind Singatt.

"The computer pilot can't chart a navigational pattern," answered Singatt. "It's best if I bring it down manually."

Beio-Rhett was thinking of saying something when he heard Prellina's voice in the chair to Singatt's right.

"Singatt's right," said Prellina, still sitting in the navigation station. "Our navigational system is going haywire." She typed on the keyboard rapidly while looking at a screen. "The Quezzes must be using radioactive gas laser bolts. If they are used in automatic blasters the chemical exhaust could stir up the weather."

At this point, Beio-Rhett felt he didn't have to say anything about the sandstorm. He fell back in a large, swiveling chair of the communications station and stared blankly at the panel.

Dembo, who was sitting at the weapons station, was looking at the targeting monitor, taking notes on a data pad. "It seems… " he muttered, stopping to look at his notes, "that the exhaust might be hot enough to rise up to the cold air causing a storm. There is less exhaust the further we go down. I think in a few minutes the computer will switch on again."

Dembo turned out to be right. After a few minutes, the computers came on.

Prellina saw her screen transmit a radar map that dotted their position, the enemy outpost's position, and the best-calculated landing spot.

"I have the coordinates," exclaimed Prellina. "They look just like the map back at the meeting room."

"Awesome," Beio-Rhett said, still reclining. "ETA?"

Prellina shrugged, "Five minutes. You think we should bring it in a bit closer since the Quezzes' visibility will be pretty shitty?"

Beio-Rhett grunted, trying to turn his mood around. *Just chill out.* "Sounds good," he said. "Don't be too assertive."

After a few minutes, Singatt had located the landing spot and brought the ship down smoothly on the desert ground. The sand blew out from under the ship and up into the sandstorm.

Beio-Rhett stood up after the ship landed and stretched, cracking his back and neck. "Where the hell's Poko?"

Dembo stood up, "I think he's in the center room. He said he wasn't going in the field."

Beio-Rhett nodded, "Yeah, I figured." He pressed the intercom and spoke into the microphone. "Poko, you coward!" his voice rang throughout the speakers in the ship.

Poko was apparently next to one of the intercoms because his voice sounded back over the communications panel, "Man, I already got shot at today. I'll keep your ship warm!"

Beio-Rhett laughed and turned to Prellina. "So will you," he said, with a very serious look.

Prellina smiled, "I'm not gonna try to be a hero," Prellina said. "Don't worry. I know the game plan."

"Remember," Singatt said as he got up to join Beio-Rhett and Dembo. "If you get a distress call, bring the ship to the west wall and be ready for a quick take off. Keep the shields up."

Prellina nodded, "I got it," she replied. "You guys be safe," she said as she walked over to the pilot station.

"Ground team?" Beio-Rhett said, looking at Singatt and Dembo. The three assembled and got ready to head out when

Poko's voice sounded again at the com station, "Beio-Rhett?"

Beio-Rhett paused and walked over to the station, "Yeah, buddy?"

"Be careful,"

Beio-Rhett smiled, "You worry too much."

The three left the bridge having armed themselves at the armory before heading to the elevator. The three had A-5000 assault rifles strapped to their backs. Singatt carried his standard issue, military pistol. Beio-Rhett still had his weapons belt with the diamond knife and his Rhaekul pistol, plus, in a satchel around his shoulder, he threw in the explosives and a few other items. Dembo kept the two submachine guns he nabbed from the Quezzes back at the space station. When it was time to head out, Singatt opened the doors and the group walked in one by one before Singatt closed the elevator doors. The floor fell beneath the three. Singatt had his arms crossed and stood up straight. However, his tail was swaying back and forth.

Beio-Rhett leaned against the wall, binding his hair with a black bandana. His boots tapped against the floor in a simple rhythm.

Dembo, who was closest to the door, leaned against the wall. He hummed a sloppy melody nervously.

The elevator stopped and Dembo opened the sliding door to a windy desert. Beio-Rhett jumped out ahead of Dembo. He looked out into the big beige blur imagining where the outpost was located, two miles away.

There was an unusually long pause before Beio-Rhett spoke, "I don't think you should come, Singatt."

Singatt swung his head around. "What?!" he asked. "I have to go in with you! You can't do this mission with only two people!"

"Singatt," he said. "If we get caught, and you're with us, this becomes a declaration of war. If Dembo and I get caught, we're just a wayward pair of rogues. You keep talking about how you want to help me. Well, this is me helping you. For the good of your people and your government, you should hang back. Stake a post near the west wall," he ordered, staring softly at Singatt. He then turned around and looked through his binoculars. "Keep your distance, from the wall, but stay close to keep an eye on everything."

With that, Beio-Rhett signaled to Dembo. The two ran

toward the enemy outpost rather quickly, before Singatt could voice any opposition. He trudged back to the ship, disappointed.

"Pick a weapon," Beio-Rhett suddenly blurted out as the two jogged towards the outpost. "We're getting close."

Dembo grabbed the A-5000 from behind his back just to play it safe, since it had the most ammo.

Beio-Rhett grabbed the same before turning to Dembo, "This was supposed to be a covert operation," he said.

"Yeah, but we both know it's gonna take some extra firepower to bust in,"

No sooner did Dembo's words leave his lips did a spray of laser bolt fire char the ground in front of the two.

"Run for cover!" shouted Beio-Rhett to Dembo.

Dembo jumped out of the path of the bolts and ran behind a large rock a few yards away. Beio-Rhett ran across the line of fire to join up with Dembo behind the rock. Along the way he fired blindly at where the shots were coming from, strafing as he darted for Dembo's rock. When he was close enough, he dropped to the ground and rolled behind the rock.

"Dembo, are you all right?" asked Beio-Rhett once he got in.

Dembo, whose back was against the rock replied, "Yeah, sure," He huffed a bit. "Scout sentries?"

"Compensating for that lack of visibility we were banking on," said Beio-Rhett as he twisted the nob off a smoke grenade. "Time to improvise," he popped out from behind the rock and threw the grenade. It exploded in midair a good distance away from the cave. A huge smoke cloud spread out in front of the wall. He then twisted the nob off of another smoke grenade and chuckled it a similar distance.

Dembo rolled his eyes as Beio-Rhett darted back behind the rock, followed by blaster fire. "Great, now we can't see them for sure," Dembo grunted. "You forget Quezzes have that infrared advantage."

"I didn't," argued Bola Rhett. "Those grenades are equipped with UV flares. They can't see shit."

Suddenly a deafening thunder of laser bolts and torpedoes struck the ground, around the rock. "As you can see," Beio-Rhett explained, "the Quezzes are firing blind!" He had to shout over the continuous gunfire. He reached into his pocket and pulled out two small goggle like devices. "Plus," he said. "I brought these to give us a real infrared advantage."

Dembo shrugged his shoulders and put on his heat seekers, "Man, what can't Poko get?" he remarked, turning the devices on. He peaked around the corner and could see very clearly five red figures, with bursts of red shooting forth from their torsos.

Beio-Rhett ran out first and started shooting madly. Through his heat seekers, he could see the enemies every move and he didn't waste nearly as much ammo as the Quezzes were. He hid behind another rock, uninjured. Dembo followed from behind, firing back at the remaining sentries.

Now that the two were behind the same rock, they stopped and listened. The gunfire had stopped. Beio-Rhett peeked around the corner. There were still five red figures, only now they were lying on the ground and slowly turning blue.

"Coast is clear," he said. "Let's go."

Dembo slowly lifted his head up from the rock and cautiously walked out from behind it. Beio-Rhett was already walking towards the billowing smoke. The two walked through the slowly lifting black fog, getting closer to the fading red figures in the distance.

"I guess that eliminates the element of surprise," commented Dembo.

"Hopefully they were too busy shooting us to warn the outpost," Beio-Rhett said.

Beio-Rhett and Dembo kept their heat-seekers on because of the smoke and made their way cautiously forward, walking past the dimming lights of the dead Quesgralions.

After walking a good few yards past the carnage, Dembo spotted a red arm up in front of him. Dembo took off his heat-seeker and saw that Beio-Rhett held his hand up signaling to stop.

Beio-Rhett whispered, "There's an electrical perimeter fence ahead."

"Can't we just blast it open? We're running out of time," said Dembo. "We've done this before."

"This one has got to have an alarm system," reminded Beio-Rhett, pointing to an unlit light at one of the posts of the fence. "We'd set off the outpost's alarm. The sentries haven't set off the alarm. I don't want to ruin that."

Dembo looked at the post, "I wonder if there's a way to

cut the circuit without setting off the alarm," he walked up to the post and examined the unlit light. "It's probably heat sensitive, right?"

Beio-Rhett held his assault rifle at his side and unsheathed his diamond knife. He touched the barbed wire briefly, but saw that the light did not go off, "Apparently," he said. "Sand probably blows against this shit all the time. It would go off continuously, if it was just touch sensitive."

"Don't cut it," Dembo said, leaning in towards the barbed wire. "I'm sure that would set it off too."

Beio-Rhett pulled the knife away and then set it under the lower most wire. He turned the knife on its side and bent the wire up with the dull side so that there was sufficient room between it and the desert ground.

"Dig, bitch!" he said smiling.

After a short delay, Dembo had dug a deep enough trench that the two could crawl under the fence without touching it. Beio-Rhett held the lowest barbed wire as high as he could with the knife without breaking it. Dembo did the same for him. Before long, the two made their way to the west wall of the outpost. It was only another hundred yards or so from the fence, but the whirling sand coupled with only moonlight made it difficult for the duo to see a few feet in front of them.

Beio-Rhett came to the wall first. "Should we look for a front door?" he asked.

Dembo chuckled and pointed up. "There's an air shaft about forty feet up. We could climb up and go in through the ducts."

Beio-Rhett nodded and struck his hand on the wall digging his claws in it. "Ha!" he laughed. "Is this outpost made out of paper mache?"

"It's just some special coating," said Dembo. "The real wall is underneath it. Not sure what it is exactly, since Hydrolettes don't have it. I remember Dresbar tried to gain access to the technology for the Rebellion's use. Never did. It's supposed to slow down light-based artillery."

"Well, it's going to speed us up," said Beio-Rhett as he began to make his ascent. After getting a few feet off the ground, he looked back to see that Dembo got the idea as he uncurled his claws and slid them out of the wall too.

The two scurried up the wall rather quickly. Beio-Rhett was the first one to reach the air shaft which was covered by a screen. The sandstorm was much worse now that the two were at a higher altitude. It was much more difficult to see.

By the time Dembo reached the air shaft Beio-Rhett had already tore open the screen. Dembo ducked and walked through the duct, which was 6 feet tall; just a bit too small for Dembo who stood just under 7 feet.

Beio-Rhett crawled in behind him walking in a lower crouch. Both Beio-Rhett and Dembo turned on their A-5000's flashlights. To avoid getting lost, they took no tributaries and stuck to the main duct.

After what seemed like a longer time that it actually was, Beio-Rhett whispered to Dembo, "I see light," Beio-Rhett squeezed in front of Dembo and reached the source of light.

It was coming from the floor of the duct. There was a large screen leading down to a room.

"Finally!" whispered Dembo. "Let's go in."

Beio-Rhett saw that the screen was weakly bolted in. With one swift slam of his tail, the screen was smashed in. Beio-Rhett jumped in, then Dembo. They were pleased to see that they had landed in the middle of an armory.

Before the two lay racks of rocket launchers, blasters, and flamethrowers. Ammo belts hung from hooks. Magazines were packed into crates, stacked to the roof.

"Shit, why'd I even bring my own guns!" Beio-Rhett quipped.

"We don't need anything here, do we?" Dembo asked.

Beio-Rhett shrugged. "I don't know how ugly it's going to get," he sifted through the crates of ammo. "Why haven't these guys started using A-5000s yet? Everyone knows they're better than those little pellet shooters," he said picking up one of the standard-issue Quesgralion assault rifles, the M-86.

Dembo smiled, "We haven't sold them any… and we probably won't now," he rifled through some other crates looking for ammo for his Quezz sub machine guns.

Beio-Rhett chuckled as he grabbed some grenades. "Well, get whatever you need and let's get going.

They hastily walked through hallways to find the detention hall. Artinuare had given them rough directions to its location, but most of the outpost looked the same, making navigation difficult. Beio-Rhett strained his eyes to read the complex Quesgralion writing on the signs. Other times he'd ask Dembo, who happened to be fluent.

As they continued creeping through the bland, metal corridors, Dembo reminded Beio-Rhett, "We won't find the detention hall here. Artinuare said it would be on level four and I think we're on level ten still.

When Beio-Rhett and Dembo turned the corner they saw two soldiers down the hall talking to each other. Beio-Rhett spotted them first.

"Drop!" shouted Beio-Rhett. He and Dembo dropped to the floor as the sound of laser bolts whizzed above their heads. With one swift movement Beio-Rhett shot a wave of bolts from his A-5000, killing both soldiers.

From behind, a few more soldiers ran toward Beio-Rhett and Dembo. Dembo saw them first and wheeled around, aiming his rifle at them and firing without hesitation.

Beio-Rhett spun around to see what Dembo was firing at. "Not this!" shouted Beio-Rhett. He lifted up his A-5000 and fired. The two stood perfectly still as they shot, until the small squadron was mowed down. Ever so slowly, they backed up toward the door where they were headed, at the end of the hall where they turned. When they were close enough to the door, Beio-Rhett pushed the button to open the door. The sliding door slowly slid open.

"Get back now!" shouted Beio-Rhett to Dembo. Dembo jumped behind the door.

Beio-Rhett was just outside the door, with his rifle still poised. He smashed the controls on the door with his tail and the doors started to close. Beio-Rhett jumped in right before they did.

Beio-Rhett took a few breaths and looked at Dembo, "Hopefully that'll slow them down."

"Yeah, so much for covering our tracks though," Dembo said, still huffing. "Always a trail of dead."

The two turned around to see that they were in another hallway. At the end of the hallway was an elevator door. Dembo was far in the lead, walking toward the elevator. Beio-Rhett got up and started running toward Dembo.

When Beio-Rhett caught up with Dembo, Dembo held a hand up in front of Beio-Rhett and shushed him, "The door ahead on the left is open, and I heard footsteps."

Beio-Rhett stopped in his tracks and stood still. He quietly stepped in front of Dembo. He quickly looked over the side of the door and pulled his head back.

"There are three, two big ones on each side of a short one."

"Are they Quesgralion?" asked Dembo.

"No, they're Kakeuwees," said Beio-Rhett with a straight face held for a few moments, before cracking a sly grin.

Beio-Rhett took another quick look. He quickly pulled his head back.

"The one in the middle looks like Nimx!"

"What's he doing here on a remote outpost," asked Dembo puzzled. "I thought all of the Teneman hide out at the Capital."

Beio-Rhett looked up at the sign above the hall. "Maybe he's hiding out here." He looked carefully at the sign until he gave up. "What's that say?" Beio-Rhett asked.

"Attack Plans Hall," answered Dembo. "Must be planning something big for it to be all the way out here."

Beio-Rhett listened carefully to the footsteps. They were coming closer.

"We're gonna have to run across the open door all the way to that elevator," said Dembo. "If we run fast enough we can make it."

"Why can't we just shoot them now?" asked Beio-Rhett. "Then we can take as much time as we need."

Before Beio-Rhett could say anything else, both he and Dembo were scared off by a thump in the air duct, thinking someone had shot them. They jumped in front of the door, in plain sight of Nimx and the two other Teneman officers.

The officers, one on each side of Nimx, started firing their standard officer's pistols at Beio-Rhett and Dembo, before they could get a chance to return fire. The two ran toward the elevator with the soldiers following close behind, their pistols held at arm's length firing at the fleeing pair. Dembo held his rifle behind him firing blindly, without much success. Beio-Rhett charged forward to the lead, trying to make it to the elevator. Nearly crashing into the wall next to it, he stopped and pressed the button to open the doors before turning around and firing at the oncoming soldiers, waiting for the doors to open. The two soldiers ducked behind the spines of the hallway still firing blindly from around the corner.

"Come on, come on!" muttered Beio-Rhett, repeatedly pushing the button rapidly. Waiting for the car to arrive, Dembo ran for his life as Beio-Rhett covered him with nonstop gunfire.

Slowly the doors opened until Beio-Rhett could finally squeeze in.

"Look out!" shouted Dembo from behind.

Beio-Rhett was shoved all the way in the elevator when Dembo ran into him. Both Hydrolettes fell over each other in the elevator. Beio-Rhett got up as quick as he could to push the button."Go!Go!Go!" pleaded Beio-Rhett to the closing doors.

The two soldiers came out from behind the spines and ran for the elevator. Nimx jogged behind them at a slower pace. "Stop them! Kill them!" he shouted.

One of the soldiers yanked a grenade from his belt and tossed it at the elevator, hoping it would slip through the closing doors.

"Shit!" Beio-Rhett shouted, seeing the grenade roll towards them as the gap between the doors closed. The doors closed on the grenade, just as it slipped through, stopping both the grenade and the doors. Looking down, Beio-Rhett saw the grenade right at his feet, still armed, stopping the doors from closing. Without a moment of hesitation, he kicked the grenade out of the doors allowing them to close and the car to descend.

Seeing the grenade roll back their way, the soldiers skidded to a stop and turned running back through the cave, motioning Nimx to turn away as well. The grenade went off, causing a shockwave that sent both soldiers flat on their faces and Nimx on his back. Debris from the grenade rained over the unfortunate trio.

"Drat! We just lost them!" shouted Nimx as he strained to pick himself up.

"They mustn't find the prisoners. We have to kill them!" shouted one soldier.

"You think they are Hydrolette military?" suggested the other.

"Impossible," thought Nimx. "No ship can make it through the blockade! And even so, there would be some report if they did. Besides, those two looked quite roguish."

"Contractors?" the first soldier asked.

"Who knows," Nimx shrugged, finally getting back on his feet. He grunted and then thought a moment. "Seal off all elevators!"

In the elevator, Dembo had already pushed level four on the panel before Beio-Rhett kicked out the grenade. They were on their way down.

Beio-Rhett cocked his A-5000 and slapped in the ammo chain, which he looped around and over his shoulder. Dembo was breathing heavily. He had no idea what would happen when the doors opened. He strapped his A-5000 over his shoulder and grabbed the two submachine guns instead, for more close quarter fighting.

The elevator stopped at level four but the doors wouldn't open.

Beio-Rhett pushed the emergency open button. The doors just jolted as if they were trying to open but couldn't. Dembo grew nervous. "Looks like our element of surprise is blown."

Beio-Rhett grunted, "No alarms... it could just be a jam." He took out his knife and pried open the control panel for the elevator. He stared at the wires blankly for a while before Dembo intervened.

"Hmmm," Dembo commented. "Easy fix," he said before cutting some wires and connecting them to other ports. After a few sparks flew, the doors jolted and finally opened.

Beio-Rhett stepped out with his rifle aimed. "We gotta move fast. The whole outpost will be on us soon."

The two stepped out into another empty hallway, with a door at the end that led to a lobby of sorts with some officers talking at a table. Beio-Rhett lifted up his A-5000 and fired a wave of laser bolts. The unarmed Quezzes rattled about as the laser bolts flew through their bodies and the furniture. Yellow blood splattered in the air. Beio-Rhett saw a guard on his left. He turned around and shot a single laser bolt through his head, sending yellow blood and green brain matter flying everywhere.

Dembo came into the lobby soon after looking around. "Look out!" he shouted pointing to another guard. He aimed with one of the submachine guns and took out the only other armed Quezz in the room.

Beio-Rhett nodded approvingly at Dembo. "Let's find this Detention Hall."

Dembo walked across one side of the room. Beio-Rhett walked across the other.

Dembo stopped at one of the doors. He read the sign. Then he whistled at Beio-Rhett. "Found it!" he shouted.

Beio-Rhett walked over. "Are you sure?" he asked while running to the door.

Dembo nodded. He looked down at the knob. He lifted his hand to the knob and opened the door. "Yep. This is the guards lobby. I think this door leads to the Detention Hall."

Both walked in. They found two prison guards towering over them.

Dembo held out both submachine guns and blew away both guards before they could even lift their rifles.

"Come on, let's hurry up," said Beio-Rhett running down the hall, stepping over the bloody corpses that clogged the entrance to the hallway.

Dembo ran down the hall at a slower pace, stopping short of Beio-Rhett. "Hold up," he called to Beio-Rhett. "I think we're in the Detention Hall now," he looked around and the dark heavy doors that lined either side of the hall. "Let me look through the signage to see if it'll lead us anywhere."

Beio-Rhett nodded and waited, leaning on his A-5000 while Dembo walked down the hall reading, "This looks like it's mostly holding cells for traitors and defectors..." he kept perusing before stopping at the end of the hall, "Hey!"

Beio-Rhett walked over. "Found it?" he asked.

"Mass holding cell!" announced Dembo. "This should be it," he said. "Unless there's another platoon of Hydrolettes trapped in here."

"Or a whole bunch of traitors," Beio-Rhett joked.

Beio-Rhett opened the door to a dark, damp jail room. On the walls were two rows of cages on top of each other. Some arms, legs, even tails were hanging out of the cages, all obviously Hydrolettes. The arms and legs sported standard beige military field uniforms, probably the same ones they were wearing when they were captured so long ago. The room reeked of feces, sweat and other bodily smells. It was nothing Beio-Rhett hadn't seen before. Although he tried to pretend the dismal scene before him had no effect, there was always a small part of him that that didn't want to see it. Perhaps it was the most important part of him. He scanned the scene indifferently, as if someone was watching him, judging any and all emotion shown as he looked at the scene. He glanced once at Dembo, who was visibly upset by the scene, though he held his weapons firm and didn't move, except to look around. Beio-Rhett knew that Dembo had seen similar scenes, which made it seem strange that he would appear so moved. He looked back at the cages to see what warranted Dembo's reaction: two children in one cage trying to reach for their mother in the cage beside them.

"Kids?" exclaimed Beio-Rhett. "What the fuck is going on here?"

Without thinking about what he was doing, Dembo pushed a green button next to the door. All the cages opened at once. Some of the prisoners were so weak they couldn't move.

A female Hydrolette gracefully leaped out of her high cage. She was tall and fit. Her hair was noticeably long, even for a female, and was tied haphazardly behind her head. Her tail swayed smoothly behind her. Her legs where quite lean and firm, as her arms. Her bust was also quite visible through her ripped military outfit. When she came to the light, Beio-Rhett and Dembo saw that she was a rare red-eyed Hydrolette like Dembo.

"I'm Lieutenant Ttaurel, leader of the platoon being held here," she said.

"Platoon?" asked Dembo. "Then what's with all the kids?"

Ttaurel shook her head. "You think all these prisoners were from only the platoon? There was a small space cruiser that was apprehended by the Quezzes for some reason. Most of the passengers were killed. Already, they executed a lot before you came. I'll tell you about it later." She kept a surprisingly straight face as she said this.

By this time, all the prisoners had got out of their cages. Ttaurel took a quick look at all of them and looked back at Beio-Rhett and Dembo. "We can't go out of the front door. I'm sure we'd run into security guards."

Beio-Rhett looked behind him to check the door. He heard nothing.

Ttaurel looked at Beio-Rhett. "They don't know you're here, do they?"

Beio-Rhett turned back to look at Ttaurel. He shrugged his shoulders. "We killed a few of them on our way in."

"Damn!" Ttaurel exclaimed. "The others are definitely

going to be looking for you. We could escape through the back door."

Just then, they heard the door to the Detention Hall slide open. "Let's go!" shouted Dembo.

"Not so fast!" ordered a calm voice from behind the door.

Dembo, forgetting his urgent mood, turned around and looked at the door to the mass holding cell. Beio-Rhett also turned around, as did Ttaurel. The prisoners stood back in fear. They all expected to see a Quesgralion Captain walk in, but never in their wildest imaginations what actually did walk through the door.

Curiously, not a Quesgralion, but a Dynothoxan walked through. Not a very tall one, still taller than Beio-Rhett. He was dressed in formal Zynoth attire. A black jacket and pants over a white shirt. However, this particular Dynothoxan seemed unkempt. The sleeves of his jacket were rolled up to his elbows and his shirt was unbuttoned and hung over of his pants. His tentacles were drawn in under his jacket so he didn't look threatening. His hair was very long and a dark hazel brown. Most of his hair lopped over to the right side of his face. Some dangled on his left. The rest was tied back in a long ponytail. Out of his mouth hung a toothpick. He stood hunched over with his hands in his pockets.

"I wouldn't run off so fast, if I were you," he said smoothly.

"Who are you?" asked Beio-Rhett puzzled.

"That's not important right now," the Dynothoxan said.

"Well, I say it is!" said Beio-Rhett in a commanding tone.

"Well," shrugged the Dynothoxan, "you may call me Deeko. I represent the Privateers."

"Privateers?" said Ttaurel in a thoughtful tone, "Never heard of them."

"Then we're doing our job right," Deeko smirked, "I'm only here to deliver a message...from Dresbar."

"I knew it!" shouted Beio-Rhett. "You're another bounty hunter!"

Deeko laughed, "Far from it. The details of my occupation are classified. Don't worry. I don't intend to take any action today. Just a message from your former employer… yours, too," he pointed to Dembo. "But about the bounty hunter, you won't have to worry about any more of those. It was a mistake to put a price on your head. We tried to convince Dresbar it wasn't gonna work, but you know how headstrong Dresbar is."

Beio-Rhett nodded, now finding himself more curious. *Privateers?*

Deeko continued, "He thought a simple bounty hunter could rake you in." he laughed. "You proved him wrong. I'd like to let you know the price has been taken off your head. Sad… it was a handsome sum, too." He cracked his neck. "However he hasn't given up on getting you. That's what we're here for,"

Beio-Rhett raised his A-5000.

Deeko laughed again, "Like I said, I'm not going to take action today. You have enough on your hands as it is." He looked back through the hallway. He scanned the area and looked back at the group. "Personally, I think Dresbar is just too cheap to pay the bounty, but either way, it's nothing you have to worry about." He checked the hallway again. "My superiors probably think I've said too much, but I think you should at least get a heads up." He checked the hallway again and then looked at his watch. "Funny how the alarms still haven't gone off yet. You can thank me for that later." He looked up at the group. The alarm sounded.

Beio-Rhett, Dembo, and Ttaurel jolted and looked around fearfully.

Deeko smiled, "Or not," with that he ran away.

Now the footsteps of guards could be heard running quickly towards the door. "Let's go!" ordered Dembo.

All the prisoners followed Dembo to the back of the room. Ttaurel fought her way to the front of the crowd and led Dembo to the back door.

By this time the security guards had opened the door all the way. However, they were unprepared for Beio-Rhett. The first few guards were shot down brutally from close range spraying yellow blood in Beio-Rhett's face.

Luckily for the prisoners, the mass holding cell room was shaped like an L, providing a corner for the prisoners and Dembo to hide. Beio-Rhett was the only one in sight of the security guards.

Dembo had opened the door. Both he and Ttaurel rushed the prisoners in until everyone went through the door.

"Come on Beio-Rhett!" shouted Dembo.

Beio-Rhett was firing at the security guards holding them off. When he saw signs of more coming, he bolted for the back door. "Go on! Catch up with the prisoners!" commanded Beio-

Rhett.

Dembo ran back through the door. Beio-Rhett followed him through a following hallway. Dembo and Ttaurel lead the prisoners through the hallway which seemed to get straighter and wider as they went. Beio-Rhett trailed the group. He took out his communicator and dialed Singatt's number

The desert had settled down a great deal from the blinding sandstorm. Small amounts of dust kicked up from the desert floor but slowly fell back down again. Singatt swished his tail back and forth through the sand as he heard his communicator beep. He picked it up and said, "Singatt."

The voice on the other line was Beio-Rhett.

"We're on the run!" Beio-Rhett shouted. "Take the ship to the west wall! Keep your distance, but get here fast! Arm the weapons just in case. When I signal the beeper, you bring in the ship, pick us up, and let's get the fuck out of here!"

"Got ya," replied Singatt. With that he ran all the way to the ship. When he got there, he opened the ships docking port and stepped in.

Leading the way through this new hallway, Dembo turned a corner and toppled over the grumbling, flustered Nimx. Nimx immediately pushed Dembo off but realized that Dembo had his rifle already aimed and ready. Nimx could not reach his pistol in time, so he put his hands up.

Dembo quickly rushed all the prisoners through the next door, holding the A-5000 firmly against Nimx's chin. Finally after Dembo came through, Beio-Rhett fired at Nimx from behind, but was to slow. Nimx ducked behind the corner just as two bodyguards popped out from the same spot and started shooting.

Beio-Rhett quickly shot and killed both of them, but took a laser bolt in the stomach.

At first Beio-Rhett felt a burn and crouched. Green blood gushed out. Beio-Rhett held his stomach and pressed as hard as he could. Luckily, the blast didn't slice right through him instead the laser just dissolved inside.

Nimx was left with no bodyguards and only a pistol while Beio-Rhett was squatting, nursing his wound.

Nimx held his pistol around the corner and shot blindly. Beio-Rhett could easily dodge these bolts even with his stomach wound. After firing a few poorly aimed rounds, Nimx pulled his pistol back and waited a few minutes against the wall, breathing heavily. Beio-Rhett hadn't made a single shot. Nimx became suspicious of the silence. When he looked around the corner Beio-Rhett was gone. He left a trail of green blood to the door. A small device sat where Beio-Rhett was hit.

"What the hell?" Nimx thought. The device had a screen, which had Hydrolette numbers counting down to zero. Nimx raised his brow and gasped, quickly figuring out what the device was. "Son of a bitch!"

Beio-Rhett stopped running through the hall and listened to the explosion. He smiled and continued to run down the hall.

"We better hurry up and find the nearest exit!" He shouted while walking past a hidden camera, before regrouping with the others.

The camera sent a signal to a rather large communication panel. A Quesgralion saw a beeper go off and looked at a screen. He saw Dembo run by, then the prisoners, then he saw Beio-Rhett limp along behind the group.

"Huh," he said, not sure if he saw what he saw. "There they are!" he signaled another Quesgralion and shouted, "Where are our guards?"

"I'm getting a negative reading from most of our sentries!" the other Quesgralion said in a panic.

"What?! How? There are only two of them! That can't be!"

"I can't get a hold of anyone. And the active sentries don't know where the hell they are!"

"I just saw them! Hallway Five, Level Four, just west of the Detention Hall!"

"Hallway Five?" the other one asked before pondering a moment, "I have an idea!" he spoke into the intercom, "Seal all doors in Hallway Five except the maze door!"

The other Quezz nodded, "Oh yeah! That'll take care of them for sure!"

Beio-Rhett asked Dembo, "Try one of the doors," as he limped along. "We can't go on like this."

Dembo stopped to try one of the doors. It didn't open. He tried the next. That one wouldn't work. After five more tries, a door opened. The door led to a hallway that turned a corner.

"Let's go," ordered Dembo. The prisoners rushed through the hallway.

When Beio-Rhett, Dembo, and the prisoners turned the corner. They faced another hallway that turned another corner. When the group ran to that corner, the hallway turned another corner!

Beio-Rhett noticed that the ceiling was twenty feet high, yet the walls went up only ten feet. He scratched his chin.

"Stay here," whispered Beio-Rhett.

Slowly Beio-Rhett climbed the wall. He could only climb with one arm because he used the other to cover his stomach wound. He found that the wall ended at a ledge. When Beio-Rhett stood up on it he saw what he had predicted he would see. The group had run into a maze! *What is wrong with these people?*

Beio-Rhett heard a thump. The ceiling started to move down. Beio-Rhett quickly jumped off the ledge. When he hit the floor, the ceiling had just came in contact with the wall. Lights lit up the maze's hallway. When he looked up he asked, "Where the hell is Dembo?"

Ttaurel spoke up. "He went back to check the door that we came in," she explained.

"And left you guys alone!?" asked Beio-Rhett furiously.

"I was left in charge," explained Ttaurel.

Just then Dembo came rushing back panting. "It's locked!"

The prisoners sighed in disappointment. Beio-Rhett slammed his free fist against the wall and cursed under his breath.

"Let's get going," suggested Ttaurel. "I should've known this would happen. I overheard them talking about this room. We have to move!"

The group started down the maze. All of them knew that a long walk was ahead.

Dembo decided which paths they would take and the pace they should keep. Sometimes the group took a wrong turn. After the first few minutes, the group was very worn out. Beio-Rhett tailed behind the group, growing weak. With every passing minute, he was another step behind the group. Everyone knew that he was losing blood and fast. Such a shot wouldn't kill him, but the blood loss might. *Ain't going out like this.* Beio-Rhett would sometimes collapse without warning, while one of the prisoners held him up.

"Dembo!" he shouted. "The explosives! We have to plant them."

Dembo stopped and turned around, "We have to find a

way out of here first, man. Remember our priorities."

Beio-Rhett only nodded, took a breath, then hoisted himself up and continued to limp forward.

After turning another corner farther down, Dembo stopped the group by raising his hand. Up ahead was a darkened area.

Beio-Rhett ran up to the lead, still limping. "Hey!" he said. "What's this?"

Dembo shushed Beio-Rhett as he looked ahead and saw the darkened area.

A low rumbling growl came from the dark area.

"Oh, fuck you!" Beio-Rhett yelled at the unseen assailant as he lifted up his A-5000 with his free hand, still nursing his wound with his other. He fired a wave of laser bolts into the darkness.

After firing for a while, Beio-Rhett lowered the heavy rifle. He was getting tired. *Gotta... rest.*

The gurgly growl came again, only closer. Beio-Rhett lifted his blaster again and fired an even longer wave of bolts. The growl came again but was much closer, now.

Beio-Rhett shouted with rage as he held the trigger for a while. A good ten inches of his ammo clip were swallowed up and spat out.

When the growl came again, everyone was worried. Even Beio-Rhett started shaking.

Dembo saw that he had to take charge now. He took his A-5000 and switched the dial from automatic to missile. He pulled the trigger and a giant blast of yellow compressed light shot out of the barrel. The darkened area filled with light from the explosion, but then it darkened again.

Beio-Rhett switched his A-5000 to missile setting as well and let out a huge blast of light at the darkened area. The darkness lit up again, then blackened. The growl disappeared but a loud clattering came toward them.

"What the hell!?" Dembo asked. "I can only think of one thing that..." he muttered, feeling for a switch in the darkness. When he turned on the switch, there was nothing! Nothing but the destruction caused by the missiles and laser bolts.

"What?" thought Beio-Rhett limping in. "Nothing!" He looked at the charred black walls from the destruction they made.

What? He heard a light chattering in the walls. *Where?* He racked his memory, thinking what he could be up against, if it was something he'd seen before. He listened to the clatter. He thought back to his times as an assassin. The clatter continued. He thought back to his times as a bounty hunter. The growl returned. He then caught on to a sliver of memory from his days with the Rebellion. He remembered that they spent most of their time underground planning their various covert strategies. The Rebellion was quite successful in their strategies, but he remembered it wasn't only soldiers that they had at their disposal. He remembered the malikae. They used malikae for missions too dangerous for Hydrolettes. Malikae were the ultimate killing machine. They were native to Quesgarlon and a few years ago were genetically enhanced by the Hydrolettes to be smarter, meaner and stronger. The Quesgralions bought the genetic information from the Hydrolettes and used it to make more genetically enhanced creatures. The Quesgralions probably used the malikae as the Rebellion did. A biological wrecking ball hidden in pits waiting for soldiers to fall into or hidden in the walls to… the *walls*… Beio-Rhett pulled himself out of his memory.

"THEY'RE IN THE WALLS!"

Ttaurel swung around. "Who?"

"Malikae!" answered Beio-Rhett. "Stay away from the walls! Dembo you lead!"

Dembo rounded up the prisoners. "Okay!" he shouted. "You heard him! Single file! Don't go near the walls!"

The prisoners lined up and started running down the maze.

Beio-Rhett, who was limping behind, stopped to look at the walls. He was suddenly knocked to the ground by a piece of wall with one of the dreaded, ferocious malikae pushing it from behind. Beio-Rhett's wound burst with blood again, as he grabbed the wall with both hands. The only thing stopping the malika from tearing Beio-Rhett apart was the piece of metal between them.

"Beio-Rhett!" shouted Dembo.

"Keep going!" shouted Beio-Rhett. "Get the prisoners out of here! I've fought these fuckin' things before! Don't worry!"

Dembo continued to run through the maze. He didn't bother shooting the malika during the genetic process they were made with exoskeletons to reflect laser bolts, a trait that made them invaluable war machines in field combat.

Beio-Rhett knew his guns were of no use either. He struggled to keep the metal plank between them. The malika lashed its whip-like tail at Beio-Rhett's leg.

Beio-Rhett growled in pain. "You're asking for it!" Beio-Rhett shouted as he lifted his tail up and swung it down hard on the malika's back.

The malika screeched in pain from the hard blow, before rearing up its barbed tail and stabbing it in Beio-Rhett's thigh.

Beio-Rhett grabbed his leg in pain. He couldn't cover the new wound because he was using his hands to hold the plank. "That's it!" shouted Beio-Rhett. He let go one hand from the plank. He reached for his diamond knife. With one hand propping the metal wall up, he held the knife as far out as he could and brought it hard against the side of the malika's horrid, growling face. He plunged the knife deep into the creature's brain, twisting the blade and pulling it out. The glimmer of the shining blade was followed by a torrential gushing of thick black blood. The malika's growls started to drown in blood, sounding more like fading gurgles. Still, the creature thrashed with its last remnants of ferocious energy. Beio-Rhett brought the knife back for another devastating plunge. More blood poured forth from the wound, as well as from its mouth now. Beio-Rhett yanked the knife out and brought it back for the finishing blow before the malikae could no longer thrash, or growl, or even gurgle, and finally fell down on the piece of wall, limp.

Beio-Rhett thrust the metal plank up and off of him. The malika's lifeless corpse slid off of the plank and landed in a bloody mess on the floor. It took him a while, but after taking a few breaths, Beio-Rhett managed to pull himself up, while still holding his stomach wound with his left hand.

"Wait!" he called out to Dembo, hoping he had not gone too far ahead. "There's a hole in the wall. We can use the wall to get to the outside!"

Dembo did indeed hear Beio-Rhett and turned the group around. However, by the time Dembo came back, Beio-Rhett was on the ground again, laying on his right side. He was holding the stomach wound on his left side. The barb wound wasn't much to worry about by comparison, except it was starting to swell and darken.

"How?" asked Dembo, holding his hand out for Beio-Rhett to lift himself up again.

Beio-Rhett grabbed Dembo's hand and pulled himself up, "Malikae are usually provided with a network between the walls of whatever building they're kept in that leads to the outside," explained Beio-Rhett slow and breathless. "We can get out through these walls easily."

Dembo thought. "How narrow are the passages. This is a maze."

Beio-Rhett took a deep breath. "When I climbed up to the ledge, I noticed that it was very wide, wide enough for malikae to crawl through. They're probably more than wide enough for us to walk through."

Dembo nodded. But as he turned to go through the wall, he asked Beio-Rhett, "What if we run into a malikae?"

Beio-Rhett took a breath. "Then run. Use grenades. Improvise. You've handled them before."

Dembo nodded, "And you?"

Beio-Rhett leaned against the wall. "Get going! I'll be close behind. I gotta do something with these explosives burning a hole in my bag."

Dembo grunted, "Forget destroying this place! They already know we're here. They probably already alerted the Capital. Let's just get these people out of here!"

"We will! That's your job! But I'm slowing you down! I can't keep up. Get them out of here. You have soldiers with you. You'll make it. I'll be right there."

Dembo paused and thought to argue, but took a breath instead and looked at the prisoners. "Quietly now, let's go through the walls. I'll lead. Children in the middle."

Dembo turned the flashlight on his A-5000 to light the way in front of the group.

Beio-Rhett was in even worse shape than before. It took him a few minutes support his weight and not lean on the wall. His leg stung where the barb stabbed him. *Damnit...* The barb was indeed poisonous. Yet another genetic modification that the Quezzes had implemented since Beio-Rhett last encountered these monsters. When he got up, he let his left leg drag since it was numb. He dropped his A-5000 as it had grown too heavy for him to carry. He reached into his satchel and produced one of the

explosives. *Now, I'm definitely not leaving without blowing up something.*
He peered into the hole in the wall and smelled a very fowl stench.
Aha... He then looked on his person for another weapon and
brought out his Rhaekul. He looked at the weapon, then at the
dead beast, then at the hole in the wall again. *Shit!*

The inside of the walls were just as twisty as the maze.
However, the group didn't run into any malikae.

"This isn't any better than the maze!" complained one of
the prisoners.

"This has to lead somewhere," said Dembo. "The malikae
must have access to the outside, or some sort of open area." He
stopped talking at the sight of a glowing sign.

Ttaurel came up to Dembo. "What the?" she asked.
"That's not Basic Quesgralion?"

"Sure isn't," said Dembo. "It's not even Galactic
Standard."

Ttaurel looked a little closer. "It's probably some sort of
malikae command," she suggested.

Dembo stepped a little closer before the ground suddenly
fell beneath him.

Ttaurel quickly knelt down to the hole Dembo fell in.
"Dembo!" shouted Ttaurel. She turned around to the prisoners.
"We got to go in and help him." She waited for a response.
Nobody answered. She scowled. "We're going down! That's an
order to my platoon! The rest of you can stay if you want," With
that, she jumped down the hole.

One by one, the prisoners decided to follow. It wasn't like
their current location was any safer. Ttaurel fell into Dembo's
arms. Before she could say anything, Dembo put his finger to her
lips and shushed her. "Be very quiet. See out there?"

Ttaurel nodded.

"There are about five sleeping malikae out there. See?"
asked Dembo, pointing to a wide, vast area. Five malikae were
definitely there. Their bodies lifting up and down, breathing.
Beyond them, was a barred door.

"We can get out through that door alive if we don't wake
them," said Dembo.

"The others should be coming soon," said Ttaurel. "Let's
give them a few minutes. When I count nineteen, then we go for
the door at your commands."

Dembo nodded.

Soon, one by one, the prisoners slid down the hole. Dembo would catch them and shush the ones that tried to scream or asked too many questions. Ttaurel made sure she counted every head. When she counted the nineteenth Hydrolette, she asked "What about Beio-Rhett?"

Dembo looked up at the hole. He kept his head up for a few minutes. After he put it down he finally spoke, "He'll make it." He stepped forward a bit into the vast area. He turned around and whispered to the group, "Walk in a group, stay close together, don't go anywhere near the malikae, and be very quiet."

Dembo took a few steps into the area. He looked back and signaled the group to follow him.

The first part of the walk was smooth, but as the group got closer to the malikae, the going was more uneasy. Some of the malikae rolled over or blinked their eyes, but soon went back to sleep. The group was getting closer to the door. Dembo still didn't rush. Finally, when the group was close enough to the door, they all huddled around it.

Dembo looked around the barred door. He saw a large red button. Dembo immediately pushed it. The button flashed. Dembo sighed in relief. Suddenly, a deafening alarm rang out, tearing violently through the fragile silence.

Dembo and Ttaurel both swung around and looked in all directions. The rest of the group ducked and covered their ears.

Dembo listened carefully over the sound of the alarm. He could just make out a low hissing. He looked straight ahead into the darkness at five pairs of glowing eyes. Dembo raised his A-5000 and backed off. Ttaurel saw the same sight and backed up all the way to the wall. The alarm stopped, and the glowing eyes got closer. The malikae's bodies started to take form and move closer. The hissing turned to snarls.

Dembo raised his A-5000, but a malika whipped it out of his hand. Dembo was up against the wall now. The children huddled together against their mother, finally reunited here at the end. Other Hydrolettes pulled on the bars on the door. Dembo looked to his right at Ttaurel. Ttaurel turned to her left facing Dembo with her hands up blocking the sight of an encroaching malika, looked back at Dembo. Dembo turned his head to look at the malikae, now getting much closer. He then looked back at

Ttaurel. "I'm sorry," he said calmly.

Suddenly, a loud explosion rung through the air. The entire group jolted. Dembo closed his eyes and looked away from the malikae. A pair of glowing eyes disappeared and its thick, reeking black blood splattered over the group.

Dembo opened his eyes and saw the blood on his steph jacket and pants. Dembo closed his eyes again at the booming sound of four more shots. The two children screamed at the sound. Some of the soldiers that were standing dropped down and covered their ears. The stench of the blood filled the room.

Dembo waited a bit and opened his eyes. He saw a figure emerge from the darkness. Dembo recognized him immediately as the tenacious bastard himself. "Beio-Rhett!" he shouted.

When Ttaurel opened her eyes, she also recognized the limping figure. Dembo walked up to Beio-Rhett, who was holding up the Rhaekul. He lowered the blaster and walked over to Dembo.

Dembo looked at the steaming black blood. "I thought they had laser reflecti..."

Beio-Rhett interrupted, "They do." He unlocked the magazine on the blaster which fell into his hand. He slid the top open and a metal bullet popped out. Beio-Rhett grabbed the thing and showed Dembo. "That's the Rhaekul for you. Solid hydrogen fueled bullets, encased in titanium. These specific rounds have explosive tips." He took a breath. "The galaxy's almost completely turned to using light-based ammunition, so the malikae are designed to be resistant to such weapons, but this..." he lifted the bullet up. "There are very few things in the galaxy this won't put a hole through.

Dembo took the bullet. "A blast from the past. Who'd a thought this retro crap would actually have a use these days."

Beio-Rhett took the bullet back and reloaded the weapon. "It's not the exact, original model. These are essentially reconstructed collector's items," he cocked the pistol. "Poko can be pretty useful at times." Beio-Rhett whispered. He handed the pistol to Dembo. "I should've given this to you earlier. Sorry, buddy."

Dembo looked at the beautiful weapon in his hands. The hand carved wooden handle was met with the cold steel of the barrel around the trigger. The barrel was long and the magazine was fed in front of the trigger, providing a large finger guard. The pistol was also equipped with a short-range scope. He smiled at Beio-Rhett and put the pistol in his holster.

Ttaurel came up to the group. "How are we supposed to get out?"

Beio-Rhett faced the group. "Now," he announced. "That button was a decoy." He limped over to the bloody bodies of the malikae. He kneeled over a dead malika. He took out his diamond knife and hacked at the body spraying more black blood. He put the knife back in its sheath and lifted his tail up over the body before smashing it against the corpse.

Part of the malika's exoskeleton fell off after the impact of Beio-Rhett's tail.

Beio-Rhett limped back to the group with the broken piece of exoskeleton.

"The door opens only when malika skin is rubbed on this scanner," he explained.

"Oh," muttered Dembo.

Beio-Rhett held the piece of exoskeleton in front of a scanner next to the button and the cage door opened, leading to a small room. Dembo went in first and looked down at a hole. Before he sent anyone down he radioed Singatt. "Singatt, are you in position for the pickup."

The Donta Ryx slowly glided along the sand. Inside the ship in the pilot seat, Singatt answered, "I'm bringing Ryx down on the west wall. Poko is arming all weapons just in case."

"Copy that," said Dembo. "Get sick bay ready. Beio-Rhett bleeding very badly!"

"Shit!" snapped Singatt. He hung up and turned to Poko, "You heard him, have everything ready. Prellina!" he shouted over the intercom, "Get sick bay ready."

"All right, let's hope that alarm was just for the malikae," said Beio-Rhett. "Let's go!"

Dembo went first through the slide, then the prisoners, then Beio-Rhett. There was only one sharp turn that sent Beio-Rhett up the side of the slide. Beio-Rhett closed his eyes as he saw the end of the slide. He flew out the end of the slide and face down on the sand. Dembo helped him up. Beio-Rhett looked at the green stain on the sand. He was bleeding still, but they were outside. Out of the base. He looked off in the distance to see the Donta Ryx hovering over the desert floor blowing sand out from under it. They had come out at the west wall as planned.

"Okay guys, let's go. Hurry before we're under attack!" It was Singatt calling. He was carrying his A-5000.

Beio-Rhett gave Singatt a thumbs up. Singatt ran over to the prisoners and huddled them together. He led the prisoners over to the Donta Ryx. Dembo and Beio-Rhett trailed holding their weapons at ready. After finally reaching the elevator, Singatt picked up his communicator. "Prellina! Fire up the engines! We're loading right now!" he shouted.

"Copy that," said Prellina. She jumped over the communications panel and leapt into the pilot seat, firing up the engines. She checked the monitor of the ship's front camera to see the commotion down by the ship, she did a quick scan over the west wall of the outpost to see if there were any following Quezzes. She turned to Poko, "Weapons?"

Poko nodded. "They're ready." Prellina tried to make out Beio-Rhett from the figures in the screen. Sick bay was ready and waiting for him when he got on board.

Down at the elevator, Singatt put the last of the prisoners up the elevator. Beio-Rhett and Dembo kept an eye out for any quezzes. When Ttaurel, being the last of the prisoners was in, Singatt jumped in. "Let's go damnit!" he shouted.

First Dembo jumped in. Then Beio-Rhett. Singatt closed the door. He radioed Prellina, "Go! Go! Go!"

The Donta Ryx lifted of the sandy ground and sped off into space. The main thrusters blazing as the ship disappeared into the night sky.

In the elevator Singatt looked at Beio-Rhett, "The explosives?"

Beio-Rhett smiled and took out the remote detonator. "It's your call."

Singatt took a breath. With his word, he knew that he would be firing the first shot in what would be yet another terrible war. He looked down at the floor then up at Beio-Rhett. "Do it."

Beio-Rhett pressed a button on the remote.

The Donta Ryx had just passed through Quesgralion's atmosphere when a huge fiery blast sprouted forth from the seemingly barren desert landscape far below.

End of Book 1

About the Author

Bennett Mohler was born in San Jose, CA in 1988. He graduated from University of Oregon with a Bachelor's Degree in English. He is an avid reader and has been writing since a very young age. He now resides in Portland, OR where he also enjoys playing music, hiking, and drinking scotch.